Trailer TRASH

MARIE SEXTON

RIPTIDE
PUBLISHING

Riptide Publishing
PO Box 1537
Burnsville, NC 28714
www.riptidepublishing.com

Trailer Trash
Copyright © 2016 by Marie Sexton

Cover art: Jay Aheer, jayscoversbydesign.com
Editor: May Peterson
Layout: L.C. Chase, lcchase.com/design.htm

"Future Shock" is copyright of *Newsweek*, November 24, 1986.
"Fact, Theory and Myth on the Spread of AIDS" is copyright *The New York Times*. February 15, 1987.

ISBN: 978-1-62649-396-4

First edition
March, 2016

Also available in ebook:
ISBN: 978-1-62649-395-7

MARIE SEXTON

For all the people who kept nagging me until I finally finished this one: Heidi, especially, but also Rowan, Troy, Rob, and Wendy.

TABLE OF

Contents

CHAPTER
One

*C*ody was at the gas station on the corner, waiting for the customers to clear out so he could buy a pack of smokes, when the new guy came in. Warren, Wyoming, was a small place. Everyone knew everybody else. This kid obviously wasn't from the area, and Cody stopped browsing the *Rolling Stone* magazine in his hand to check him out.

He was seventeen or eighteen years old, just like Cody, but dressed like a preppy boy from one of those John Hughes films—deck shoes, pegged jeans, and a golf shirt with the collar turned up. He probably had hairspray in his hair, for fuck's sake.

There were two possibilities: the first, and most likely, was that he was just another schmuck who'd tried to take a county road shortcut from I-80 to Yellowstone and had stopped for directions. The second was that he'd just moved into town.

Cody watched, intrigued, as the stranger walked right up to the counter, cocky as could be, and asked Vera for a pack of Marlboro Reds. She glanced around the station like Cody knew she would, noting the other shoppers—Tammy, with her bawling kid; old Jerry, who was apparently searching for the perfect packet of beef jerky; and Lucy, wearing her house slippers. Then she turned to the new guy. She smacked her gum once and said, "You got an ID, kid?"

"Of course." But he didn't reach for his wallet.

"You gonna show it to me?"

Cody couldn't see the boy's face, but he didn't need to.

"No cigarettes unless you're eighteen."

"Oh," he said, as if he hadn't thought of that. "Okay. Thanks."

The newcomer started studying the gum display next to the counter. Ms. Thomas, the music teacher from the high school, came in then, and Cody gave it up for a lost cause and left the store.

Ms. Thomas and Vera didn't like each other too much, but they made a good show of it any chance they got. They'd be yacking for ages.

Cody leaned against the side of the building and pulled out a cigarette. The wind was blowing like it always did, and he had to go behind the big ICE cooler to get it lit. When he looked up again, the preppy boy was standing there, watching him. The wind blew his blond hair into his eyes. He pushed it off his forehead and said, "Hey, man, can I bum one of those?"

Cody only had two left. Still, saying no felt like an asshole move. "Sure."

He shook one loose from the pack and offered his lighter. When it was lit, the new kid leaned against the ice machine. He was a bit taller than Cody. Then again, just about everybody was. "What's your name?"

"Cody."

"Cody," he said, like he was tasting the name. He must have liked it, because he smiled. "My friends call me Nate."

Did that mean Cody already qualified as a friend? The possibility surprised him.

"Can't believe she carded me," Nate went on. "Nobody at home ever cared."

"Vera doesn't care either, but she's worried others do. One of the PTA moms finds out she sells us smokes, and she's out of a job. You gotta wait till everybody else is gone, then she'll sell to you, no questions asked. Beer too, once she knows you."

"And she knows you?"

"Well enough." His mom'd been sending him there to buy stuff since he was old enough to cross the street.

Nate turned his head, seemingly so his blowing hair would be behind him, but all it did was wrap around the other side and back into his face. "Does the damn wind ever stop blowing around here?"

"Only when it snows."

"Man. I've only seen snow once in my life, and that was enough."

The statement struck Cody as funny, and he laughed. He figured Nate was just being a smart-ass and doing a piss-poor job, but then he realized maybe not. "You serious?"

"Lived in Texas my whole life. It'd freeze a couple of times a year, but the only snow I ever saw was last year. The entire city had to shut down."

"We sure as hell don't shut down for snow around here, I can tell you that. Did you just move here?"

"Last week."

It was odd timing. With the oil and coal booms over, more people were moving out of Wyoming than were moving in. "Where do you live?"

Nate gestured to the northeast. "Up in Orange Grove."

Orange Grove. That figured. Orange Grove was Warren's rich neighborhood. Never mind that nobody in the history of the world had ever managed to grow any kind of citrus in Wyoming.

"Where is everybody, anyway? I mean, you know, where's everybody hang out?" Nate had only smoked half the cigarette, but he tossed it into the gutter.

Cody resisted the urge to smack him. He'd smoked his down to the filter, and he dropped it on the pavement and ground it out with the toe of his shoe. He was trying not to resent Warren's newest resident for wasting half of his second-to-last smoke. He was also trying not to resent him for being from the fucking Grove. He could get past the first. The second, though? That one pissed him off for no good reason. "Who exactly are you looking for?" he asked. "Rich kids like you?"

He could tell Nate didn't know how to answer. "I suppose. Anyone our age, really."

Cody knew his attitude was unwarranted. It wasn't Nate's fault his folks had money any more than it was Cody's fault that his didn't. He sighed. "The people you're talking about will be at City Drug. It's on Main Street."

"A drug store?"

"It's like a general store. It's old. They still got one of those old-fashioned fountains, you know? Like from the fifties." It was actually a pretty cool place, if you didn't mind the preps. They made killer malts, had Ironport on tap, and sold limeades that were actually fresh squeezed. "That's where your type will be."

Nate grinned. His hair was blowing in his eyes again. "And what about the ones who aren't 'my type'?"

Cody frowned. He resisted the urge to take out his last cigarette and light it. "The cowboys'll be at the old rock quarry, south of town. I don't know what they do there, and I probably don't want to. The burnouts and the trailer-park kids hang at the bowling alley. It's only got three lanes, but there's a Pac-Man, and Centipede, and pinball, and a foosball table."

He could have told him that the pinball machine tilted if you breathed on it wrong, and the foosball table was missing four of its men, three from red and one from blue, but he figured Nate didn't need to know quite that much. "Then there's just the Mormons, I guess. They stick together. Mostly hang at each other's houses, I think."

"And what about you? Where do you hang?"

Cody laughed. "I guess right here, behind the ICE cooler."

"There must be someplace else?"

Cody studied him, weighing his odds. "Maybe."

Every school had its outcasts, and at Walter Warren High School, that role was filled by him. If he had to pick a crew, it'd be those losers at the bowling alley, but he didn't trust them. He knew from experience they'd turn on him in a heartbeat if it suited them. So on one hand, it was kind of cool to think about having some company for a while. On the other hand, school started again in three weeks. And when that happened, it'd be over. It was a safe bet it'd only be a few days before Nate was in tight with the jocks and those preps from the Grove, looking right past Cody in the halls like they'd never met.

Still, that wouldn't be until September, and this was August. Bright and sunny and blowing like a motherfucker. Right at that moment, he didn't have a damn thing to lose.

"I'll take you somewhere," he said. "But first, let's buy another pack of smokes."

Nate assumed they'd leave right away, but Cody had him wait. Finally, when the last customer left the gas station, he took Nate's money and went inside. He came back out with a pack in each hand, one of Marlboros, one of Camel Lights. He shoved the latter into his jacket pocket, and tossed the Reds Nate's way.

He didn't say anything. Just headed off down the sidewalk. "Where are you going?" Nate called.

Cody turned on his heel. "Thought you wanted to go somewhere?"

Ah. Cody expected him to follow. On foot. "Why don't we drive?" He nodded toward his car, and Cody's eyes followed the gesture to the brown Mustang parked at the end of the lot.

Cody looked at it for a minute, and Nate didn't miss the resentment on his face. He thought about the way Cody had said, *"Rich kids like you?"*

"Yeah, okay," Cody said.

Nate got in the car, and Cody came back and got in the passenger side without meeting his eyes. "Nice car." But it was clear he only said it because he figured Nate expected it. He glanced around. "Convertible, even."

"I had the top down the first day. It's a lot less fun here than at home." Having the wind in his face was one thing. Having it buffeting him from every direction was another. "My dad wants me to sell it and buy a truck."

Cody shrugged. "Truck'll do you a lot more good in the winter."

True enough, probably, but the fact was, the car had somehow become the centerpiece of his battle with his dad. First, his parents had ruined his life by deciding to divorce. Then, his dad decided he needed a new start in a brand-new town. Nate had wanted to stay in Austin with his mom, but his folks decided that wasn't how it should be, Nate's feelings on the matter be damned. So here he was, in the middle of godforsaken Warren, Wyoming, population 2,833 (and he thought that might have been a generous estimate). He didn't want to be here. Selling his car and buying a four-wheel-drive truck like the local yahoos drove would make him one of them.

And he had no desire to ever be one of them.

"Which way?"

Cody pointed down the street, and Nate started to drive. A minute later, Cody leaned forward to touch the stereo, a shy grin on his face. "Eight-track. That's crazy."

"I don't even know if it works. I used the radio at home, but the only station I could find here was playing country."

"That's out of Casper. The closest rock station's in Salt Lake. Might be one in Laramie, too, but we're in the middle of fucking nowhere, man. We're like the black hole of modern civilization. Don't even have a damn record store."

"I saw some cassettes at the gas station."

He laughed. "Sure, if you like Hank Williams."

On the west end of town was a trailer park. Cody directed him all the way through it. On the far side, the road turned south and dipped under the train tracks. It came back up in what might have been a trailer park in its good days. Now it was like something out of a horror movie: four bedraggled trailers with nothing but dirt for yards, tattered sheets in the windows in lieu of curtains, and one mangy dog growling at them from under a rusty car on cinder blocks.

"Park here," Cody said.

He did, and then followed Cody out of the car and up to a barbed wire fence. Cody ducked through.

Nate stopped, suddenly having second thoughts. He eyed Cody, wondering what he was up to. Nate was no fool. He could look at Cody and figure the score. Faded, off-brand jeans with a ratty T-shirt, a denim jacket that was falling apart at the seams, and that wary, accusing look that told him Cody was probably used to being on the wrong side of every line anybody had ever drawn.

Nate's dad would take one look at him and say he was a bad egg. He'd tell Nate to stay away.

Of course, that was the exact reason he'd decided to talk to Cody in the first place. Still, it was one thing to piss off his dad. It was another thing to get arrested for trespassing.

"Will we get in trouble?" he asked.

"Nah. This is Jim's land. He don't care, so long as we don't mess with his cows."

Nate followed him through the fence. They jumped an irrigation ditch that stunk of cow piss, and walked on through the field. Ahead of them, to the west, he spotted the highway that would eventually lead to the interstate. From here, they were close enough to see the cars, but too far away to tell makes and models. To the south, a herd of cows grazed. A couple raised their heads to regard them, but mostly they just chewed their cud and ignored the human interlopers.

A few more steps, and the land dropped several feet, forming a small bluff. Below was a graveyard of sorts. It was obviously the place where Jim and his family had dumped unneeded vehicles for the past hundred years. There was a rusted cab of an old pickup truck, a few tractors looking like decrepit skeletons, and a couple of things Nate couldn't even begin to identify—maybe farming equipment of some kind.

On the face of the bluff, wedged halfway into the dirt, was an old wagon. The wheels were gone. Its axles must have been buried in the embankment underneath it. There were still arching metal bands that had once held a canvas cover. It sat in the ground at nearly a ninety-degree angle. Cody stepped over the topside and slid down to sit on the downhill edge. The bed of the wagon made a sort of reclining seat that looked out over the prairie.

He pulled his cigarettes out. He took the last one from the first pack, wadded the empty package up and stuck it in his coat pocket, then lit the smoke with practiced ease. "Watch your butts out here. Gets pretty dry. I imagine Jim'd skin me alive if we burned down his field."

Nate slid down the wooden bed of the wagon and sat next to him. Being inside of it at least took the edge off the wind.

"What do you do out here?" he asked.

Cody leaned back and closed his eyes. "Nothing."

"Nothing?"

Cody smiled but didn't open his eyes. "I smoke. I read. I nap. I jack off." Nate wasn't sure if he meant that literally, or if he meant it as a synonym for goofing around. His stomach fluttered a bit as he pondered it.

"So this is it?" Nate asked. "This is all anyone does?"

"This, or get high."

"You get high?"

"No. But lots of them do. Especially those of you in the Grove with money to spare."

Nate had always been a good kid at home. Sure, he'd snuck a few beers through the years, but he wasn't into drugs. He took his own pack of cigarettes out of his pocket and looked at it. The truth was, he'd only started smoking two weeks before, and he'd only done it to piss of his dad.

"Class of '87," Cody said. "You'll be a senior this year?"

Nate wondered how he knew, then realized Cody was looking at his class ring. "Yeah."

"Me too."

Nate straightened the ring on his finger, remembering how excited he'd been as he chose the designs back in tenth grade. Of course, he hadn't known then that they'd be moving before graduation. Now he'd have to serve out his senior year in Warren, Wyoming. Only one year in this joke of a town, and he'd be able to leave. That's what he held on to. "You play any sports?"

Cody laughed. "Yeah, man. I'm the captain of the football team. Whatta you think?"

It had been a stupid question. If he'd thought about it for half a second, he would have known that.

"What about you?" Cody asked.

"Tennis. And I was on the swim team."

"Only swimming pool here is the outdoor one. It's open about three months outta the year."

"Yeah, I saw it." It was nothing more than a square, cement hole in the ground, full of squealing kids. It wasn't even close to Olympic size, even if there had been lanes. Next to it was the tennis court—singular, not plural—the cement cracked and overgrown with weeds and grass. Nate had counted five empty beer bottles but not one tennis ball.

He swallowed hard against the sudden lump in his throat. He fought to turn his frustration into anger. It'd serve him better that way.

"I guess I don't do anything anymore." But he didn't sound nearly as casual as he'd hoped. He knew his bitterness came through.

For the first time, there was no resentment or disdain in Cody's eyes. It looked more like pity.

"You're in hell, Nate," he said without a hint of humor. "This place will eat your soul."

CHAPTER
Two

Nate offered to drive Cody home, but Cody said dropping him back at the gas station where they'd met would be close enough.

"Want to hang out tomorrow?" Nate asked. "I can meet you at the wagon after lunch."

It took Cody a second, like he hadn't quite understood the question, or couldn't believe he'd actually heard it, but then he smiled. Not the cynical smile Nate had seen earlier, or the one that told him Cody thought he was a preppy fool. This was different. It made him look younger than he really was. It was sweet, like a secret smile Nate suspected few had ever seen.

"Cool," Cody said. Nothing more. But Nate had a feeling he was looking forward to it.

He drove up the hill to Orange Grove with a familiar feeling of dread in his gut. His dad was the newest officer with the Warren PD. The oil boom had brought lots of people to the state in the seventies and the first part of the eighties, but now, the boom was over, and people were fleeing Wyoming in droves. Towns were shrinking, and unemployment was higher than it had ever been. Fully a third of the houses in Orange Grove were empty, dented For Sale signs standing in the front lawns, bowing before the wind. Unfortunately, higher unemployment and a hard-hitting recession meant an elevation in crime. Nate's dad had managed to get a job with the police department because he had years of experience on his résumé, but Nate had never understood why they had to leave Austin at all, and moving to a town that had already peaked and was now declining into ruin was the last thing he'd wanted to do.

He found his dad at the dining room table with open folders full of paper spread out all around him. "Where've you been?" he asked. Not accusing. Not worried. Just genuinely curious about Nate's day.

"Out."

Nate saw the pain in his dad's eyes at his elusiveness. He and his dad had always been pals. But that had been before.

Before the affair. Before the divorce.

"Did you meet some kids?"

"One. We hung out."

"That's good. I'm glad you're making friends. Boy or girl?"

"A boy. He'll be a senior, like me."

"That's great. What's his name?"

"Cody."

"What's his last name?"

Nate knew he was only asking because he wanted to know if it was a name he'd find on the lists of habitual offenders. Nate was happy to be able to honestly say, "I don't know. I didn't ask."

They lapsed into an uncomfortable silence, his dad fiddling with his pen, Nate staring at his toes. He wanted to say more. He wanted to say, *Cody took me to a field where we smoked half a pack of cigarettes because there's nothing else to do in this goddamn town.* He wanted to say, *He told me everybody from this part of town gets high.* He wanted to say, *You've brought me to the shittiest place on earth. Cody says it will eat my soul, and I think he's right.*

What he actually said was, "What's for dinner?"

"I was thinking Chinese?" It sounded more like a question than a statement. "I noticed a place on Main Street."

"They don't have a Pizza Hut or a McDonald's, but they have a Chinese restaurant?"

"There's actually a pretty rich Asian history in this area. A lot of Chinese helped build the railroads. I was in the library today, and they had a book on—"

Nate cut him off before he rambled on for ages. "Chinese is fine."

The diner was like a trip back in time, with little individual jukeboxes at each table. A dial on top flipped the pages, like some kind of storybook, showing them the available tunes. They pumped in a few dimes, just for fun. There wasn't much pop, but Nate picked "It's Raining Again" and "One Thing Leads to Another." His dad hunted for Bob Seger, but the only one they had was "Tryin' to Live My Life Without You," and it seemed that one hit a bit too close to home, so he played "Down Under" and "Jack & Diane," and for a few minutes, it was almost fun.

The food turned out to be better than Nate anticipated, too. They had sweet and sour pork, and ham-fried rice, which they both agreed was way better than regular old "pork-fried" rice. Nate'd grown used to awkward meals with his dad. This one wasn't as bad as some, but it still felt wrong. His dad attempted to make small talk, as if nothing had changed. As if Nate's mom wasn't missing from the picture. As if they weren't sitting in a ridiculously tiny Chinese diner in the middle of Wyoming, with the wind blowing outside like it couldn't wait to get the hell into some greener state.

And who could blame it if it did?

"I saw a truck for sale today," his dad said. "A Ford. A little rusty, but those things'll run forever. I think it would be a good investment."

"I'm keeping my Mustang."

"Once winter comes—"

"I know."

They lapsed into another uncomfortable silence. They seemed to have those more often than not lately.

"I know you don't want to be here," his dad said quietly. "But there weren't that many jobs to choose from."

"I don't see why we had to leave Austin at all. You had a job there."

"Your mom wanted the house, and I didn't want to fight her for it."

"You didn't fight for *anything*."

"I wanted you," his dad said, his voice quiet. "I fought for you."

Nate slumped, having no good way to tell his father he shouldn't have bothered. Besides, he'd heard it all before. "Whatever."

"I couldn't stay in Austin after the divorce. I just couldn't. I needed some distance—"

"Well, you got that, didn't you?"

His dad rubbed his forehead. "I know you think I should have tried harder to make things work with your mom, but—"

"You didn't try at all."

"That's not true," his dad said with seemingly infinite patience. "You have no idea how wrong you are about that."

"If you'd really tried, we wouldn't be here. We'd be at home in Austin. With Mom."

His dad sighed. He sat there in silence for a moment, and then he dug in his pocket, and pushed a dime across the Formica. "How about another song?"

Cody walked home from the gas station feeling uncharacteristically cheery. Yes, he'd only have a few weeks before school started and the normal social politics of high school took Nate away, but until then, it seemed he had friend. He hadn't really had one of those in a while.

The three trailers near his seemed more oppressive than usual. One housed Ted, an unemployed alcoholic in his forties who lived alone. Vera from the gas station lived in another, with her invalid mother. And the third belonged to Kathy Johansen and Pete Jessup, who might have made a living selling drugs if they hadn't used more than they sold. They were arguing like they always did, their shouts easily overheard through the thin walls. Cody heard a crash inside their trailer as he walked past. The only thing louder than Kathy and Pete's frequent arguments were the trains that came through every other day, shaking Cody's entire trailer as they passed.

Nate had offered to drop Cody off at his house. He had no idea they'd been right there, practically at Cody's front door, but there was no way Cody wanted a rich kid from Orange Grove to see where he lived. Nate'd find out more than Cody wanted him to know soon enough.

He was surprised to see his mom's car parked out front. She was sitting on the couch when he walked in, a cigarette smoldering between her fingers and two empty beer cans on the coffee table in front of her. She should have been at work.

"They were slow today," she said, answering his unasked question. "Ralph sent me home."

His mom worked as a waitress at a truck stop on I-80. It was a forty-minute drive each way, and the pay was shit. She spent more than half of what she earned on the gas it took to get there and back each week, but there weren't any jobs to be had in Warren. Besides, they'd gone through plenty of stretches with no income at all. This was better, albeit not by very damn much.

"What's for dinner?" he asked. Occasionally she'd bring home a leftover hot beef sandwich for him, but there was no takeout container on the countertop today.

She shrugged and ashed her cigarette into the dead plant on the end table. "Whatever you can find."

He opened the cabinet and stared at the contents as if he hadn't seen them before. Ramen noodles, the generic equivalent of SpaghettiOs, and a mostly empty jar of peanut butter.

"Do we have any bread?"

She didn't answer. That meant no.

From the kitchen, he could only see the back of her head as she watched *Wheel of Fortune*. It came in a bit staticky because the tinfoil-wrapped rabbit ears on top of the set were crap, but he could still see it was the end of the round, when the winner looked through the showcase and used their prize money to buy things.

"I'll take the ceramic dog for $317," today's winner said. "And the color TV for $625."

Cody wondered as he always did what it would be like to spend money like that. Those people had no idea how lucky they were. *Yes, Pat, I'll take the spaghetti sauce for $3. Not the generic kind with the black-and-white label, but the Prego, if you please. And a loaf of Wonder Bread for $2.50.*

Nate probably had bread at his house. Cody wondered if Nate's mother sat on the couch, drinking her dinner while chain-smoking her way through her second pack of the day.

"The check didn't come," his mom said.

Cody stared at the back of her head as her words sank in. Whatever giddiness he'd felt after his time with Nate died a quick and painful death. "He's months behind. He promised he'd send it."

"You think I don't know that, Cody?"

"School starts in less than a month."

She sighed. She still didn't look away from the TV.

"Yes, Pat," the woman on the TV said, smiling her perfect smile. "I'll take the gold money clip for $120."

"Mom," Cody said, doing his best to keep his voice level and rational rather than letting himself whine. "None of last year's clothes fit anymore."

"You can go to the Basement. I have a bit of tip money you can use."

One of the churches in Warren ran a small used-clothing shop out of their basement. Secondhand shoes and secondhand styles. The worst part was, it was all donated by people who lived in town. "I hate shopping there."

"It's not that bad."

She didn't know what it was like, but he still remembered very clearly the humiliation he'd felt in junior high when some jock laughingly pointed out that Cody was wearing the shirt he'd tossed out the year before.

"I don't want to buy my school clothes there." Now he *was* whining. He knew it, but he couldn't seem to help it.

"What the fuck do you think I can do about it, Cody?" She finally turned to look at him. The lines in her face seemed more pronounced than usual. She looked far older than she was. "Money doesn't grow on trees."

Christ, like he needed her to tell him that. If it did, he figured they'd have a damn loaf of bread. Then again, there weren't all that many trees in southern Wyoming. Even if money did grow on them, it'd probably all be the same place it was now—up in goddamned Orange Grove.

Cody bit back his frustration. He wished, not for the first time, that he'd quit growing. His toes were jammed uncomfortably into the end of last year's sneakers. He was wearing the one pair of jeans he owned that didn't show most of his ankles. He'd mowed a few lawns over the summer, but the money he had left wouldn't be nearly enough.

His mom turned back to her show. Back to the people who could spend $175 on a magazine bin that was imported from Italy and still ugly as sin.

"You'll live," she said.

Pat, I'd like a new fucking life for ten thousand dollars. Just take the money off the tree. The one up by Nate's house.

He thought about the Sears catalog in his room. He'd spent weeks poring over it, circling things, making lists, adding and subtracting, figuring out how he could get the most useful assortment of clothes for the money his dad had promised to send. Winters in Wyoming sucked, and in the end, he'd decided to forgo fashion in lieu of warmth. Jeans, shoes, and a few shirts of course, but he'd planned to use a large chunk of the money for a new winter coat. Now, he'd have none of it.

He closed the cabinet door, his hunger suddenly gone. At least he still had most of a pack of cigarettes in his pocket.

"I'm going out."

She didn't answer.

He went back outside. The dull sounds of Kathy and Pete's latest argument echoed around the lot, sounding desperate and pitiful. Cody sighed and plopped down on the steps. He had no idea where he was going. Back to the wagon in Jim's cow field, or back to the gas station? He could go to the bowling alley and hang with the burnouts. Or out to the rock quarry, just so the cowboys could kick his ass. They hadn't done that in a couple of years. Maybe this time they'd do it right and put him out of his misery.

It almost seemed like a good idea.

Jesus, Cody. Melodramatic much?

Yeah, he was laying it on thick, but it was either that or cry. The former seemed better than the latter.

He lit a cigarette and looked west, toward the highway. He imagined the distant interstate, full of people who were going somewhere. How many of them had money? How many had families in their car? How many never had to worry about whether or not their deadbeat dad sent the court-mandated payment or not?

At that moment, he would have traded places with any damn one of them in a heartbeat. No questions asked.

CHAPTER
Three

ate had told Cody he'd meet him after lunch, but he ended up going to the field right after he got out of bed. It was a bit after eleven when he arrived, and Cody was already there, a half-empty pack of cigarettes in his hand.

"Wind's still blowing," Nate said as he sat down.

"Welcome to Wyoming."

He didn't even glance Nate's way. A brand-new day, and somehow Nate knew he was starting fresh with Cody. Whatever camaraderie they'd shared the day before had been wiped away in the night.

"I hear it's really nice up in the northern part of the state," he said, in an attempt to make conversation.

Cody sighed and tapped a cigarette into his hand. "I hear that too. I wouldn't know." He tucked the rest of the pack into the upper pocket of his jean jacket and pulled out a lighter. Nate waited while he turned away, cupping his hand against the wind to get it lit.

"How long have you lived here?"

Cody blew smoke, his other hand clenching around his lighter. "My whole fucking life."

"Well, you graduate this year, right? Then you can leave. Maybe go to college—"

"Ha!" Cody shook his head, leaning forward to put his elbows on his knees. "Yeah, right. College."

Nate wasn't sure what that meant. Maybe his grades weren't good enough, or—

"There's no leaving this town. Didn't I tell you it's the black hole of modern civilization? I meant it, man. There's no escape. You're born here, you knock up some chick, then you die here. That's how it goes."

"Uh . . ." Nate had no idea how to tackle that happy thought. "You're planning on knocking somebody up?"

Cody laughed without much humor and contemplated the smoldering cigarette between his fingers. "Pretty sure nobody actually *plans* that. Don't change anything, though. Gotta have money to leave, and by the time you've got it, it's too late."

"I don't care what you say. I'm leaving, as soon as I can. Packing up my car the night before graduation and leaving five minutes after they put that diploma in my hand."

"And going where?"

"Home, I guess, for the summer at least. Then I'm moving to Chicago."

Cody frowned at him, and Nate hurried to elaborate.

"My aunt lives there. She's a real estate agent, and she owns a bunch of houses and apartments. She has one she said I could use while I go to school." Although the idea of putting in college applications in a few months turned his stomach to knots.

Cody ground out the last of his cigarette against the side of the wagon and tossed the butt angrily into the wind. "Lucky you."

Nate studied him for a moment, taking in the ripped knees of his jeans and the way they ended a bit short of his ankles. The arms of his denim jacket left his bony wrists exposed. His tennis shoes had holes in both toes.

A small knot of shame formed in Nate's stomach as he finally realized it wasn't grades standing between Cody and college. He thought about Warren—windblown streets lined with lifeless, dusty buildings. No flowers. No joy. No jobs. Even the houses seemed to droop in defeat. The people he'd seen didn't look much better. Dead-eyed women not much older than him dragging their screaming kids through the grocery store. The line of rusty pickup trucks parked outside the shitty, seedy bar on the far side of town, no matter what time of day it was.

Maybe Cody was right. Maybe there was no escape.

Nate cleared his throat, trying to think of something that hinted at hope. "My mom always says, 'Despair is anger with no place to go.'"

Cody chuckled and put his head down. He ran his hands through his straight black hair. "I guess that makes me Despair, then."

"My mom also says, 'When it's dark enough, you can see the stars.'"

"Oh yeah? Well, my mom says, 'If the world didn't suck, we'd fall off.'"

Nate laughed. He wasn't sure if Cody had intended it as a joke or not, but either way, Nate couldn't help it. Cody looked over at him in surprise.

"Well," Nate said, still laughing a bit, "at least I know where you get your cheery disposition."

Cody blinked at him once as if trying to decide how to take that comment, but then he gave Nate a grudging smile. "And I guess I know where you get yours."

"Yeah." Now it was Nate's turn to duck his head in hopes of hiding his expression. It was true his mother had always been happy and upbeat. Right up until May, when she'd walked into Nate's bedroom and casually told him she was leaving his dad.

"Your mom sounds like some kind of brainiac or something."

"She's an English teacher."

"Will she be teaching at the high school?"

"No." Nate couldn't look at him. He twisted the class ring on his finger, watching the way the sun glinted off the light-blue stone. "She didn't move here with us. She's still back in Austin."

Cody didn't respond right away, and when Nate finally glanced up, he found Cody looking at him with more compassion than he'd seen from him before. "That sucks."

"You have no idea." As soon as Nate said the words, he realized maybe he shouldn't have. He didn't know anything about Cody's family situation. It was possible Cody knew exactly how Nate felt. He wondered if he should apologize, but Cody didn't seem bothered.

"When I was a kid, it seemed like I was the only one whose parents were split." Cody looked toward the distant motion of the highway again, as if it held some kind of answer. "People were always asking me why my last name was different from my mom's. Used to piss me off. But the older I get, the more it seems like the norm, you know? I don't know if there really are more divorces now, or if it's just because I'm more aware of it."

Nate had always known about divorce, but he'd always assumed it only happened to kids with fucked-up family lives. Somehow, he'd thought the "broken home" came first, and the divorce second. He hadn't quite realized the divorce was often what made it "broken."

"I guess I thought it couldn't happen to me," he said.

He hated it. Hated his life and his parents and the fact that he was now one of *those* kids. He hated coming home to a house where his mother's music wasn't playing. He hated having to do his own laundry and the fact that there was never a pot of soup on the stove or a batch of cookies in the oven, and the fact that he never, ever woke up to pancakes and bacon for breakfast. He hated knowing he'd taken those things for granted for so many years. And more than anything, he fucking hated Wyoming.

"Hey," Cody said, and when Nate looked over at him, Cody smiled. "When it's dark enough, you can see the stars."

Nate tried to smile back, but failed. "I only see the dark."

"Me too." Cody nudged Nate's knee with his own, and this time, Nate did manage to smile a little. "Guess it gives us a reason to keep looking up."

They spent a stupid percentage of the next couple of weeks sitting in the middle of a goddamn field, smoking until their throats burned.

"Seriously," Nate said sometime during their second week together. "What the hell do people do around here?"

Cody lit a cigarette from a book of matches, shaking the used match to extinguish the flame, as if the wind hadn't done it already. "You got a gun?"

The question alarmed him. "No! Why would I?"

Cody shrugged. "Lots of people shoot squeakies in the summer."

Nate blinked, trying to wrap his head around that sentence. Lots of people shooting was scary enough to begin with. "What the hell's a squeakie?"

Cody squinted at him. "You know. Squeakies."

Nate could only shake his head in bafflement, and Cody rolled his eyes before elaborating. "What, you don't have squeakies in Texas?"

"I guess not. What are they?"

"They're little rodents that burrow in the ground."

"Like prairie dogs?"

"Smaller."

"Like, a chipmunk?"

"No, man. Like a squeakie! People shoot 'em. Or they find a field full of 'em and spin donuts in their cars, seeing how many they can run over."

"Are you serious?"

"And when they get bored of that, they chase the antelope, trying to run them down. And if that ain't cool enough for you, I hear they got dogfights up by Farson."

"Dogfights?" Nate gripped his head with both hands, horrified, wishing he'd never heard anything Cody had said. "Like, where the dogs get killed?"

Cody blew smoke and shrugged again. "That's what they say. I ain't never seen one. Can't really see why that'd be fun. Never understood why shooting squeakies was fun either, but you asked what people do." He held up both hands. "That's about it."

"Oh my God." Nate hadn't ever killed anything in his life, unless he counted the occasional insect or spider on the bathroom floor, but he'd seen a cat get run over once in Texas. He didn't ever want to see anything like that again. "I think hanging out in this field is better."

Cody smiled at him. "See? You're getting used to Wyoming already."

Once he was back home, Nate went to the bookshelf in the family room and scanned the spines of the set of encyclopedias his parents had bought two years before. *S* comprised two full volumes. He pulled out the second one and sat cross-legged on the floor as he flipped through the pages.

No "squeakies."

"Whatcha doing?" his dad asked, startling Nate from his contemplation of the book. "School hasn't even started yet, and you're doing research?"

"What's a squeakie?"

"Squeakies." His dad chuckled. "I wondered the same thing. Turns out they're some kind of ground squirrel, although I'm not sure which kind. Jake said a Thompson's ground squirrel, and Fred told me they're actually Uinta ground squirrels, and Susan told me they're

Wyoming ground squirrels." He scratched his head and shrugged. "Not sure who's right or what the difference between them is anyway. Why? Somebody ask you to go shooting with them?"

"Not exactly, but I heard that's what some people here do for fun."

"Yeah, I've already been on a couple of calls because of it. People shooting guns in city limits, or on someone's private property. For what it's worth, I'd rather you didn't participate in that particular local custom. It's bound to get you in trouble sooner rather than later."

Nate was perfectly happy to promise he wouldn't go out shooting innocent ground squirrels anytime soon, but for the rest of the night, he brooded over his conversation with Cody. He imagined squeakies—they looked like prairie dogs in his mind, no matter what Cody said—running for cover, and antelope fleeing pickup trucks, and dogs, forced to fight to the death while a bunch of rednecks laughed and drank.

This was what passed for entertainment in Wyoming?

He took a deck of cards to the field with him the next morning. It was almost impossible to keep them from blowing away, but over the next few days, they managed a few games of Go Fish, Crazy Eights, and War. They were attempting a game of Five Card Draw when Cody suddenly asked, "So, why'd your folks split?"

Nate squirmed. He wasn't sure he wanted to talk about it. Then again, he had a feeling Cody would understand, seeing as how his own parents weren't together either.

"My dad had an affair."

"Suppose that'd do it."

"I guess." Nate didn't know the details. His parents hadn't ever told him, but he'd overheard his aunt and uncle whispering about it.

He didn't want to think about his parents. He scowled down at his cards. He didn't even have a lousy pair. "I fold."

Cody laughed as he gathered Nate's discarded cards. "Bad move. I didn't have shit."

They weren't playing for anything, so it didn't matter. Nate's hair was blowing in his face again, and he pushed it off his forehead. He kept thinking he'd buy a baseball cap, but he had yet to find one in Wyoming that didn't have either a John Deere logo or some redneck slogan on it.

He glanced at Cody who was shuffling the cards, a cigarette dangling from his lips. "What about yours?"

Cody frowned as if he hadn't considered that Nate might turn the tables on him. He cleared his throat, and took the cigarette out of his mouth. "My dad was sort of in and out all along, you know? But I guess he's been mostly 'out' since I was ten or eleven. He lives in Worland."

Nate didn't know where Worland was, but figured it didn't matter. "Do you ever see him?"

"Not for a long time."

"Do you miss him?"

Cody scowled, his eyes turning dark. Nate wasn't surprised when his answer was more attitude than anything. "Why the fuck would I? He's a jerk who can't even bother to send me a goddamn birthday card. Fuck him." When he was done, he sucked long and hard on his smoke, not meeting Nate's eyes.

"I miss my mom." Nate figured he sounded like a whiny kid when he said it, but he didn't care. "I thought maybe I could go visit for Christmas, but my dad keeps putting me off, saying 'maybe.'" He watched as Cody started dealing, tossing cards by Nate's knee onto their makeshift seat. "Like I don't know that means no."

"You got a car. Why can't you just go?"

Nate blinked at him, stunned by the idea. "I hadn't thought of that."

"Fuck, man. If I had my own car, I'd have ditched this shithole ages ago."

Nate thought about that. "What about high school?"

Cody shrugged, but Nate suspected his nonchalance was just for show. "What about it?"

Nate picked up his cards and fanned them out, his mind a mile away. He knew Cody didn't consider college of any kind an option, but giving up on high school seemed reckless, even for him. "There must be a community college in Laramie or something." He glanced up at Cody, trying to gauge how close he was to pissing him off. Cody's expression was still stony, but not quite angry. "Don't you have any plans for after high school?"

"Always figured I'd end up in either the oil fields or the coal mines, like everybody else who grew up here." He dropped a couple of cards and took some off the stack. "I'm taking two. How many do you need?"

"Is that what you want, though? To dig coal or be a roughneck?" Nate only knew the term because of his dad.

"Jesus, nobody wants to be a roughneck, but what the fuck else is there around here? You think I'm gonna take up ranching instead? Buy a couple of cows and spend my days worrying about whether there's enough rain this year to make hay?"

"I don't—"

"Just 'cause you got your life all planned out, don't mean the rest of us do."

Nate didn't have his life all planned out. Not by a long shot. He wasn't even sure he wanted to go to Chicago, or to college, but it was what he and his parents had planned back before the divorce. He figured he'd live in the apartment his aunt owned and scope out the schools. Maybe he'd take some accounting courses at the community college, or see about learning computers. His aunt seemed to think there'd be a lot of jobs in that field someday. "I didn't mean—"

"It don't matter." Cody ran his fingers through his hair and forced a smile. It looked more like a grimace. "We playin' poker or what?"

"Yeah."

"Then either tell me how many goddamn cards you want, or fold."

Nate folded, even though he'd been holding a pair of kings.

CHAPTER
Four

*W*ith the exception of Cody, Nate had yet to meet a single kid his age in Warren. Yes, he'd seen a couple in the neighborhood, or passed them in the grocery store, but he'd intentionally avoided the places Cody had named as the popular hangouts, not because he was shy, but because he wasn't ready to deal with high school bullshit yet. Cody made Walter Warren High School sound like a cliquish hell. The longer Nate could avoid it, the better. When he saw other teenagers around town, they gave him curious looks, but none of them spoke to him, and he chose to return the favor.

A week before school started, his luck ran out.

"Hey, Nate," his dad said one afternoon, just as Nate was about to leave the house. "How about we go uptown and get some lunch?"

"Why's it 'uptown' here? In Austin, we went 'downtown.'"

His dad cocked his head, his lips pursed. "I have no idea, now that you mention it. Maybe bigger cities have 'downtown,' but small towns go up?"

Nate shrugged. "Whatever."

They were quiet for the few minutes it took to drive into what qualified as "uptown" in Warren. It wasn't until his dad was parking the car that Nate realized where they were headed.

"The drug store?"

"Joe tells me it's a great place to grab a bite."

"Let's go get some ham-fried rice instead."

"We've had Chinese food twice in the last five days!" He was right, of course. Nate was getting tired of it too, but if he told his father the real reason he didn't want to go inside, his dad would never understand. Nate sighed and followed his father in.

The near side of the store was much like any other drugstore, only smaller. Greeting cards, ChapStick, cheap toys. But the entire length of the back wall was taken up by the counter and stools of the old-fashioned soda fountain. At the far end were a couple of booths, and that's where the teens were, some lounging at the tables, some occupying the stools across from them.

Nate and his dad chose stools at the counter on the near side, as far away from the teenagers as possible, and Nate did his best to ignore their curious stares. He and his dad ordered grilled ham and cheese sandwiches and vanilla malts. The lady working the counter even asked if they wanted them thick or thin (the former for his dad, the latter for Nate). Afterward, his dad excused himself to use the restroom. Nate didn't want his dad to leave him there alone, even for a minute, but he resisted the urge to follow him like a little kid.

"You're the new guy," one of the teenagers said to Nate as soon as his dad was gone. The teen in question was the perfect prep—letter jacket over a polo shirt with the collar flipped up. Nate could imagine Cody's disdain, and it was safe to assume that attitude went both ways.

"Yeah," Nate said, seeing no way around it. "Nate Bradford."

"We've seen you around."

What was he supposed to say to that? They sat there awkwardly for a second, until one of the girls stepped forward.

"We're going out to the old mine tonight," she said. "Why don't you come along?"

"Yeah," one of the other girls said. She had poofy, permed hair and bangs that stood straight up like a tidal wave. "You're just two doors down from me, you know. You can ride with me."

"I don't know—" Nate started to say, but the first boy cut him off.

"We scored some beer."

Nate wasn't sure if that made it more tempting or less. Unfortunately, his dad came around the corner just then. The guy who'd mentioned the beer did his best to look casual. The girl with the tidal wave bangs smiled at Nate. "I'll pick you up at eight?"

"I'm not sure I can go," Nate started to say, but this time it was his dad who cut him off.

"Why not?" he asked. "You should get out of the house more."

Nate got out of the house plenty. What his dad really meant was, Nate should meet more people his age, and it wasn't like Nate could argue with his new "friends" listening in.

"Great," he said, wondering if his severe lack of enthusiasm was evident. "See you at eight."

The girl with the tidal-wave bangs showed up promptly at eight. She told him her name was Jennifer. Nate climbed into the passenger seat of her Toyota Tercel, and wondered for the hundredth time what he was getting himself into.

"There's an old mine northeast of town," she told him. "We're not supposed to go in there, but we do. We have bonfires and stuff."

And stuff. Nate was afraid to ask what that meant.

There were two guys in the group: Brian, the one with the letter jacket from the drug store, and Brad, who was smaller and obviously spent most of his time in Brian's shadow. There were three girls. Two were named Jennifer, and the third one was named Christine. The Jennifers didn't seem to like her, and it took him a bit, but Nate finally figured it out.

There was nothing like fashion to build the brick wall between the "haves" and the "have nots," and in high school, being a "have" was the only thing that mattered. Those with money proved it by sporting labels—Guess, Gitano, and Esprit, accessorized with Swatch watches and Reebok tennis shoes. If you wanted to look like a rebel without looking like your folks were dirt-poor, you went for the acceptable alternatives: Converse, Doc Martens, and Levi's 501s. The Jennifers were designer all the way, from their United Colors of Benetton earrings to their scrunchy Gap socks. Christine, on the other hand, had none of it. Everything she wore had probably come courtesy of the Sears or JCPenney catalogs, and not the high-dollar pages either.

The Orange Grove residents may have had more money than the rest of Warren, but despite what Cody seemed to think, none of them were rich. Not by the Texas standards Nate was used to, at any rate. They were solidly middle class. Upper middle class at best. What truly seemed to set them apart wasn't so much their money, but their attitude and their awareness of the outside world.

"Can you believe we *still* don't have MTV here?" Brian said to Nate. "It's like living in the Old West or something."

"It isn't as bad as I thought it'd be," Nate confessed. "I was worried we wouldn't even have cable."

"Warren's all right," Christine said. "My parents say there's nothing worth watching on cable anyway, and the antenna works well enough."

"Well enough for *what*?" Brian asked. "Jesus. I get static more often than not, and the radio's worse."

"Cable, but no MTV," Jennifer said. "I mean, they have it in Casper and Laramie, but not here. And I wish we didn't have to drive all the way to Colorado or Utah to find a mall!"

"There's a mall in Casper," Christine said, but all the others immediately laughed.

"Eastridge barely qualifies," Brad said.

"It isn't fair," Jennifer went on. "Laramie's less than an hour from Fort Collins, and only another hour past that to Denver. Evanston's an hour from Salt Lake, and people up in Sheridan can get to Billings. But we're stuck in the goddamn middle of nowhere. It's an hour and a half to Rock Springs, and that's barely even a town!"

"The shopping isn't the worst of it," Brad said. "It's the music! I wish we didn't have to drive eight hours to see a damn concert."

Nate wished they'd quit talking about it. They were only making him hate Warren more than he already did.

Brian tossed Nate a can of Old Milwaukee. "You're cool, right? You won't tell your dad or anything?"

It seemed a bit late for them to be asking that question, but Nate said, "No. I won't tell."

Over the next hour, the sexual dynamic of the group became clear. One of the Jennifers—the one with smaller bangs—liked Brian. Brian liked big-bangs Jennifer, who seemed to be focused on Nate. Brad was clearly trying to get into Christine's pants, and despite her obvious desperation to fit in, Nate had a feeling the only reason she'd scored an invite at all was because Brad wanted to get laid.

"Where've you been hanging out?" Brad asked.

Nate swallowed a bit of beer, debating his answer. "Nowhere."

"I saw him with Cody Lawrence," Christine volunteered. "At the gas station." She looked around for some kind of approval of her statement. "Last week, and again yesterday."

They all looked at Nate. Brad smirked. "Cody? He's a loser."

Christine scowled and crossed her arms. "He's nice. Just because he isn't from Orange Grove—"

"He's worthless trailer trash," Brian said, as if it were the final verdict.

Christine looked away, biting her lip. Nobody else spoke. Nate took a long pull on his drink and wondered what to do. Cody was the only friend he had, but even he could see that they were from different worlds. Cody seemed to assume Nate would end up being friends with this group—the "rich kids" from Orange Grove. Nate wasn't sure if he wanted to fit in with them or not.

A few minutes later, Brian pulled a cigarette out of his pocket. Except on closer inspection, it wasn't exactly a cigarette. He lit it and made a show of taking a big hit and holding the smoke in his lungs as he passed the joint to his left. Nobody commented on it, and Nate's heart began to beat faster than normal. He'd tried pot once back home, but it had been with friends he was comfortable with. None of them had been serious about it, and he was pretty sure none of them had actually inhaled. But everybody in this group seemed to be fairly familiar with it.

Cody had told him to expect it. Still, Nate was beginning to see just what being in such a small town meant. Back in Austin, there'd been all kinds of people to hang around with. If he was uncomfortable with one group, he could just move to another. There was lots of overlap between the cliques. People he knew from the swim team or the tennis team might also be on student council, or in metal shop, or in the chess club. The lines were fluid, and it allowed for a great deal more individuality. At the time, he hadn't appreciated it, but looking back, he could see now that his social options had been limitless.

But here in Warren, his choices were few. And just as Cody had said, there wasn't much to do. No movie theaters. No malls. No arcades, libraries, or skating rinks. There was nothing but a run-down bowling alley, a soda shop that closed at five, a rock quarry where the cowboys hung out, and apparently an old mine, where the preps and jocks got high. There was beer, and weed, and guessing from the activities going on between Christine and Brad on the other side of the fire, plenty of sex, but not much else.

The joint inevitably came to Nate, and he tried not to be too obvious about taking the smallest hit ever.

"You going out for football?" Brian asked as Nate passed the joint on.

"I doubt it."

"Wrestling?"

Nate sighed. His dad would certainly like it if he made an effort, but he had no desire to appease him. Besides, Nate didn't know the first thing about wrestling. "I don't think so."

Brian finished off the joint. It wasn't long before he gave up on the Jennifer he obviously preferred and started making out with the one who wanted him. Brad and Christine hadn't come up for air in ages. That left Nate and big-bangs Jennifer, who scooted closer, looking hopeful. He felt trapped and completely out of his element.

Dear God, get me out of here!

His dad's policy had always been "call if you need a ride home." He claimed it didn't matter where Nate was or what kind of situation he'd gotten into, his dad would rather Nate call than ride with somebody who'd been drinking, or stay at a party where Nate was being pressured to do something he wasn't comfortable with. Nate had always laughed at the idea before, but suddenly, he wanted more than anything to take his dad up on that offer. He wanted to beg his dad to take him home, even if "home" meant their house in Orange Grove. But he was a long way from a pay phone. More people were arriving too, all of them eyeing him, sizing him up. He didn't want to deal with any of them.

He made a show of looking at his watch. "I need to get home. My dad'll kill me if I miss curfew."

Jennifer squinted at the three Swatches on her left wrist. "It's only ten thirty."

"I know, but he's pretty strict. Can you give me a ride?"

"I'll come with you," a girl who'd just shown up said. "I'm out of cigarettes, and we can pick up more beer on the way back."

Nate ceded shotgun to the newcomer, who introduced herself as Michelle. She and Jennifer hit him with a barrage of questions as they made their way through the winding, unpaved county roads. Where was he from? Why had he moved to Wyoming? Where had he been hanging out? Did he have a girlfriend back in Texas? Nate answered in a monotone without ever saying Cody's name. He just wanted out of the car.

He breathed a sigh of relief when they finally entered Orange Grove. There was a house for sale on every block. So many homes, most of them less than ten years old, but nobody was buying. At least a third of the empty houses had broken windows and graffiti spray-painted across their sides.

It was downright depressing. No wonder getting high was such a popular pastime.

"Back already?" his dad asked when he walked in. "You're an hour before curfew. Did you have fun?"

"It was kind of lame."

He went upstairs and showered, washing the smell of bonfire smoke from his hair. He climbed into bed and thought about Austin. About the tennis team, which he was no longer a part of, and his old bedroom, and his friend Mike, and all the times they'd complained that there was nothing to do in Austin.

What a fool he'd been.

CHAPTER

"Have you been to the Basement yet?" Cody's mom asked a week before school started. She'd come home from work and gone straight to the shower, and now she sat with her hair combed but still dripping, the shoulders of her Led Zeppelin T-shirt soaked through, a cigarette smoldering between her fingers. She kept her eyes glued on the TV, even when she asked him a question.

"Not yet."

She'd given him a bit of money from her tip jar the week before. It wasn't much, but he knew it wasn't her fault. She worked hard waiting tables, and there were too many expenses and not enough left over in the end. Cody tried looking for work of his own every so often, but there weren't many jobs in Warren to go around, especially now that the boom was over. With too few businesses and too many unskilled workers, most of the entry-level jobs went to adults, many of them fresh out of high school and already trying to support kids. The few spots left for teenagers usually went to family members and friends, and Cody was neither. Sometimes there was seasonal work to be had—mowing lawns, painting houses, shoveling snow—but those never lasted, and neither did the few dollars they brought in.

He appreciated that she'd given him what she could. Yes, he wished like hell there was more, but at least she tried, and he recognized that every time she handed him money—even a few dollars—it meant something she was giving up for herself. Maybe it was only a couple of drinks at the bar, but it wasn't like she hadn't earned them. If a few beers on Thursday night was the high point of her week, Cody understood. In a place like Warren, you took what distractions you could find.

For himself, he had a new distraction: Nate. Every evening, when Nate dropped him off at the end of the day, he'd say, "Want to meet again tomorrow?"

Cody's heart did the same funny little dance every time. He tried not to get his hopes up too high—it was only until school started—but like his mom with her drinks, he chose to take what happiness he could when the opportunity presented itself. When they got tired of playing cards, they drove around town. They even stopped at a yard sale and picked up an eight-track tape for fifteen cents, just to test the player in Nate's Mustang. It turned out it still worked, and after that, Nate stopped at every yard sale he found in search of more. Cody couldn't help counting those coins as Nate handed them over, thinking how he could have put them to better use, but it was Nate's money, and it made the afternoons a bit more fun. They ended up with a ridiculous collection—everything from KISS to the Bee Gees to the soundtrack from *Pete's Dragon*—but it was better than the country station out of Casper and the static that filled the rest of the radio bands.

His mom was watching him now, waiting for him to elaborate on his answer. "Maybe I'll go tomorrow." The truth was, there was a better store in Rock Springs, but he hadn't worked up the nerve yet to ask Nate for a ride.

His mom went back to watching TV, but a minute later, she ground her cigarette out and stood. As she passed him, heading to the kitchen, presumably to scrounge up something to eat, she laid a bundle of folded bills on the coffee table in front of him.

Cody's heart sank a bit.

She didn't say a word. Just opened the fridge, pulled out a beer, then stood there staring in, the unopened beer in one hand while she contemplated their severe lack of food.

Cody licked his lips, debating. Leaving it lying there wouldn't change what had been done. He picked it up and unfolded the small bundle with shaking hands. It was more money than his mom should have made waiting tables. He closed his eyes, trying to find his center. Trying to find that quiet place inside of him where he didn't have to feel anything.

He wished he'd never made a big deal out of it. He wished he'd never even mentioned his clothes not fitting.

Too late now.

The money felt dirty in his hands. He imagined he could feel its taint seeping into his flesh, leaking into his bloodstream, rushing headlong for his heart. He didn't want these crumpled, fading bills, but telling her would only make him look even more ungrateful.

He opened his eyes, trying to feign an innocence he didn't feel. "Where'd you get this?"

"I had a good night." Punctuated by the *click-fizz* of her popping the tab on her beer.

Cody's bile rose, and he forced himself to take slow, even breaths. He was torn—grateful for the money, but ashamed of it. Embarrassed for her, annoyed at himself, angry at his no-good father for forcing their hands.

"Mom . . ." He wanted to say, *I'm sorry.* He wanted to say, *You don't have to do what I think you did.* But her back was rigid as she stared resolutely into the fridge, and Cody said the only thing he could. "Thank you."

"Don't blow it on records."

Cody couldn't remember the last time he'd bought music of any kind. That was a luxury he'd long ago learned to live without, Nate's sudden infatuation with eight-tracks notwithstanding. "I won't."

He slid it into his back pocket, trying to let go of his misgivings. Maybe she'd been saving up for a while. Maybe there'd been a really big table, or one high-roller who liked the way his mom smiled.

Anything was possible.

Anything was better than the truth.

When Nate wandered into the field the next day, he found Cody sullen—even moodier than usual, and that was saying a lot. Nate didn't tell him about the encounter with the Grove clique. He knew bringing it up would only drive Cody deeper into his anger. Cody expected him to fall into line with that group once school started, and although he couldn't quite picture it, he kept hearing their voices in his head.

He's a loser.

He's worthless trailer trash.

Nate studied his class ring, remembering the second day he'd spent with Cody, and his assertion that there was no escaping Warren,

Wyoming. What if he was right? What if this really was a black hole nobody managed to leave? Nate felt like he could barely breathe, just thinking about it. School was only four days away, and he was dreading it more than ever.

"There must be something around here we can do," he said at last. "Besides shooting things, I mean."

Cody shrugged as he ground his cigarette out against the side of the wagon. There was a pretty substantial black mark there from all the times he'd done it in the past. "I don't know. There's the places I told you—City Drug, and the bowling alley." He looked down at the toes of his shoes. "I can take you to the bowling alley, but no way in hell I'm going where all the preps hang out."

"Well, I have a car, you know. What about if we left town? What's the closest place to go?"

Cody blinked at him in surprise. "Rock Springs."

"Is there anything to do there?"

Cody's eyes shifted to the side, and he bit nervously at his lip. He obviously had something in mind but didn't seem to want to mention it.

"What is it?" Nate prodded.

"Well," Cody glanced sideways at him, "there's a store there."

"What kind of store?"

A slow blush started to climb its way up Cody's cheeks. "A clothes store."

Nate wasn't sure what he'd been expecting, but that sure as hell wasn't it. "You want to go shopping? Are you serious?"

Cody blushed even more, and ducked his head. "Never mind," he said, his voice quiet.

Nate was confused by Cody's sudden embarrassment. He'd been teasing, but this was clearly something Cody couldn't handle being hassled about.

"Cody?"

Cody looked cautiously toward him. His cheeks were still bright red.

"It's cool, man. I'll take you. Anything's better than sitting here."

A flash of hope lit Cody's eyes, but he seemed to smash it down, grinding it out like he had his cigarette. "The thing is, it's . . . Well, it's a thrift shop, you know? Like, used clothes people donate."

Used clothes?

Suddenly, the reason for Cody's embarrassment was crystal clear, and Nate couldn't even blame him for it. Secondhand stores were something he was vaguely aware of, but he'd never set foot inside of one. He'd always thought of them as places homeless people and bums went. Somehow, it hadn't ever occurred to him that regular people shopped there. People his age.

People like Cody.

Cody was still looking at him, his cheeks red and a mute plea in his eyes—not asking if Nate would take him to Rock Springs, but asking Nate to please, *please* not laugh at him for this.

In some past life, he might have done just that. But not now.

"They have a McDonald's there too, right?" Nate asked.

"Yeah."

"I'd kill for a Big Mac right now."

Cody gave him a big, broad smile that was cute as hell, and utterly contagious. "Two all-beef patties, special sauce, lettuce, cheese—"

"Pickles, onions, on a sesame seed bun."

"Let's go," Cody said.

But Nate was already on his feet and running for the car.

They drove south to the interstate, then turned west. The sun was shining, semis blasting past them in the left lane, and the farther they got from Warren, the more Cody seemed to shine.

It was as if all his anger and resentment and embarrassment burned away as they drove, left somewhere behind them on the shimmering, hot asphalt. He smiled more. His laugh came easier. He fiddled with the radio and finally managed to tune in a rock station broadcast out of Salt Lake. It was more Cody's music than Nate's—Van Halen, Def Leppard, the Scorpions—but they both agreed it was better than nothing. By the time they pulled into the McDonald's parking lot in Rock Springs, Nate was marveling at how much of Cody's usual hostility seemed rooted in the dusty streets of his hometown.

Cody excused himself to use the bathroom as soon as they walked inside, and by the time he came out, Nate had already paid for a double order of Big Macs, fries, chocolate shakes, and apple pies.

And just like that, Cody's newfound happiness wilted a little. The pained look that always haunted his eyes came back as he scanned the tray full of food. "I can pay you back."

"Forget it," Nate said, wanting only to see him relax again. "What the hell else am I going to spend my allowance on?"

They slid into opposite sides of a booth. Cody unwrapped his hamburger first, but Nate was dying for french fries.

"What in the world are you doing?" Cody asked as Nate took the lid off his chocolate shake and dipped a fry in it.

"I've been craving this ever since we moved." He held the shake out to Cody. "Seriously, you've never dipped your fries into your shake?"

"No."

Nate was about to say his mother had introduced him to the idea, but that seemed like a good way to wipe the smiles off both their faces fast. Instead, he ate another milkshake-coated fry, pushing the open cup toward Cody again. "Go on. Try it. You'll never want ketchup again."

Cody didn't look too sure of the idea, but he obediently dipped one of his fries into the shake and put it in his mouth.

"Good, right?"

Cody tilted his head, still chewing, seeming to put way too much thought into whether or not he liked it.

"You know what I really miss?" Nate asked.

Cody swallowed. "Besides a swimming pool and MTV and a mall with an arcade?"

Nate laughed. "Yeah, besides those things. I miss grits."

Cody stopped in the middle of taking the lid off his own chocolate shake. "What are those?"

If anyone had told Nate two months earlier that he'd be talking to somebody who'd never heard of grits, he would have called them an idiot, but he'd checked the grocery store in Warren. There were no grits to be found. Not even the instant kind. "They're like Cream of Wheat, I guess, but not really." He unwrapped his hamburger, thinking about all the things he couldn't find in Warren. "I miss fried okra too. And you know what else?"

"What?"

"Collard greens cooked with bacon. I didn't even think I liked them that much till I found out I couldn't get them. Now, every night at dinner, I sit there wishing we had them."

"Isn't spinach the same thing?"

"Not even close." For a while, they ate in silence, although Nate was pleased to see he'd converted Cody to the world of chocolate shakes in lieu of ketchup on his fries. And Nate's Big Mac was the best damn thing he'd ever tasted.

"You don't have much of a Texas accent," Cody said as he wadded up his empty hamburger wrapper.

"No. It's 'cause my folks are damned Yankees."

Cody wrinkled his brow, and Nate laughed, realizing the joke was lost on him.

"It's something they always say in the South. The difference between a Yankee and a damned Yankee is that a Yankee's here to visit, but a damned Yankee's here to stay." He shook his head, realizing that his "here" had become "there." He still thought of himself as a Texan.

"Anyway. My mom and dad were both Air Force brats. They lived all over growing up. They moved to Austin the year before I was born, but the southern drawl never really rubbed off on them. Plus, you know, my mom's an English teacher, so she's big on proper grammar. She likes telling me how 'y'all' isn't in the dictionary." Why did he always end up talking about his mom? "Anyway, as far as I'm concerned, you're the one with the accent."

Cody stopped, a fry halfway to his mouth. "I don't have an accent."

"You do. You and everybody else in Warren. You sort of . . . twang."

Cody dropped his fry, sitting back as if Nate had slapped him. "I don't 'twang.'"

"You do. It's kind of cute, really."

Cody just stared at him, and Nate suddenly regretted having said that last bit. He crumpled up his Big Mac wrapper, searching for something else to say that didn't feel so stupid. He glanced out the window, at the cars headed downtown.

Or was it "uptown" in Rock Springs?

"Hey," he said, struck by a new thought. "Is there a record store in Rock Springs?"

"Pretty sure there is."

"Then hurry up and finish your pie. I never managed to buy *Lifes Rich Pageant* before I moved."

"Who?"

"R.E.M."

Cody groaned as he started to gather their trash onto the tray. "Thank God your car doesn't have a cassette player."

Cody could tell Nate was uncomfortable when they entered the thrift shop, but he seemed to be doing his best to act casual about it. The place had the same sour, musty smell as every other used clothing store Cody had ever been in. The front of the store was all women's clothing, and Nate followed him past the racks of clothing to the men's section. Cody tried to tell himself he had no reason to be embarrassed as he started sorting through the options.

"How about this?" Nate was on the other side of the rack of clothes, directly across from Cody. He held up the ugliest sweater Cody had ever seen.

"No."

Nate put it back without a word. Thirty seconds later, he said, "This?"

This one was bad enough it made Cody think better of the first one. He couldn't tell if Nate was seriously offering him the sweater, or if he was intentionally picking things he knew Cody would hate. "No."

"This one?" The shirt Nate held up this time was almost identical to the one he was wearing, right down to the little horse embroidered on the chest.

Cody shook his head. "Nate, look at me. Then look at you. Then look at that shirt. Now tell me, who're you kidding?"

Nate actually blushed a bit as he put the shirt back. "Just trying to help."

So he had been serious. Now Cody felt bad for being a smart-ass. "What I really need are pants."

"I saw some parachute pants over there." Nate pointed to the end of the row.

"Please tell me you're joking."

Nate shrugged. "Eddie Van Halen wears them."

"Maybe you ain't noticed, but I'm *not* Eddie Van Halen. And neither are you."

"I don't know. I think you could pull it off. It's that whole 'bad boy' thing. You just need a leather jacket to go with it."

Again, he couldn't tell if Nate was serious or not. He didn't know if he should bother pointing out that if he was buying his jeans secondhand, it was a safe bet he couldn't afford a leather jacket. Instead, he chose not to respond at all. He went back to sorting through jeans.

"You want me to pick you up on Tuesday?" Nate asked.

Cody winced, hoping Nate didn't notice. "For what?"

"For school."

"What do you mean?" It was a stupid question. Really, he was just stalling for time. He'd been anticipating this conversation, but having it now, in person, in a public place, was a lot more difficult than he'd pictured it being.

"What do you think I mean, genius? Do you want a ride to school?"

"I'm totally out of your way."

"Cody, the town is two blocks wide. There's no such thing as 'out of my way.'"

He was exaggerating, but not by much.

"I thought it'd be cool if you'd hang out with me, you know?" Nate said, seemingly oblivious to Cody's discomfort. "I mean, you're the only friend I have. I don't know my way around. I don't even know where the school is, now that I think about it."

Cody took a deep breath and made himself say the words he'd rehearsed in his head a hundred times, although he couldn't look Nate in the eyes as he did. "You don't want the others to know we're friends."

"Why not?"

"Because—" Fuck, what was he supposed to say? He made himself meet Nate's confused gaze over the rack of clothing. "Because you don't. That's all."

"You're too cool to hang out with the preppy guy from Orange Grove? Is that it?" Nate actually seemed upset by the idea.

"Yeah, that's it. I'm worried you'll ruin my rep."

Nate actually looked a bit hurt by that comment, like he didn't quite realize Cody was being sarcastic.

Cody sighed and tried a different tactic: the truth. "Think about it, man. Have you seen anybody else in Warren speak to me?"

"We hang out in a cow field. I haven't seen anybody out there at all."

Good point. Still, he didn't understand. How could he? But once school started, he would.

"The thing is, you're gonna be in classes with all those assholes from the Grove. They're gonna be curious about you, trying to figure out if you're cool or not. And they're gonna tell you things about me." Cody stared at the hangers on the metal bar in front of him so he wouldn't have to see Nate's face. "Some of what they tell you will be lies, but some will be true. And either way, you won't want to be seen with me after that." There was *not* an itch in his throat as he said those words. He refused to acknowledge it. "Being the new kid is tough enough. No need to make things worse by showing up on your first day with the class pariah."

Out of the corner of his eye, he saw Nate duck his head. Nate started sorting through the shirts in front of him, even though Cody didn't think he was seeing any of them. When Nate finally glanced up again, his cheeks were red. Was he embarrassed, or mad?

"I'll be at the gas station at seven thirty," he said. "You better be there."

CHAPTER

A new coat was going to have to wait, but the money from his mother was enough to cover a couple of pairs of jeans, a few T-shirts, a hooded sweatshirt, and—best of all—a pair of barely used black Converse that actually fit. Cody had always hated having to buy shoes secondhand, but at least he'd managed to score a pair that didn't scream "trailer park." Hell, even those assholes from the Grove wore Converse.

He was more nervous than usual on the first day of school. Nate had made him promise more than once that he wouldn't stand him up. He was like a damn dog with a bone, stuck on the idea that having Cody with him on the first day would somehow make it easier. No matter how many times Cody tried to tell him the opposite was true, Nate insisted, which was how Cody found himself at the gas station, climbing into Nate's car at seven thirty in the morning on the day after Labor Day.

He'd gotten used to his car, but Nate looked different. During the few short weeks of their friendship, he'd let his preppiness slide a bit. Cody hadn't quite realized he was doing it until he saw Nate all decked out for school with his collar flipped up and his newly cut hair all moussed into place. He was even wearing a Members Only jacket, with the sleeves pushed partway up his forearms.

Christ, he was going to have some girl from the Grove following him around like a lost puppy by the end of the day.

"You look ridiculous."

Nate didn't even blink. "You need a haircut."

That was true, but Cody chose not to answer, turning to look out the window as Nate pulled out of the gas station and turned toward the school.

"I still think you should have gone for the parachute pants and the leather jacket."

Cody laughed, despite himself. "Maybe next time."

His stomach clenched as they turned into the parking lot. Already, the groups had formed—the preps and jocks by the big Walter Warren High School sign in front of the school, posing so everybody could see which brands they were sporting. The cowboys were gathered near the corner of the building, keeping to themselves. A few of the nobodies who didn't fit in anywhere were huddled around the flagpole, talking quietly and doing their best not to be seen. Cody wished he could be one of them—one of the regular students who mostly went unnoticed—but even that didn't seem to be an option for him. And off in the corner of the parking lot were the few people Cody might have called friends, the other trailer-park residents, gathered in a circle as if that could hide the cigarettes they were smoking.

All those little cliques, and Cody imagined every single one of them turning to watch as Nate parked. Jennifer Parker raised her hand to wave at them. Well, to wave at Nate, at any rate. Then she glanced at Cody, and her brow wrinkled in confusion. She leaned toward her friends, and they all started talking, glancing pointedly toward the Mustang.

"I take it you've met her already?" It surprised Cody, because Nate hadn't mentioned it.

"Once." Nate didn't seem inclined to elaborate. He killed the engine and sat there, fiddling with his class ring, sizing it all up. "It's so small. I mean, is this everybody?"

"I'm sure there are a few more inside."

"How many students, though?"

"About two hundred total."

Nate whistled through his teeth and looked down at his class ring. "My graduating class alone back in Austin was four hundred and thirty two." He scowled. "I guess it isn't my graduating class anymore." He scanned the groups again. "Do they ever mix?"

"On the surface, sure. I mean, like you said, the school isn't that big. We all have classes together. Or, you know, some of the cowboys are on the wrestling team and the football team with the jocks. But once lunchtime rolls around—"

"Or parties on the weekend?"

"Right. Then you gotta know where you belong. And if you don't, they'll sure as hell let you know." Nate glanced Cody's way, and Cody shook his head, refusing to meet Nate's eyes. "There's a few people who manage to sort of float between them all, you know? Like Logan Robertson and Christine Lucero."

"Christine? I think I met her too."

Cody looked over at him, his curiosity piqued. "When was this?"

"Last week. The day before we went to Rock Springs. I went out to some mine with a few of them."

For some reason, that hurt. Cody couldn't quite say why. "Why didn't you tell me?"

"Because I knew you'd make a big deal out of it." And Nate's tone told him that was exactly what he thought Cody was doing.

"What'd they say about me?"

"Nothing."

Cody knew he was lying by the way he clenched his jaw and refused to look at him, but they must not have given him the full scoop, or Nate wouldn't have insisted on Cody riding to school with him. "Did you bang Christine?"

Nate's head whipped his way. "What? No!"

"Somebody did. Logan can go from group to group because he's the quarterback, and he does what he wants. That's just how he is, but Christine only manages because she puts out." He felt guilty for saying it though. He liked Christine. "It ain't her fault, you know. Her dad makes my dad look like Father of the Year. Show me a girl who can't say no, I'll show you a girl who's spent too many birthdays staring out the window, waiting for her daddy to show. Seems like having a deadbeat dad's harder on girls than it is on us, you know?"

This was met with dead silence, and Cody squirmed, wondering why he'd said so much. He finally made himself look over at Nate. He couldn't read Nate's expression—he was either impressed, or sad, or both. "No, I didn't know. I hadn't ever quite realized that, but you're right. The girls I knew back home with that kind of reputation . . ." He leaned back in his seat, tapping his fingers against the steering wheel, staring at some distant point in the sky, miles beyond the high school. "So what happens to boys with deadbeat moms?"

Cody frowned, wondering how he'd managed to make Nate so somber. "They become serial killers. Whatta you think?"

Nate laughed, like Cody'd hoped he would, and it felt like they were back on solid ground again.

"Christine's cool. She's a year behind us. Her brother Larry is our year though, and he's the world's biggest asshole. Just so you know."

"Can't wait to meet him."

Cody sighed, noting the way the Orange Grove residents were all watching them while trying to look like they weren't. "They're gonna give you hell for giving me a ride. You should tell 'em we just met, and you felt sorry for me."

"I'm not telling them that."

Cody rubbed his forehead, wondering how many times he'd get his ass kicked this year. Then he glanced at Nate and wondered the same thing about him. Of course, once Nate was in tight with the preps, he'd only have the cowboys to worry about. Cody, on the other hand, was pretty much fair game. He felt like the minute he and Nate walked through the front doors, he'd be alone again. No matter what Nate said now, he wouldn't want to keep being seen with Cody. Not once he heard what those Orange Grove assholes had to say. But putting it off wasn't going to make it any easier to lose the best friend he'd had in years.

"Well," Cody made himself say, "I guess it's now or never."

"Guess so."

The first bell rang as they climbed out of the car. On a normal school day, that would have meant five minutes before first period started. Today, they followed the crowd into the gym to pick up schedules and locker assignments. Lines were forming based on the first letter of last names. Not surprisingly, the *B*s and the *L*s weren't in the same line.

Cody's stomach squirmed. A lump started to form in his throat, and he swallowed hard, telling himself to stop being such a sentimental fool.

Nate took a deep breath. "I'll see you at lunch, right?"

Cody shoved his hands deep into his pockets and stared at the toes of his shoes. After the trip to Rock Springs for clothes, he was down to his last five dollars, and he wasn't about to spend it on a school lunch. He'd scarfed down a peanut butter sandwich for breakfast. That and a smoke at lunch would have to tide him over until after school. But no way in hell was he telling Nate any of that.

"Right," he lied.

"Okay. Here goes nothing."

And just like that, Cody was alone.

Not like it was the first time or anything, but it felt a bit lonelier than it ever had before.

Nate found the line for seniors with last names starting with letters *A* through *C* and took his spot at the end, right behind Brian.

"Hey!" Brian said, as if they were long-lost friends and not two guys who'd barely spoken as they'd passed a joint around a campfire. "Nathan, right?"

"I go by Nate."

"Where've you been, man? Nobody's seen you around at all."

Nate glanced over at Cody, still waiting in line for his own schedule. He had his arms crossed protectively over his chest and his head down. "At home."

"Well hey, don't worry about being the new kid. I got your back, you know?"

Somehow, that didn't make Nate feel any better. "Thanks."

They collected their schedules and locker assignments, and Brian stepped close to compare them. They were almost a perfect match.

"Come on. I'll show you where the lockers are before first period starts."

Nate looked around for Cody. It took him a few seconds, but he finally spotted him against the far wall. Cody was chewing his lip, staring at his own slip of paper. Nate wondered how many classes they'd have together, or if their lockers were at least close.

Brian caught the direction of his gaze and laughed, throwing his arm over Nate's shoulder. "Don't worry about him. I don't know how you got stuck giving that loser a ride, but he'll leave you alone now that he knows you're one of us."

Nate had a feeling that was more true than even Brian knew. Cody looked up right then, his eyes meeting Nate's for only a fraction of a second. One brief moment, with Nate trying to say, *Don't leave me.*

He had a feeling what Cody was saying was *Good-bye.*

Nate hardly saw Cody the rest of the day. The passing periods were too crazy, with Nate trying to find his way around a brand-new school while Brian and Jennifer introduced him to the rest of their Orange Grove friends. He'd already met Brad, Michelle, and the other Jennifer, but there were nearly a dozen more, across all four grades, all of them in designer jeans and Members Only jackets. By lunchtime, Nate wished his mom had never bought his. He hid it in his locker and looked for Cody.

But Cody was nowhere to be seen. It pissed Nate off a bit. Cody could lay the blame on the Grove and the cliques all he wanted, but the way Nate saw it, Cody was the one abandoning him, not the other way around. It wasn't until social studies, the very last class of the day, that he saw Cody again. Nate had been placed in the advance classes for every subject, and it seemed Cody hadn't, but social studies was one of the few classes that wasn't broken into levels. It was also one of the few classes where they were able to choose their own seats. Nate was sitting behind Brian, with Jennifer on his right and another of their Grove friends to his left. His heart skipped a beat when Cody walked in. He found himself smiling, willing Cody to catch his eye.

Cody scanned the desks quickly, his eyes wary. He stopped on Nate, pursing his lips. Nate waved, trying to beckon Cody to come over. The seat behind Nate was still empty, and he wanted nothing more than to have Cody there, at his back.

"What are you doing?" Jennifer whispered, pulling his hand down. "We don't want him by us!"

Nate was about to protest, but it was too late. Cody had already chosen a desk on the far side, near the back of the room, right by the door. He stared resolutely at the desk in front of him, refusing to look

Nate's way. Once class ended, he was out the door again before Nate could even gather his things.

Nate cursed under his breath, although whether he was cursing himself or his new Grove friends or Cody, he didn't know. He assumed he'd give Cody a ride home, and he waited at the car for fifteen minutes. Cody never appeared, and Nate finally admitted to himself that Cody'd chosen to walk rather than ride with him.

Wednesday was much the same. Nate went to the gas station at seven thirty to pick Cody up, but Cody wasn't there. Nate waited a few minutes, fuming. He wanted to go to Cody's house. To confront him. To tell him he was being a fool. If Cody'd just lighten up and trust him, he could make things work. He could bridge that gap between Cody and the preps. But he had no idea where Cody lived. He didn't even know his phone number. It was a shocking realization. He felt like they'd been friends over the summer, but the truth was, unless Cody was at the gas station or in Jim's field, Nate had no way of finding him.

He'd talk to Cody after social studies. He'd be ready as soon as the bell rang, and he'd run if he had to. He'd force Cody to ride home with him. Cody wanted to shut him out, to pretend they'd never sat across from each other at McDonald's, dipping fries into their chocolate shakes. He wanted to pretend like they hadn't talked about their moms and what it felt like to have only one parent around. It felt like Cody'd locked himself away in some secret room, but Nate intended to beat down the door. He'd tear the walls down with his own hands if that's what he had to do.

That's what he told himself, at any rate. But when the last bell rang, Jennifer was flirting with him, and Brian was talking about the bonfire they were having on Friday after school, and Michelle was talking about the new Dead Milkmen album and how Nate just had to hear it.

And, in the end, he didn't even notice when Cody ducked out the door.

CHAPTER
Seven

Cody had known from the beginning that he'd lose Nate once school started, but knowing didn't make it any easier.

It wasn't as if Nate ignored him completely. It was true he made no effort to talk to Cody in social studies, but on the rare occasions when they passed each other in the hall, Nate still said hi, or at least raised his hand in greeting. But Cody felt the hostility of the Grove residents in Nate's company. He heard their snickers as they passed. Once, he heard Brian say, "Why do you still talk to that loser?" And so Cody changed his habits. He learned when and where he was most likely to see Nate, and he altered his course through the school in order to avoid him.

Even he couldn't have said whether completely avoiding Nate made things better or worse.

To his surprise, Logan turned out to be his savior.

Logan's little sister, Shelley, was a sophomore, and she was Orange Grove all the way. Logan, though, was the exception to every rule, partly because he was so big nobody dared mess with him, partly because he was the quarterback and the star of the football team. He had plenty of family in Wyoming, but his parents had moved to Warren three years earlier to open a steakhouse. Having come from California garnered him a certain amount of credibility, and a fair share of leeway. He was the only kid in school who could pick and choose who to hang out with from day to day. Logan spent a lot of his time at the bowling alley, but he was in the advanced classes in English, math, and science, and he played football. He smoked, which should have made him ineligible for football, but it wasn't like the coach was going to bench his best player. He was in 4-H, but drove a shiny black Camaro. Those things alone made him hard to pin down, but he refused to conform to clique standards when it came to clothing, too. Most days, he wore 501s and a denim jacket, which would have pegged him a burnout, but he wore them with pastel polo shirts, tailored sweaters, cowboy boots, and a cowboy hat.

Nobody else in the school could have made that work, but he did.

Logan had always been friendly toward Cody. Not like they ever hung out or exchanged phone numbers, but Logan had never avoided him like the others, and he'd certainly never called him names.

Not to his face, at any rate.

Still, Cody was surprised on Friday when Logan not only sat next to him in social studies, but leaned across the aisle to talk to him.

"Hey, man. I've been trying to pin you down in the smoking section all week, but you're never there when I am."

Logan had been looking for him? "I only go out at lunch." He'd been trying to cut down on how much he smoked, mostly because he was a buck twenty away from being flat broke.

"Listen. You know the Tomahawk Saloon?"

Sure, he knew it. Not that he'd ever eaten there. The Tomahawk was what passed for fine dining in Warren. "Yeah. Your family owns it, right?"

"My dad owns it. My Uncle Frank manages it. Anyway, I've been washing dishes there part-time since last spring."

The room was getting loud as more students came in and claimed their desks. Jimmy Riordan and Larry Lucero sat behind them and did their best not to look interested in whatever it was Logan had to say to the class freak.

"Okay," Cody said, wondering what this had to do with him.

Logan glanced at Jimmy and Larry, then leaned closer to Cody, practically blocking the aisle with his bulk. He lowered his voice. "Well, our other dishwasher got canned last week, so they're looking for help, and I told Frank about you."

Cody's heart leaped. "You did? Why?" After all, there were plenty of other people in Warren looking for work.

"I thought you might like to earn a bit of cash, that's all. It's just washing dishes, and it's only minimum wage. But otherwise, it's just gonna go to some dick-weed like Larry back there, or some addict like Pete Jessup who'll only show up half the time and be high the other half. And frankly, I figured you could use it more."

It was said without pity. Without judgment. Just a fact. It might have felt insulting if Cody hadn't been so surprised. "Would he really hire me?"

"You bet. I told him we'd painted houses together last summer, how you were the only one who showed up on time every day. The hours kind of suck but—"

"Okay, people!" Mrs. Simmons said as the bell rang. "Enough chatter. Let's talk about last night's homework. How many of you did the reading?"

"Think about it," Logan whispered before straightening back up into his own seat.

Cody sat there, stunned. It was true he'd had a house-painting job with Logan the summer before their junior year, but it'd only been a couple of weekends, and they'd barely spoken to each other during that time. Cody was surprised Logan even remembered. He was even more surprised that Logan would stick his neck out for him. Part-time at minimum wage wouldn't be much, but it'd be a hell of a lot better than nothing. He might even be able to get a new coat before the snow started to fly.

He spent the rest of the class dreaming about that first paycheck.

Washing dishes was more enjoyable than Cody had expected. Sure, the water was gross and his hands ended up looking like prunes, but he was sequestered in a back corner, alone more often than not, which suited him just fine. Frank didn't mind if he took smoke breaks, as long as he was all caught up, and best of all, the waitresses occasionally gave Cody dinner—a steak returned for being overcooked, or a baked potato that wasn't supposed to be loaded but was. Cody was amazed at how many perfectly good dinners came back to the kitchen untouched, and unless somebody wanted them, they went into the trash.

He'd never eaten so well in his life.

The downside was that being alone, up to his elbows in soapy water, he had way too much time to think about Nate. He remembered afternoons spent playing cards. He dreamed up a hundred new trips together to Rock Springs or Casper. He often imagined Nate and his father out in the dining room, perusing the menu, not even bothering to check the prices before they ordered. He wondered if Nate ever thought about him.

It was stupid, but it was hard to stop daydreaming about having his one and only friend back.

Well.

One of his *two* friends, as it turned out.

Cody and Logan mostly worked opposite shifts, but every once in a while, they'd overlap. Saturday nights especially were often busy enough to warrant both of them, and Logan liked to talk. He talked about football and how his parents hoped he'd get a scholarship. He talked about the trip to Orlando he'd taken with his family that summer, and about the trip to Mexico they'd take after Christmas. He talked about school. About the Grove residents and their weird obsession with what name brands were selling in cities where shopping malls actually existed. He talked about the trailer-park kids at the bowling alley, and the cowboys who were in 4-H with him, and the girls . . .

Good lord, he liked to talk about girls. He especially liked to talk about Jamie Simpson, the daughter of a cattle rancher who lived a few miles north of Warren. Cody mostly knew her as the girl who'd beaten Larry Lucero's ass on the playground back in fifth grade, but she'd made more of a name for herself in the last couple of years by taking first place two years running in both bareback bronc riding and breakaway roping at the rodeo, beating all the boys from Warren in the process.

Yeah. Logan talked about her a lot.

It wasn't that he was a gossip. It was more like he was a sponge, soaking up information all day long, and when he found himself in the back corner of the kitchen with Cody, he had to wring it all out. His mouth just started running, never really bad-mouthing anybody. Just stating the facts, as he saw them. He asked a lot of questions too, and Cody answered, hesitantly at first, but growing more confident as the weeks passed. Logan never passed judgment. He never laughed at Cody. He never seemed surprised or shocked by the things Cody said, and Cody found himself revealing more of himself than he normally did. He talked about his dad, and about not having a winter coat, and about his summer.

He talked about Nate.

He hadn't quite realized he was doing it until one night when Logan said, "Sounds like you guys were thick as thieves before school started."

Thick as thieves. Seemed like a damn stupid saying, but it made Cody realize how often Nate's name had fallen off his tongue. And once he realized it, he couldn't *stop* realizing it. Sometimes it felt like every third word out of his mouth was Nate's name, and he began to hate himself a bit more with each one.

He didn't hate Nate, though. Somehow, he couldn't ever manage that.

"Did you hear about Jerry Smith?" Logan asked one Saturday in mid-October. The wind was howling outside, and everybody was predicting the first snow of the year, but in the back of the kitchen, it was warm and steamy and comfortable. Cody was washing while Logan put away what was already clean. Some of the shelving was pretty high, and at just over six feet tall, Logan had a lot of reach on Cody, who was closer to five seven.

"Who?"

"Jerry Smith. He used to play for the Redskins. Retired with the most touchdowns by a tight end in NFL history."

"No. What about him?"

"He died of AIDS on Wednesday."

Cody went cold, suddenly afraid to look at Logan, feeling uncomfortable with him for the first time in weeks. "What's that got to do with me?"

"Nothing. Just making conversation."

And it was true, he didn't sound disgusted or accusatory. Still, it made Cody nervous. He tried to keep his voice steady as he said, "Seems like more and more people are dying of it every day."

"Does it worry you?"

"Why would it?" But he knew he sounded too defensive.

Logan sighed. "Look, man. I know what they say about you."

Cody's heart tripped into high gear. "Who?"

Logan shrugged, putting a stack of big silver mixing bowls back on a shelf. "Everybody."

"What exactly do they say?" Even though he already knew the answer to that question.

"That you're gay and you have the hots for Nate Bradford."

Well, he thought he knew, at any rate, but he'd only been half right. He stopped in the middle of scrubbing a frying pan, his heart pounding, his stomach doing strange, fluttery things. The part about him being gay wasn't a surprise, but he hadn't expected Nate to be dragged into it, especially since they hadn't even spoken since the beginning of school.

Logan was sorting through the clean silverware, separating forks, knives, and spoons into separate bins, but glancing Cody's way every few seconds, waiting for an answer. It took a couple of tries to make himself speak. "You trying to ask me if it's true?"

"No. I'm trying to tell you, I don't really care either way. I mean, I don't see how you could look at a dude and actually want to see him naked, let alone kiss him. Or, you know . . . do other things with him." He cleared his throat, and Cody ducked his head, hoping his too-long hair hid the burn of his cheeks. "But the thing is, there aren't exactly a lot of babes in Warren, Wyoming, and I figure the less competition I have for Jamie, the better."

"Oh." Cody didn't know what to say to that. He'd never imagined anybody in Warren, Wyoming, might be so blasé about his darkest secret. He'd also never fully considered his feelings for Nate. Sure, he liked him. Sure, he missed him like crazy. And yes, his heart ached a little bit every time he thought about him. He could remember the exact cadence of Nate's laugh, and the way he tilted his head when Cody gave him a hard time, and the exact curve of his lips when he smiled. But never once in their time together had Cody seriously considered kissing Nate, or even trying to hold his hand, mostly because he figured that'd send Nate running for the hills.

Or for Orange Grove, at any rate.

But Logan's question brought him up short. His stomach continued to feel too wiggly and too light and altogether too uncomfortable, but in a way that was kind of exciting. He imagined how it might feel to kiss Nate, and smiled at the sudden tingle in his groin.

Did he really have a crush on Nate?

"But, you know," Logan said quietly, interrupting Cody's thoughts, "just out of curiosity, you don't have the hots for Jamie, do you?"

Cody laughed, confident that in this at least, he could speak the truth. "No. As far as I'm concerned, Jamie Simpson is all yours."

"From your lips to God's ears, my friend."

Over the first few weeks of the school year, Nate seemed to see less and less of Cody, and more and more of the people from the Grove.

He didn't like them. It didn't take him long to figure that out. Yes, in some ways they were more like him than Cody was, but there was a rebelliousness there that made him uncomfortable. And despite his dad's claim that there was a rich Asian history in the area, nobody would guess it by looking at the inhabitants. With the exception of one Hispanic family, every single kid at Walter Warren High School was Caucasian. Nate thought no racial tension should have meant no racism, but the Orange Grove residents displayed a casual prejudice toward anybody who wasn't white, as well as toward anybody who lived in the trailer park.

Nate had never heard so many racist jokes in his life.

There was also way too much sex. Nate was a virgin. He'd had a couple of awkward make-out sessions with girls back home, but he'd never felt compelled to test the girls' boundaries by sliding his hand into their shirts or down their pants. The kissing had never exactly felt right, and he assumed someday he'd meet a girl who did feel right. Until then, he figured he'd have to wait.

Except suddenly here he was, in the windblown boonies of Wyoming, with girls coming on to him in ways they never had back home. Christine Lucero and Jennifer Parker both made their interest in him quite clear. It should have been flattering—maybe even arousing—but it wasn't. He'd been embarrassingly familiar with his right hand back in Texas, but since moving to Warren, even masturbation didn't appeal to him the way it used to.

And the sex was only the beginning. There was more alcohol than he was used to. More marijuana. More of everything. Two weeks into the school year, he let Brian and Brad drag him to a party in the Grove. It was at Jennifer Carrington's house, because her parents were out of town, but Nate had a feeling the gathering hadn't been her idea. He could tell by the way she rushed around putting coasters under drinks and telling people not to smoke that she was nervous about her parents finding out.

Nate downed a beer and was handed another. Logan and a couple of jocks were playing quarters on the coffee table with three of the cheerleaders. Another group was stair surfing. The entire room was sweet with the tang of marijuana. Three boys in the corner were laughingly contemplating the possibility of burning down one of the haystacks in a field outside of town.

"What if the whole field burns down?"

"That'd be rad!"

Nate walked on.

He found a small group in one of the bedrooms, gathered around a dresser. Brian and Brad, plus another guy and a girl who Nate had seen at school but didn't know. Brian glanced up as Nate walked in, then smiled.

"Hey, man. Just in time. I swiped this from my dad's dresser this morning."

"Won't he notice?" the girl asked.

"He never has before."

Nate assumed it was pornography of some kind, and he moved closer, trying to get a glimpse between the bodies. But what he saw made him stop short.

It was a marble cutting board with white powder already sorted into neat little lines. "Cocaine?" he said, stunned.

"Shh!" they all said at once, turning toward him, and Nate felt his cheeks begin to burn. He'd seen cocaine in movies and on TV, but at a party? No. None of his friends in Texas had ever even considered it. But once again, here in Wyoming, he found himself the odd man out, feeling like the lone prude in a group that seemed to know far more about the world than he did.

Didn't they even care that his dad was a cop?

He waited until they'd all turned back to the tray before ducking out of the room. He left his half-full beer on the coffee table and walked home. Brian and Brad cornered him the next Monday in school, wanting him to promise that he wasn't planning to tell his dad.

"It's not a big deal," Brian told him. "Just keep it to yourself, all right?"

"Of course," Nate promised. He had no desire to cause trouble. But he had no desire to get into trouble, either, and when his dad told him a few days later that somebody had lit a haystack on fire and inadvertently destroyed two fields and killed a couple dozen head of cattle in the process, Nate bit his tongue, not wanting to tell his dad he knew who'd done it.

His conscience nagged at him, though. Burning down fields and killing cattle wasn't a victimless prank. It was a serious blow to some poor rancher's livelihood, and Nate vowed to distance himself from the Orange Grove group as much as possible. By the time October rolled around, he was looking for excuses to avoid Brian and Brad. He didn't want to be one of them. What he wanted was to be with Cody, but Cody had become inaccessible. On several different occasions, Nate wandered into the field, looking for him, but Cody was never there. Nate found only their deck of playing cards, wrapped in a plastic baggie to keep it dry, tucked into the corner of the wagon. In social studies, Cody always sat by the door, although these days, he talked to Logan more than he talked to the rest of the student body put together.

Jealousy burned in Nate's chest every time he saw them with their heads together in class. Everybody liked Logan except Nate, leaving him the odd man out again.

Once, Nate tried waiting outside the classroom, determined to stop Cody at the door. He planned to tell Cody that he was sorry, that he'd rather be friends with him than any of the Orange Grove residents, but Cody arrived next to Logan, so lost in conversation that he didn't even notice Nate standing there, and Nate hung his head in defeat as he made his way to his desk. Cody didn't even look his way, although Logan gave Nate a look he couldn't quite interpret.

When class ended, Nate gathered his books as fast as he could, but he couldn't get past the crush of students in order to reach Cody in time. He stepped into the hallway, looking both ways, trying to see which direction Cody had gone.

He caught a glimpse of black hair a few yards away, but he only made it three steps before he was stopped short by Christine Lucero.

"Hey, Nate. We're having a party on Friday at Jimmy Riordan's. You want to come with me?"

It was the third time she'd invited him to a party with her. The first had been to a gathering at the mine, with the Grove residents. The second party had been at the rock quarry, with the cowboys. Nate had declined both times, confident he'd be horribly out of place. But this one would be at Jimmy's place. Nate knew who Jimmy Riordan was, even though the only classes they had together were PE and social studies. Jimmy lived in the trailer park. He was one of the "burnouts," as Cody called him, often ditching class to smoke cigarettes in the parking lot, but he seemed like a nice enough guy.

Nate hesitated, contemplating. Would Cody be there?

"Sure," he said, as noncommittal as he could manage. "Maybe. I'll have to see."

"It'll be cool, I promise."

She touched his arm before walking away, and Nate watched her go, sure the exaggerated sway of her hips was just for him. She glanced over her shoulder once, blushing when she caught him still looking at her.

"You know she puts out, right?" Brian said from behind him.

Nate jumped, wishing he'd seen Brian coming so he could avoid him. "That's what I've heard."

"It's true, man. She doesn't even make you work for it. I went to her house last week. Wasn't even inside five minutes before she was in my lap."

His triumphant grin filled Nate with a deep sense of shame, and a fair amount of sympathy for Christine. "Show me a girl who can't say no, and I'll show you a girl who's spent too many birthdays waiting for her daddy to come home."

Brian blinked at him, his brow wrinkling, but only for a moment. Then he laughed. "Show me a girl who can't say no, and I'll ask her to homecoming."

That night, Nate dreamed of Christine Lucero.

She was in his bedroom. He didn't know how, or why, but she was in his bed, in his arms, lying beneath him.

Nate kissed her, thinking even as he did it how he wasn't sure he wanted to. He thought about all the guys who had kissed her before him. Brian and Brad, and God only knew who else. But it didn't matter. Nate was hard and ready, and he didn't necessarily want what they were doing to stop. He just wished it was with somebody else. Like maybe Jennifer Parker. Or Jennifer Carrington. Or Amy Prescott. Or maybe Cody.

Cody?

He saw Cody's smile. He heard Cody's laughter in his ears. And suddenly, that's who was under him. Cody gave him that secret smile Nate suspected only he had ever seen. He was laughing at Nate, yet somehow encouraging him too—an invitation in his dark eyes that made Nate ache in the most wonderful, erotic way. Cody was perfection, so sweet and sexy and shy and unapologetic, all at the same time, and Nate wanted him in a way that made no sense whatsoever.

He kissed him. He pulled Cody close and pushed slowly inside of him.

It was strange, because in his dream, Cody was like a girl down there, and Nate knew that wasn't right, but he also knew he didn't care. However things were fitting together below the waist didn't matter nearly as much as how it made him feel. And God, it felt good. *Cody* felt good. Somehow in Nate's dream, he was kissing Cody, but still seeing his face, seeing the way his neck arched as he threw his head back, feeling the length of Cody's body against his, thrusting into him again and again—

It peaked far too soon.

The intensity of it woke him, breathless and panting, still pushing against his mattress as he came. He didn't want to leave the dream behind, and he held on to the image of Cody underneath him. He lay there in the sticky pool of his own mess, his body still thrumming from the strength of his orgasm, remembering how it had felt to kiss Cody. It had felt like a miracle. Like an epiphany. Like a revelation.

It scared the hell out of him.

It was time to face reality. He rolled over and looked at his clock. It was 7:04. In a minute he'd have to get up and do something about his stained sheets before he went to school. And at school he'd have to deal with the Grove group. And Christine.

And Cody.

His dream left him feeling edgy and spacey and uncomfortable. He was halfway relieved when Cody continued to avoid him, but he found himself searching the rows of lockers again as he hadn't done since the first week of school, hoping to catch a glimpse of his thick, black hair. Hoping to hear his laugh echo through the halls. Not that Cody laughed much at school, and if he did, it was bound to be at something Logan said.

Still.

He desperately wanted to see him.

Nate raced to his locker before last period, determined to get to social studies early so he could grab a desk next to Cody. Who cared that nobody switched seats in that class? He was sick of being stuck with the Orange Grove assholes. He swapped textbooks and stopped to check his hair in the mirror on the inside of his locker door.

"Hey, Nate." It was Christine again. She moved to stand between him and his open locker.

"Uh . . . Hey." He glanced toward social studies, trying to see if Cody was there yet, but couldn't see much past the crush of people.

"Listen, about tonight. Jimmy's mom changed her plans, so party's off."

That was something of a relief, actually. "Okay."

"But I might go out to the quarry with Tom Watson and Lance Donaldson. You want to come with me?"

"I can't. Really. Thanks for the invite." He backed away, hoping she'd get the message and move so he could close his locker door. "I appreciate it, but I don't really know those guys—"

"That's okay. You could still—"

"Look, I've gotta go. I'm sorry. Maybe next time?"

"Oh. Sure." She finally moved aside, letting him slam the metal door shut. "See you around."

He raced for social studies, but it didn't do him any good. Cody was already in his seat, as was everybody else. Nate's usual seat was open. There were always a few open desks because there weren't enough students in the class to fill them all, and Nate took one near the back, but on the opposite side of the room as Cody. It was the only open desk that allowed him to see Cody without turning around in his seat. He ignored the confused looks of the Orange Grove group as the bell rang, and class began.

They were studying the end of World War II, and Mrs. Simmons was babbling on about the Universal Declaration of Human Rights and the Marshall Plan, but Nate didn't hear any of it. He was two rows back and three over from Cody, giving Nate a side view of the back of his head. When Cody looked at his textbook, he tipped his head down, and his thick, black hair fell forward, hiding his face from view. When he was listening to the teacher, he turned slightly Nate's way, allowing Nate to see his cheek and the shell of his ear. And when Cody leaned across the aisle to talk to Logan, his T-shirt rode up in the back, giving Nate a brief glimpse of the pale skin above his waistband.

Nate found that expanse of exposed flesh intriguing. He imagined touching it, maybe running his hand up the inside of Cody's shirt.

Cody went back to listening to Mrs. Simmons, and Nate propped his chin in his hand, studying the lines of Cody's neck, analyzing the way his shoulders hunched when the teacher looked his way, and the way they relaxed again when the teacher moved on. Nate thought about his dream. In the bright light of day, it seemed hazy and surreal, but he could still remember the exact look on Cody's face as they'd kissed.

Nate's stomach fluttered a bit at the thought, and he felt a familiar twinge of arousal in his groin.

It made him uncomfortable, realizing he was thinking about his best friend in such a blatantly sexual way. Cody wasn't supposed to make him feel like this. Cody wasn't supposed to turn him on. But watching Cody now, seeing the tender curve of his neck, the smooth line where it met his shoulder, Nate had the undeniable urge to run his fingertips over that bit of skin. He wanted to explore it with his lips and his tongue, to see if Cody made the same sounds in real life as he did in Nate's dream.

The possibility made him breathless.

"Mr. Bradford!"

Mrs. Simmons had the annoying habit of addressing everybody by their last names, so Nate didn't realize the teacher was addressing him until the student next to him kicked his chair and hissed, "That's you, dumbass!"

Nate jumped. Mrs. Simmons was looking right at him, her fists on her expansive hips and her eyebrows up.

"Yes?" Nate felt his cheeks burning. He risked a glance Cody's way. Cody's eyes were determinedly glued to his textbook. Logan, on the other hand, was staring at Nate with obvious puzzlement and more than a bit of amusement. "I'm sorry. What was the question?"

"We're talking about the Servicemen's Readjustment Act of 1944, otherwise known as . . ."

"Uh, the GI Bill?"

"And what was the purpose of this bill?"

"To help soldiers returning from the war buy houses and go to college and, uh, stuff like that."

"Yes, 'stuff like that.'" Mrs. Simmons almost smiled. "You don't pay attention in class, but at least I know you did the reading."

She moved on, letting Nate off the hook.

And Nate went back to studying the perfect curve of Cody's neck.

CHAPTER
Eight

Nate ventured out to the field on Friday night, but once again found the wagon empty. He spent the rest of the evening watching TV with his dad. He checked the field again three times on Saturday, but Cody wasn't there.

Where the hell could he be? He wouldn't go to the rock quarry or the mine. He wasn't in the field. It was possible he was sitting at home by himself, but Nate dismissed that possibility, not because it was unlikely, but because he hoped it was wrong. After all, he still had no idea where Cody lived, so the only chance he had of finding him was if Cody was somewhere other than home.

It wasn't until he was driving back to Orange Grove and spotted Logan's Camaro in the parking lot of the bowling alley that Nate realized how stupid he'd been. Hadn't Cody told him the bowling alley was the only hangout he'd go to? And if Logan was here, Cody probably was too.

Nate tried not to be nervous as he stepped inside.

The bowling alley smelled like every bowling alley Nate had ever been in, except more so, the foul odors condensed in the relatively small space. Sweaty feet, disinfectant spray, and stale beer, undercut by the tantalizing aroma of hamburgers and the acrid tang of lots of cigarette smoke. There were only three lanes, two of them being used by a group of adults. A chain of empty beer bottles lined the counter behind them. To the right of the door was the shoe rental counter. The employee working it took one look at Nate and went back to reading his *Mad* magazine. To Nate's left was the source of the more pleasant aromas—a food counter, with a pegboard menu boasting burgers, hot dogs, and chili-cheese fries. And just past that, Nate found the other high school students. They were lounging around a half-dozen tables that trailed from the makeshift café to the half-assed arcade in the corner.

Nate approached slowly, his heart sinking. He couldn't picture Cody here, and his eyes skipped from face to face, confirming what he'd already suspected. No Cody. The few people who bothered to notice his arrival quickly dismissed him.

All but one.

Logan maintained eye contact, and Nate shifted from one foot to the other, debating. The obvious answer was just to ask Logan, but Logan wasn't alone. Larry Lucero, Amy Prescott, and Jimmy Riordan were with him. Their conversation died as Nate edged closer.

"You look a bit lost," Logan said, although his tone was friendly enough.

"Yeah." Nate glanced at the others, wishing they'd all find something else to occupy their attention, but their eyes were glued on him. "I'm looking for Cody."

Larry laughed. Not a nice laugh, either. It was full of mockery. "He ain't here."

Amy and Jimmy glanced sideways at him. Logan ignored him completely.

"I can see that," Nate said. "I just . . . I couldn't think where else he'd be—"

"He doesn't come here much anymore," Amy said.

"Not since we all learned he's a fag." That was Larry again. And just as before, Amy and Jimmy threw awkward glares his way while Logan ignored him.

"Amy's right," Jimmy said. "Cody doesn't really hang out here. Not since—"

Larry laughed again. "Not since Dusty—"

Amy jumped to her feet, staring at Larry. "Shut up. Jesus, you're such a pig. What's Cody ever done to you?"

Larry only laughed, and Nate focused on Logan again. "Do you know where he lives?"

"He lives in the fucking Hole, man," Larry crowed. "How trashy can you get?"

Logan finally turned his icy gaze Larry's way. "Not like that's his fault."

"Guess his mom doesn't make enough as a lizard."

"That ain't his fault either."

"Everything else about him is, though."

Nate cleared his throat. He hated how soft and weak his voice sounded when he spoke. "Like what?"

The triumphant smile on Larry's face was enough to turn Nate's stomach. "Like that he's a fag."

Nate sighed. "I get it. You don't like him. That doesn't mean—"

"No, man." This time, it was Jimmy who spoke, not with Larry's gleeful hatred, but in a tone that was almost apologetic. "He's right. Cody's— Well, he's a homo. He's into guys. Everybody knows it."

"Yeah?" Logan said, suddenly pushing to his feet. "So what?"

Jimmy shrank a bit, backing down in front of Logan's obvious threat, but Larry wasn't so easily cowed. "'So'? He probably has AIDS, the fucking queer."

Logan shook his head. "Jesus, you're an ignorant hick, you know that?"

"I don't believe it, anyway," Jimmy said without meeting anybody's eyes. "I mean, I've hung out with him a bit. We had slumber parties when we were kids, and he never came on to me."

Larry rolled his eyes. "Right. And God knows no fag could resist you, right?"

Jimmy shrugged, trying to look unconcerned, although he looked more embarrassed than anything.

"Who cares anyway?" Logan asked.

They were all standing now, moving away from the table, closing in on each other. The other teenagers in the bowling alley began to look their way, like sharks sensing blood in the water.

"You telling me you don't care that he takes it up the ass?" Larry asked.

Logan shrugged. "That's what I'm telling you, yeah. Like Amy said, he's never done anything to you, has he? And it's nobody else's business anyway."

Amy looked pleased that Logan agreed with her. Larry, on the other hand, rolled his eyes. "Gimme a break, Logan. You just like thinking you're better than us."

"Better than you, at any rate." Larry opened his mouth to speak, but Logan rushed on before Larry could interrupt. "You know what? My whole life, my Aunt Nadine's lived with a chick. We call her Aunt Mabel. And if you ask my mom, she says Nadine and Mabel are just good friends. But I'll tell you what, I've been to their house, and they only have one bedroom."

"They're dykes!" Larry said.

"Maybe they are, but so what? They're cool, man. And I'd rather have them than my Uncle Frank. He's a drunk, and he beats on my aunt, and he beats on my cousins, and he harasses all the waitresses at work. Everybody knows he fucks around with any woman whose pants he can get into. So am I supposed to be proud of my good ol' Uncle Frank and ashamed of my aunts because they like each other more than they like guys?"

For a moment, nobody spoke. There was only the *wocka-wocka-wocka* of the Pac-Man game behind them. Everybody else was watching now, edging closer, trying to hear what was being said. Jimmy was the one who broke the silence.

"I didn't know that about Frank." His voice was low, pitched so the others couldn't hear. "I didn't know he hit Lorraine."

Nate couldn't help but think he was intentionally missing Logan's point.

"So you like your dyke aunts," Larry said, apparently unwilling to let the point go. He allowed his voice carry, seemingly pleased at the crowd that was drawing nearer. "You probably think about them while you're jacking off. You probably love imagining them in bed together."

Logan took a step toward Larry, and Jimmy and Nate both put a hand out at the same time to stop him, although Nate doubted they would have been able to hold him if he decided to really make a move.

"Or maybe you don't," Larry went on. "Maybe you think about Cody. Maybe you're a fag too."

Logan relaxed, his anger fading into a snide smirk. "You know I'm not gay. I fucked your sister." He glanced at the group of onlookers. "Of course, who here hasn't?"

The grin fell from Larry's face.

"Everybody's fucked her." Logan hooked his thumb over his shoulder. "Even Nate here's fucked her."

Nate shifted on his feet, wishing Logan hadn't dragged him into it. Maybe he should speak up and say it wasn't true, but Logan didn't give him a chance.

"Everybody's fucked her. Everybody except Cody, and you. And let's face it—she'd put out for Cody too, if he bothered to take her up on it." Logan's smile was mean, his eyes hard. "Must be frustrating, being the only guy in town she won't spread her legs for."

Larry flew at Logan. It was lucky Jimmy was both faster and bigger. Several other guys moved in too, some helping to hold Larry back, some putting their hands against Logan's chest, as if that would have been enough to stop him. Larry was flailing, swearing, screaming, spit flying from his mouth as he fought to get to Logan, and Logan just stood there and smiled. He shook his head, chuckling.

"You're an idiot." And with that, he turned on his heel and headed for the door. "You coming, Nate?" he called over his shoulder.

Nate glanced once at Larry, who was still blustering, his face so red Nate half wondered if the guy was having a heart attack, and Jimmy, trying to talk him down, telling him not to listen to Logan, and all the other teenagers who were staring, starting to put their heads together and whisper.

He didn't fit in here any better than he did with the Orange Grove clique.

"I'm coming."

He didn't quite run, but he walked as fast as he could, trying to catch up with Logan's long strides as he followed him out of the bowling alley, into the cold Wyoming night.

Logan was still chuckling when he finally stopped on the far side of the narrow parking lot. He leaned against the driver's side door of his Camaro and pulled out a pack of cigarettes.

"Why'd you do that?" Nate asked.

"Do what?" Logan shook one smoke free and offered the pack to Nate.

Nate shook his head. He hadn't smoked much since he'd lost touch with Cody. "Why'd you mouth off to Larry like that? And why'd you stick up for Cody?"

Logan lit his cigarette and pocketed the lighter. He blew smoke and tucked his thumbs into the front pockets of his jeans, looking at Nate like he was the biggest fool he'd ever seen.

Hell, maybe he was.

"'Cause Larry's an ignorant prick, and 'cause Cody doesn't deserve that shit." He took another drag off his cigarette, eyeing Nate through the smoke. "Unless maybe you think he does."

It sounded like a question. "No. Of course he doesn't." Nate wrapped his jacket tighter around himself. Cars drove past, their lights wedging between the vehicles parked at the bowling alley, but he could see Logan's expression well enough, thanks to the streetlights. "But is all that true?"

Logan crossed his arms, squinting at Nate. "All what?"

"The stuff he said."

Logan shook his head. "Nuh-uh. I ain't gonna make it that easy on you. You got a question, you ask it. Then I'll decide if I'm going to answer."

Nate sighed, thinking back through the entire thing. "He said Cody lived in the Hole."

"Well, you know where Cody lives, right?"

"No." He was glad it was dark so Logan couldn't see how much it pained him to admit it. "He never let me see. He always had me meet him at the gas station."

Logan's lips turned down. Not quite a frown, but a look of puzzlement. "Huh."

"What do they mean, anyway? What's the Hole?"

Logan scuffed the toe of his boot against the concrete, considering. Finally, he pointed down the road. "You're talking about that gas station on the corner of Front and El Paso, right?"

"Yeah."

"Okay. You know the trailer park just down the street from there?"

"Yes."

"And have you ever driven through that park?"

Nate's stomach sank, seeing where the conversation was headed. "You mean, under the tracks?"

"Right. You've seen what's there?"

"A dirt lot."

"And a handful of the rattiest trailers in town."

Nate stared down at his feet. "I've seen them."

"Everybody calls it the Shit Hole. Like, the last place all the trash in this town goes before it dies."

"And Cody lives there?"

Logan squinted at him through the haze of his cigarette. "Maybe you should ask him."

Nate pinched the bridge of his nose. Somebody drove by blasting Van Halen, David Lee Roth encouraging them to jump, before the truck rounded the corner and the music faded into the night. "What about the rest? Something about his mom? And lizards? And Cody?" He had to take a deep breath to make himself say the words. "Is he really gay?"

Logan didn't answer, and Nate finally dropped his hand and faced him. Logan still had his arms crossed. He'd almost finished the cigarette. It smoldered between two thick fingers. "The way Cody tells it, you guys were pretty close over break. Seems like you were friends."

"We were."

"But then school starts, and you just run off with your buddies from the Grove without a backward glance."

"No!" He wasn't sure if he was angry or just frustrated as hell. "That's not how it happened. He's the one avoiding me! I've looked for him. I've tried to find him. Jesus, that's why I came here tonight, to this fucking joke of a bowling alley, trying to figure out where the hell he's been hiding!" He sighed, scrubbing his hand through his hair, his sudden burst of temper already burned out. "It's like he's afraid of me or something."

Logan dropped his cigarette and ground it beneath the toe of his boot. "Or something."

He obviously knew Cody better than Nate at this point, and Nate tried not to hate him for it. "Look, are you going to tell me where he is or not?"

"At work." Logan put his hands in his jacket pockets. Nate expected him to pull his cigarettes out again, but he didn't. "He's been washing dishes with me up the Tomahawk."

Nate certainly hadn't expected that. "Since when?"

"Since school started. We alternate Mondays. He works Wednesday and Friday, so I can play football. I work Tuesday, Thursday. We both work Saturdays, sometimes together, sometimes back-to-back."

Okay. Here was information Nate could really work with. He felt a small surge of hope. "So he's there right now?"

"He's scheduled to work till ten."

"And what about tomorrow?"

"Sunday? Tomahawk's closed on Sundays."

Of course it was. Nate still wasn't used to living in a town that shut down completely every seventh day. Only Pat's, the bar on the edge of the town, was open on Sundays, and from what Nate could see, it seemed to do pretty good business too. "Will you see him before then?"

Logan cocked his head, studying Nate as if he couldn't quite tell if he was a butterfly or just a dumb old miller moth. "Maybe."

But the way he said it clearly meant, *If I decide I want to.*

"Will you ask him to meet me? Tell him I've been looking for him. Please. Tell him I'll meet him tomorrow at noon. At the usual place. Tell him—" He almost said, *Tell him I'm sorry,* but he stopped himself. Cody deserved to hear his apology in person. "Just tell him to come. Will you do that for me? Please?"

Logan pushed off the side of his car and turned to unlock the driver-side door. "For you? No. I won't do a goddamned thing for you." He didn't even glance over his shoulder as he climbed inside. "But I'll do it for Cody."

Cody was glad when ten o'clock rolled around. Logan had left at eight, and without him to talk to, the last two hours of Cody's shift had crawled by. He could have left early—they weren't all that busy—but unless Frank specifically told him to clock out, Cody kept working, doing the math in his head over and over, trying to determine exactly how much his next paycheck would be worth. It was late October, and the bite of winter was in the air. It was a miracle they hadn't had snow yet, and all Cody could think about was whether or not this paycheck would give him enough to get a coat.

Not if he wanted a brand-new one from the Sears catalog. He'd need several more weeks for that. He thought of the secondhand shop Nate had taken him to in Rock Springs.

There wasn't much chance of getting a ride from Nate this time around.

He pushed through the back door of the Tomahawk into the employee parking lot, already reaching for his cigarettes. He was surprised to find Logan there, leaning against the fender of his Camaro and smoking.

"What're you doing here?"

"Came to give you a ride."

"Oh." Logan had given him rides home before, but only when they both got out of work at the same time. Making a second trip back to pick him up was unexpected, but not unwelcome. Sometimes Cody didn't mind the one-and-a-half-mile walk back home, but he sure wasn't going to complain about getting to skip it. "Thanks."

Inside, the Camaro was still warm from the drive over. Cody knew from past trips that Logan didn't mind people smoking in his car, so he lit one up and cracked the window a bit to let the smoke out.

The engine rumbled to life, and Logan edged them out into the street, turning west. The car had a cassette player, and Logan had some kind of country music on low. Cody wasn't much into country, but he figured it was better than R.E.M. or Depeche Mode.

"I saw Nate tonight."

Cody froze, his stomach fluttering. So that's why Logan had come by—to talk about Nate. Cody kept his eyes averted, staring out the passenger-side window. "So?"

"At the bowling alley."

That got his attention. His head whipped Logan's direction. "Nate went to the bowling alley?" He couldn't even imagine it—Nate walking into that dive, all the burnouts lounging against the video games, smoking so much the ashtrays were overflowing halfway through the night. "Why?"

Logan glanced pointedly his way. "Looking for you."

Cody's heart did a funny little dance. He didn't know if it was from excitement or dread. "What'd he want?"

Logan's shrug was dramatically casual. "Well, if you had to ask me—and it turns out, you do—I'd say he misses you."

"I don't think so."

"I told you, man. He's been trying to get your attention in social studies all week."

Cody turned away to stare out the window again. "Not trying too hard, is he?"

Logan made a snorting, scoffing sound of disgust. "You're not exactly being fair. You think I don't notice how hard you work to *not* see him looking over at you every five minutes? Jesus, he was staring at you so long on Friday, he didn't even hear the teacher call his name."

"You're full of shit."

"Yeah. Okay." But he could hear the amusement in Logan's voice. "That's how it is. I'm the one who's full of shit. You betcha."

Logan could almost always make him laugh, but not this time. "He has his new friends now. All those assholes from Orange Grove. He's probably just going to ask me to buy him some beer so he can look cool for Jennifer Parker. He knows Vera will sell to me. Then he and his rich pals can all have a good laugh about it."

"Jesus. Only you could come up with something so pessimistic, you know that?"

Cody didn't answer.

"Listen, I've been up to the mine with those assholes from the Grove. I've been to their parties. I've seen Nate there with them. And I know you don't want to believe me, but he doesn't fit in with them as well as you think. Hell, he didn't even last thirty minutes at Jennifer Carrington's party a couple of weeks ago. Ran out of there like his life depended on it, except, you know, trying to look all casual while he did it." Logan laughed. "I heard he walked in on Brian and Brad doing lines. I think your boyfriend's too uptight for that scene."

Cody turned reluctantly toward Logan again, not wanting to expose too much of himself, but wanting to see Logan's face so he could judge how much of what he said was true and how much was bullshit. He didn't even bother to contradict the "boyfriend" remark. "But he's one of them."

"He has the clothes, I'll give you that, but that's as far as it goes. He always sort of hangs back, looking like he'd rather be anywhere else in the world than where he is."

Cody hadn't expected that.

They turned into the trailer park, and Logan slowed the car to a crawl on the speed bumps. Cody tossed his smoke out the window and watched the trailers creep past. They dipped under the train tracks, and Logan braked to a stop outside Cody's trailer. Cody was already reaching for the handle, anxious to escape their awkward conversation.

"Wait."

Cody did. It'd be damn rude to do anything else after Logan had gone out of his way just to give him a ride.

"He wants to see you. He wanted me to tell you he'll meet you tomorrow at noon. He said 'in the usual place,' whatever that means."

Cody closed his eyes, trying to stop the little glow that blossomed in his heart. It felt like hope, but hope was a lie. Hope was dangerous. Hope would make him bleed like nothing else in the world could. "Okay."

He started to pull the handle, but Logan spoke again before he could open the door.

"There's more."

And based on the tone of his voice, Cody wasn't going to like it.

"Jimmy and Larry were there, and Larry gave him an earful, man."

Cody closed his eyes, leaning his temple against the cold window. "Was this before or after Nate said he wanted to see me?" Because it was possible Nate had asked to see Cody, but then changed his mind after Larry flapped his fat mouth.

"Before. Larry went off. You know how he is. He's a loudmouth asshole, and he started saying, well . . . He said—"

"I know what he said. I know what they all say."

"But after that, Nate and I left, and he asked me if any of it was true."

"And what did you tell him?"

"I told him to ask you."

Cody wasn't sure if that made him feel better or worse. He appreciated that Logan wouldn't talk shit about him, and yet it almost would have been easier to let Nate get the confirmation he needed from somebody else so that Cody wouldn't have to see the disgust on his face when he found out the rumors were true.

Some of them, at least.

"And even after all that, he asked me—no, man, he practically fucking *begged* me—to tell you that he wanted to see you. I think he really misses you." Logan's voice was quieter now. Upsettingly gentle. "But I thought you deserved fair warning, so you could decide what exactly you wanted to say."

Cody nodded. He couldn't deny just how far Logan had gone, not only to deliver Nate's message, but to make it easier on Cody. "Thanks. For the ride, I mean, and—" *for being my friend.* But he wasn't sappy enough to say it out loud. "Thanks for everything, man."

He went quietly into the trailer. His mom's car was gone, so either she was working, or she was at one of the local bars. He was glad to have the house to himself.

He wouldn't lie to Nate. That was the one thing he knew. Whatever Nate asked, Cody would tell him the truth. It'd be a relief to finally have it out in the open.

And then?

That was the part he wasn't sure of.

He brushed his teeth, changed into a pair of sweats, and lay on his bed, staring at the ceiling, imagining all the ways their conversation could go.

Some of them ended with them as friends.

Some ended with Nate turning his back on Cody forever.

A few strayed into a place he hadn't dared imagine before—a place where Nate took Cody's hand. Where Nate leaned forward and kissed him while the Wyoming wind tried to blow them both away.

He wasn't sure which possibility scared him more.

ate spent half the night thinking about the things Larry had told him, and about Logan's refusal to give him straight answers. He suspected Larry hadn't lied about the Hole. As much as Nate hated to think it was true, it fit. Why else would Cody have worked so hard to hide his home from him? It bothered him that Cody hadn't trusted him.

As for the rest of the things Larry had said?

Nate was pretty sure those would turn out to be nothing more than teenagers being assholes. He spent the next morning debating whether or not to confront Cody with Larry's lies.

Nate arrived at the Hole just before noon. He parked his car where he always did, on the edge of the dirt lot that held the four decrepit trailers. He climbed out of his car and glanced at them, each one somehow seeming worse than the last.

Yes, he was pretty sure Cody lived in one of them.

He ducked through the barbed wire and headed into the field. He didn't really expect Cody to be there, even if Logan had delivered his message.

He pulled his coat tighter around himself as he trudged through the field. The cows barely spared him a glance. The sun was shining. At almost seven thousand feet above sea level, the rays were intense, but the wind was bitterly cold. They'd have to find a better place to spend their time. Hanging out in a damn field obviously wasn't going to be an option for very much longer.

With the wagon sunken into the earth facing the highway, he couldn't tell if Cody was at their meeting spot or not. Not until he was right on top of it, at any rate. But when he finally reached the upper edge of it and looked down, he found Cody there, grinding a cigarette out against the sun-bleached planks of the wagon.

For a moment, Nate just stood there, suddenly unsure what to say. Everything that popped into his head felt ridiculous after a month and a half of barely speaking to each other. He shifted awkwardly back and forth on his feet, debating.

"You gonna sit down or what?" Cody asked without even glancing up at him.

So much for niceties. Nate stepped over the upper edge of the wagon and slid down to the side that served as their bench. "I wasn't sure if you'd be here."

Cody shrugged, hunching his shoulders and rubbing his hands together. He was only wearing his usual too-small jean jacket with a zip-front hoodie over it. Nate wondered if the shirt underneath at least had long sleeves.

"Aren't you freezing? Why didn't you wear a coat?"

Cody ducked his head and crossed his arms, tucking his hands under his armpits. "You're the one who wanted to meet out here."

Nate sighed, feeling defeated. He'd clearly said the wrong thing. Again. He wasn't sure if he was really as clueless and clumsy was Cody made him feel, or if Cody was overly sensitive. Maybe a bit of both. But he hadn't pictured things starting out so wrong. He'd come here to try to reclaim his friendship with Cody, and so far, Cody hadn't even looked his way.

"Look, Cody. I'm sorry, okay? I'm sorry about how things have gone this year. I never meant—"

"It doesn't matter."

"It does though. I'd like for us to still be friends."

"Why bother?"

That hurt, no matter how much he wished it didn't. "You don't want to be friends, then? Is that what you're saying?"

"No. It's just, this was always how it was going to be. It's not a big deal. I knew you'd get in tight with that Grove clique, and I'd—"

"But I'm not 'in tight' with them. That's what I'm trying to say. I don't even like them, to tell you the truth. And I don't know how you and I ended getting separated in the first place. I mean . . ." He floundered, running his hands through his hair in frustration. "Jesus, you're the one who's been avoiding me, not the other way around!"

He waited, expecting Cody to deny it, maybe even to lash out, but Cody said only, "I know."

Nate sat back, stunned. "You do?"

Cody shrugged. "I figured it'd be easier that way."

"Easier for who?"

"Look, I know how people in this town see me. I know the things they say, and I figured once you heard all that, you wouldn't want to hang out with me anyway. And you wouldn't want to have to tell me. And I wouldn't want to be hanging around, watching you tiptoe around it. So I just split, all right?"

It was insane that Cody's ridiculous reasoning almost made sense. "But—"

"And I was right, wasn't I? Larry Lucero told you everything."

Nate looked down at the toes of his sneakers, his stomach suddenly twisting into knots. "I don't care what Larry says."

"Maybe you should."

Once again, Cody's answer surprised him. He remembered the day at the secondhand store. Cody had said, *"Some of what they tell you will be lies, but some will be true."* Nate's mouth went dry. "So, Larry wasn't lying?"

"Well, it depends. What did he tell you?"

"He told me you live in that little trailer park."

"Is that how he worded it?"

Nate had been trying to keep things civil, but it seemed Cody wasn't in the mood for having things sugar-coated. Nate took a deep breath and dove in. "He said you lived in the Hole."

"That part's true."

Nate had suspected as much, but having Cody admit it bothered him. It meant Cody had deliberately misled him.

"So each day last summer, you'd leave your house and walk to the gas station, and then I'd drive us right back to your house in order to walk out here? And at the end of the day, we'd walk past your house to my car, and I'd drive you to the gas station, just so you could turn around and come back to where you started?"

It was absurd, but he knew it was true. He could tell by the way Cody's cheeks turned red, and by the way he refused to meet Nate's eyes. But Cody didn't duck his head. He didn't try to hide. He kept his gaze straight ahead, locked on the distant highway.

"Why would you do that, Cody?"

"Why do you think?"

Nate scrubbed his fingers through his hair again, debating that. So Cody lived in the absolute crappiest, poorest corner of town. It didn't matter, did it? And yet, Nate couldn't quite deny that he might have thought worse of Cody on that first day if he'd known the truth. But that had been months ago. Certainly Cody trusted him by now?

"What else?" Cody asked.

"They said something about your mom. That she's a lizard?"

Cody still didn't look over, but his eyes flashed and his jaw clenched. He gripped the side of the wagon, as if anchoring himself, as if to keep himself from flying into a rage. "That's *not* true. She's a waitress. That's it."

That confused him. He wanted to ask Cody what exactly the term meant, but he could see how angry Cody was at the insinuation, so he kept his mouth shut.

"Is that it?" Cody asked. But Nate could tell by his voice that he knew it wasn't.

"No." Nate didn't want to say the rest though. If the comment about Cody's mom made him this angry, he didn't want to know how Cody would respond to the slurs against him. He fiddled with his class ring, wondering whether he should tell Cody to forget it.

"Go on." Cody's voice was quiet. "You can say it."

Nate blinked, stunned at his sudden realization: Cody already knew. This wasn't about Cody finding out what they'd said. He'd faced it all before, God knew how many times. This was about making Nate face it.

"They said that you're . . ." He wasn't sure what to say. He didn't know how to word it.

Cody did though. "A faggot?" He didn't seem angry. If anything, he seemed detached. They might have been discussing lunch. "A homo? A queer?"

"Yes."

Cody sighed, and for the first time, he ducked his head, looking down at the toes of his sneakers. "That part's true too."

It took a minute for those words to register. They were the last ones Nate expected to hear. Denial, anger, resentment, yes. Those he was ready for. But not this quiet acceptance.

"Really?" Nate asked, and immediately kicked himself mentally for asking something so utterly stupid.

Cody took a deep breath, as if gathering his nerve. "Three years ago, there was another boy here. His name was Dusty. His family only lived here for a few months. It was right at the end of the oil boom, and he never quite fit in. Tried to hang with the Grove group, but they never really took to him. The hicks didn't want him. He thought he was too good for the burnouts, and he sure as hell wasn't going to hang with the Mormons. And I guess I was the last option left. We had almost every class together, and he was cool to me. So one day he shows up at my place with a bottle of schnapps he'd swiped from his dad's cabinet. My mom was working, and we sat in my room and drank that bottle."

It was strange, listening to him. Nate's heart was pounding. He wanted to know what Cody would say next. He wanted to hear it in a way that made his cheeks burn. It made his palms damp and his stomach flutter.

Cody's eyes were still on the distant promise of the highway, but his focus was inward. "We finished the bottle, and then he started touching me. And kissing me." The image was vivid in Nate's head. He could imagine Cody in the bedroom he'd never seen. And thanks to his dream, he could imagine the look on Cody's face. The heat in Nate's cheeks spread, down his spine, past his anxious stomach, to settle into a deep, low hum between his legs.

"Oh?" he tried to say, trying to prompt him. God, he wanted to hear more.

"He was all over me. And fuck, Nate, I could tell you it was just being drunk that made it feel so good, but I'd be lying. I came so hard, I saw stars."

The hum between Nate's legs grew. He fought to keep his breathing normal, pulling his jacket tight around himself to hide the growing bulge at his groin.

"For three weeks, it was like that. He'd go try to hang with the others, but at some point, he'd be lonely, or maybe just horny as fuck; I don't know. And he'd find me. He'd knock on my window just after sunset, and I'd let him in."

And do what with him? Nate wanted to ask. *Tell me exactly what you did. Tell me everything you did together.* But his tongue was glued to the roof of his dry mouth, his voice gone.

"But then, his parents decided to split. He had to move away with his mom, even though he wanted to stay with his dad. And I don't know if he was mad at me, or mad at them, or just mad at the world, but he went out one night with those assholes from the Grove, and he told them everything. Except, you know, not *everything*. Because he made it sound like it was all me. Like I'd come on to him, and he hadn't ever wanted it. He made it sound like I showed up at his house, instead of him showing up at mine. He told them that I begged for it. Even that I paid for it. He told them all what I am.

"And then he moved away."

That tantalizing ache in Nate's groin seemed to waver. His desire to hear more of what Cody had done with Dusty, alone in his room, in the middle of the night, warred with the anger that swelled in his heart. He could imagine all too clearly how it had been in Cody's room—the lights out, the frantic, desperate touches, the whispers and the stifled moans as they fought to keep from being heard. He could picture it with a clarity that made him breathless. But how could anybody do that with Cody, share that kind of intimacy with him, and then turn around and betray him? How could Dusty take those private, stolen moments and turn them into something ugly? It made Nate angry. It made him want to cry for Cody. It made him want to reach out and touch Cody and tell him he'd never do what Dusty had done.

But something stopped him. He couldn't quite bring himself to bridge the gap. He grasped about for something to say, his mind reeling.

All the rumors were true. Cody really was gay.

"Aren't you worried about AIDS?" He hated himself the minute the words left his mouth. Was that really the only thing he could come up with to say?

Cody laughed. It was a laugh Nate had heard many times—a laugh that told him Cody thought he was being a dumbass. "It's an STD. You know what that stands for? Sexually. Transmitted. Disease. That means I'd have to actually have sex with somebody to catch it."

"What about Dusty?"

"First of all, he was my first. And I was his first too. So there's no way either of us had it when we started. And second, he and I . . ." Cody kept his face averted, rubbing the back of his neck. "It's not like we did *everything*, you know? I mean, we fooled around, yeah. But, well, I don't know exactly about the things we did, to tell you the truth, whether it can spread like that or not. But we never, well, you know, we never fucked, okay? And like I said, neither of us had ever done anything like that before, so there's no reason to think either of us would have it now."

"Right." Nate wasn't as embarrassed for asking as he was for having forced Cody to answer. "I guess that makes sense. I just hadn't ever thought about—"

"Do you think it gets spread through blowjobs?" Cody suddenly asked. "I've kind of wondered that, but I don't know who to ask."

"Hell, I don't know." The question triggered a flood of erotic images in Nate's brain—Cody naked, Cody with an erection, Cody with a cock in his mouth, Cody on his knees, looking up at Nate with those teasing eyes of his, and suddenly Nate's erection was back, the longing in his balls stronger than ever. Jesus, what was wrong with him?

"I figured handjobs were safe enough," Cody said, his words gaining momentum now that the truth was out, as if he'd been dying to ask somebody this question. Maybe he had.

But all Nate could think about was Cody's warm fingers wrapped around his cock. Or maybe his lips. He wanted to know how that would feel. Nate's erotic dream starring Cody was bright and vivid in his mind, and he wanted desperately to kiss Cody for real, to touch him, to make him come as hard as Dusty had, but Cody was oblivious to his discomfort.

"Nobody's ever told me if you can catch AIDS from a blowjob or not. I tried looking in the school library, but of course they don't have anything like that there. I guess it don't matter, 'cause I knew Dusty and I were both clean, but—"

"Stop." Jesus, he had to get away. He would have stood up and left already if he weren't worried about Cody seeing his erection. "Look, I need to go."

Cody sighed. "I figured. You can't hang out with the kid from the Hole."

"I don't care about that."

"Okay. So what's the problem? Is it the lies about my mom? Or is it what I told you about Dusty?"

Nate hung his head. He was embarrassed to say it, but he couldn't deny how aroused he was, listening to Cody talk. "Dusty," he whispered.

"I won't hit on you or anything, I promise."

"That's not the problem." Or maybe it was.

"You afraid it's contagious? You afraid I'll make you a fag too?"

Nate shook his head. "No."

But he couldn't say it. He couldn't possibly tell Cody the real reason he was suddenly so desperate to escape. Even now, his erection refused to wane.

Cody didn't say anything else. Nate waited for his next accusation, but it didn't come. The silence stretched on for ages.

Finally, Nate forced himself to look over. He couldn't hold his head up and face Cody directly, but he glanced at him sideways to try to gauge his reaction.

Cody was staring right at him, obviously waiting for him to make eye contact. He didn't say a word. He kept his eyes locked on Nate as he slowly reached across the expanse between them. He put his hand on Nate's thigh, and every inch of Nate's body seemed to come alive. It was as if his entire awareness shrank—or maybe it expanded—to that one spot where Cody's hand rested on his leg. That tiny bit of contact made his blood race.

"Is this why?" Cody asked quietly.

Oh God, yes, this was why! The fact that Cody was all he could think about. That his smile took Nate's breath away. Nate couldn't even look at him without longing for him to be closer, but that was wrong. He needed to pull away, to run back home, to hide in his safe, Orange Grove world, because his only other option was to push much, much closer, and he was terribly afraid to let that happen.

He did nothing. He stayed there, the heat of Cody's hand burning through his pant leg, his cock hard and aching, chafing in the confines of his jeans.

Cody stood up, moving slowly as if approaching a wary animal, and Nate supposed in a way he was. With him standing and Nate still sitting on the edge of the wagon, they were exactly the same height. Cody's hand strayed a mere half an inch upward, and it was enough to make Nate hold his breath. He had to brace himself to keep from sliding down in his seat in order to make Cody's hand drift higher.

Cody inched closer. "Do you want me to stop?"

No, Nate didn't want him to stop. That was the last thing he wanted. He tried to speak, but couldn't. All he could do was shake his head.

Cody smiled, that gorgeous, secret smile that haunted Nate's dreams. He moved so he stood between Nate's knees. He had one hand on each of Nate's thighs now, and Nate's breath caught in his throat. He shut his eyes and let the heat of Cody's touch warm him. It tingled in his groin, up his spine, wiggling all the way to his fingertips like electricity crackling through his veins. He might have moaned, but he wasn't sure if it actually happened or if it was all in his head, but Jesus, Cody's touch felt good.

"Nate?" Cody's voice wasn't much more than a whisper. "Do you want me to touch you more?"

Just the words made Nate ache. His entire body felt weak, insubstantial, nonexistent except for the desperate need Cody had kindled in him. He made himself nod.

Cody kissed his jaw, his breath warming Nate's cheek. And then his hands moved in tandem, up Nate's thighs until his fingers touched Nate's erection. Even through his jeans, it was almost enough to make Nate come. The sound he made this time was closer to a whimper than a moan. His eyes were still closed, but he knew Cody's hands. He knew the length and shape of his fingers, and he couldn't seem to think of anything else at all as they touched him through his pants.

"Do you want me to kiss you?" Cody asked.

And this time, Nate could talk. The word burst out of him before he had time to think. "Yes!"

Cody's lips brushed his, and it was all Nate could do to hold still, to hold on, to keep on breathing as the tip of Cody's tongue teased against his lips. Nate felt as if every bit of him was wavering, melting, thrumming with impatience. The gentle pressure on his erection felt like bliss, and Nate parted his lips. He grabbed Cody and pulled him closer to deepen their kiss. Cody tasted like smoke and sugar, and Nate moaned, desperate to feel more of him. He held his breath, bracing himself as Cody undid Nate's pants and slipped his hand inside, hoping he didn't come the minute Cody touched him.

It was a near thing. Feeling Cody's fingers wrap around him almost sent him over the edge, but he fought back his orgasm, his breath coming in sharp little gasps. He hung on to Cody, lost in his kiss, lost in the feel of the cold air and Cody's hand stroking him, urging him to climax. One glorious, amazing minute of feeling better than he'd ever felt, knowing this was what he'd been dreaming of all along. Nate cried out against Cody's lips as he came.

And then it was over, so quick it made Nate dizzy. Cody moved his hand away to wipe it on his jeans, and Nate gasped, the cold wind on his wet groin suddenly feeling icy. It was like waking from a wonderful dream. Like plummeting from some great height to crash into the rocks below. He was embarrassed and ashamed and confused. He fumbled to wipe himself clean, to cover himself up. He tried to look away from the obvious bulge in Cody's pants.

Jesus, how had he let this happen? He'd wanted to talk to Cody. He'd wanted for them to be friends again, but this . . .

"Nate?" Cody said.

Nate couldn't face him. He covered his eyes with his hands, struggling not to cry.

"That never should have happened. Oh my God, that never should have happened!"

The silence that followed was horrible. The still, pregnant silence of hurt. The painful, awkward silence of betrayal.

"Funny," Cody said at last. "That's what Dusty said too."

Even over the wind, Nate heard the swish of the grass as Cody climbed the embankment and walked away.

CHAPTER
Ten

*H*ow'd it go?" Logan asked Cody the next day in social studies. "Did he apologize?"

Cody chewed his lip. He didn't want to have this conversation at all. Then again, at least Logan cared. At least Logan didn't treat him like some kind of pariah. "Kind of."

Logan's smile wilted a bit. "'Kind of'?"

Cody cleared his throat, wishing his chest wasn't so tight, wishing there was no itch behind his eyes. Logan leaned closer, his long legs and bulky frame filling the aisle between the desks, and Cody pitched his voice low so nobody else could hear. "He asked me about all the stuff Larry told him."

"And?"

"And I told him." He couldn't even look at Logan as he said it. "And then . . ."

"Then?"

"We . . ." His cheeks burned. "Well, we—"

"Holy shit!"

"Yeah. Exactly. But afterward, he freaked right the fuck out and bolted."

"But . . ." Logan sounded as confused as Cody felt. "I thought—"

"It doesn't matter." But it did. God, as much as he hated to admit it, it did. "Forget it, all right? It's over."

Logan didn't mention Nate again the rest of the week, but Cody noticed how he glared at Nate off and on during social studies. It was almost enough to make him smile.

Almost.

But even Logan's outrage wasn't enough to ease Cody's heartache. He'd never felt so alone. He didn't dare think about the field. For one brief, miraculous moment, he'd been lost in the sheer exhilaration of knowing Nate wanted him the same way he wanted Nate. But he'd felt that freeze go through Nate a half a minute after he'd come, and when that happened, every emotion in Cody's heart seemed to disappear. He was as barren as the Wyoming plains, the wind scouring his insides clean until there was nothing left but bone.

Friendship with Nate had never really been an option. A romance with Nate? Well, that had been a stupid dream at best, too foolish to even think about. Cody kicked himself again and again for ever daring to believe it might be possible. He replayed their encounter in the field, wondering how different things might have been if he'd only lied. Or if he'd never reached across the wagon and put his hand on Nate's knee. How much better might this have ended if he'd never known the way Nate's breath caught in his throat at Cody's touch?

No, he never should have let that happen.

Too late now.

He was glad for work, thankful for an excuse to be away from his dank little trailer. He threw himself into the mindless task, basking in the hot, soapy water as cold descended outside, hoping to wash away the pain, to see all his loneliness and anger go spinning the drain.

It never did, though.

Two days after the incident in the field, somebody knocked on Cody's front door.

He was at the kitchen table, working on math homework, while his mom watched TV. They looked at each other, both of them seeming to ask the same silent question. *You expecting anyone?*

Cody's mom shook her head.

Cody was closer, so he went to the door and opened it a crack. What he saw through the screen made his heart sink.

"It's the police," he said to his mom, without opening the storm door, and without taking his eyes off the man on the other side of it. He was in uniform, but he wasn't anybody Cody recognized.

His mom came to the door, edging Cody out of the way and blocking the entire opening with her body, as if she could shield Cody from whatever this was.

"What do you want?"

The cop squinted at her. "Are you Cyndi Prudhomme?"

"Yes."

"I'd like to talk to you for a few minutes. Can I come in?"

"You have a warrant?"

"No."

She held up her hands, as if it were somehow out of her control and she wasn't the one denying him entrance. "Guess you're not coming inside, then."

"Is your son at home?"

"You know he is. You just saw him."

"I need to speak with him."

"My son's not eighteen yet, so if you have something to say, you can say it to me."

Cody smiled, despite himself. He'd be eighteen in only a week, but it was nice that his mom seemed so determined to stand up for him.

"Ma'am—" the cop started to say.

"It's okay, Mom," Cody said. "I haven't done anything."

She glanced over at him, her lips narrowing. "You never do, but it sure doesn't stop them from knocking on our door every time something goes wrong."

But she moved out of the way and let the police officer step in. He stopped just inside the door, clearly waiting to be invited to sit down, but Cody wasn't feeling that generous. "What do you want to talk to me about?"

"You're Cody?"

"Yes."

"Cody, I'm Officer Bradford. I—"

"Bradford?"

Now it was the cop's turn to look confused. "Yes."

"Nate's dad?" Because suddenly, this was looking far worse than he'd ever imagined.

The man's eyes narrowed. "Yes."

Was he here because of what had happened with Nate? Had Nate told him that Cody had forced himself on him? Cody's cheeks burned. He glanced toward his mother, wondering if he could ask her to leave without arousing any suspicion.

"I need to know where you were last night," Nate's dad said.

Cody blinked, surprised. So it wasn't about what had happened on Sunday with Nate. "What time?"

"Any time."

"Well, I went to work right after school. I was there until nine. Then I came home."

"Where do you work?"

"At the Tomahawk."

"Doing what?"

"Washing dishes." He wished he could have said something better—something that didn't make him sound like such white trash—but at least he was working.

Officer Bradford turned to Cody's mom. "Can you corroborate that?"

If the word "corroborate" confused her, she didn't let it show. "He was at work, then he came home, just like he said. Why? What's this about?"

"Your neighbors reported a break-in."

"Oh, for fuck's sake," his mom mumbled.

"Which neighbors?" Cody asked.

"Kathy Johansen and Pete Jessup."

"Oh, for fuck's sake!" his mom said again, louder this time.

Cody's heart began to pound a bit faster than usual, but he fought to keep his tone level. "Is that it?" Cody asked, knowing it wasn't. "Somebody broke in? Or is there more?"

"Some money was taken."

Just like his mom had said—as soon as something went wrong, they came looking for either Cody or his mom. "I didn't have anything to do with it."

"They say they saw you hanging around—"

"Of course they saw me hanging around. I live right next door."

"They think maybe you were casing their house."

Cody almost rolled his eyes.

Almost.

"Look, if I was gonna go casing people's houses and then breaking in, don't you think I could find somebody with more money than Kathy and Pete?"

"I don't know. Could you?"

Cody took a step back, feeling like he'd walked right into a trap. "I didn't mean it that way." He regretted letting his temper get the better of him. He knew from past experience it wouldn't do him any good. "I just mean, I haven't stolen anything. Not from anybody, but certainly not from them."

"So, you wouldn't mind if I checked in your room?"

"I—"

"No!" His mom stepped forward like she was going into battle. "We're done here." She pointed to the door. "You have no warrant and no grounds for a warrant—"

"If your son's innocent, you have no reason to deny the search."

"What would you even look for?" she asked. "Cash? He has cash. He just told you he's been working part-time up at the Tomahawk. I can tell you right now, if you search his room, you'll find a bit of money. But do you have any way of proving it came from their trailer? You got serial numbers or something for the money Pete and Kathy say was stolen?"

Officer Bradford clenched his jaws. "No."

"So you're gonna go in there, find the money Cody earned working after school, and based on that, you're gonna say he's a thief?"

"No." Officer Bradford shook his head, holding up a hand to calm her down. "I'm not here to lay blame—"

"Bullshit. That's exactly what you're here to do."

"Ma'am—"

"Enough. We're done talking." She pointed to the door. "You want to search any part of my house, you come back with a warrant. But we both know you ain't gettin' one based on the word of two drug dealers, so you can just turn around and go right back out the way you came."

Nate's dad scowled. He clearly didn't like being told what to do, but he also didn't have any other options. He left without saying another word, and Cody's mom closed the door behind him, latching the dead bolt as if he might try to break in next.

"Mom," Cody said, his heart still pounding, "I didn't—"

"Of course you didn't. If you were gonna resort to stealin', I imagine you would've done it a long time ago, not waited till you had an actual job."

"Maybe we should have let him search. I mean, he isn't gonna find anything that belonged to Pete or Kathy in my room."

"To hell with him." She pulled a beer from the fridge and cracked it open. "I'm sick of them actin' like you're some kind of criminal when you ain't done nothing wrong."

She returned to the couch and her static-filled TV, and Cody took that as his cue to return to his homework.

Nate's dad hadn't come about what happened in the field. That was a relief. And Cody's mom had stood up for him. That had been nice too. But he couldn't help but think that if he hadn't already ruined everything with Nate, the visit from the police would have put an end to their friendship anyway.

Nate's entire week was miserable. His dad was starting to harass him about college. Nate had applications for several universities in the Chicago area stuffed into a folder in his desk drawer. Most of them needed to be sent in by the first of February, but he hadn't filled out a single one. He had a hard time picturing himself at any of them, and he couldn't seem to focus enough to crank out the required paperwork and entrance essays.

He had a hard time focusing on anything but his disturbing sexual problems, really.

Cody continued to avoid him, and Nate did the same, taking refuge with the Grove residents. Homecoming was less than a month away. Back in Texas, his homecoming had been in early October, but at Walter Warren High School, it was held in late November, the weekend before Thanksgiving. The hallways and classrooms were abuzz over who was going with who, and who would be crowned king and queen. Flowers and balloons appeared daily as boys made their moves, inviting whichever girls they fancied. Nate sat still and silent in social studies while his so-called friends joked and laughed about what they'd wear and whether or not they'd be able to sneak in alcohol. He couldn't bring himself to look over at Cody, but he didn't miss the glares Logan threw his way every time they passed in the hallway.

"You know a kid named Cody?" his dad asked him on Tuesday night. "Is that who you were hanging around with at the end of the summer?"

Nate's heart seemed to miss a beat. He tried to swallow, but his mouth was too dry. "Yeah. Why?"

"I don't want you seeing that boy anymore."

The phrase "seeing that boy" felt loaded with innuendo. Nate scrambled, wondering if his dad somehow knew what had happened. "Why?"

"You don't need to be friends with kids like him, that's all."

Kids like him. That phrase felt loaded as well.

"Don't worry," Nate said, feeling as if his heart might break. "Cody and I haven't really been friends since school started, anyway."

It was true enough that their friendship was over, but no matter how hard he tried, Nate couldn't stop thinking about the things Cody had said, or about how good it had felt to let Cody touch him. It wasn't supposed to be like that. He was supposed to think about girls when he masturbated, not boys. One evening, he locked himself in his bedroom and pulled out the *Playboy* magazine he'd stolen from a friend's house back in Texas. He refused to let himself think about Cody as he did it. He focused on those beautiful women as he stroked, forcing himself to imagine it was one of them touching him.

It worked, more or less.

He felt better after his orgasm, although his hands shook as he slid the magazine back between the mattress and the box spring. He knew, in some deep corner of his mind, that he didn't enjoy looking at it as much as some of his friends back home had.

Maybe it was too clean. Maybe the women were just too polished, or too refined. Maybe if he had one of those *other* magazines—the ones his friend Mike had told him about during a sleepover, his voice a hushed whisper as he described how those women looked between their legs—maybe then Nate would find them more exciting. He'd never seen that part of a girl before, not counting the cartoonish black-and-white drawing in his health textbook back in ninth grade. The most he'd seen was the triangle of hair up front. Maybe if he could see those secret folds of flesh, he'd react the way he was supposed to. Maybe seeing those ladies with their legs spread would make him as anxious and aroused as his friends.

He had to find out. He had to find a way to get one of those magazines. Or . . .

There was another possibility. One he was almost afraid to think about, but which couldn't be denied.

Maybe he needed to see the real thing. He was almost eighteen now, after all. At least half of his friends back home had lost their virginity already, and he was pretty sure everybody from the Grove was more experienced than him. Losing his virginity here in Wyoming seemed a lot easier than it had in Texas.

He tried to picture it. Maybe in the backseat of his Mustang with Jennifer Parker or Christine Lucero. He tried to imagine kissing one of them, unbuttoning her jeans, sliding his hand inside to explore that warm place between her thighs. It was an exciting thought. He was relieved at the gentle twinge in his groin. *See?* he told himself triumphantly. *Women turn me on too!*

He wondered how it would feel to spread their legs, to put the tip of his erection in that place—would he even know where to put it? Well, it couldn't be too difficult to find the right spot, could it?—and push slowly inside.

It had to be wonderful. It had to be life-changing, given the way the boys in both Texas and Wyoming talked. It had to be far better than his hand, of that much he was sure. After all, that spot—that place, that secret little opening he'd never seen and could barely even imagine—had been designed, either by God or by biology or both, to wrap around a man's penis. It had been created to give pleasure, and then to give life.

And Cody? Well, Cody didn't have any of that, did he? Cody would look—

Nate stopped himself there. Cody was male, and that was all there was to it. Nate wouldn't think about whether or not Cody's penis looked any different than his own. After all, it didn't matter. He wouldn't think about if Cody's might be bigger or smaller or somehow shaped different. He wouldn't think about how it might feel to wrap his fingers around it—

Nope. Not thinking about that at all.

It was better to think about girls. Better to contemplate his chances of finally losing his virginity.

Luck seemed to be with him, because the following Monday, a week after the embarrassing encounter with Cody in Jim's cow pasture,

Christine found him. They were between third and fourth period, and Nate was pulling his English book from his locker when she suddenly appeared next to him.

"Are you busy Friday night? My mom will be in Cheyenne for the weekend, so Larry and I are having some friends over. You wanna stop by?"

Did he? Not really. He and Larry Lucero hadn't ever been friends, and things certainly hadn't improved after Nate's one trip to the bowling alley, but Christine's invitation seemed like a sign.

This was exactly the kind of opportunity he'd been hoping for.

"I'd love to."

She seemed to smile the rest of the week. She waved at him and giggled with her friends every time they passed in the halls, and Nate tried to convince himself he'd done the right thing. Christine was nice. She was friendly. She was pretty, he supposed, even if she wore a bit too much makeup and her teeth weren't quite straight. She also wasn't from Orange Grove, and that seemed important for no reason he could put into words.

And everybody knew she was easy.

This last thought gave him pause each time. He wanted to lose his virginity, yes, but he couldn't stop hearing Cody's words in his head. *"Show me a girl who can't say no, I'll show you a girl who's spent too many birthdays staring out the window, waiting for her daddy to show."*

It wasn't as if Nate intended to force himself on her. On the contrary, he was desperately hoping she'd be the one to make the first move, because he wasn't sure he could. But even assuming she was willing, Nate worried he'd be taking advantage of her.

Maybe it was wrong. Maybe his plan was stupid. Maybe going to her house in hopes of having sex with her was the worst thing he'd ever done. It certainly gave him a dark, sinking feeling, like he was letting somebody down. It made him feel dirty in a way that was new. Masturbation, pornography, his secret thoughts about both women and Cody—none of those things made him feel as icky as the thought of trying to seduce Christine.

Well, sex or not, he'd already told her he'd be there. He wouldn't back out of it now. And besides, maybe it would be fun. It'd be one Friday night he didn't have to spend avoiding the Grove clique, or going along with them only to wish he hadn't, or wishing he could spend it with Cody.

No. He wasn't thinking about Cody.

That's what he told himself all week, at any rate. But no matter how hard he tried not to think about Cody, he failed. Night after night as he lay in bed, he found his mind straying to that forbidden, shameful possibility. He was obsessed with the idea of kissing Cody again. Of touching him and being touched by him. Of seeing him come. On Friday morning, Nate gave in as he masturbated under the hot spray of his morning shower and let himself imagine Cody. He imagined it was Cody's hand stroking him. He imagined Cody there, in the shower with him, and the result was undeniable. He was glad his dad had already left for work, because he was sure he'd cried out at the end. His knees feeling like rubber, his body shuddering over and over, his loins still aching.

Jesus, there something wrong with him.

He wondered who he could talk to. His family didn't go to church, so there was no youth pastor or confession booth. There was no counselor at school he trusted. He sure as hell wasn't going to bring it up with his father.

His mother?

Maybe. He kept that possibility tucked away in the back of his mind. He only talked to his mother once a week—always on Wednesday evenings, always for exactly twenty minutes. His dad was usually on the other side of the room, trying his best to look like he wasn't listening. But maybe Nate could ask his dad to leave the room. Maybe he could tell him how he needed to talk to his mom in private.

He hated the idea, but as lame as it was, it was still the best one he had.

Nate spent the rest of Friday morning contemplating lies he could tell Christine to get out of going to her house. *I'm sick. I'm grounded. I have too much homework.*

But at the end of the day, when Christine stopped by his locker and said, "See you tonight?" Nate choked on the words, his heart pounding. His need to know if Christine could turn him on as much as Cody was suddenly stronger than his conscience.

"Yeah," he said. "See you tonight."

CHAPTER
Eleven

Christine lived near Cody, in the trailer park, but in the more respectable portion where tenants had actual lawns with grass, and wind chimes hanging on their front porches. By the time Nate arrived a little after eight, the party was already in full swing. Van Halen blasted from the stereo while at least a dozen teenagers milled about inside the cramped trailer.

Larry Lucero scowled at Nate, but Christine hugged him, and Jimmy handed him a red Solo cup full of beer. Nate drank it gratefully and let Christine take his hand and begin leading him through the party.

His heart pounded as she introduced him to people and told him jokes. Nate did his best to laugh at the right times, but his mind was racing the entire time. She smiled at him, moving closer, an obvious invitation in her eyes, and Nate had to fight the urge to run.

I don't want this. I don't want her!

But that was wrong. He was supposed to want girls. He probably did want girls. He just hadn't been able to prove it yet.

Once I'm alone with her, everything will be fine.

He drank another cup of beer, then remembered he'd have to drive and found a can of soda instead. Christine hadn't let go of his hand since he'd come in, and he studied her in a way he never had before. She was wearing tight jeans and a low-cut sweater. She kept pressing her breasts against him as she talked. It was distracting. Almost arousing. And when she finally stood on her toes and kissed him, he sighed with relief.

Yes, this was why he'd come here tonight. He needed to know.

Somebody catcalled, and Christine laughed against his lips and pulled away to smile up at him. "You want to go to my room?"

He couldn't quite speak, torn between curiosity and arousal and gut-wrenching fear. He nodded, and she took his hand again and led him down the hall.

Her bedroom was done all in pink, with stuffed animals on the bed and a collection of porcelain dolls on the shelf, but the walls were covered with Van Halen and Ratt and Mötley Crüe. Christine casually closed the door, stepped close, put her arms around his neck, and kissed him again.

Her lips were warm, and Nate moaned, falling into it, wanting desperately to feel something. He pulled her close and concentrated hard on kissing her, and feeling the way she fit into his arms. The way her lips felt under his tongue, and her breasts pressed against his chest. His heart was pounding, but that was probably normal. It was normal to be nervous, right? Normal to be so afraid of whatever came next that it was easier to simply wait and let her lead the way.

It's okay, he told himself. *This is good. This is what you need. Now you'll find out you like girls just fine.*

She pushed him backward until the backs of his knees came up against her bed, and he sat down. She straddled his lap, still kissing him. She was breathing hard, and there was a bit too much saliva, but Nate embraced it, trying to let himself become aroused as they kissed and her soft little moans filled his ears. It was awkward, like every other kiss he'd ever shared with a girl, but he figured he'd get the hang of it eventually.

He sensed she was impatient—that he was doing something wrong—and he realized that although he was kissing her, he wasn't doing anything else. His hands were near her waist, not moving, just sitting like fat lumps on her hips.

He slid one up to cup her breast. She let him, sighing against his lips, leaning closer, and he grew bolder. He slid his hand inside her sweater to caress her, feeling the hard bud of her nipple through her bra.

Nothing about it felt right, and when she reached behind her back and unhooked her bra, he balked, wanting nothing more than to pull away and put a stop to it.

No! You want this! You're supposed to want this!

He let his hand slip under the loose bit of elastic, cupping her bare breast in his hand. It made his heart pound, but not in the way he'd hoped.

She took his other hand and guided it to her thigh, grinding against him a bit as they kissed, and Nate tried to ride the thrill to its obvious conclusion. He tried to tell himself this was good and right and wonderful, even though his stomach was in knots and his penis definitely wasn't doing what he knew she'd expect it to do.

Christine moved off him quickly, and he felt an instant of relief, thinking maybe he'd screwed up enough that she'd given up, but no such luck. She pulled off her sweater and let her bra drop to the floor, leaving her naked from the waist up. Her breasts were smaller than he imagined, her pink nipples hard and pointing his way. She undid her jeans and peeled them off before kicking them away. She was wearing only a lacy pair of black panties.

She put her hands on her waist, throwing one hip out, striking a pose, giving him a teasing pout. "Is that all the reaction I get?"

He cleared his throat, trying to think of what to say. Seeing her almost naked was exciting, in its own way. He'd never seen naked breasts outside of magazines or movies. But he was still pretty sure he wasn't reacting the way he should. His stomach felt like it was full of lead. His palms were beginning to sweat.

"You're beautiful," he told her. It was true, even if he wasn't able to put as much desire behind it as he would have liked.

She smiled and moved back onto his lap, kissing him again.

Touching her breasts felt awkward, so he put his hands on her thighs. Her skin there was warm and silky smooth. He wasn't sure he wanted things to go any further, but he had to know. He had to find out if he could make himself enjoy this as much as other boys seemed to.

He slid one hand upward until he found the place between her legs. She gasped, rising a bit to give him room, and he wiggled his fingers under the elastic, exploring more than stroking, although she didn't seem to mind. He found hair, and hot flesh, and there, in the center, a slippery entrance. He tested it, circling, pushing just a bit, surprised at how wet it was, and how warm, but he felt nothing beyond a bit of curiosity. He wasn't even remotely aroused. It was nothing like when Cody had touched him.

Jesus, maybe he really was gay.

And Christine had spent too many birthdays watching out the window for her father.

And none of this should be happening.

"Stop," he said, pulling his hand from under her. "I'm sorry. We shouldn't be doing this."

"It's okay. My mom won't be home until tomorrow, and my brother doesn't care."

"I don't think it's a good idea."

She leaned back a bit to look at his face. "Really?"

He remembered again Cody's comment about girls who couldn't say no. He hated what he'd let himself do. A moment ago, he'd been curious, but now, he felt nothing but shame. "I'm sorry. I shouldn't have let things go this far—"

"What are you talking about? I wanted you to." She smiled flirtatiously and slid her hand down his chest toward his groin. "We could do more, if you want." She unzipped his pants, and Nate jumped in alarm.

"No!" He stopped her hands, hoping she didn't hear how close he was to panic.

Or to tears.

"I'm sorry," he said again, feeling like an idiot for repeating himself over and over, but he didn't want to hurt her feelings. "I'm so, so sorry. I just . . ." He sighed in frustration, putting his face in his hands. Unfortunately, one of them now smelled wrong, and he jerked it away, his stomach turning. He wished he'd never come to Christine's stupid party.

"Is this a religious thing?" she asked. "Are you freaking out because it's a sin?"

"Yes!" It was a lie, but he grasped at it readily enough. "I'm still a virgin." And maybe he should have been embarrassed saying it, but he wasn't. He moved her carefully off his lap and stood, zipping his pants as he did. He picked her sweater up off the floor and handed it to her, trying not to see her naked breasts as he did, just wanting her to cover herself so he'd be able to look at her again. "I'm sorry. I know it was terrible of me to take advantage of you like that. I know I shouldn't have. I know it was wrong. I just got carried away, and—"

"Stop!" she said, smacking his shoulder playfully. To his surprise, she was laughing. Her breasts swung as she leaned over to pick up her bra. "You didn't take advantage of me, you big prude. I'm the one who dragged you into my bedroom. I'm pretty sure I jumped you, not the other way around."

"I . . . uh . . ." His heart was still pounding, his hands shaking, his stomach twisted with shame. He just wanted to get out of her bedroom and out of her trailer and away from Warren, Wyoming. "So, you're not mad?"

"Why would I be? Because you're not falling all over yourself trying to get in my pants?"

"Yes. I mean, no. Because I *did* get in your pants, but I didn't want to. I mean, I didn't mean to. I just—"

She pulled her shirt on and bent to pick up her jeans. "You're forgiven."

He blinked at her, stunned. "Just like that?"

She grinned at him as she wiggled into her tight jeans and buttoned them. "You're not the only fish in the sea, Nate. I mean, you're cute and all, but it ain't like I can't find another guy."

"Right. Of course." And probably any other guy at the party would be happy to be pulled into her bedroom. They wouldn't be afraid and embarrassed about touching her breasts or that warm place between her legs. They wouldn't have a hard time getting critical parts of their anatomy to cooperate.

What was wrong with him?

"No hard feelings, right?" she asked.

It seemed like he should be the one saying that to her. "Of course not."

"Cool."

She opened her bedroom door and went back to the party, leaving Nate standing like an idiot in the middle of her room.

He'd had his chance, and he'd felt nothing. He was pretty sure his erection had never made it past half-mast, at best. He was glad she hadn't tried to touch him there. He would have been beyond embarrassed to have her discover his lack of arousal.

And what about that? What exactly did that mean?

Maybe if you'd let her touch it, you'd have gotten hard.

Maybe. But shouldn't just the thought of her touching him have been enough? His mind drifted back to that one amazing day at the wagon, when Cody had unzipped Nate's pants and slipped his hand inside. His penis stirred at the memory, far more than it had at the actual possibility of being touched by Christine.

He'd had his chance, and all he'd proven was that he was a coward at best.

A fag, at worst.

Nate fought back the lump threatening to fill his throat. He made it to his car and halfway home before he started to cry. It wasn't sobbing or wrenching or painful. Just hot tears running down his cheeks, and he had no way to stop them.

He'd never been so confused.

The difference between his experience with Christine and the one with Cody baffled him. Touching Christine had been uncomfortable and awkward. But Cody . . .

He'd never felt anything so piercing and perfect as when Cody's lips had touched his. And the rest of it—letting Cody tease him into an orgasm—had been the most amazing thing he'd ever experienced. It couldn't be right, but nothing about it felt wrong.

Nate thought of all the words he'd heard people use. All the cruel slurs tossed around.

Homo.

Queer.

Faggot.

Pansy.

I can't be one of those things!

But on the tail end of that thought came the memory of Cody's acceptance of being called those names. Cody hadn't bothered to deny what he felt.

What they both felt.

"I'm not like him," Nate said out loud. The croon of the Bee Gees from his eight-track player did nothing to ease his mind.

The TV was on in the living room when he got home, and he rushed upstairs to his bedroom, not wanting his dad to see him with his eyes red and swollen and his cheeks wet. He washed his hands until he could no longer smell Christine's very feminine musk on them, then sat on the edge of the bed with his head in his hands, trying to tell himself he wasn't going to keep crying like a five-year-old, but he couldn't stop the tears welling up in his eyes.

Who could he talk to?

Cody.

No. Not Cody. Anybody but Cody.

Who else?

Maybe somebody from Texas? One of his friends?

Yeah, right. He hadn't even heard from any of them since moving to Wyoming. Even if he was allowed to make long-distance calls, he couldn't imagine calling one of them up now. *Hey, Mike. How's tennis going? Sure is windy here in Warren. By the way, you ever look at another guy and have the irresistible urge to see him naked, or maybe to jack him off? No? Okay. Just checking.*

He hadn't ever felt this way back in Texas. Maybe this was all simply a symptom of having moved to Warren, Wyoming, where there wasn't a damn thing to do except get high or get laid. Maybe if he found a way to go back home, all of these horrifying feelings he had for Cody would go away. Surely there was a girl back in Texas with big hair and a familiar southern drawl who could make his heart race and his loins tingle.

His dad's heavy treads thumped up the stairs, stopping outside Nate's room. He knocked lightly on the door. "Nate? You in there?"

"Yeah." Nate wiped his face as his dad cracked the door and poked his face through the gap.

"I didn't expect you home so soon." His brow wrinkled. "You okay?"

"Fine."

"You sure?"

"Yeah. I'm just tired."

"Okay." He didn't look convinced, but it seemed he wasn't inclined to press the issue. "I'm headed to bed myself."

"Good night, Dad."

Nate waited, listening to his dad bustle around in the room next door. He watched the clock on his nightstand, counting the minutes until at last the house lay silent. He gave it an extra thirty minutes after that, just to be sure his dad was asleep.

Finally, he crept out of his bedroom and tiptoed down the stairs to the kitchen. He might get in trouble when the phone bill came and his dad saw the long-distance call, but there was only one person left on his list of people he might talk to.

The dial tone seemed ridiculously loud in his ear. Luckily, the cord was long enough to reach all the way to their pantry. He closed the door behind him, sinking down to sit on the floor, surrounded by shelves of cereal and Hamburger Helper. It was pitch-dark, but the keys on the handset were lit, and he dialed the number that he'd thought of as his own for nearly eighteen years.

It began to ring as the call went through. It was an hour later in Texas, which meant nearly midnight. He figured his mom might still be awake. Even if he woke her up, she'd probably be happy to hear from him. He wasn't quite sure yet what he was going to say, but he knew the gist of it: he wanted to go home. He hated Wyoming, and he intended to beg his mother to let him move back to Texas, where it was warm and the wind rarely blew semis over on the interstate and where he didn't have embarrassingly erotic dreams about other boys.

"Hello?"

It was a man's voice. Nate froze, his mind reeling. Had he dialed the wrong number?

"Hello?" the man said again, sounding annoyed this time.

Should he hang up? Dial again?

"Hi," he made himself say. "Maybe I have the wrong number. I'm trying to reach Susan Bradford."

The man made a noise—something similar to a growl. "Her name's Susan Jennings now."

"Oh. Right." Although it felt like a knife in his heart, hearing his mom called by her maiden name. Worse than that, this meant he did have the right number. It was almost midnight, and his mom had a man in the house.

A man who was most definitely not his dad.

"Is she there?"

"Hang on."

Nate waited, his heart pounding, his stomach twisting painfully. "Babe?" he heard the man say. "It's for you."

"Who is it?" Definitely his mother's voice.

"Hell if I know."

There was the usual jumble of clunking as the handset changed hands, and then his mom said, "Hello?"

Nate swallowed, suddenly unsure. "Mom?"

"Nate? What's wrong, honey? Is everything okay?"

Was it? He had no idea how to answer that question.

"Are you hurt or something?" she asked. "Where's your father?"

"He's in bed." And now, Nate's mind was scrambling for purchase. "I wanted to talk to you. I needed—"

"Nathan, you're only supposed to call on Wednesdays. You know that."

She didn't sound angry, though. Just . . .

Sad?

Guilty?

"Who was that?" he asked, unsure if he wanted to hear the answer.

"Who was who?"

Such a stupid question. Such a ridiculous pretense, to pretend she didn't know what he was talking about. "Who was that guy who answered the phone?"

"Oh. Well, just a friend—"

"He called you 'babe.'"

"Oh." Her voice suddenly sounded very small. "Oh, honey. I didn't want you to find out like this."

"Is he living there?"

She didn't answer, but the silence told him everything.

"For how long?"

"Since . . . Well, since—"

"Since we left?" Because suddenly, it was all clear. He'd heard his aunt and uncle whispering about an affair. He'd seen the way his parents couldn't look at each other anymore. And all along, he'd assumed it was his father. All that time, moving to Wyoming, being dragged to this shithole of a town, he'd blamed his dad. And all along, his mom had been at home with another man already warming her bed.

Nate hung up. He sat there in the dark, clutching the phone to his chest, just long enough to be sure the line was dead. He put it to his ear, checking for the dial tone, which would soon become incessant beeping of a phone left off the hook too long. Then he stuck the phone between the Froot Loops and Honeycomb cereal and shut the pantry door. If his mom called back, she'd get a busy signal.

And eventually, she'd give up on calling, just like she'd given up on her family.

Nate awoke the next day with his eyes scratchy from the tears he'd shed into his pillow the night before. He felt like he'd lost his mom all over again. Even worse, his dreams had been full of Christine laughing at him, and Brian and Brad tapping out lines of cocaine on a mirror, telling him it was his turn, and Cody yelling at him, telling Nate he should be ashamed of himself for taking advantage of Christine. And through it all, Nate tried again and again to tell Cody that his mom already had a new boyfriend, but Cody never seemed to hear him.

He found his dad in the kitchen, making French toast. The phone was back on the wall. His dad looked at him strangely but didn't ask.

After breakfast, his dad left to go grocery shopping, and Nate dug the Warren phone book out of the junk drawer in the kitchen. It was tiny. He'd laughed when he'd first seen it. The phone book in Austin had been two separate books—one for white pages, one for yellow—and both had been enormous. Here, the white and yellow together were only as thick as one of the single-subject spiral notebooks he used in school.

He looked for "Lawrence" first.

None.

He scratched his head, puzzled, then remembered what Cody had said. *"People were always asking me why my last name was different from my mom's. Used to piss me off."* Nate slumped, feeling defeated. How in the world could he get Cody's phone number?

Logan.

He looked up Robertson. There were three listings. He called the first and asked for Logan.

"Wrong Robertson," the man on the other end said. "You're looking for my brother's son." He rattled off a phone number, and Nate hurried to grab a pencil and scribble it down. It helped that every single number in Warren had the same prefix.

He called the second number and asked for Logan.

"That's me."

He should have recognized the voice. "Hey. Um, it's Nate Bradford."

There was a stony silence, and then Logan said, "Okay. What the hell do you want?"

"I need to talk to Cody."

"Yeah, you said that once before, but it doesn't seem like it went all that well."

"I know, but—"

"If you want to talk to Cody, why the hell are you calling me?"

Nate put his head in his hand. "Because I don't know his number."

"Are you kidding me?"

"He never gave it to me."

He could practically hear Logan scowling at him. "Did you ever ask?"

Nate sighed. It annoyed him how Logan could make him feel so small, even over the phone. "Look, can you help me or not?"

"Why should I?"

Nate traced his finger over the wood grains of the tabletop, debating ways he might convince Logan. He had a feeling Logan wouldn't forgive him until Cody did, but maybe he'd meet him halfway. "Can you at least tell me his mom's last name?"

A second went by. Then another, and another. Finally, Logan said, "Prudhomme." It sounded like he hated himself for letting it slip.

Nate was already flipping through the pages, running his finger down the lines of names, the black ink smearing beneath his fingertip. "Powell. Powers. Probst. Prudhomme! Cyndi? Is that it?" It had to be. "Thanks, Logan. Really."

"You're welcome." Although his voice said otherwise. "And Nate?"

"Yeah?"

"Fuck with his head again, and I'll skin you alive. Got it?"

Nate swallowed, wondering if he was making the biggest mistake of his life. "Got it."

His heart pounded as he dialed the number. It rang once, twice, three times. Somebody picked it up midway through the fourth ring.

"Hello?"

Cody's voice. Nate tried to swallow, but his mouth was too dry.

"Hello?" Cody said again, sounding annoyed. It was oddly reminiscent of Nate's call home the night before, and suddenly Nate's hands were shaking, his throat too tight to speak. What the hell was he doing? What exactly did he think he could say to Cody now? *I'm sorry. I screwed up. I'm confused. I want to see you. I've lost my mom. I'm lonely as hell, and you're the only friend I have.*

He couldn't say any of it, though. His grip on the phone was tight, his heart in his throat, the pressure in his chest almost more than he could bear.

"I'm hanging up," Cody said. "Speak now or forever hold your peace, man."

Nate sat there, silent and confused, until the line went dead.

CHAPTER
Twelve

*L*ogan was already at work when Cody arrived Saturday afternoon. The back of the kitchen was steamy as a sauna.

Well, steamy as Cody imagined saunas to be, at any rate. He'd never actually been in one.

The brisk walk from home had kept him warm, despite the ice-cold wind and his insufficient jackets. All but his hands, at least. They were frozen stiff, and he rubbed them together, not wanting to plunge them into the hot water quite yet.

Maybe he'd ask Logan for a ride to Rock Springs. He had a feeling Logan would do it. He might not even laugh at him. Granted, he probably wouldn't buy Cody a Big Mac and hassle him about his Wyoming twang as they both dipped their french fries into their chocolate shakes, but a ride would be enough, even if it made Cody's heart hurt, thinking about it.

"How was your morning?" Logan asked, his arms elbow-deep in dishwater, his eyes uncharacteristically bright and expectant as he waited for Cody's answer. "Anything interesting happen?"

"Not really." It seemed like an odd question, even from Logan. "You wanna switch and let me wash?"

"Hell, yes."

Logan had to stoop to reach the sink, and Cody couldn't reach half the shelves to put stuff away. With them both there, it didn't make much sense to do it any other way. The water was already pretty foul though, so Cody flipped the lever under the sink to let it drain.

"So, *nothing* happened this morning?" Logan asked, watching Cody carefully.

Cody wrinkled his brow, trying to figure out what Logan was getting at. "The phone woke me up at ten, but nobody was there. We're out of milk, so I ate my cereal dry, and my mom was still asleep when I left. She's working evenings now, so she gets up after I'm gone for the day and doesn't get home until I'm asleep." He shrugged. "That's the sum total of my morning so far." He watched the last bit of water twirl down the drain. "How'd the game go?"

"We won."

"Good."

"I threw for one hundred ninety-eight yards, and had three touchdowns." He wasn't bragging. It was said in the same matter-of-fact tone he used for just about everything. "Coach says there might be scouts from the University of Wyoming at the homecoming game next week."

If scouts were coming to Warren, it could only be to see Logan. Cody heard enough talk at school to know Logan was the star of the team. "You think they'll offer you a scholarship?"

"My parents think so, but what do they know?" Logan was rinsing the dishes he'd already washed, sorting them into neat rows on the drying rack. "That reminds me though—I wanted to ask you something."

Cody flipped the lever back in place to plug the drain and turned on the water, testing the temperature as it began to fill the enormous sink. "Okay."

"You want to go to homecoming with me?"

Cody blinked, sure he'd misheard. "What?"

Logan laughed awkwardly, looking uncomfortable for the first time ever. "I didn't mean it like that. Not, you know, *together*."

Thank goodness. As nice as Logan was, the thought of dating him was horrifying. "Aren't you going with Jamie Simpson?"

Logan scowled, tossing a handful of clean forks into the utensil bin with a bit more force than the occasion demanded. "She's going with Tom Phillips."

"Tom Phillips?" Cody added a generous squirt of Dawn to the sink, thinking. "Didn't he graduate three years ago?"

"Yes."

It wasn't uncommon in Warren for teenage girls to date guys in their twenties. High school girls bringing guys in their thirties to prom wasn't unheard of.

"So?" Logan prodded. "What do you say?"

"You want me to go to a high school dance with you?"

"You don't have to say it like that."

"Like what?"

"You make it sound weird. But it's no big deal, you know. Lots of people go stag. And Frank's giving us both the night off."

Cody would have preferred to work. He felt like he was in a race against Mother Nature to see whether or not he'd manage to buy a coat before the snow started to fly. He waited while Logan took the clean silverware to the front to be wrapped in napkins by the hostesses.

"So, what'll we do there?" he asked, once Logan was back. "Stand against the wall looking like idiots while everybody else makes out?"

Logan laughed. "Have you ever even been to a school dance?"

"Whatta you think?"

"First of all, they won't let anybody make out at the dance. There are chaperones to make sure nothing kinky goes down."

"Yeah, 'cause that'll stop everybody from having sex."

"It'll stop 'em from having sex there in the gym, at any rate." He shoved a stack of bowls onto the shelf in the corner. "But not many people actually dance with their dates. I mean, like I said, half the school goes stag anyway. The girls mostly dance together in one big pack, and the guys hang out and bullshit. I mean, it'll be the usual cliques, you know? The cowboys in one corner; the Mormons in another; the Grove pricks hanging out in the parking lot, getting high; and all the burnouts sneaking out the back door for a smoke."

"So why do you want to go at all?"

Logan turned toward him, leaning his thigh against the long metal sink. "Because we're seniors, man. This is it! Our last homecoming. Our last prom! This is the kind of shit we'll be reminiscing about when we're forty, rotting away in the nursing home."

Cody laughed, finally plunging his hands into the blissfully warm water. "I think you have to be a lot older than forty to get into one of those places."

"Whatever. You gonna come make a damn memory with me, or are you gonna sit on your stinking couch watching *Spenser: For Hire*?"

Cody sighed as he grabbed a sponge off the sideboard. He wasn't used to having anybody ask him to do anything. He certainly wasn't used to being coerced into school dances. "Can I ask you something?"

"Sure."

"Why're you so determined to be my friend when you know the rest of the town hates me?"

Logan shrugged. "I don't know. Maybe 'cause you're not an asshole, and there's nobody else to talk to while I'm at work, and Jamie Simpson won't give me the time of day. Is that enough of a reason for you?"

Cody smiled, despite himself. "I guess." He felt around in the water, searching for the silverware at the bottom as he debated. He'd taken a chance once before, with Nate. Even now he couldn't quite say if it had been worth it or not. "Do you think . . ." He stopped, considering his words while scrubbing a fork that was already plenty clean.

"Spit it out. Do I think what? Do I think you're an idiot? Yes. Do I think you need a haircut? Yes. Do I think—"

"Do you think you could take me to Rock Springs on Saturday? Before the dance, I mean."

"Sure. What for?"

"I need to get a coat."

"Don't you have a Sears catalog?"

Cody made himself say the words. "I can't afford one of those. But there's a secondhand store in Rock Springs—"

"No way, man."

Cody winced. He'd hoped Logan wouldn't laugh, but he hadn't been expecting such a blatant refusal. "Okay. Sorry I asked."

"No, I mean, no way do you need to go to that stupid store. Who knows where that shit comes from. I have at least eight coats in my closet that don't fit me. Half of them ain't even been worn yet. My grandma sends them all the time, but she keeps forgetting I'm not still twelve. I'll bring you one of them, and then you can save your money for something cool."

Cody glanced over at him. Not a bit of mockery in his eyes. Not a bit of pity, either. Just a matter-of-fact assessment of the situation. "I don't mind paying—"

"Don't be stupid. So, are we going or not?"

"To Rock Springs?"

"No! To homecoming."

Cody shook his head, wondering how he'd ever gotten into such a ridiculous conversation. "Maybe." He chewed his lip, debating. "Am I supposed to dress up or something?" Because if that was the case, he was screwed.

"Just wear your best jeans and a clean shirt."

"You sure that's good enough?"

"Which one of us has been to more school dances?"

"Fine."

"Then I'll pick you up at seven thirty."

Cody turned back to his work, smiling down at the soapy water. "Whatever." But as hard as he tried to act like he didn't care, he did. He was filled with something that might almost have been happiness. "Just so you know, I don't put out on the first date."

"Good. Then there's no reason to buy you a corsage."

And just like that, Cody had a not-quite date for the dance.

If Nate thought he'd been miserable after his sexual encounter with Cody, it was nothing to how he felt after failing to feel anything with Christine.

He was different. He knew that now, without any doubt. After his mother's betrayal, and his failed phone call to Cody, he'd locked himself in his room and debated simply climbing into his car and driving home to Austin.

It wouldn't help. As much as he'd tried to convince himself that his shameful desire was somehow the result of Wyoming, he knew it wasn't true. When he finally sat back and looked at it objectively, he could admit he'd never really been attracted to a girl at home, either. He'd watched other boys in the locker room on occasion. Usually, there hadn't been anything erotic about it, but looking back, he began to take note of the times his heart had raced and his palms had grown damp at the sight of some boy undressing next to him. At the time, he'd chalked it up to nerves and self-consciousness. It had never progressed to anything more than that. But now, when Nate thought about those boys, and thought about how it might feel to touch them, he couldn't deny the way it made him feel. In the clear, cold light of morning, he was able to admit something to himself he'd never realized before.

He was gay. Or queer. Or homosexual. He liked that term a bit better. But whatever anybody called it, the fact remained: he was far more attracted to males than to females.

And from there, it was easy to take the final leap.

He wanted Cody.

It was that simple. He was obsessed with Cody. Enamored of him. Maybe even in love with him. He fell asleep every night thinking about him, remembering how it had felt to kiss him, wondering if he'd ever have the chance to do it again. The thought of never again sharing that kind of intimacy made his heart ache.

But he didn't have the faintest idea what to do about it.

Homecoming week arrived, and it seemed to be all anybody was talking about. Nate found himself avoiding Christine, as well as the Grove residents. He once again switched seats in social studies, choosing a desk in the front row on the right-hand side. He'd planted himself squarely in the middle of the Mormons, who all smiled nervously and said hello. He had classes with many of them, and they were always polite but distant.

Polite but distant suddenly felt like the greatest kindness in the world.

He heard the disturbance behind him as Cody and Logan came in. He'd bumped Logan's entire row back a seat, which meant he'd have a harder time talking to Cody. That wasn't why Nate had done it. He'd just wanted to get away from anybody who might talk to him about homecoming and sit in a place where he wouldn't be tempted to stare at Cody the entire period but he figured breaking up Logan and Cody was an added bonus.

But he couldn't bring himself to initiate contact with the object of his desire. He sat tense in his seat, listening to the quiet cadence of Cody's voice as he talked to Logan. He secretly wished Logan would come down with a bad case of the mumps. He wasn't even sure if the mumps were still a thing, but he didn't care a bit. Anything that would ruin Logan's perfect face for a few days at least, and get him away from Cody.

By Wednesday, the Mormons were talking to Nate, and inviting him to sit with them at lunch as if he were one of their own.

Nate had been vaguely aware of Mormonism back in Austin, but he'd always thought of the Church of Jesus Christ of Latter Day Saints as an odd little cult. The people he knew talked about Mormons with the same confused contempt they used when talking about Jehovah's Witnesses or Hare Krishnas. But in Warren, Mormons were the majority. Easily more than half the town's residents were technically members of the church, but most of them, including Cody and his mom, were what Cody called "Jack Mormons," meaning they belonged to the church in name only.

The ones who were true Mormons—the ones who actually followed the church's many rules—formed their own little clique. There were four of them with him in social studies: Stacy, Lisa, Grant, and Nephi. Nate was surprised to find they weren't anywhere near as weird as he'd been led to believe. They didn't drink, or swear, or smoke, but other than that, they seemed to be into all the same things the other teenagers were.

That night, Nate's dad knocked on his bedroom door. "Seven o'clock," he said as he poked his head in. "Time to call your mom."

Nate was at his desk, doing math homework. His heart clenched. He couldn't meet his father's eyes. "I don't want to talk to her."

His dad didn't respond. For several seconds, there was only silence, Nate staring blindly at his math book, his dad like a statue in the doorway. Finally, his dad spoke, his voice gentle. "I talked to her on Sunday, Nate. She said you called late Saturday night. She said—"

"I don't want to talk to her!"

"You can't avoid her forever, son."

Nate put his pencil to paper, biting his lip, trying to direct his attention back to limits and differentiation. Trying not to think about whoever had answered the phone at his old house in Austin.

Eventually, his dad left, closing the door behind him.

The following afternoon, Lisa tapped him on the shoulder and said, "Are you going to homecoming on Saturday?"

Nate turned in his seat, hoping she wasn't about to ask him on a date. "I don't think so."

But it was Stacy who spoke next. "You can come with us, if you want."

"Yeah," Grant said. "It'll be fun. The guys are meeting at Adam Sullivan's house at five. We'll have pizza and watch a movie or something until the girls are ready. Then we'll all head over together."

Nate glanced cautiously back at Cody, who was studiously ignoring him, and Logan, whose long legs were stretched out into the aisle, his cowboy boots strangely at odds with his hot-pink polo shirt. Logan was glaring at him, and Nate averted his eyes quickly, remembering Logan's threat to skin Nate alive if he fucked with Cody's head.

Don't worry, Logan. I'm too busy fucking with my own head, and Cody's forgotten I exist anyway.

But despite everything—Cody and Logan, Nate's wayward sexual desires, and his mom's new boyfriend—Nate suddenly didn't want to miss the dance. It was his senior year, after all, and going with a group seemed safe enough.

"Sure." But his eyes lingered on Cody as he said it.

Not much chance of Cody being at homecoming.

He was in a good mood until he arrived home Friday afternoon and found a letter waiting for him in the mailbox. It was from Mike, and Nate stared at it for a moment, trying to decide what he felt.

On one hand, it was nice to know that Mike still thought about him enough to write a letter. On the other hand, Nate felt so detached from his old life, he almost wanted to throw the letter away unopened.

"Don't be stupid," he mumbled to himself. He dropped his backpack on the living room floor and took the letter upstairs before plopping down on the bed to read it.

Nate,

Hey, man. What's up? Nobody's heard from you since you moved to Wyoming. It must be more fun than you expected.

Our tennis team is awesome this year. Too bad you're not here. We're second in the division, and might even take state. I got my letter. I failed my math test because Ms. Carter is a bitch, but I was still eligible, so it's cool.

Jason and Lisa broke up last week, right in the middle of *Top Gun*. They got kicked out of the movie theater and everything. It was totally embarrassing. And Tony went to homecoming with Carrie, but says he didn't even get to first base. Have you had homecoming yet? Met any hot babes up there? According to David Lee Roth, farmer's daughters make you feel "all right," so at least you have that going for you, right? (And yeah, I know it was a Beach Boys song first, but David Lee Roth is way cooler.)

Speaking of cool, have you bought the Beastie Boys record yet? Check out the album cover in a mirror, if you haven't already. They're my new favorite band. My mom hates them, which makes it even better. You gotta fight for the right to party, know what I mean?

Guess that's about it.

Write back soon.

Mike

Nate's hands were shaking by the time he finished the letter. The tennis team was doing great without him, and his friends were going to movies and to homecoming and listening to music as if Nate weren't stuck in the windiest version of Hell ever. Nate didn't even care that Tony hadn't made it to first base. To hell with Tony. Warren didn't even have a movie theater. The closest Nate had gotten to *Top Gun* was seeing the commercials on TV. Some of the people from the Grove had driven to Casper to see it, but he hadn't wanted to go with them, and he sure wasn't going to go by himself. And as for the Beastie Boys . . .

Who in the world were they?

The one static-filled station he managed to pick up in Warren played country, and there wasn't a single record store in town. *I want my MTV!* had been spray-painted across the side of the bowling alley, but so far, nobody had complied. Some weekends, Nate managed to stay up late and to watch *Night Flight*, always hoping for a few music videos, but he was pretty sure he hadn't seen anybody called the Beastie Boys.

He really was in the black hole of modern civilization.

"Fuck you," Nate said aloud to the room. He crumpled the letter into a ball and threw it toward the trash can in the corner. It bounced off the wall and landed in the middle of the room. "Fuck you, and fuck David Lee Roth too."

CHAPTER

*T*he coat Logan brought Cody on homecoming night—"Better than a corsage, anyway," Logan had said—was a bit too big, and still had the tags on it. Cody felt like a fool for taking it, but only until he put it on and walked outside into the Wyoming wind. A glance at the sky was all it took to tell him snow was coming.

To hell with pride. The coat was warm, he'd beaten the snow, and he still had all his money. Maybe now he could buy some good boots, or a pair of gloves.

"Don't you have a truck you can drive in the winter?" Cody asked as he climbed into Logan's Camaro.

"Hey, as long as the roads are clear, I'm sticking with this one." He started the car and turned it around in the dirt lot that counted as Cody's front yard. "You gonna talk to Nate tonight?"

Cody shook his head, trying not to chuckle. "Gee, I'm so anxious to discuss Nate for the eight hundredth time this week."

"You know he's going to be there, right?"

"How would I know that?"

"Don't pretend like you didn't hear them talking about it in social studies."

"I don't listen to anything he says."

"Liar." Cody kept his gaze averted as they drove under the train tracks and surfaced on the more respectable side of the trailer park. "Have you talked to him at all?"

Christ, Logan could be persistent. It was hard to fault him for it, but they seemed to have this conversation over and over. He was tired of talking about a relationship that only existed in Logan's imagination. "Why would I?"

"How many times do I have to say it? He misses you."

"No, he doesn't."

"I think he's trying to find a way to break the silence."

"By what? Switching desks in social studies. So what? It doesn't mean a goddamn thing."

"There's something else. Something I didn't tell you before. Last week—"

"Logan, stop. I know you're trying to help, but seriously, let it go, okay? Concentrate on your own lousy love life, and leave mine alone."

Logan braked at the stop sign at the entrance to the park. There was nobody behind them, and they sat there for a minute. Cody didn't look over, but he felt the weight of Logan's gaze on him. He squirmed a bit under the scrutiny. Maybe he'd been too harsh. Maybe he was overreacting. Maybe—

"Okay," Logan said, his voice quiet. "I won't mention it again."

For some reason, Logan's acquiescence didn't feel as good as Cody had hoped. Having Logan actually drop the subject felt like giving up on Nate all over again. It felt like finally admitting defeat. But it was what he'd asked for, so Cody forced himself to say, "Thanks." He hated the awkward silence though, so he cleared his throat and said, "How'd the game go last night?"

Logan smiled. "It was awesome. I mean, we lost, but only because our defense sucks, and I actually had a pretty good game. I was afraid knowing the scouts were there would make me nervous, and I guess it kind of did, but it seemed like a good kind of nervous. I threw for two hundred and twenty-seven yards, and rushed for one touchdown. Coach thinks I'll hear from the university by Christmas."

"That's great." He couldn't even envy Logan his success, although he couldn't help but wish somebody would offer him a ticket out of Warren too.

Cody felt like an idiot walking into the dance. He was sure everybody would see him and wonder why he was here, but if anybody noticed, they didn't make a big deal out of it, and an hour later, Cody grudgingly admitted it didn't suck nearly as much as he'd expected. It helped that Logan was there, trying to keep up a good front despite watching the girl he was crazy about rub herself all over some guy who was old enough to legally drink.

"Forget her," Cody said, in an attempt to cheer Logan up. "Ask somebody else to dance."

"Maybe." Logan eyed the group of girls huddled in the corner to their right. "If you do."

"No way."

"Why not?"

"You know why."

"Yeah, but they don't. Have you ever thought about trying to prove the rumors wrong?"

Cody looked up at him, trying to search Logan's face as the red and blue lights from the dance floor flashed across it. "Are you serious?"

"Sure. Just a couple of dances, maybe take one of them on a date or something, and then all the trash talk might go away."

Cody pondered that. Maybe Logan was right, but it wouldn't change the facts. Even if he could find a girl willing to date him, how long would it take her to figure out that he had no interest in her? "I'd hate to put one of them in the position of having to tell me no."

"What if they said yes?"

"That'd almost be worse." Because he knew without a doubt that it'd never go further than that. He'd had plenty of time to consider the fact that girls had no effect on him whatsoever.

He was saved by Logan's sister, Shelley, who tapped Logan on the shoulder and said, "Hey, I had an idea." Logan turned away, stooping a bit so they were eye to eye and he could converse with her without having to yell over the music.

Cody leaned against the wall, his eyes scanning the gym. It wasn't too bad, really. Sure, the music sucked, and Logan was his only friend, but things could've been worse.

Then his eyes landed on Nate and Stacy.

Yeah, Cody. It's worse.

He'd somehow avoided looking at Nate up until this point. He'd almost even avoided thinking about him. But now, Nate was all he could see. He wanted to look away—wanted to walk outside and have a smoke, at the very least—but he couldn't take his eyes off Nate. And then Nate and Stacy turned his way, doing that stupid little circle that apparently qualified as slow dancing at school dances, and Nate's eyes locked on to his.

It made Cody's stomach squirm and his heart do horrible, fluttery things. It made him want to hide, to dive deep into that quiet place inside where he didn't have to feel anything, but at the same time, he wanted to stay right where he was, just soaking Nate in. He was scared and thrilled and utterly powerless to do anything but watch Nate.

Nate, dancing with Stacy.

Except, maybe not really. Because Cody felt sure Nate wasn't thinking about Stacy at all. He felt sure something was happening that had nothing to do with her and everything to do with Nate and Cody, as if everybody else in the gym had disappeared and they were the only two people left on earth.

It was ridiculous. Nate had practically run screaming in fear after Cody had spilled his guts about being gay. And why in the hell had he started babbling about blowjobs and handjobs anyway? He could have kicked himself for being so stupid, but it had felt like such a relief to finally say it out loud. To finally have somebody he could voice his uncertainties to. And then, to actually kiss Nate, to see the way Nate responded to his touch. It had felt absolutely perfect.

Right up until Nate bolted, at any rate.

But Nate wasn't bolting now. He wasn't moving closer either, but Cody was sure that was only because of where they were. Because of the dance, and Stacy, and the knowledge that whatever happened between them would be seen by everybody in school. Stacy moved closer to Nate, and Nate settled his cheek against the side of her head, but still, his eyes stayed locked on Cody's. Nate's hands moved on Stacy's hips, the casual motion somehow significant, somehow making Cody's skin tingle. Somehow making him sure Nate was thinking about him.

But why would he be?

Cody winced and ducked his head, not wanting to see Nate and Stacy together anymore. He'd been jealous his whole life. Jealous of people with money and new clothes, of kids who had fathers there for the birthdays and mothers who had respectable jobs. He was jealous of many things, yes, but he'd never been so jealous of a girl simply for being where she was. But seeing Nate with Stacy, Cody was filled with a jealousy so strong and foul, he was almost ashamed. Stacy seemed like a nice enough girl. She'd certainly never done anything to Cody. But why did her happiness have to include Nate? At that moment, Cody would have done anything to be the one in Nate's arms.

That thought hit him like a bolt of lightning, almost blinding him with its brilliance. It wiggled down his spine, making his stomach do somersaults, making him feel suddenly too hot and too itchy and entirely too exposed. Cody found himself again staring into Nate's eyes.

Jesus, why the fuck was he such a goddamned fool? What was he doing here, leaning against the gym wall, trying to communicate with Nate from what felt like half a mile away, while still feeling as if Nate was in his space, in his face, in his head, seeing every insecurity he'd ever had? He wanted to cry. Or to run. Or maybe just to give up and tell Nate that he was so fucking crazy about him he couldn't even think straight.

That thought almost made him smile.

Can't even think straight.

Except, Nate *was* straight. And Cody was the town's biggest idiot.

He turned away—away from the dance, away from whatever it was Nate was trying to tell him from across the room—and headed for the door. At least he had a warm coat now. Walking home would be better than staying there, seeing Stacy have the only thing in the world Cody really wanted.

He'd barely made it out the open door of the gym before Logan caught him in the hallway, laying one big hand on Cody's shoulder.

"Cody, wait." Even in the hallway, the music was loud, but at least the lights were on. Logan bent his head closer to Cody's to talk, rather than shouting. "You leaving already?"

He knew Logan would make a big deal out of it, so he shrugged. "Maybe I'm just going for a smoke."

Logan didn't look convinced, but he obviously had something else on his mind. "Yeah right. Hey, listen. I need a favor."

"Anything."

"Can you cover for me at the Tomahawk next Saturday?"

"After Thanksgiving, you mean?"

"Right. You don't have plans, do you?"

Of course he didn't, and Logan knew it. It was a day they'd been booked for overlapping shifts, Cody for only a few hours in the first half of the day, and Logan arriving later. "Why? What's up?"

"Shelley wants me to take her to Casper on Friday so she can go shopping with our cousins on Saturday. She's gonna spend the weekend there. I could come back that night and work my shift, but then I'd have to drive to Casper again on Sunday to pick her up. It'd be easier if we both just stayed the weekend and came home Sunday evening. I know you've worked almost every Friday night during football season, and you shouldn't have to work all day Saturday too—"

"It's cool." After all, he had nothing better to do with his weekends, and a few extra hours on his paycheck would be nice. It'd mean working a ten hour shift, but so what? "I'll cover for you. I don't mind."

"Are you sure?"

Cody grinned. "Well, I'll have to cancel that hot date I had with Jamie Simpson, but for you, I'll do it."

Logan laughed and threw his arm around Cody's shoulders, turning him toward the outside door just as Jimmy Riordan and Larry Lucero came through it. "You're the best." He tugged Cody to the side to let Jimmy and Larry by, nearly pulling him off his feet as he dragged him closer, his face bumping the top of Cody's head as Cody fought for his balance. If he didn't make it as a quarterback in college, Cody figured Logan had a shot as a defensive lineman. "I owe you."

"Yeah, you do."

They strolled toward the door, Logan's arm still draped comfortably over Cody's shoulders.

"You're not just going out for a smoke. You're bailing on the dance, aren't you?"

"Yeah."

"At least let me give you a ride home."

Even in his new coat, a ride in Logan's Camaro would sure beat walking. "I'm still not putting out on the first date."

"How do you feel about first base?"

"That's the second date."

Logan laughed again. "I was planning on breaking up with you before then anyway."

Nate arrived at the dance with nearly a dozen Mormons, from all four grades. The overhead lights in the gym were out. A mirrored ball hung over the center of the floor. Christmas light had been strung all over the place, and streamers were abundant, but it still looked and smelled like the same gym they all had PE in.

Several couples were already on the dance floor, along with a small group of girls, dancing in a circle. He followed the Mormons to the right, circling away from the Grove clique, but Nate's eyes met Brian's for a moment, and then Brian leaned toward Brad and Jennifer, whispering something that made them both look Nate's way.

Nate's stomach knotted, some small seed of discomfort wiggling there, almost like a warning, and Nate tried to tell himself it was nothing. So the Grove kids were talking about him. Why should he care? He was the one who'd abandoned them, not the other way around. Maybe he didn't quite fit in with the Mormons, but at least he didn't have to worry about them peer-pressuring him into a bottle of Blue Maui, or pushing him toward a few lines of cocaine.

Eventually, the group he was with moved onto the dance floor, Stacy pulling Nate along with them. They danced a few fast dances, Nate feeling awkward and ridiculous, but confident at least that he looked less foolish than Jimmy Riordan, who seemed to be having convulsions on the far side of the room.

And then, the thing Nate had been dreading happened: the slow dance.

Some of the Mormons left the floor. Some of them paired up. A few of them stayed put, glancing awkwardly at each other. His eyes met Stacy's. He cleared his throat, trying to think of what to say.

"Do you want to—"

"Sure!" She stepped closer, putting her arms around his neck.

Nate had intended to say, *Do you want to get some punch?* He hadn't intended to ask her to dance, but there wasn't a graceful way out now.

He put his hands on her waist. She was shorter than him, a bit overweight, but pretty enough, he supposed. They moved their feet a half inch at a time, slowly turning in circles, not speaking, their eyes averted. Nate had no idea what to do with his hands. Were they too close to her breasts? He wasn't sure, but if he lowered them, they were too low on her hips. His elbows seemed to be sticking out way too far. He glanced at the couples around them and noticed that most of the guys had their hands all the way around their partner's waists, but then he'd have his hands practically on her ass. Not only that, it'd mean drawing her a lot closer to him than she was now.

They were on their second rotation when he spotted Cody.

He was so surprised, he stopped short. Cody was the last person he expected to see at the dance, but there he was, not only present, but actually laughing like he was having fun. He was standing next to Logan. Of course. Logan always seemed to be near Cody these days. Nate couldn't help but hate him for it. But as he watched, Logan's sister walked up and tapped Logan on the shoulder. He turned to talk to her, leaving Cody alone for the moment.

Nate and Stacy kept turning, taking Cody out of his view, but not out of his thoughts. Had Cody seen him? Had he wondered why Nate was here with Stacy? Had he made assumptions about Nate's intentions or about his exact relationship with her? He turned his head as they neared a complete rotation again, wanting to find Cody.

He was still right where he'd been before, but this time, he was looking at Nate. It was unnerving, and yet, Nate didn't want to turn away. Cody looked the same as always—in a pair of jeans and one of his least-ratty shirts, his hair beginning to hang in his eyes because he hadn't had it cut in a while, and Nate stood, transfixed, no longer thinking to keep up his slow rotation with Stacy. She moved closer. Nate noted how warm she felt. How scratchy her dress was against his wrists. She was about the same height as Cody, and with the same black hair, even though hers was longer. She settled her head on his shoulder. And still, he kept his eyes on Cody, wondering if that's how Cody's hair would feel too.

His pulse quickened, blood suddenly heading for places below the belt. Nate scooted back a bit, trying to think of other things, not wanting to pop wood while dancing with the good Mormon girl. He succeeded, but he couldn't stop wondering how it would feel to dance like this with Cody.

He wanted to find out. He knew that with the same surety he knew the sun would rise in the east. Whatever was happening with

Stacy didn't matter a bit. All he wanted was to walk over to Cody. To hold out his hand and pull Cody onto the dance floor.

Not that he seriously considered that an option. They'd be lucky if they managed to get kicked out of the dance before somebody kicked their asses. But still, he kept his eyes on Cody, trying to somehow tell him he was sorry, that he was wrong, that he was an idiot.

Cody turned away and walked out of the gym, and Nate watched as Logan caught up to him in the hallway. Logan was at least six inches taller than Cody, and he ducked his head, leaning close, displaying an intimacy that made Nate's stomach writhe with jealousy. They talked for just a moment, and then Logan put his arm around Cody's shoulders, turning him toward the door just as Jimmy Riordan and Larry Lucero passed them. He suspected neither Logan nor Cody saw the way Jimmy and Larry both turned to watch them together as they passed. Logan pulled Cody close, their bodies fitting together like puzzle pieces, and then—

Logan kissed him.

It was brief. Just a peck on the top of Cody's head, but Nate went cold, all the way to his toes. He felt as if his stomach had somehow fallen past his legs to land on the dirty gym floor.

"Guess the fag got himself a new boyfriend," Larry said to Jimmy as they walked past where Nate and Stacy were dancing.

And the worst part was, there was nothing in the world Nate could do about it.

CHAPTER
Fourteen

*I*t was snowing when Nate left the dance, and for a minute he simply stopped, staring up at the cold sky. Huge, fluffy flakes landed on his cheeks. It should have been dark out, but it wasn't. Clouds obscured the moon and stars, but the sky glowed faintly white, reflecting light from the streetlamps, making it almost as bright as daytime, except that the entire world had been muted to shades of gray.

"It's snowing!" he said. He thought he might have laughed with delight if his heart weren't aching so much over Cody.

The Mormons all shook their heads, chuckling at him good-naturedly. "You won't be that excited about it when it's still snowing in March."

It continued all night, and all day Sunday, and Nate sat staring out the window, going around in circles in his head, arguing with himself endlessly until he thought he was going mad.

Cody's dating Logan.

No, he isn't. That's ridiculous. Logan isn't gay. You heard him say so himself at the bowling alley.

But boy, he was awfully defensive when Larry Lucero called Cody a fag. He was pretty quick to say that it wasn't anybody's business. Maybe it was because he really is like Cody. Maybe he said that to cover the fact that he's sleeping with Cody.

No. They're friends. Nothing more.

But he kissed Cody. Right there in the school, with me and Larry and Jimmy all watching.

That doesn't mean anything.

It means everything.

Nate was glad they only had two days of school the next week. Only Monday and Tuesday to see Logan and Cody in social studies, ducking their heads together across the aisle to talk before the bell rang, both of them chuckling, even if Cody's smile did look a bit forced.

By Wednesday, the first day of Thanksgiving break, the snow had stopped. The sky was clear and brilliantly, shockingly blue, the wind stronger than ever, so icy it seemed to cut right through every coat Nate owned. There'd been no talk of him going home for Thanksgiving. It hadn't even been an option before Nate's phone call home. It was even less of one now, in his mind at least. Still, he knew he couldn't avoid the subject of his mother for a second week in a row.

Sure enough, his dad knocked on his bedroom door on Wednesday evening.

"Nate?" He'd just come home from work and was still wearing his uniform, his gun belt hanging from his hips. "Time to call your mom."

Nate was lying on the bed in the darkness, staring at the blank ceiling above him. Howard Jones was spinning on the turntable, telling him things could only get better, but Nate found it hard to believe. He'd spent the last hour trying not to wonder what Cody was doing. Trying not to wonder if he was with Logan. Trying not to imagine Cody touching Logan and kissing him and whispering secrets to him in some dark, distant room.

Nate reached over and hit the button to lift the needle from the record, letting silence fall.

"I have nothing to say to her."

His dad crossed his arms, resting against the doorframe even though it must have made his gun belt dig into his hip. "Are you okay, Nate?"

"I'm fine."

His dad rubbed a finger over his mustache. "I know you never wanted to move here. I thought things'd get better once school started and you met kids your own age, but it seems like it's going downhill. Seems like things are getting worse instead."

Nate sat up on his bed, crossing his legs, thinking about everything that happened since he'd first talked to Cody behind the ICE cooler.

Could he talk to his dad about it?

He'd dismissed the idea before, but then again, he didn't have much to lose. "I don't belong here, Dad. I don't fit in anywhere."

"Oh, I'm sure it isn't that bad."

Of course he'd say that. His dad had no idea how claustrophobic Walter Warren High School was, with its tight cliques.

The bed shifted as his father sat down next to him. "What happened two weeks ago that made you want to sneak downstairs and call your mom?"

"I was going to ask her to let me come home."

"Well, I figured that much. But what I'm asking is, what happened that night to make you want to go home right then? We've been here since August, but something happened this month that made things worse."

Nate fidgeted with the hem of his jeans, debating. It all started with Cody. "I did something . . ." He shook his head, trying to come up with a way to tell his dad about it without actually telling him anything at all. "Something maybe I shouldn't have." But whether he meant letting Cody touch him and kiss him, or whether he meant pushing Cody away afterward, even he couldn't have said.

"Are we talking about something illegal? Or . . . breaking rules?"

"No."

"Cheating on a test? Stealing? A prank that went wrong?"

"Nothing like that."

"Did you get in a fight?"

Did he? It almost felt like it. "Not really, but . . . an argument, maybe."

"With somebody at the dance?"

"With the only real friend I have."

"Ah." He patted Nate's shoulder. "Well, these things happen. Friends argue sometimes, but it'll be okay. You'll see."

"It wasn't okay with you and Mom."

"That's different."

"Why?"

His dad took a deep breath, tilting his head back to stare up at Nate's bedroom ceiling. He didn't answer though.

"Somebody else answered the phone at our house."

His dad blew out a puff of air. "Yeah, that's what she told me."

"He's living there, isn't he?"

"Yes."

"Who is he?"

His dad's shoulders slumped. The answer came out a growl. "Greg."

"Greg who?"

"Greg Merriman. They met at the gym."

The gym? Nate thought of all the times his mom had come downstairs with a smile on her face and her workout bag slung over her shoulder, telling him she'd be back in a couple of hours. "All this time, I thought you were the one who had the affair. But it wasn't you, was it?"

His dad leaned forward to put his elbows on his knees. "No."

"Why didn't you tell me?"

"She begged me not to."

"But . . ." It seemed so feeble. So ridiculous. She'd torn their family apart, and yet his father had let Nate put all the blame on him. "That's why you wouldn't let me stay in Austin?"

His dad stood up, still staring at the ceiling as if it held some kind of answers. "I don't want to talk about this again. We've been over it a thousand times—"

"But you never told me the truth, did you? Well, I want the truth now. No more lies. No more treating me like a little kid." Even if he felt like one, at the moment. "Was it because Mom didn't want me to know about the affair? Is that why I couldn't stay?"

"That was part of it."

"What was the rest?"

"Greg wanted . . . Well, he didn't want . . ." He paced as he talked, as if searching for the right words. He ended up at Nate's dresser, eyeing the frame of the mirror. Nate had wedged snapshots into it when they'd first arrived—one of the tennis team, a couple of him and his parents together as a family, some of friends from Austin—but he'd taken them all down in the past week. His dad frowned, eyeing the empty spaces where the pictures had been as if he couldn't quite believe they were gone.

Nate watched his dad's face in the mirror. "Greg wanted what, Dad?"

His dad sighed. "He didn't want you. He knew you'd hold a grudge against him and he—"

"What?" Nate jumped off the bed, advancing on his father, even though he wasn't the one Nate was angry with. "And Mom was okay with that? She just shipped me off like I was nobody, all so she could be with him?"

His father turned to meet Nate's gaze, squaring his shoulders, reminding him he was still several inches taller. "She didn't 'ship you off,' Nate. I wanted you with me, and with Greg in the picture, she agreed that was probably for the best."

Nate fell back against his desk, stunned. "That's why you let me believe you were the one who had the affair—just so I wouldn't know that Mom didn't want me."

"Son—"

"Does she love me at all?"

His father laughed. It was dry and humorless and awkward, but it was a laugh nonetheless. "Of course she does. More than anything. She just . . ." He threw up his hands, looking powerless, even in his full cop getup. "She's in love. I know you don't know what that's like yet, but someday you will. And when you love somebody like that—" His voice cracked. "The only thing you want to do is to be with them, whatever it takes. It isn't logical. It doesn't make sense. It's just how it is."

Nate sat down heavily in the desk chair, his heart seeming too big and too fragile. *The only thing you want to do is to be with them, whatever it takes.*

"I think maybe I do know what that feels like." His voice sounded small and ridiculous, even to him.

His dad blinked, processing, but then a grin spread quickly across his face. For the first time in ages, it looked like a real, heartfelt smile. "Really?"

Nate squirmed in his seat, feeling like an idiot, but the words felt true. They felt right. "I think so. I don't know. It's so confusing and scary, and it doesn't really make any sense, but—"

His dad laughed. "Yeah, that sounds like love." His dad was still smiling ear to ear. "I'm glad to hear that, son."

It was the last thing he'd expected to hear. "Why?"

"I don't know. I guess because there's nothing in the world like that first time. I sound like a damn greeting card saying it, but somebody around here may as well get something good out of this situation." He shook his head, still grinning like a fool. "Well, who is she?"

And just like that, the spark of hope in Nate's chest went out. What in the world could he say? What would his father think when he found out his son was a fag? And what did it matter anyway when Cody wasn't even speaking to him? But luckily, his dad asked another question before Nate even had time to answer the first one.

"Is that who you argued with?"

Nate slumped, relieved he didn't have to tell him quite yet. "Yes."

His dad sat down again on the edge of the bed. "Well, I wish I could tell you it will all work out, but when it comes to things like this . . ." He shook his head. "Sometimes love sucks."

Nate chuckled, remembering one of his first conversations with Cody. "If the world didn't suck, we'd fall off."

His dad's brow wrinkled in confusion, but he smiled. "I guess."

"I'm sorry I was such a jerk to you. All this time—"

"It doesn't matter." His dad glanced at his watch. "It's after seven. If we're going to call—"

"I really don't want to talk to her right now."

"You can't put it off forever."

"I know."

"Fair enough." His dad stood up, but didn't move to leave. "I'm working tomorrow. Most of the weekend too. Low man on the pole and all that. I bought you a turkey TV dinner. Not much of a Thanksgiving feast, but at least you won't go hungry. And there's money on the kitchen table if you need to get anything from the grocery store."

"That's fine."

His dad made it as far as the door before stopping again. "Nate?"

"Yeah, Dad?"

"That guy on your record is right, you know. It really does get better. I know high school seems like the whole world right now, but ten years from now, none of this will matter a bit. You'll have forgotten about most of it."

Nate nodded, not knowing if he believed his dad and Howard Jones or not.

Thanksgiving Day wasn't so bad. Sure, Nate was home alone for much of the day, but having admitted to himself how much he cared about Cody had somehow lifted a weight from his shoulders. His dad was working again on Friday, and Nate drove to the grocery store in search of junk food. The roads were clear, thanks to the wind more than rising temperatures, and Nate marveled at the drifts on the western sides of the buildings. Many of them were taller than he was. He spotted a group of kids sledding down a drift from the roof of their garage, laughing in delight even though their cheeks were bright red from the cold. It was almost enough to make him wish he were still a kid.

At the store, he grabbed a six-pack of Coke, some microwave popcorn, and a bag of M&M's. The cover of *Newsweek* caught his eye as he stood in the checkout line.

AIDS was printed in huge, block letters. And below that: "How the spreading epidemic will affect health care, government policy, civil liberties and attitudes toward sex."

Nate's heart burst into gear. He glanced around, seeing if anybody was watching, before admonishing himself for being stupid. He was only reading a magazine cover, after all. And it wasn't as if he actually had AIDS, but having finally admitted to himself how much he wanted Cody seemed to have opened up a whole-new, wider world to him. A disease he'd dismissed until now as something that only happened to "them" had suddenly become something that might happen to him. And he hadn't forgotten Cody's question in the field about whether or not it could be spread with oral sex.

"You ready?" the man at the register asked.

"Yeah." Nate grabbed the magazine and placed on the checkout stand with the soda, candy, and popcorn.

The cashier eyed it skeptically, then turned his gaze on Nate, as if asking a question.

"It's for a research paper." Nate hated the way his hands shook as he reached for his wallet. He shouldn't have to justify something so simple as buying a magazine.

"Serves them all right if they die, if you ask me," the man said as he started ringing up the groceries.

Nate did his best to ignore him, but he wondered, as he gathered his groceries and headed for his car, if he looked guilty.

Back at home, he settled on the couch to read. The article was scary, but depressingly uninformative. "By 1991 an estimated 5 million Americans may be carrying the AIDS virus." The article talked a great deal about how the disease that many had assumed was confined to homosexuals and intravenous drug users was sure to sweep through the heterosexual population next. It was estimated that sixty percent of the heroin addicts in New York State were infected, and the idea of those people carrying the virus back home, to their presumably straight wives and girlfriends, or to prostitutes, had experts predicting an outright epidemic. But other than suggesting more care in selecting sexual partners and encouraging the use of condoms, there was very little practical information.

Could it be spread by a blowjob? Nate still had no idea.

He wanted to talk to Cody about it, but how could he, after the way he'd acted?

This week, he'd do better. This week, he'd make himself walk up to Cody and apologize.

That was easy to say when he was home alone, but by Saturday, Nate's resolve was fading. Come Monday, he'd be right back where he'd been before the dance, trying to avoid at least half the people in the school while longing for the one person who wanted nothing to do with him. He found himself dwelling on that moment at the dance, replaying the scene over and over again—Logan putting his arm around Cody's shoulders and kissing the top of his head.

It doesn't mean anything.

It means everything.

He wished he knew which one was true. He was beginning to think he truly hated Logan. The one kid in school who everybody loved—the star quarterback, honor roll student sure to be named valedictorian, the one person with enough self-esteem to do his own thing regardless of what anybody else thought—and Nate found himself wishing Logan would disappear. Wishing he'd suddenly pack up and move far, far away.

By Sunday, he'd worked himself into a real funk. He'd wasted his entire holiday weekend staring at the TV, and what had Cody done?

He had no idea, of course, but that didn't stop him from imagining all kinds of scenarios, most of them featuring Logan.

The weather had been cold but mild all week, but a freak snowstorm blew in early Sunday afternoon, gusts of wind bending the trees and making the windows creak in their panes. Nate watched out the window as the snow started to fly, almost horizontal in the wind.

Maybe he could call Cody. Maybe he could go to the Hole, knock on trailers until he found the right one. Maybe he could . . .

What? Suddenly declare his love for Cody?

Yeah. Great idea.

Six o'clock rolled around. They had leftover Chinese takeout in the fridge, but Nate figured he'd wait for his dad to come home so they could eat together. He suddenly felt more connected to his father than he had in a long time.

But his dad didn't arrive.

It wasn't unusual for him to be a bit late, but by the time eight o'clock had come and gone, Nate was beginning to worry. He could call the station, but that was generally frowned upon. Besides, his dad was unlikely to be hanging around there after the end of his shift. Maybe he'd gone out for a drink with some of the other cops? But no, that seemed unlikely. He did that on occasion, but rarely on Sundays, and never without calling to let Nate know.

It was nearly nine when his dad came in, the Wyoming wind throwing the door back against the wall, carrying in a flurry of snow. His dad shoved the door closed and dropped his hat on the coffee table. His face was pale and gaunt.

"Dad, what happened? Why are you so late?"

His dad crossed the living room in three long strides and pulled Nate into his arms. He was shaking as he held Nate close.

"Dad?" Nate's face was squished against his dad's cold, wet cop coat. It wasn't so much that Nate objected to being hugged as that it was a bit unusual. "What's going on?"

His dad let him go, pushing his hair back from his face. "Something's happened, Nate." He shrugged off his coat and turned to hang it in the closet, still talking. "I've been trying to decide if I should tell you. I'm not supposed to, but you'll find out anyway. I just—" He turned to face Nate. "You can't tell anyone. I'm sure it'll spread through the school like wildfire, but it can't start with you. Do you understand?"

Nate swallowed, his heart beginning to race. "Yes." Was it his mom? His grandma? No, that didn't explain why his dad was late, and it certainly didn't fit with his dad's warning about keeping quiet about it. "What is it?"

"There's been an accident. Some kids from your school—"

"Is it Cody?"

"Cody?" His dad frowned. "No. It has nothing to do with him."

Nate fell back onto the couch, his hand to his chest. No, not Cody, thank God. But somebody his dad expected him to know. "Who?"

His dad sank down to perch on the edge of the coffee table, their knees vying for space. "A boy and his sister. Logan and Shelley Robertson. Do you know them?"

Nate's heart skipped a beat. For half a second, his brain screamed, *You did this! This is your fault!* He'd been wishing for Logan to go away, but not like this. He'd never wanted anything like this. "I know Logan. I've met his sister, but—"

"You're friends with him?"

Nate hesitated, flashing through every conversation he'd ever had with Logan. "Not quite friends, but— Jesus, Dad. What happened? Are you telling me they're—"

"They were driving home from Casper. God knows what they were doing in a Camaro in this storm, but they must have hit a patch of ice. They collided with a semi. They—" He shook his head, placing his hand on Nate's knee. "Jesus, I don't think I'll ever be able to get those images out of my head. Just so much blood, and those two kids looking so small—"

"Oh my God! They're dead?"

His dad's head jerked. Not quite a nod. Not quite a gesture of denial, either. "The girl is. She died on impact. But Logan . . ." He swallowed. "He's in the ICU in Casper."

That brought a surge of hope. "He's alive, then? He's okay?"

But he knew he wasn't. He could see it in his father's eyes. "It doesn't look good, Nate. The doctors say even if he lives, he'll never be the same."

Nate felt as if the bottom had dropped out of his world. He wanted to go back in time. To take back every bad thought he'd ever had about Logan, as if that could somehow change what had happened. *"He'll never be the same."* Nate didn't even want to consider what those words meant. He thought he might be sick. Knowing it wasn't really his fault didn't make him feel any less guilty.

"I'm buying you a truck. I don't want any arguments. I won't even make you sell the Mustang, but I won't have you driving it around on the icy roads."

"Okay."

"I have a squad car for the next few days. I want you to take my Jeep until then." His dad's jaw clenched. "No arguments, all right? The Mustang isn't safe."

Nate nodded, feeling completely helpless and tiny and terrible. "I understand."

CHAPTER

onday started out bad and went downhill from there. Nate felt like he was toxic, the horrible knowledge of Logan and Shelley's accident tucked into some dark corner of his heart. He'd prayed for the first time in years the night before, asking a God he'd never believed in to please make Logan better. Please let Logan come out of this unscathed. In the cold light of morning, it seemed feasible.

Logan was hurt, but he was strong. He was huge. He was larger than life. If anybody could beat this, it was Logan.

Nate walked into the school with a small seed of hope in his heart. He couldn't say anything, and so he watched.

First period was small. It was calculus, and being the most advanced class the high school offered, not many people took it. Only half a dozen students normally, but on this day, they numbered only five. Nate eyed the empty desk that was usually filled by Logan's giant frame.

By second period, people were starting to whisper. He spotted a couple of sophomore girls with their arms around each other, crying. Shelley's friends, he assumed.

Third period was when it got real. The teacher was late arriving, and when she did, her eyes were red and swollen. The unruly class quickly settled, somehow sensing that their world was about to change.

It was clear she'd been told exactly what to say, and equally clear that in every classroom in Walter Warren High School, teachers were making the same announcement.

"Some of you may have heard rumors, but we've just received word." She put her hands over her lips, visibly trying to steady herself. "There was an accident last night, up by where 220 meets 287. Shelley and Logan Robertson—" She gasped for air. "I'm afraid they're—"

"Only Shelley," somebody said. "I thought Logan was in the hospital."

The teacher shook her head. New tears welled up in her eyes. "He was, but . . . not now. Not anymore."

The tiny piece of hope in Nate's chest shattered. For the rest of the period, the students were hushed and somber. Grief counselors would arrive the next day from Casper, but until then, there was nothing but an entire school of numb, shocked people.

Nate stumbled through the rest of his day. Teachers were quiet, not bothering to teach, some of them openly weeping. And the students . . .

The students.

Before the accident, Nate hadn't thought he could hate Walter Warren High School more than he already did, but as the day wore on, his anger mounted. What should have been mourning was quickly growing into some kind of sick competition. Every girl seemed to be claiming she'd dated Logan. Every boy said he'd seen Logan just the other day. He had no doubt that the same thing was happening amongst the sophomores with Shelley.

"I talked to him on the phone on Friday."

"I told her not to go to Casper."

"He said we'd go out on a date this weekend, but I guess now it will never happen."

"I know she was going to ask me out."

"I wish we'd never broken up."

I, I, I. That was all Nate heard: people trading memories that seemed to grow by the minute, trying to prove they had the most reason to grieve, vying for attention as they sobbed in the halls.

All but one.

Nate didn't have to see Cody to know he wouldn't be trading stories by his locker, or hugging it out next to the water fountain. He searched for him in the hallways, watching for that familiar shock of black hair. He arrived early to social studies and perched on the edge of his seat amongst the Mormons, wanting to catch Cody as soon as he came in.

"My mom's helping plan the funeral."

"My dad said the car was totaled, the top of it just torn right off."

"They won't be able to have open caskets."

Nate waited, his foot bouncing nervously as the seconds ticked by.

Cody entered just before the bell rang. One look at him was enough to break Nate's heart. There was no sign of tears, but there was something so *wrong* about Cody—some terrible stillness that Nate couldn't begin to describe that told him he was right—that the person who would probably mourn Logan the most was the one person nobody bothered to think of.

Cody stopped a foot inside the door, his eyes locked on the desk where Logan normally sat. His jaw clenched. His eyes closed. For one fraction of a second, Nate thought Cody was going to fall apart right there in the classroom. But just as the bell rang, Cody turned on his heel and walked out the door.

Nate jumped to his feet, made it half a step before he remembered his books. He turned to grab them, wanting to call out to Cody but unwilling to draw attention like that—

"Mr. Bradford, take your seat please."

Nate stopped, his books a jumble in his arms. "But—"

"I know this has been a tough day for everybody, but the bell has rung." Mrs. Simmons seemed to be holding her neck at an odd angle so as to look at Nate without seeing the horribly empty desk three seats behind him. "Take your seat, please."

Everybody's eyes were on him, and God only knew where Cody was by now. Nate sank into his chair, defeated.

But only for now. Class was forty-five minutes long, and after that, he'd find Cody, no matter what it took.

Cody had noticed everybody in school whispering and crying, but he hadn't thought much of it. Nobody ever bothered to tell him gossip, and there was nobody he could ask except for Logan, but Logan hadn't been around.

It wasn't until third period that he found out the two things were related. He felt like he'd been in a trance since he'd first heard those terrible words.

"Logan Robertson is dead."

He'd only survived the day by diving for that deep, cold place inside of himself where he didn't have to feel happiness or pain or heartache. It was a defense mechanism he'd learned as a kid. There hadn't been an option. It was an instinct born of nights cowering beneath his blankets as his parents fought in the living room, and days waiting on the front porch for a father who never arrived, birthdays that went unmentioned and Christmas mornings when the only gifts were a mushy orange in his stocking and a packet of socks underneath the tree. It wasn't that his mom didn't try, but he suspected she'd learned long ago to do what he was doing now: killing everything inside. Locking away any dream of a real life was the only way to survive. There was no such thing as hope. There was just this moment, bleeding into the next, and into the next, slowly trudging toward the sunburnt patch of brown grass where residents of Warren were finally dropped into the cold, hard ground, with only a flat, gray stone to mark the spot.

And now, Logan would be there, long before his time.

Cody walked home, buffeted by the wind, warm in a coat that was suddenly more precious than it had ever been. His mom was gone when he got home, either at work or at the bar, and Cody sat in the empty, silent living room, a cigarette slowly burning to the butt between his still fingers, holding himself in that lonely, safe place. He had to be careful not to move.

Careful not think.

Careful not to hear Logan's laugh echoing in the distant corners of his mind. Otherwise, he might not make it. He might fracture and break, shatter into a hundred pieces, fall apart on their filthy living room floor.

No, he couldn't do that.

And so he sat, watching the smoke from his cigarette curl toward the ceiling, convincing himself that this was all there would ever be— this moment, and this numb emptiness keeping him from the pain.

The room was deep in shadows when the knock came. It was only four o'clock, but the sun was low in the sky, ready to be swallowed by the barren, wind-blown earth.

The knock came again, and this time, Cody stirred, turning toward the sound.

Nobody ever knocked on their door except the cops and the occasional Mormon missionary. Even they hadn't been around in a while.

Knock, knock, knock.

Cody dropped his cigarette butt into the ashtray and pushed himself off the couch, moving slowly to keep from losing his center. The room seemed to tilt around him, everything going left while he went right, and he flicked the light switch by the front door, illuminating the porch, before opening the door. His heart missed a beat when he found Nate waiting on the other side of the torn screen. The careful stillness that sheltered Cody threatened to crumble, just seeing Nate standing there with the wind blowing his hair into his face, his eyes so full of concern that Cody could barely stand to look at him.

"I wasn't sure which one was yours. I tried that other one first, but—"

"Why are you here?"

"I wanted to see you."

Cody did his best to sound angry. "Well, now you have. Is that it?"

Nate didn't even blink, as if he'd expected Cody's hostility. "Can I come in?"

Cody hesitated, but only for a second. What was the point? He'd dreaded this moment since the day they'd met. He'd tossed a pack of cigarettes to Nate and climbed into his car, and ever since then, he'd done everything he could to keep Nate from seeing his real life, but he didn't care anymore. It was time for all pretense to be tossed aside. Time for all his careful dissemination to be discarded like the stack of crumpled yellow butts in the ashtray. What the hell did it matter anyway, with Logan gone?

He turned away without opening the screen door, but Nate opened it anyway and followed him inside. Cody glanced around and the familiar space—sagging couch, threadbare armchair, dingy curtains, the whole place reeking of cigarettes and stale beer, a bit of smoke still lingering in the air. He wondered how it looked through Nate's eyes, but when he turned to face him, to try to gauge his reaction, he realized Nate wasn't seeing any of it. Nate, it seemed, only had eyes for him.

And Jesus, those eyes. Cody knew in that instant that Nate had come for him. Despite everything that had happened, despite the fact that they hadn't spoken in weeks, Nate had seen what nobody else had. He'd recognized that Logan's death would break Cody's heart. And he'd come to the Hole, knocking on doors, until he found the right one.

Nate said only, "I was worried about you."

Cody's stillness cracked right down the middle like the earth in some Hollywood movie earthquake, everything he'd been steeling himself against welling up through that breach. He turned away, trying to stamp it all down, trying to locate that safe place he'd found earlier, but it was out of his reach. He wanted to run, but he only made it as far as the kitchen, where he came up short against the refrigerator, the stupid stained towel with the crocheted hook hanging from the handle, and Cody hung there as well, his shoulders and jaw tight, his teeth clenched, his knees threatening to give out.

"Cody, I'm sorry."

Cody bit his lip, shaking his head, wishing he could send Nate away.

"I know you must be upset."

"I'm fine," Cody choked out, but he wasn't fooling anybody. Not even himself.

"Look, I know you probably hate me. I know I've been an asshole. But I just—" He sighed. "I care about you—"

"Stop."

"And I'm sorry about what happened between us. But most of all—"

"Don't."

"I'm sorry about—"

Cody put his head in his hands, trying to cover his ears, trying to block out the words. "Don't say it!"

"I'm sorry about Logan."

Cody couldn't handle that. Couldn't face the wave of emotions rising over him, threatening to drown him. He put his head against the freezer handle, clenching his eyes shut. He wanted to quit fighting it. He wanted to scream at Nate, to tell him to go to hell, to go away, to leave him the fuck alone.

But most of all, he wanted to bury his face in Nate's chest and cry. He wondered if that would feel as good as he'd always imagined, to have somebody hold him while he let go.

God, he couldn't let that happen.

He took a deep breath, his lungs aching. "I need you to leave."

"No."

"I don't want you here."

"I know, but you shouldn't be alone."

Alone. Alone sounded good. Alone sounded safe. "I want—"

"I know you're upset. I know you must be devastated, Cody."

Devastated. One simple little word to describe the horrible turmoil in his heart, the awful emptiness in his life, the Logan-shaped void nobody else would ever be able to fill, just standing there next to him at work, talking about girls while he put away the dishes.

Talking to Cody like he wasn't so bad after all.

"I know he was your friend."

"My friend," Cody managed to whisper. "Oh God, Nate. He was my friend. He was my *only* friend."

"I know."

And then it all hit him at once, that hot, horrible weight he'd worked so hard to avoid suddenly filling his chest, rising into his throat, and Cody bent forward, gasping, trying to hold it in, wanting to just *maintain*. Just keep himself together.

"Cody." Nate's hand on his shoulder was so soft. So gentle. "It's okay to cry."

Cody shook his head, choking on his tears. "No, it isn't."

"It's okay to miss him."

That was the worst part, knowing he'd go on missing Logan like this forever. That nothing he did could change it. A sob burst out of him, wretched and humiliating but such a fucking relief after fighting so hard, and Cody gave up. He surrendered at last to the pain, shaking as he cried, almost falling to the floor as his knees gave out.

Good thing Nate was there to catch him.

CHAPTER

*N*ate ended up sitting on the kitchen floor with Cody curled against his chest as he cried. It was painful, witnessing Cody's grief, feeling the way Cody's entire body shook with the force of his sobs, but Nate just held him, feeling strangely at peace. Holding Cody felt as natural as breathing. There was none of the strange terror like when he'd touched Christine, or the awkwardness he felt when he danced with Stacy.

It went through his head, over and over again as Cody's tears finally began to slow.

This is right.

Although after half an hour or so, Nate's backside was beginning to hurt. For the first time, he noticed how uncomfortable he was, scrunched against the cabinet, but he wasn't about to disturb Cody now. Nate glanced around at the sad state of Cody's home, and his heart ached for him anew. Even in the dim light, it was easy to see that the floor probably hadn't been mopped in ages and the cracked linoleum was curling at the corners. Several of the cupboard doors hung crooked on their hinges. One was gone completely, revealing a shelf that contained only a couple of cans of soup and a jar of peanut butter, all generic brand. No Campbell's or Skippy Extra Chunky for Cody. Probably no Coke or Pepsi in the fridge to wash it down with, either.

It was just one more thing Nate had taken for granted his entire life.

Eventually, Cody's breathing slowed, although his chest still hitched every few seconds. Nate ducked his head, burying his nose in Cody's dark hair, breathing in the clean smell of shampoo and the familiar tang of smoke.

"I'm sorry," Cody whispered, between hiccups.

"For what? Being upset? You don't need to apologize for that."

"Do you know..." Cody had to stop and take a deep breath. Then, his voice even quieter, "Do you know how it happened?"

Nate had to think for a second about exactly what Cody was asking. "How he died?"

Cody nodded without moving his head from Nate's chest.

"Didn't you hear at school?"

"I heard a car wreck, but..." He shook his head. "I didn't want to hear any more. I didn't think I wanted to know, but now—"

He choked again, his shoulders shaking, and Nate hurried to fill the gap. He didn't have to rely on the little information he had from his father. He'd heard plenty at school. "He was coming home from Casper with Shelley. Remember how it started snowing all of a sudden yesterday afternoon? I heard they stayed at his cousin's through dinner, thinking the weather would clear, but it didn't. And since it was a school night—"

"He should have stayed."

"I know."

"He shouldn't have been in that stupid Camaro this time of year."

"I know."

"If I hadn't traded shifts with him, if I'd just told him no, maybe he wouldn't have gone to Casper at all and none of this would have happened."

Nate wasn't sure exactly what Cody was talking about, but it didn't matter. "Maybe. But that doesn't make it your fault. You had no way of knowing."

"He just wanted to trade shifts."

"You didn't do anything wrong. There was no reason for you to say no."

"I wanted the hours! How could I think the hours were more important than him?"

"You didn't." Nate shook his head, rubbing Cody's back as he tried to piece together what must have happened. "He asked for a favor, right? And you said yes. That's all. You had no way of knowing."

Cody shuddered. "And Shelley. God, I haven't even thought about Shelley."

"You didn't know her as well."

"All I can think about is going to work and not having him there to talk to. Or going to school and not having him sitting next to me in social studies." He sniffled. "All I can think about is *me*, and how much I want him back."

Nate stroked his hair. "I know."

"Does that make me selfish?"

"I think that makes you normal. I think the rest will come later."

"It should have been me." He was crying again, although not the gut-wrenching sobs of before. This was quieter. "Logan was going to college. He was probably getting a football scholarship. He could have done anything."

"I know—"

"He wouldn't have been stuck here, don't you see? He had more than the oil wells or the coal mines to look forward to. It should have been me! Nobody would care if I died."

"That's not true," Nate said, holding Cody tighter. "I'd care."

"I wish it had been me."

"No," Nate said simply, shaking his head. "No."

Cody settled closer, his tears subsiding again. One arm snuck around Nate's waist, and Nate's heart swelled. He rubbed Cody's back, making soft shushing sounds until Cody sighed and shifted his weight, pulling away a bit and tilting his head back to look up at Nate. The light from the porch fell through the kitchen window to be reflected off Cody's damp cheeks.

"Thank you for coming over."

"You're welcome."

"I feel like a jerk for crying all over you."

"I don't mind."

Quite the contrary. He didn't like seeing Cody in pain, but he appreciated having an excuse to be so close to him. It might have been arousing if Cody hadn't been so distraught. Nate brushed a lingering tear from under Cody's eye, then continued the caress, letting his fingers tangle into Cody's black hair. They were almost nose to nose. It would have taken so little to close that gap—to simply claim Cody's lips with his own. Nate knew how he'd taste—how the tears would have turned his tongue salty—and he almost moaned with the desire that rose up in him, seeing Cody look at him like that.

But he stopped himself.

This wasn't the time. Not when Cody was wracked with grief over Logan.

"He wasn't your only friend, you know. I'm sure that's how it felt, these last few months. And that's my fault, for being such an idiot, but I won't leave you like that again." He wasn't sure if he saw doubt in Cody's eyes, or if it was only his own guilt making him think so. "I promise, you still have one friend left."

Cody leaned closer, and for one amazing second, Logan thought maybe Cody would take matters into his own hands and initiate a kiss himself, but he didn't. "Promise me something else?" His voice almost cracked as he said it.

"Anything."

"Let your dad buy you a truck. Please. Don't make me lose you too."

Nate almost laughed. He'd already made the agreement with his dad anyway. He wasn't giving up his Mustang, but that didn't mean he had to court death. "Okay."

They stayed like that for a moment, lingering on that promise. Nate thought again how easy it would be to kiss Cody, but he found himself thinking of Logan. Wondering when Logan had last kissed Cody. Wondering how long it would be before Cody could kiss somebody and not think of Logan while he did it.

Now who's being selfish, Nate?

Cody sat back on his heels and wiped his face. The motion moved him away, taking him out of Nate's reach. Nate mourned the loss a bit, but he was also relieved to be able to stretch his legs and his back. And seeing the peanut butter had made his stomach grumble.

"Are you hungry?"

"No."

Nate waited, trying not to smile. It seemed wrong to smile. "Have you eaten anything today?"

"No."

"Are you *sure* you're not hungry?" Because Nate knew how grief could make somebody forget to check in with their stomach.

It took Cody a second to answer. "I guess maybe I am."

"We could go downtown—"

"Uptown."

"Uptown, then, and get ham-fried rice and sweet and sour pork." The black-and-white labels in the cabinet caught his eye. He had no idea how much money Cody made at the Tomahawk, but he didn't want that to be an issue. "My treat."

Cody shook his head. "I don't want to go in there." Already, his voice was threatening to crack again. "All those people. Everybody will be talking about—"

"You're right." In such a small town, something as juicy as two teenagers dying in a gruesome car wreck would certainly have everybody buzzing. "How about if I go pick it up and bring it back here instead?"

Cody looked like he was trying to smile, even if he wasn't exactly doing a bang-up job of it. "I haven't eaten there in years."

"Does that mean yes?"

"Do they still have those little fried crab things? The ones with the cream cheese?"

"I have no idea, but if they do, I'll get you some."

This time, Cody's smile looked a bit more genuine, even if it didn't quite reach his eyes. "Okay."

Cody pushed himself to his feet, then held a hand down to Nate and pulled him up too. Nate was a bit disappointed that Cody let his hand go as soon as he was standing.

Cody followed him to the door, lingering in the doorway as Nate stepped onto the porch and zipped up his jacket. Nate sensed his hesitance, and he wasn't surprised when Cody reached out and grabbed his sleeve.

"You're coming back, right?" Even now, it was as if he hardly dared to hope.

"With fried rice and crab wontons." And just to seal the deal, Nate kissed him. Not on the lips, because he wasn't brave enough for that yet. But he kissed Cody's forehead, even though Cody went stiff as he did. "Twenty minutes or less, I promise."

Cody didn't answer. Didn't respond at all. Didn't even move. But Nate found himself smiling all the way to the restaurant.

Cody didn't have much of an appetite despite not having eaten since breakfast, but Nate had gone to so much trouble that he felt compelled to eat. The food was good, but each bite hurt, as if daring to enjoy anything good about the world was a betrayal to his grief. How could he be excited about crab wontons, knowing Logan and Shelley were lying in a morgue in Casper?

"Nobody's at the Tomahawk." It came to him all of a sudden, and he had to set his fork down to fight the knot in his throat again.

Nate froze with his fork halfway to his mouth, his brow wrinkled in confusion. "What do you mean?"

"We alternate Mondays. It was Logan's turn." He felt like he should have remembered. Like he should have gone in to cover Logan's shift for him, but the thought of standing by that sink again filled him with a horrible sense of despair. How would he ever get through his shift on Wednesday? He felt tears welling up again and hurriedly wiped them away. He was sick of blubbering in front of Nate, but his eyes weren't cooperating.

"Why don't you go watch TV or something?" Nate suggested. "I'll put the leftovers in the fridge for you."

Cody nodded, but it took a minute for the words to register in his brain. He made it to the couch before realizing the remote was out of his reach. Whatever. He didn't want to watch TV anyway. The metal rabbit-ears on top of it had been a bit out of whack for a week, barely picking up anything anyway. He laid his head on the arm of the couch, curling halfway into a fetal position, finding some strange comfort in the worn, threadbare upholstery. At some point, Nate put an afghan over him, and Cody drifted in a warm place where he couldn't quite remember how horrible the day had been.

He didn't realize he'd fallen asleep until Nate gently shook his shoulder. He opened his eyes to a completely dark room.

"I'm late for curfew. I didn't want to wake you, but—"

"What time is it?"

"A little after ten."

Cody sat up, rubbing his eyes. He had no idea what time it had been when he'd first lain down. Everything about the day felt distorted and surreal.

"I'll pick you up tomorrow morning, okay?"

Cody blinked, confused. It was too dark in the room to see Nate's expression. "For what?"

"For school."

"No." Cody shook his head, trying to clear it. "You don't want the others to know. If they see us together, they'll make assumptions."

"To hell with them." Nate took Cody's hand and squeezed his fingers. "There's nothing wrong with us being friends."

Cody wanted to argue. He wanted to tell Nate he had no idea what kind of trouble he was flirting with, but he couldn't do it. Nate's hand felt so warm and solid and perfect holding his. There was comfort in his voice and in his presence, and Cody found himself relenting. "I can meet you at the gas station."

He couldn't see Nate's smile, but he heard the soft exhale of breath that was almost a laugh. "Jesus, don't start that shit again. I said I'd pick you up, and I will."

"Okay."

Cody stayed on the couch, tracking Nate's movements around the room more by sound than by sight. When Nate finally had his coat on and keys in hand, he stopped in the doorway. "You'll be here tomorrow, right? You're not planning on leaving before I get here or some dumb thing?"

Cody smiled, despite how lousy the day had been. "I'll be here."

"Good."

The door creaked open, and Cody spoke quickly to catch him in time. "Nate?"

"Yeah?"

"Thanks, man. For . . . well, you know. For dinner and everything."

"You're welcome."

Cody was apprehensive the next morning when he climbed into Nate's car, not because of Nate, but because he wasn't sure he'd be able to get through a day at school without bursting into tears like a damn kid. Nate distracted him during the drive by asking seemingly random questions. Where was Cody after first hour? When was he in the senior hallway? Where did he go every day at lunchtime? It wasn't until the first passing period that he realized Nate had been figuring out his class schedule, making sure he could check in at least a few times throughout the day.

It seemed like a lot of trouble for him to go to, but Cody didn't mind the extra company.

The "grief frenzy"—dubbed so by Nate, his voice thick with disdain—seemed to be in full swing for the second day in a row, everybody trying to one-up each other in their sadness. Other than talking to Nate, Cody kept his head down and did his best not to hear what was being said. There were sign-up sheets to talk to grief counselors. Nate stopped Cody in front of one and nodded toward it without saying anything, his raised eyebrows turning it into a question.

On some level, Cody knew it made sense, but he couldn't make himself put his name on that sheet. He didn't need some stranger asking him how he'd known Logan, or how close they'd been. He just shook his head, and Nate shrugged and moved on.

Cody had shared two classes with Logan, the first one being PE. Although Logan had always been friendly toward him, they were definitely in very different worlds when it came to sports, and so Cody was used to only saying hello in the locker room and not much else. But social studies was different. That was the place he'd counted on Logan the most, and walking into that classroom took more strength than he expected. It helped that Nate was right behind him, but he still froze two steps into the room, causing Nate to bump into him.

"Go ahead," Nate said quietly, almost in Cody's ear.

Cody eased into his seat, steeling himself for the grief, feeling almost as if his desk were a trap that might spring on him at any moment. He held very still, trying not to think about how much he still hurt. Nate took the open desk next to him—the desk that should have been Logan's. It was strange, having him there. Wrong somehow, because Cody desperately wanted to see Logan's long legs blocking the aisle as he leaned over to chat, and yet having Nate there was still so much better than having the seat be empty.

After class, Nate followed him out of the classroom, practically knocking over a freshman to stay on Cody's heels.

"I'm okay," Cody said. "I can go to my locker without falling apart, I promise."

Nate smiled. "I know, but then you'll try to sneak past me and walk home rather than letting me give you a ride."

Cody grudgingly admitted to himself that he might have done exactly that. In the end, Nate drove him home, then spent half an hour fiddling with the foil-wrapped rabbit ears just so they could watch TV. It was like having a babysitter, but Cody appreciated the company.

By Wednesday, the grief frenzy was beginning to abate. Still, it was with a heavy weight in his stomach that Cody asked Nate to drop him off at work after school, rather than take him home.

The back area of the Tomahawk was the same as always—warm and steamy, the air heavy with the smell of soap and the clatter of noise from the kitchen. Cody made it through half of his shift before he started crying. Standing there up to his elbows in dishwater, he could almost hear Logan's voice. He could imagine him working right behind him, stretching to put the bowls on the shelves Cody couldn't reach.

"You okay, sugar?"

Cody jumped, trying to wipe his eyes with hands that were wet and prune-y. It was one of the waitresses. She was in her early thirties and always worked the dinner shift. Cody didn't know her name, had barely exchanged more than a few hellos with her, but she pulled him into a hug, holding him in a way nobody but Nate had done in a long time. It was surprising and awkward, but it felt genuine.

"It's a shame," she said, still hugging him. "We'll all miss him."

She patted him on the back and left him with the dishes, somehow feeling a bit less alone than he had before.

By Thursday, the school seemed almost back to normal, and there was no school at all on Friday, because that was the day of the funeral.

Cody wasn't sure if he wanted to go, but Nate insisted. It was held at the biggest church in town, which still turned out to be too small. Cody sat next to Nate in the back pew as the room filled around them. The two caskets at the front of the room were closed. Cody was almost relieved he wasn't expected to walk up there and see Logan's face again. He wasn't sure he could have handled that.

He started out listening, but it didn't take him long to realize the funeral had nothing to do with Logan and Shelley. There was a lot of talk about God, and the Kingdom of Heaven, and Cody grew more and more agitated as the speakers droned on. They weren't talking about Logan at all. Nobody mentioned how friendly he was, or how he stood out at Walter Warren High School simply because he refused to conform to social expectations. Nothing about the funeral captured Logan's spirit, or his laughter, or his larger-than-life presence.

Cody glanced around, wondering if Shelley's friends felt as unsatisfied as he did, but found no answers.

Still, he was glad Nate had made him come.

"Do you want to go to the graveside part now?" Nate asked as they made their way back to Nate's new-to-him Toyota truck.

It was sunny out, but the wind was worse than normal, howling across the plain, bending Warren's few trees, ripping at their jackets as they walked.

"No. It'll just be more prayers." And although he felt the cumbersome weight of unshed tears in his chest and his throat and behind his eyes, he knew standing there watching them lower Logan and Shelley into the ground would only make it worse. "Besides, I told them I'd be at work early." They'd already told him they didn't intend to replace Logan at the Tomahawk. Business had been waning since fall. They'd recently let two waitresses and one of the cooks go, and more and more of the work was being done by the Robertson family. Cody'd be able to pick up a few extra hours, but not nearly as many as he would have liked.

It wasn't until he was climbing into the cab of Nate's truck that it hit him—he'd seen everybody in the school grieve in one way or another.

Everybody, that was, except for Nate.

He debated his words as Nate started the engine, but he didn't manage to speak until they were pulling out of the parking lot.

"You're the only one who isn't sad."

Nate frowned. "I wouldn't say that."

His tone was guarded, and Cody waited, feeling like there had to be more coming. Several seconds passed in silence, and Cody finally prodded Nate by saying, "And? Is that it?"

"I feel guilty," Nate confessed at last.

Cody hadn't expected that. "Why?"

Nate hesitated, braking at a stop sign and spending a long time checking to make sure the coast was clear before moving again. Cody was pretty sure he was just biding his time, trying to decide what exactly to say. Finally, he sighed. "I think I almost hated him."

Cody couldn't even comprehend such a sentiment. "You hated Logan? Why? I thought everybody liked him." Just the thought of somebody disliking Logan made him angry. "What'd he ever do to you?"

"Nothing. He didn't do anything. It's just . . ." A slow stain of red was beginning to creep up Nate's neck. "I was jealous, that's all."

"Why? Because he was popular?"

"No." Nate's voice was tight but level. "Because of you."

Cody blinked, stunned. "What? Why?"

"You guys— It just seemed like you were so close, you know?" His cheeks were now bright red. "It feels petty now that he's dead. I almost feel like I made it happen by wishing he'd disappear." He glanced hesitantly Cody's way before turning back to the road. He must have seen the incomprehension on Cody's face, because he rushed on, trying to explain. "I was jealous because he had the part of you that I wanted most."

Cody sat back, even more confused than before. He couldn't even begin to wrap his head around that last statement.

They were silent for the rest of the drive. Nate pulled into the Tomahawk's lot and parked. He left the engine on, but sat staring at the keys hanging from the ignition. Cody could tell he was working up his courage for something, but after admitting his inexplicable envy of Logan, Cody couldn't begin to imagine what could be coming next.

"Did you . . ." Nate took a deep breath, as if forcing himself to go on. "Did you love him?"

Cody shook his head, feeling as if he were a mile behind in their conversation. "What?"

"Did you love him?" The question seemed to come easier the second time.

Cody wasn't sure exactly what Nate meant. There were lots of kinds of love, and it seemed ridiculous that Nate would be asking.

"We were friends." It was the only thing he could think to say.

"Yeah, but you were more too, right?"

Cody blinked at him again. "What?" It felt like he'd asked that a hundred times in the short drive over.

"I saw you with him at the dance."

"At the dance," Cody admitted. "But not, like, *with him* at the dance."

"I saw him kiss you."

Cody's head bumped the passenger window as he reeled backward. "*What?*"

"I saw him—"

"Are we even talking about the same guy?" He held his hand up, over his head. "Like, six foot two. Quarterback of the fucking football team? The guy who had half the girls in school trailing behind him, no matter where he went?"

"Yeah, I know, but—"

"What, you think I was doing some kind of favors for him? Like the only way he'd be friends with me is if I was blowing him on the side?"

"No! Jesus, I never said that!" Nate's cheeks were redder than ever. "But I know what I saw."

Cody shook his head again. "I'm pretty damn sure Logan never kissed me. I mean, Christ, I think I'd remember if he had!"

Nate wrapped his hands around the steering wheel as if grounding himself. Another gust of wind hit them, rocking the truck a bit. Sunlight flashed off the light-blue stone in the senior ring Nate still wore, even though it was for the wrong school. "You were in the hallway, right before you left. He had his arm over your shoulder, and Jimmy and Larry were walking by, and he pulled you close and he . . . he kissed your hair."

Cody remembered the moment. He remembered the way Logan's face had bumped into his head. He hadn't even realized it had been intentional. And now here was Nate, freaking out over *that*?

"On the head?" Cody asked, pointing to the very spot where Logan's lips must have touched, fighting hard not to laugh, because laughter seemed so wrong. "You thought something was going on because he kissed me *on the head*?"

Nate sighed. "I guess."

Laughter rose up in Cody's chest before he could stop it, and the next thing he knew, he was doubled over in the passenger seat, laughing in a way that felt close to hysteria. His chest ached. Tears streamed from his eyes. Some part of his brain told him to get his shit together, that he was acting like a nut job, but it felt too good to let go. To just let the sheer idiocy of the entire incident take over.

"Oh God," he finally gasped, clutching his stomach. "I wish he was alive to hear that. He'd have gotten a real kick out of it."

Saying it out loud made it real—he could see the expression on Logan's face and hear the exact tenor of his laugh—and then Cody wasn't sure if he was laughing or crying. It felt like some strange mixture of both. After all the time Logan had spent telling Cody that Nate missed him, and their jokes about whether or not Cody would put out after homecoming, and then to have Nate misinterpret something so simple as a friendly kiss, if it had even been that—Cody still wasn't convinced it had been anything more than a clumsy head bump—was more than he could stand. When he finally got control of himself again, he realized Nate was sitting stone-still in the driver's seat, his cheeks still red, his jaw tight, obviously hurt by Cody's laughter.

Cody wiped his eyes as his laughter subsided, watching the way the sunlight shone through Nate's carefully moussed blond hair. He didn't know how he could feel so many things at once. Logan's death still hurt more than he could bear, and he dreaded another shift without him at the Tomahawk, but his laughter had made him realize that it wouldn't be that way forever. The conversation with Nate, as ridiculous as it may have been, made him see that remembering could bring joy as well as grief.

And Nate had given him that, whether he'd meant to or not.

Cody leaned across the seat and grabbed him, pulling Nate by the front of his jacket until they were face-to-face. He felt like he'd said "thank you" so many times since Monday, but it wasn't enough this time. He wanted to hug Nate, except there was no space to do it properly. He wanted to kiss him, but he was afraid of making that mistake again. He found himself staring into Nate's eyes, trying to gauge the length and breadth of what he saw there.

They stayed like that for a moment, Cody debating what to do, Nate just watching him, until Cody finally realized he needed to speak. He needed to say something to let Nate know that he'd done everything right.

"I missed you like crazy," Cody finally said. "I'm really glad to have you back."

And the smile Nate gave him was like warm August sunshine on the icy mass of his grief.

CHAPTER
Seventeen

ody gave up trying to explain to Nate why they shouldn't let their friendship be seen at school. Nothing he said changed Nate's mind, and Cody was happy enough to have the desk next to him in social studies not go empty.

Every morning, Nate picked Cody up on his way to school, then drove him home or to work at the end of the day. Sometimes he even picked Cody up after work and drove him home. And any hour that wasn't taken by school, the Tomahawk, or sleeping, they spent together. Sometimes they watched TV or played with the deck of cards Cody had retrieved from the wagon. Sometimes, if the weather was nice, they drove around in Nate's car, exploring the back roads that surrounded Warren. Weeknights were often spent doing nothing more than sitting at Cody's kitchen table working on homework together. And if Cody felt Nate's gaze on him more often than seemed normal, if he noticed the way Nate sat a bit too close on the couch or found any excuse at all to touch him, Cody chose to chalk it up to friendly concern.

Some nights, Cody found himself drifting in that warm, surreal place between sleep and reality. Sometimes, in those hazy moments, he imagined kissing Nate again. Sometimes he replayed a moment from the day when Nate had found a reason to reach across the table and take his hand. But when consciousness came, he steadfastly refused to acknowledge those thoughts. The memory of more than a month of the silent treatment was enough to keep him grounded in reality. He'd risked everything once, only to have Nate turn his back. He couldn't bear for that to happen again.

Besides, he had bigger things to worry about. Namely, his mother. Or, to be more accurate, the complete absence of his mother.

She'd switched to the evening shift a few weeks before homecoming. It meant she didn't get up until Cody was already at work, or at school. She left before he got home, and didn't come home herself until he was asleep. It meant they rarely saw each other. It was something that had happened before, and Cody was used to taking care of himself.

But at some point, he'd begun to realize that she wasn't coming home at all. The pile of unopened mail on the countertop grew taller. Some of them were coming with "past due" stamped in red across the envelopes.

The Tuesday before Christmas break, Cody woke to the sound of a train barreling down the tracks less than twenty yards from his trailer. He glanced out of habit at the digital clock radio next to his bed. The display was blank, and Cody frowned, sitting up to rub his eyes. What the hell time was it? The house was still dark, as was the sky outside. That meant it was before seven, but he had no way of knowing how long he had before Nate arrived.

He wandered into the kitchen. Nothing happened when he hit the light switch. He squinted at the old-fashioned battery-powered clock hanging on the wall, and finally determined it was six thirty. He had plenty of time, but having the power out was going to make for a damned cold shower. It happened on a regular basis in the spring and fall when lightning storms were common, but it generally only happened in the winter if they had a blizzard. The ground was still blanketed with snow from the last storm, but the roads were dry, so it hadn't snowed during the night.

He caught sight of Vera through the window and rushed onto the front porch to catch her before she climbed into her car, undoubtedly headed for the gas station.

"Hey, Vera?"

She turned toward him, although her expression was lost in the dim light. "Yeah?"

"Is the power out at your place?"

"Nope. Working just fine."

Cody's heart sank. Vera had power, but Cody didn't. There was only one explanation.

He took the pile of mail, sat down at the kitchen table, and started opening envelopes. He was still sorting through it when Nate arrived, and he had to hurry to get dressed while Nate waited, his brow furrowed with curiosity.

"Do you think you can take me uptown after school?" Cody asked, once they were in the car.

"I still can't figure out why it isn't 'downtown.' I mean, it's downhill from most everything else."

"From Orange Grove, maybe."

Nate shook his head, looking amused. "Whatever. I can take you. Why? What's up?"

Cody hesitated, unsure how much he wanted to say. It was true Nate knew most of the sordid truth about his home life now, but this felt extreme. He chose to change the subject rather than answer. "Are you going home for Christmas?" It was something he'd been wondering, but hadn't asked. He'd been afraid of the answer.

"No."

"Oh." That surprised him, and Nate must have heard it in his voice, because he sighed.

"Remember how I told you that my parents split up because my dad had an affair?"

"Yeah."

"Well, I was wrong. Turns out it was my mom. And her new boyfriend is already living there with her, in the house I grew up in, and he doesn't want me around."

Cody knew exactly how it felt to have a parent not want you around. His own father hadn't even bothered sending a birthday card in years. "That sucks."

Nate's shrug was a bit too forced to be casual. "I don't mind, to tell you the truth. I'd rather be here with you anyway."

It took three stops after school to pay the rent and the more urgent of the bills. The electric company promised to have the power back on in a day or two. In the meantime, Cody had to hope it didn't get too cold. He almost wanted to cry as he handed over his money. He'd only been a few dollars away from a brand-new pair of snow boots. Now, he'd face the winter in his Converse. Still, he didn't resent the loss of footwear so much as the simple loss of his money.

Somehow, having that bundle of cash tucked into his drawer had given him hope. Each dollar he added felt like a promise. Now, he was back to less than ten dollars in his pocket until payday rolled around again. At least with Christmas break starting soon, he'd be able to pick up a few extra shifts.

The days rolled by with no sign of his mother, and he began to worry. She'd been gone before for a few days here and there, but never this long. They didn't have long-distance service, so one afternoon, Cody walked to the gas station and pumped two dollars in quarters into the pay phone in order to call the truck stop, but they said only, "She isn't here right now," before hanging up.

On one hand, that made it sound like there was no reason to panic. On the other hand, she still hadn't come home. He felt like he should call somebody, but he couldn't think who. His mom's parents were both deceased. Her sister, Shirley, lived in Cheyenne, but Cody hadn't seen her since he was ten years old. It would have cost him another two dollars to call her. It seemed like a waste when he was ninety-nine percent sure his mom wouldn't be there. Any other family Cody might once have had were on his father's side. He hadn't talked to any of them in years and was pretty sure his mom hadn't either. He debated calling the police, but what good would it do? It'd just be one more mark against his family in their book. And besides, it might be Nate's dad who showed up to take the report, and that scared him for some reason he couldn't quite explain.

School ended, and Cody signed up for every shift at the Tomahawk he could find that needed to be covered. He saw the way Nate frowned when he told him. He knew Nate had been counting on him for company over the break, but Nate didn't have to worry about things like waking up to find the power had been turned off. Nate at least had one parent who paid the bills and made sure he was home by curfew and took the time to put food in the pantry.

As for where Cody's mom was, there seemed to be two options. Either something had happened to her and she wasn't able to get home, or she'd simply decided to leave.

He wasn't sure which possibility bothered him more.

She'd be home for Christmas. He hung on to that thought like a talisman. Certainly she wouldn't leave him alone for Christmas morning.

The Tomahawk was closed on Christmas Eve, and Nate's dad had to work, so Cody and Nate spent the entire day in Nate's family room, watching Christmas specials on cable TV. Nate and his dad had a giant tree covered with lights and brand-new, store-bought ornaments. Cody counted at least two-dozen presents under the tree. Nate popped popcorn and did his best to be cheery, but between Logan's death and his mom's absence, Cody couldn't manage to match his mood.

They left Nate's house shortly before his dad was due home. Nate kept glancing Cody's way in the gloom of the little pickup truck's cab. Cody found himself thinking of the Robertson family, wondering how they'd celebrate this year with both of their children gone. Wondering if they'd still take that trip to Mexico. He knew reveling in his melancholy did no good, but he couldn't seem to stop.

"Maybe I should come in," Nate said as he parked in front of Cody's trailer.

"Your dad'll be waiting. You should be with him."

Nate glanced at the dark windows of Cody's home. He reached over and took Cody's hand, his warm fingers wrapping around Cody's. "You shouldn't be alone on Christmas Eve."

"It's okay. I'm used to it." And at least he'd had most of the day with Nate.

"I'll come over as soon as I can tomorrow morning."

"You don't have to do that. Your dad will want—"

"He works at noon anyway."

Cody sighed, relenting. Having Nate there would certainly make the day more bearable. "Okay."

He moved to open the door, but Nate didn't let go of his hand. "Cody?"

"Yeah?"

Nate took a breath, but didn't speak. Cody waited, trying to read Nate's expression in the dark. He wondered if Nate would ask about his mother. If he'd tell Cody how sorry he was that Cody didn't have a better life. Sometimes Cody wanted that confirmation, sometimes he didn't. Sometimes, it felt too much like pity, and pity made him uncomfortable.

"Merry Christmas," Nate said at last.

Cody only nodded, but Nate finally let go of his hand and let him go inside.

Cody fell asleep that night dreaming of Christmas. He dreamed of magical mornings where he emerged from his room to find a tree in the living room, bright and gaudy with decorations, and a modest pile of presents underneath. He dreamed of a single stocking, hung with a tapestry pin from the back of the couch. He was younger in his dream, although his exact age seemed to ebb and flow, but however old he was, he still had the bright, unabashed hope of youth.

The belief that Santa could perform miracles.

He didn't want to open his eyes when he awoke the next morning.

The house was silent. He sat on the edge of his bed for several long minutes, steeling himself for what he knew he'd find. It took only a glance out the window to see that his mom's rusty Duster hadn't appeared. There was no tree in the living room, no stocking stuffed with candy, no presents to unwrap at all. There was no Santa, and no magic, and no reason to even get out of bed.

Not until later, at least, when Nate would show up.

He spent the morning looking through the bills again. It had become his primary pastime when Nate wasn't around to see. He'd taken care of the most urgent ones, but more were due each day, and the late fees on a few were as much as the original bill. He counted the hours he'd worked since his last payday and tried to figure out exactly how much would be deducted before he even saw the check.

He wouldn't have enough to cover them all. That much was clear. He'd have to prioritize, pay what he could, knowing the others would have past-due notices by January. Was this why his mother had left? Because she'd finally gotten tired of staring at that pile of paper on the counter, knowing she'd never be able to make ends meet?

He showered and dressed, not wanting to be in sweats when Nate showed up, then made himself breakfast. He'd used the last of his money two days earlier to buy bread, peanut butter, a box of off-brand cereal, and a half gallon of milk. He hadn't wanted Nate to know, so he'd gone to the gas station after Nate was gone. He knew it was stupid—the food there cost more than it did at the grocery store—but the grocery store was two miles away, and the gas station offered a certain amount of comfort. Vera hadn't said anything when he put the food on the counter, but when he'd come up seventy-two cents short, she'd frowned. Cody had eyed the groceries, trying to decide which thing to put back, but she'd taken his money and started putting the food in a bag before he could choose.

"But, I don't have enough—"

"I'm sure I got that much in my purse, and if don't, then it won't matter none if the drawer's a few cents short. Sometimes my countin' ain't so good anyway. What'll they do? Fire me?"

He swallowed, torn between embarrassment and gratitude. "I don't want you to get in trouble."

"I think you got enough troubles of your own, kid. Don't worry none about mine."

He hadn't argued, and he said a silent thank-you to her again as he ate a bowl of cereal on Christmas morning. He stashed the bills out of sight, turned on the TV, spent a good fifteen minutes adjusting the antenna to get the picture as clear as it could be without cable, and waited for Nate to arrive.

He came shortly after noon, as promised. He was smiling ear to ear, his cheeks red from the cold, a big basket wrapped in plastic tucked under his arm.

"It's snowing!" he said as Cody let him in. "Everything's white and clean, and it sparkles in the sunlight. It's amazing. It's just like Christmas in a movie."

Cody forced a smile, thinking how his dank, dusty living room was about as unpicturesque as could be. "Not like Texas, huh?"

"Not even close. Here." Nate shoved a giant gift basket into Cody's hands. "Hang on. There's more."

He disappeared back outside, and Cody stood, staring at the gift. It was crammed full of oranges and grapefruit, half a dozen tiny bricks of cheese, and a summer sausage, with little bags of candy and nuts stuffed in between. He set the gift on the kitchen counter, his hands shaking. He heard Nate come back inside, but he didn't turn to face him.

"I can't take this."

"Sure you can. It's from the station. All the cops got one. My dad said I could have it."

That made him feel better. It would certainly be nice to have something other than peanut butter to eat, and at least Nate hadn't spent any money on it. "Oh. Okay."

But then he turned to find Nate holding four more boxes, each one wrapped in bright-colored paper with smiling Santas and dancing reindeer. Nate shoved the stack into Cody's hands and turned to shed his coat.

Cody's heart sank. He felt like an idiot. He hadn't even considered the possibility that Nate might buy him a gift, and now here he was with a stack of them, and Cody had nothing at all to give in return. He put the boxes on the counter, next to the shrink-wrapped food that rightfully belonged to Nate's dad.

"Nate." He hated the way his voice shook. He hated the way his throat burned. He almost hated Nate for putting him in such a stupid position. "You shouldn't have bought me anything."

"Why not? It's Christmas."

"I know, but..." Cody eyed the presents again. Some childish part of him wanted to tear them open and see what was inside. If only he'd thought to buy Nate a gift. Of course, that would have meant losing electricity or telephone service. "I didn't have enough money—"

"I know." The way he said it reminded Cody of Logan—no pity or disgust in his voice—just matter-of-fact acceptance. "It's okay. I wasn't expecting you to buy me anything."

"I feel terrible."

"You shouldn't."

"But Nate—"

Nate stepped closer, backing Cody up against the counter. "I'll make you a deal." He took the top box off the stack and laid it in Cody's hands. It was small and easily identifiable based on its size and shape—a cassette tape. "Just open this one. I'll take all the others back if you want. But this one, I really want you to have." His voice sounded as shaky as Cody's had, and Cody glanced up to find Nate watching him, his eyes unreadable, his cheeks slowly turning red. He moved a bit closer. "Go ahead. Open it."

Cody nodded, his resolve weakening. "Okay." It was only a cassette, after all. It wouldn't have cost much. What kind of tape would Nate have picked for him anyway? He was pretty sure they had zero in common when it came to music. He wondered if he could sufficiently fake gratitude if it was Pet Shop Boys or some weird European band he'd never heard of.

He unwrapped it slowly, wanting to make this one stupid gift last all day.

It wasn't an album. That much was clear immediately. It was a tape Nate had obviously made himself. The spine was decorated only with Cody's name, and a little red heart. The song list was printed down the front part of the insert in Nate's small, perfect penmanship. Madonna, Cyndi Lauper, Mr. Mister, Pat Benatar, plus a bunch of bands Cody had never heard of—Crowded House, Yazoo, Modern English. But the song titles jumped out at him, somehow saying everything: "Something About You," "Against All Odds," "We Belong," "Crazy for You," "Time After Time."

Cody's heart seemed to patter out several extra beats in a single breath. His hands started to shake again. Jesus, did this mean what he thought it meant? He didn't know most of the songs on the list. Maybe it wasn't what he thought.

Or maybe it was.

"Say something," Nate said, his voice almost a whisper.

"You made me a tape."

"I did."

"I, uh . . ." Cody stumbled, afraid if he said much more, he'd start crying after all. "I didn't get you anything."

Nate moved closer, the distance between them matched exactly by the tape in Cody's hands, as if it were the only thing keeping them apart. He touched Cody's arm, his hand warm and gentle and wonderfully familiar. "You should know by now there's only one thing in the world I want anyway."

Cody finally looking up at Nate, wanting to know if this was really what it felt like.

And before Cody could say a word, Nate kissed him.

It was awkward at first, their lips not quite lining up, Cody's arms pinned between them. Only for a second, though. Only long enough for Cody to catch his breath, and then he dropped the wrapping paper and wiggled his arms around Nate's neck, the cassette still tight in his hand. He relaxed into Nate's embrace, parting his lips to let Nate kiss him deeper, and the next thing he knew, Nate was pushing him back against the counter, leaning against him, kissing him harder, his hands seeming to be everywhere—under Cody's shirt, in his hair, his fingers warm and soft on the back of Cody's neck—and Cody found himself suddenly balking, shocked at the sudden onslaught and the urgency in Nate's touch.

"Wait," he said, trying to pull away even though he had nowhere to go. Nate had him trapped, and Cody wasn't all that sure he wanted to escape anyway. "Nate, hang on."

Nate didn't stop kissing him. He just moved away from Cody's lips to kiss his neck instead, pulling Cody tight against him. "What?" he asked, his breath warming Cody's ear, making him shiver. "What's wrong?"

"I, um . . ." Jesus, would he ever have a moment with Nate where he didn't feel like he was about to cry? Cody's throat was tight, his eyes welling up. Nate's caresses were becoming difficult to resist, the hard bulge in Nate's pants making everything seem far too real. "I don't want it to be like last time." And damn it, now his tears were coming faster, and he didn't even have a graceful way to wipe his cheeks with Nate holding him so tight. "I can't have you walk out of here and ignore me again. I can't do that again. I can't— God, I can't—"

"That's never going to happen." Nate cupped Cody's cheek in his hand, wiping at Cody's tears with his thumb. "I told you before: I won't abandon you like that again."

"You will, though. We'll graduate, and you'll move away. You'll go live in that apartment in Chicago and have a brand-new life, and I'll still be here, only I'll be more alone than ever."

But Nate was already shaking his head. "I'm not going anywhere without you."

"No." Cody blinked, his tears forgotten as he tried to interpret exactly what that meant. "You don't want to stay in Warren. Nobody wants to stay in Warren."

"Then I guess you'll just have to leave with me."

"Wh-what?"

"There's no reason you have to stay here either. You can come with me. We can share the apartment there. We can live there together."

Cody gulped, trying to imagine it how it would feel to wake up next to Nate every day in a brand-new place so far from Wyoming that even the wind couldn't find them.

God, it couldn't be that simple, could it?

"Do you mean it?"

"Of course I mean it."

"But it's Chicago!"

"So what?"

"I can't live in Chicago! The biggest city I've ever been to was Casper, and I was ten! Chicago's *huge*. Chicago's—"

"Then *not* Chicago," Nate said, laughing. "We'll find someplace else. I don't really care where we go. I just want to be able to kiss you without worrying about who sees."

"Oh God," Cody whispered, suddenly not sure his knees were even working. It was possible Nate was the only thing keeping him on his feet. "You can't want that. Jesus, why would you want that? It doesn't make any sense! Why would you want this? Why would you want *me*?"

"Because I think love you."

"No."

"I mean, I *know* I love you."

"Stop."

"But I think—"

"No!"

"I think I'm *in* love with you."

"*No!*" Cody covered his ears, despite still holding the cassette, trying to block the sound of that word. Nobody said that word. Not here. The inside of his crumbling trailer had never heard it uttered.

Love.

He had the irrational urge to run, to put as much distance between them as he could, but Nate was still holding him. Still smiling at him. Still standing here after saying he loved him, and Cody had no idea what to do or what to say. He took a deep breath, trying to steady his pounding heart, trying to find his focus. His eyes fell on the cassette tape, still clutched tight in his hand.

"I don't have a tape player."

It was such a stupid thing to say, after Nate had laid his heart on the line, but Nate just laughed. "I got you one of those too. Come on." He stepped away, turning to grab the last three presents on the table. "You may as well open them."

He sat down at the kitchen table, and Cody followed, his feet heavy, feeling like he was still in one of last night's dreams. He sank slowly into a chair. "It isn't fair for you to buy me all this stuff."

"For crying out loud," Nate groaned in exasperation. "Look, Cody. I know things are different for me than they are for you. I live in the Grove. You live here. I get a weekly allowance, and money from my grandparents for Christmas, and money from my mom just because she feels guilty about running off with some new guy, and I know you don't get any of that, and it sucks. It isn't fair at all."

Cody thought he'd realized the full extent of his envy, but hearing Nate lay it all out like that made his anger feel somewhat justified. And yet, he also knew it wasn't Nate's fault.

"The thing is," Nate went on, his voice quieter now, "none of that matters to me. You can't afford to spend money on stupid shit. I know that. But I can." He pushed the stack of presents a bit closer to Cody. "And I wanted you to have presents on Christmas."

Cody turned the tape over in his hands. A tape Nate had made, just because the songs made him think of Cody.

Maybe it was selfish. Maybe it made things between them even more lopsided than before, but he wanted to listen to it.

He eyed the presents again, his resistance crumbling. It was Christmas, after all, and Nate had gone to the trouble of wrapping them and everything. Would it really be so bad to accept a couple of presents?

"Jesus," Nate chuckled, shaking his head. "And I finally get a smile out of you." He picked up the top box and held it out to Cody. "Open the damn thing, already."

Cody laughed and set the tape aside in order to take the second present.

The tape player wasn't much of a surprise, since Nate had already told him about it, but that didn't mean he was any less happy to receive it. It was smaller than a boom box, but with a handle and a built-in radio. Not that there were many stations to pick up in Warren, but still.

"I debated a Walkman instead, but this seemed more versatile."

"It's fantastic."

The next gift was a pair of headphones, and the last box held a pair of ski gloves.

"I've never been skiing in my life," Cody said.

Nate laughed. "It's not like they *only* keep your hands warm on the slopes, you know."

Cody pulled one on, thinking how much better his walks to and from the Tomahawk would be now.

"I wanted to get you that leather jacket we talked about, but they were a bit out of my price range."

"It's okay. I like the coat I have anyway." He set the gloves aside and put his hand on Nate's knee, narrowing the distance between them. "Thank you."

"You're welcome."

Cody hesitated, feeling like he should say more. So much had happened in such a short amount of time, and he still wasn't entirely sure what to believe. He was afraid to put too much faith in Nate, but he was pretty damn tired of being alone.

And God, at that moment, he loved Nate with a fierceness that took his breath away. He'd tried for so long to tell himself his feelings were a mistake, but now . . .

"We'll have to be careful. Maybe it's okay in other places, but not here. Not in Warren—"

"I know. But it's only for five months. Once we graduate, we don't have to spend another minute in this damn town."

Cody chewed his lip, considering. "But what if—"

"Stop." Nate leaned forward in his seat, bringing them closer together. Only a few inches kept his lips from Cody's. He ran his hand up Cody's arm and over his shoulder to brush his fingers along the curve of his neck. "I feel like this is the only thing I've thought about for months. You're going to ask me if I'm sure, and I'm telling you once and for all: I am. If you don't feel the same way—"

Cody put his fingers over Nate's lips, stopping the words. It was hard to speak, but he made himself say, "I do." Saying it out loud made his chest ache. It made him feel like he'd been given a magical Christmas after all. He found himself grinning, suddenly almost giddy. "I do."

Nate's answering smile was the most amazing thing Cody had ever seen. "That's the only thing that matters to me."

He pulled Cody forward and kissed him. It felt more natural than before, like Cody had been made for this one simple moment. Forget his mom and Warren and the Grove and everything about the world that seemed to keep him from being happy. Warren had done its worst, and it hadn't been enough to keep Nate away.

It hadn't beaten them.

The kiss started out sweet, but quickly grew in urgency. He wanted to undress Nate. To touch every bit of him. To feel Nate touch him back. Before long, there was no more room for thought. There was only the simple joy of pushing Nate down the hall, into the bedroom, onto Cody's bed. Climbing on top of him, not daring to look into his eyes, because he wasn't ready yet for what he might see there.

It was easier to let their bodies take over. To let clothes disappear. To burrow under the covers together, making their own heat as the snow fell outside. There was nothing but them pushing closer, sharing breath and space, letting their frantic moans be their only form of communication as their passion grew. They were naked, skin to skin, but Cody was suddenly afraid to ask for more. It was left to Nate to finally take Cody's hand. To guide it between them. He moaned deep in his throat when Cody's fingers finally closed around him, and then it was Cody's turn to moan as Nate returned the favor, and they found a new level of bliss.

Nate used his free hand to grab a handful of Cody's hair, pulling his head back so he could look into Cody's eyes as they caressed each other. It may not have been the first time Cody'd had another boy in his bed, but it was the first time it'd felt this intimate. What he'd shared with Dusty had never been so intense, or so terrifying. Nate had stripped him bare in more ways than one, torn him open in some new, exquisite way. The pleasure was overwhelming, the knowledge that Nate was as lost as he was somehow humbling, and Cody tried to hold back. Tried to hold on.

As if there were any chance of succeeding.

Even after it was over, Nate didn't pull away. He rolled them so he was on top, but he never stopped touching Cody, or kissing him, despite the mess between them. His voice was hushed, his tone reverent and sweet.

"You have no idea how many times I've thought about this. Or how long I've wanted it to happen, but I never knew what to say. I never knew how to make things right between us again. And then Logan— God, Cody, I'm sorry. I'm so sorry. I'm sorry about Logan, and I'm sorry I was such an ass."

Cody shook his head. Maybe it was wrong, but he didn't want to think about Logan right now. "It's okay."

"It isn't, though. I was so afraid, but I'm not now, I promise. I don't care what else happens, as long as you're with me. If Chicago's too big, we'll pick someplace else. I don't care. Wherever you want to go—"

Cody held Nate close, shivering for no reason he could explain. "Don't, Nate. Don't make promises you might not want to keep."

Nate chuckled in Cody's ear. "To hell with that. I'll make whatever promises I want. I love you. God, I love you so much. It feels good to finally say it."

The truth of those words seemed to sink into Cody's heart, warming him from the inside out. He couldn't quite say them back— not because he didn't feel the same way, but because it scared him too much. Instead, he said, "I think I understand your mom's saying."

Nate pulled back to look down into his eyes. "What?"

"It makes sense now. I know exactly what it means." He couldn't seem to stop smiling. "'When it's dark enough, you can see the stars.' And I think I do."

Nate shook his head and kissed Cody again. "I only see you."

Those four words were the best Christmas gift anybody had ever given him.

CHAPTER

Eighteen

*C*ody worked on December thirtieth, but Nate picked him up at the end of his shift.

"I promised my dad I wouldn't go out tomorrow night," Nate told him. "But he'll be working all night, so you could come to my house, if you want."

They were a lot more careful about fooling around at Nate's than they were at Cody's, because there was no telling when his dad might come walking in. But Nate had cable, and a huge TV to watch it on, and a pantry full of snacks. The limit on sexual activities aside, Nate's house was a much better place to pass the time.

"Sounds good," Cody said.

Nate pulled out of the Tomahawk's parking lot, heading for Cody's house. They'd have a couple of hours together before Nate had to be home for curfew, and the warm cab of the truck seemed thick with possibility as Nate drove. They'd spent a great deal of time since Christmas exploring all the ways they could use their hands and their mouths to make each other feel good, and Cody knew they were both thinking a lot more about the time they'd have alone in Cody's bedroom tonight than about New Year's Eve.

But any excitement Cody felt about the evening died when they drove under the train tracks. There, parked in front of his trailer as if it had never left, was his mom's car.

Nate braked to a stop next to it, glancing Cody's way. He'd never asked about her absence. Cody wasn't sure if Nate realized she'd been gone, or if he simply assumed she was always at work.

"Do you still want me to come in?" Nate asked as he put the truck in park.

Cody's heart was racing, his stomach queasy with nerves. The shifting light against their thin curtains told him his mom was in the living room, watching TV. "Maybe tonight's not so good."

"Okay." Nate reached over and took his hand. They wouldn't kiss here—even inside the truck, chances of being seen by the neighbors was too great—but their hands were low enough to be out of sight. Cody took comfort in the gentle pressure on his fingers. "You can call, if you want. Just not after ten."

Cody nodded, hesitating, wanting to stay hidden in Nate's truck forever. Maybe they could just turn around and leave. Head for the interstate and drive until they passed the state line. At that moment, he didn't care which direction they went. It didn't matter if they ended up in Utah or Colorado or Nebraska, just as long as it wasn't Warren, Wyoming.

Yeah, Cody. You'll get real far with five bucks in your pocket and half a tank of gas in Nate's truck.

He squeezed Nate's hand one last time before stepping out of the truck. He climbed the front steps slowly, trying to decide what he felt. He wasn't sure if he was relieved to have her home, or just really angry that she'd been gone at all.

She didn't turn when he came in. She must have showered as soon as she'd come home, because her hair was still half-wet. She was watching *Simon & Simon*, an open can of beer on the coffee table, a cigarette burning between her fingers.

"You're home," Cody said. Stating the obvious was the only thing he could manage.

She nodded, the motion seeming jerky and abrupt. "Yeah." Her voice was tight, her shoulders tense, but whether she was angry or embarrassed or just didn't want to talk to him, Cody could only guess. She leaned forward to ash her cigarette into the overflowing ashtray. "I was worried, but . . ." She cleared her throat awkwardly. "You did okay?"

Anger won out over relief, his calm snapping all at once. "'Okay'? Yeah, if you mean having the power turned off and having to pay all the bills and running out of money and barely being able to afford some damn peanut butter doing 'okay,' then I guess I did. No thanks to you."

She nodded again, the same abrupt motion as before. "Good." Her voice was still strangely off. She took a final drag of her cigarette before grinding it out in the ashtray. "I didn't mean for you to be left alone like that."

He was tired of staring at the back of her head. He moved to the armchair, watching her carefully as he sat down. Her face was drawn and pale, the bags under her eyes more pronounced than usual. She didn't look at him. She took out another cigarette and lit it. The quiver of the Bic's flame gave away the shaking of her hands.

Cody gripped his knees, trying to keep his voice calm and level. "Where were you?"

"Forget it, all right? I just couldn't get home and—"

"And you couldn't call?"

"I did. A couple of times, actually, but you weren't here." She cleared her throat nervously. "Look, I'm sorry—"

"I don't care if you're sorry. I want to know why you couldn't come home? Were you with a guy or something? Do you have a new boyfriend? You met somebody who was more important? What?"

She shook her head. Cleared her throat again. Scanned the ceiling as if searching for a way out. Finally said, "I, uh . . . I got picked up."

"Picked up?" There were two possible meanings to that phrase, and Cody's stomach clenched. He wasn't sure which one was worse. "You mean you went somewhere with somebody you met? Is that what you mean? Climbed in with some trucker and decided to take off for a month?"

She blew smoke and ashed again, leaning forward to rest her elbows on her knees. Her head jerked an inch to the side, indicating no, but only barely.

"You got arrested?"

Her lips narrowed. She stared at the ashtray. "I don't want you to have to know about these things."

He understood at last. She wasn't angry. Or not at him, at any rate. She was humiliated, and still trying to protect him from a truth he'd worked hard to deny. "Mom," he said, feeling a gentleness now he hadn't expected, "I'm not a kid anymore."

She nodded. "I know." She wiped angrily at her eye, brushing a tear away before it could materialize. "I was glad I could tell them you were eighteen, that you could take care of yourself. They wanted to send child services, but I told them not to. I told them you were a good kid. That you were used to fending for yourself."

He wasn't sure anybody had ever referred to him as a "good kid" before. "What happened?"

She sighed, her shoulders slumping. "The car broke down on my way to work. I managed to pay for the tow and the repairs, but just barely. I didn't have enough gas to get home. We were behind on the bills. And Christmas was coming—" She shook her head again. "I was just trying to earn a little extra cash."

Cody closed his eyes, breathing deep, trying to tame his fierce hatred of Warren, Wyoming, and everything that drove his mom to such extremes. "You should have told me. I would have given you money—"

"You shouldn't have to give me money." She wiped her eye again. "You're my son, and I should be able to at least keep the electricity on. I should be able to—"

"Stop." His hands were shaking, and he clenched them between his knees. There was no point is forcing her to justify it. "So what happened?"

She scrubbed her cigarette out, but didn't reach for a new one. She seemed to be breathing easier now that they were really talking. "I couldn't afford bail, so I had to sit." She chewed her lip. "If it'd been my first offense, he probably would have let me off with time served but—"

"What? What do you mean it wasn't your first offense?"

"I got picked up the first time last year. Remember right before your junior year, when I was gone for a few days?"

"You told me the car broke down and you were staying with a friend."

"I didn't want you to know the truth." She squeezed her temples with one hand. "That time, they gave me time served. More a warning than anything. But this time . . . I told them, I was just trying to pay the bills. He could see I wasn't a junkie, so he took it easy on me." She shrugged, but the motion was too stiff and forced to be casual. "He only gave me four weeks. They released me this morning, and some of the girls at the truck stop pitched in for gas so I could at least drive home."

Cody pinched the bridge of his nose. Rick and A.J. were bickering on TV like they always did. Sometimes they made him laugh, but not tonight. "I wish you hadn't done that, Mom. I just . . . I wish you wouldn't, that's all."

"I know. But it's my job to put food on the table—"

"No—"

"And I'm not afraid to do what needs to be done. I'm not proud of it, but I won't apologize for it, either. Your dad left me here with you and that piece-of-shit Duster, and the only place I can afford to rent is this crappy trailer in the shittiest corner of town. It's bad enough we have to deal with Ted and Kathy and Pete. The least I can do is make sure we don't freeze to death in our own beds."

Cody went back to holding his hands between his knees. The worst of the shock had worn off, leaving him numb and uncharacteristically tired. "I didn't know what to think. I didn't know if you were hurt or if you'd just run off—"

"I wouldn't do that to you."

He felt better, hearing her say it. "I paid the electric and water, and the rent. There's a bill for trash, and one for gas, and the phone bill. They're all overdue. I get paid again in two days, so I'll have a bit of money, but with the late fees, it's not enough—"

"It never is." She picked up her cigarettes, but didn't move to take one out. "The truck stop will take me back, but I lost my shift. The only thing he can give me is graveyards, and only three nights a week."

"Only waiting tables though, right?"

"I promise. I can't risk anything else so soon after getting out, anyway. But I ain't even told you the worst part yet."

Jesus, what could be worse than getting picked up for prostitution? "What?"

"I have to pay a fine. Seven hundred dollars. They're lettin' me do it in payments, but—"

"So they know you were only doing it because we don't have money, and then they expect you to somehow come up with seven hundred dollars? How does that make sense?"

"It don't. But that's how it is."

Cody shook his head, thinking. Graveyards meant shitty hours and shitty tips to boot, and with only three nights a week, it'd barely be more than she paid for the gas to drive there and back. And it wasn't like she could get a job in Warren. "I could quit school—"

"No."

"I'd be able to work full-time at the Tomahawk. Maybe just get my GED—"

"Don't even think about it, Cody. We'll get by, one way or another. But quitting school . . ." She shook her head. "That's how it starts. That's how I ended up here. That's how everybody ends up here. You either drop out or you get knocked up or both." She leaned forward, meeting his eyes directly for the first time since he'd walked in the door. "I don't want that for you. I wouldn't wish that for anybody, but especially not you. We're not that desperate yet. You hear me?"

He nodded, glad she'd shot the idea down, but feeling guilty for it. "Okay." He hesitated, wondering if there was more to say, but his mom had already turned back to the TV. Cody stood up, thinking maybe he could stretch the phone cord to his bedroom to call Nate. Or maybe he'd just fall into bed, secure in the knowledge that his mom was once again just down the hall. He was surprised at how much it meant, knowing she hadn't intentionally left him. "Mom?"

She looked over her shoulder at him. "Yeah?"

"I'm glad you're home."

She smiled, possibly the first genuine smile he'd seen on her face in months. Maybe even years. "Me too."

Nate drove home on autopilot as he thought about Cody's mom.

He was pretty sure Cyndi hadn't been around for several weeks at least, but nothing made Cody defensive faster than asking about his mother, so Nate had kept his suspicions to himself. But now, contemplating her return, Nate remembered the things he'd heard about her. The night he'd gone to the bowling alley, Larry had said Cyndi worked as a lizard. Nate still had no idea what the term meant, but it had been the one point Cody had adamantly denied.

What exactly was a lizard?

Once home, Nate did the only thing he could think to do—he went to the encyclopedias on the bookshelf and pulled out the

L volume. He sat cross-legged on the floor and flipped through the pages. He wasn't surprised to find that the only entry for "lizard" was the obvious one referring to reptiles.

"Working on a research paper?" his dad asked from the doorway. He'd just come home and was still wearing his uniform.

"Do you know what a lizard is?" Nate asked. "I mean, not like actual lizards, but when it's used to describe a person?"

His dad crossed his arms, leaning back to look up at the ceiling. Nate recognized the expression on his dad's face. It was the same one he'd had years earlier when Nate had asked him what a blowjob was after hearing the term at school. It meant his dad knew what the term meant, but he wasn't sure if it was something he should share with Nate. Finally, he sighed. "A 'lot lizard' is what they call the girls who work the truck stops."

Nate thought about what he knew about Cyndi. "Like, the waitresses?"

His dad shook his head. "No, not like that." It was obvious his dad had hoped he wouldn't have to clarify. He took a deep breath and said, "There are girls who actually work the lot, going truck to truck. They knock on the passenger side door and see if . . . well, if anybody needs some company."

Understanding dawned, and Nate sat back, stunned. "You're talking about hookers?"

His dad scowled. "Prostitutes."

Nate wasn't sure why the distinction mattered, but either way, it certainly explained Larry's derision and Cody's defensiveness.

"What's this about?" his dad asked.

"Nothing, I just—"

"Are you talking about Cyndi Prudhomme?"

Nate felt as if the air had been sucked from the room. He swallowed, his mouth suddenly dry. He wasn't sure how to answer, but the fact that his dad, who had access to the criminal histories of Warren residents, immediately associated the term "lizard" with Cody's mom was telling, in and of itself.

"Have you been seeing that boy Cody?"

Now Nate's heart kicked into high speed. "Wh-what?"

"I told you back in the fall that I didn't want you hanging around with that boy, and I meant it."

"Dad, Cody's not a bad kid."

"You don't know the things I know—"

"Like what?"

"Like—like— *Things*, all right? Things you don't need to hear about."

Was he talking about the rumors that Cody was gay? Or was there more to it than that? "Has he ever actually done anything wrong?"

"His name comes up now and then—"

"That's not what I asked. Has he ever been convicted of anything? Has he ever actually gotten into trouble?"

"That isn't the point."

Nate stood up, letting the encyclopedia fall to the floor. "That *is* the point. Innocent until proven guilty, right?"

"He comes from a bad family."

"His mom's a waitress. That's all."

"That's not all, and his mom's only half of it. His dad's in prison—"

"What? Since when?" Because he was sure Cody would have told him. He may have covered for his mom, but he wouldn't have lied about his dad.

"Since October. He went down for vehicular homicide. He was driving drunk up in Worland and killed a woman and her two-year-old daughter."

"That isn't Cody's fault! Cody hasn't even talked to his dad in ages, and—"

"So you have been seeing him."

It was more a statement than a question, and Nate froze, his heard pounding. He could tell his dad was furious by the slow tick in his neck and the way he clenched his jaw. Nate considered the words. *"So you have been seeing him."* What would his dad think if he knew exactly how much of Cody Nate had seen, or touched, or tasted? The pleasure they shared in Cody's bed felt like the most natural thing in the world, but his dad certainly wouldn't see it that way.

"We're friends," he said, his voice shaking. His dad may disapprove, but no matter what happened, Nate wouldn't turn his back on Cody again. Not even if it meant facing his dad's anger. "We're friends, and he's not a bad kid. I don't care what his parents have done. Cody isn't like that. Cody—"

"Enough!" His dad took a step forward, and Nate backed away on instinct. His dad hadn't spanked him since he was a boy. He hadn't raised a hand to him in years, but the threat was clear. "There are plenty of other kids in this town—"

"Oh, sure. Kids who go out shooting squeakies for fun, or drive through fields trying to run over antelope. Or maybe I should hang out with the kids who go to the dogfights up by Farson. Would that be better? Are those really the types of kids you want me to spend time with?"

"Those aren't your only options—"

"Yes, they are!" He was almost yelling. He knew it was a mistake, but he couldn't seem to stop. "You have no idea what you're talking about. Those *are* my only options! I can kill things for sport, or I can go out and get laid at the old mine—"

"Nobody's supposed to be up there—"

"Do you really think that's stopping them? And, Jesus, going to an abandoned mine isn't even the worst of it!"

"Hanging with trailer trash will eventually land you in trouble! Why can't you see that? There are plenty of kids in Orange Grove—"

"Do you really think the kids in the Grove are better? You actually think the kids with money are the ones who behave? Are you really that stupid?" His dad took another step toward him, his jaw tight, his fists clenched at his sides, but Nate wasn't about to back down. "The Grove group are the worst of the lot, Dad! They're the ones burning down fields and slashing tires. Hell, last time I went to a party with them, Brian and Brad were doing cocaine, for God's sake!"

His dad seemed to deflate, his shoulders falling, his jaw dropping. "What? Are you sure?"

"Well, unless there's some other white powder people chop into little lines and snort through a rolled-up dollar bill, then yeah, I'm pretty damn sure! So I can go with the Grove kids and do a bit of coke before catching somebody's field on fire and burning a few cows alive, or I can hang with the trailer-park kids, who only smoke weed because it's all they can afford. Or I can be friends with Cody, who doesn't do any of that stuff and gets a bad rap just because he has a couple of lousy parents!"

Nate was breathing hard, his heart racing, but he was glad to see his dad's anger had waned. Not only that, he seemed to be considering what Nate had told him. "And what about this girl you've been seeing?"

It felt so far out of left field, Nate was taken aback. "What?"

"This girl you've been dating, whoever she is. You've obviously been spending a lot of time with her since Thanksgiving. And based on the goofy grin you've been wearing since Christmas, things must be pretty hot and heavy with her. So, I'm asking, where does she fit into all this?"

Nate faltered, glancing around the room as if it might provide some answers. But no. There was nothing but the couch and the bookshelves and an open encyclopedia still lying on the floor. He'd talked himself into a corner now.

"Is it the girl you took to homecoming?"

"Yes!" Nate snatched at the obvious answer. "Stacy. Her name's Stacy."

"Stacy what? What's her last name?"

"Miller." He just had to hope that his dad didn't automatically have some dirt on Stacy or her family. Given that they were rule-following Mormons, he figured he was safe. "She's friends with Cody too." It was a blatant lie, but it seemed safe enough. Plus, it would give him a reason to stand by Cody's side rather than terminating their friendship, despite his dad's wishes. "And no matter what his parents have done, he's not a bad kid, Dad. Neither is Stacy." He bent over and picked up the encyclopedia. "Neither am I."

"I know you're not. But once you start spending time with the wrong kinds of people—"

"But I'm not. That's what I'm trying to tell you. I'm the one who goes to school with them. I'm the one who's been to their parties and seen who's doing what. And I'm telling you, there are tons of high schoolers in this town who get in way more trouble than Cody." He slid the book back into place between *K* and *M* before turning to face his dad again. "It all boils down to trust. Either you trust me, or you don't. So which is it?"

His dad sighed, rubbing the back of his neck. "I worry about you."

"That's not what I asked."

"I wish we'd never moved here."

It surprised Nate. It also surprised him to realize that he no longer regretted the move at all. Yeah, Warren sucked. Maybe it was the black hole of modern civilization like Cody said. There was no tennis and no swimming and the goddamn wind never stopped blowing. But having met Cody made up for all of it.

"Brad and Brian," his dad said, still rubbing his neck thoughtfully. "Brad Williams and Brian Anderson? Is that who you're talking about?"

Nate's heart began to pound again. "You can't bust them. If they find out I told you—"

"Do you know where they got it?"

"Brian said he stole it from his dad's drawer. But listen to me, if they find out it was me who told—"

"Don't worry. If I have to trust you, the least you can do is trust me."

It seemed turnabout was fair play, but it didn't make Nate feel any better.

School started again after New Year's, and Nate and Cody fell into an easy routine. Nate drove Cody to school every morning, and nearly every moment that wasn't taken by school, the Tomahawk, or sleep, they spent together. They went to Nate's if his dad was working, although even then, they were very careful about what they did there. Nate was too paranoid about his father catching them. If Cody's mother was gone, they went to Cody's. Sometimes, if the weather wasn't bad, they found a back road and Nate let Cody drive his Mustang. Cody had a license, even though he never drove his mother's car, but he'd never driven a stick, and teaching him how to operate the clutch kept them occupied for a few weeks.

But like any teenagers, they lived for the weekends. Friday and Saturday nights, Cyndi was always gone, and they had several hours after Cody's shift ended but before Nate had to be home for curfew, and they spent most of those hours sequestered in Cody's room.

Nate finally understood all the hype about sex.

They never engaged in actual, penetrative sex. Neither of them seemed inclined to venture there just yet. Besides, there were plenty of ways to make each other feel good using only their hands and their mouths.

Nate thought he'd become used to Warren, but being so close to Cody brought some of the uglier parts of small-town life home. The train schedule seemed sporadic, but when it came through Warren, it shook Cody's entire trailer. Police showed up at Kathy and Pete's place so often that Nate realized it was a miracle he'd managed to keep his friendship with Cody hidden from his dad for as long as he had. It was only a matter of time before his dad responded to a domestic disturbance call and saw Nate's truck parked out front. Toward the end of January, Vera knocked on Cody's door and asked if he'd seen Ted.

"I usually see him go past the gas station on the way to the liquor store," she said. "But I ain't seen him for three days, and I can hear that dog of his barking to go out from my bedroom."

Cody's cheeks paled, his eyes sliding to the most distant trailer in the lot. "I haven't seen him."

Twenty minutes later, Nate's dad and another police officer arrived and pounded on the front door of Ted's trailer. Eventually, they busted in, and then the ambulance arrived, but without lights or a siren. The dog was loaded into the back of a police car. A bit of careful questioning with his dad at dinnertime confirmed that the occupant had been found dead inside, apparently having drunk himself to death sometime earlier that week, and the dog had been taken to the shelter in Rock Springs. Nate stupidly hoped the poor thing didn't get put down, but he had no way of knowing its fate. Meanwhile, two pregnant girls at Walter Warren High School—one senior and one sophomore—dropped out, more families moved away, and Nate heard Brian bragging in English about the coke he'd managed to score from a friend of his father.

The sooner he and Cody got out of Warren, the better. It was something they talked about often. Whether sequestered in Cody's room because his mom was home, or cuddling on the couch while she was away, Nate and Cody spent hours talking about what might happen after graduation. Nate knew Cody was studiously saving every penny he could, but Nate also knew that wasn't adding up nearly as fast as Cody would have liked. Although they never talked about it, Nate suspected Cody was paying a fair share of the bills. He'd cut down to only two or three cigarettes a day, simply because he could no longer stand to part with several dollars a week to support his habit.

They were in agreement that there must be places in the world where homosexuality didn't seem like such a crime. They'd both heard jokes about San Francisco their whole lives, but huddled together on Cody's couch, with the lights low and the curtains all drawn tight so nobody could see them from outside, they talked in hushed tones about where else they might go.

They talked about AIDS.

It was impossible not to. It was mentioned every night in the news. It was on multiple magazine covers. Nate bought each one, not only because he wanted to make sure they knew as much as possible about the disease, but because he hoped he'd find little nuggets of info buried in the articles. In places that weren't Warren, Wyoming, whole communities of men and women in same-sex relationships lived their lives as if it were the most normal thing in the world, and Nate longed to know where those places were.

"You gotta stop buying these, man," Cody said one afternoon when Nate brought him a *U.S. News & World Report* with *AIDS* in bright-red letters across the cover. Cody sat on his couch, eyeing the magazine on the coffee table as if it were a venomous snake that might strike at any time.

"We'll bury it in the bottom of the trash after we read it," Nate said, tossing his jacket aside and sitting down next to him.

"That's not what I mean. Eventually, somebody's gonna notice that you buy every magazine about fags and AIDS. Somebody's gonna put it together."

"I make sure I go to different cashiers every time, and if they ask, I tell them it's for a school report." Nate reached out and took Cody's hand. "And we're not 'fags.' Don't say it that way. That's like using the n-word. We're gay, that's all. Or homosexual, if you like that better. But don't use their words against us."

Cody only shrugged, and Nate tried not to be frustrated. It wasn't that Cody actually thought they were doing anything wrong, but after hearing the word so many times, he'd somehow grown used to it. It was almost as if by refusing to let something as small as a word bother him, he might prove he was stronger than the town thought. At the very least, he could prove that he was above the rumors.

Nate understood, on some level, but he couldn't quite subscribe to the same mind-set, no matter how hard he tried. He grew hyperaware of every time the word "fag" was used at school.

It was a lot.

And more and more often, it was directed at him.

The stack of college applications in Nate's desk drawer remained blank. There wasn't much he could do about school until he knew where they were going. Maybe he'd be stuck at a community college instead of a university, but he was okay with that. When his dad asked, Nate flat-out lied and told him he'd applied.

He'd have to deal with the truth eventually, but he wanted to have more answers first.

On February fourth, Liberace died. Nate was sure most of the people at school had never even listened to his music, but suddenly, Nate felt the stares of the other students more often. He saw them ducking their heads to whisper as he and Cody passed. A few days later, somebody scrawled the word "fag" across his locker door with a thick, black marker.

"We need to cool it," Cody told him that afternoon as Nate drove him to the Tomahawk after school.

It was one of those days where the sun was shining and the sky was bluer than it had ever been in Texas, but the steady wind was cold enough to numb any exposed flesh. Nate kept one hand on the steering wheel and held the stiff fingers of his other hand in front of the car's vent, waiting for the heat to come up to temperature. "Cool what?"

"This. Us. Always being together."

"What, we're supposed to stop being friends just because they don't like it?"

Cody sighed, leaning his head against the passenger window, rubbing the fingers of his right hand together and bouncing his knee in a way that told Nate he was dying for a cigarette but trying to fight it. "We're more than that, aren't we?"

"You know we are. Why? Is this your way of breaking up with me?"

Cody's head jerked Nate's direction. "Breaking up? You make it sound like we're going steady or something."

Nate shrugged and gave up on the heat in order to use both hands on the wheel as they turned onto Main Street. "I don't know. You have another name for what we've been doing?"

Cody almost smiled, turning away to look out the window. "Guess I just hadn't thought of it that way."

"So if you're not breaking up with me, then what? What're you worried about?"

Cody pulled the pack of cigarettes from his pocket, but didn't move to shake one loose. "Look, I'm not saying we should actually stop seeing each other. I'm just saying, we stop letting *them* see it, that's all."

"As far as they know, we drive to and from school together, and we sit next to each other in social studies. That's it. We're not doing anything wrong."

Cody didn't argue. He gave up and lit a cigarette instead.

Valentine's Day fell on a Saturday. It was also the day of the high school girl-ask-boy dance, and the day before Nate's birthday. He spent the entire week leading up to the dance trying to avoid any girl who might ask him. Luckily, that list seemed to have decreased significantly since fall. Only Stacy Miller approached him, and Nate lied and said he was grounded for the weekend.

He didn't tell Cody about his birthday, either, only because he knew Cody would feel bad about not getting him a gift. Besides, what Nate wanted most couldn't be bought in a store.

Saturday evening, Nate told his dad he was going to the dance with Stacy. Then, he picked up Cody from his shift at the Tomahawk as usual. Cody's mom was gone for the night. Nate knew Cody would want to shower as soon as he got home. Sometimes, Nate showered with him, but tonight, he had other plans.

Once he could hear the shower running, he got to work. He started by pushing the furniture out of the way, as well as he could on his own. The couch would have to stay, but the coffee table and chair were easy enough to move. He had a bag full of candles he'd bought earlier that day. He set them up around the room, lit them all, then turned out the lights.

The effect wasn't quite as romantic as he'd hoped in Cody's dingy trailer, but it'd have to do.

The tape player he'd given Cody was already in the living room, and Nate was pleased to find the tape he'd made in it. He spent a while rewinding and fast-forwarding, trying to decide exactly which song to start with.

Which song should be playing when they danced together for the very first time?

Maybe it was silly. He had a feeling Cody would think so, at any rate. But after staring at Cody across the dance floor at homecoming, and seeing the buzz of excitement in the school leading up to the dance, Nate had found himself feeling uncharacteristically angry. He wanted to put on a dress shirt and pick Cody up at his house, like any other date. He wanted to walk into the school gym hand in hand, to stand in line for pictures, and—more than anything—to take Cody onto the dance floor when a slow song came on.

Of course, none of that was possible. Not here in Warren, Wyoming, at any rate. So Nate decided to settle for the next best thing.

"I knew you were up to something," Cody said when he finally emerged, scrubbing a towel over his still-wet hair. He'd put on jeans, socks, and a clean T-shirt, but no shoes. "You were acting kind of goofy."

Nate hit Play on the tape deck. He'd ended up on Madonna's "Crazy for You," more because he'd run out of time than because he'd actually chosen it. He held his hand out to Cody, his cheeks beginning to burn.

"Can I have this dance?"

Cody froze, the towel held to the side of his head, his eyes wide. "You're kidding, right?"

At least he'd accurately anticipated Cody's reaction. "It's Valentine's Day, and we can't go to the dance." He smiled. "Oh. And did I mention that tomorrow's my birthday?"

"Shit."

"And I know you didn't buy me anything, and that's fine. But I really want this. Please."

Cody shook his head, grinning, and tossed the towel aside. "Not afraid to play dirty, are you?" Still, he hesitated, staring at Nate's outstretched hand. "Never really done this before."

"I know."

Cody sighed. "This is stupid, Nate." But he took Nate's hand. He let Nate pull him close.

It was a pretty well-established fact that when dancing, boys put their arms around the girl's waist, and girls put their arms around the guy's neck. Nate had unwittingly taken the "guy" role. He wondered if he should have mentioned that first, maybe asked Cody his preference, but if Cody noticed or cared, he chose not to mention it. He simply put his arms around Nate's neck.

And they danced.

It was perfect, as far as Nate was concerned. Far better than it would have been at the school, because there were no prying eyes. No chaperones to tell them they were dancing too close. There was just the two of them, and the candlelight, and the music. Nate held Cody tight, smelling the clean, shampoo scent of his freshly washed hair, letting his hands wander slowly over Cody's slender body as one song became two, and two became three.

And the best part of all was the way Cody reacted.

They'd fooled around enough since Christmas for Nate to recognize Cody's arousal, and not just because of his erection brushing against Nate's as they moved. Cody's breathing became shallow and ragged. He shivered as Nate's hand moved up the curve of his spine. He whimpered when Nate lowered his mouth to Cody's throat, letting lips and tongue play over his pounding pulse. And when Nate pulled back enough to see Cody's face in the flickering light, he could see the need he'd kindled in Cody, as much by accident as by design.

"Still think this is stupid?" Nate asked.

Cody moaned in frustration, practically melting against him, guiding Nate's lips to his own. "God, yes."

One little kiss, and Cody was clutching at him, struggling toward the couch, his desperation making him clumsy and impatient. Nate barely had time to lower him onto the couch, to unzip Cody's pants and slip his hand inside before Cody was gasping, arching into him, crying out as he came.

"Jesus," Cody gasped at last. "That was—"

"Seriously hot?"

Cody laughed. "I was going to say it was pretty shitty of me, considering you're the one with the birthday."

Nate chuckled, adjusting his jeans over his own erection. They still had plenty of time before curfew, and Cody had never left him hanging for long. "How about this for my present: next time I ask you to dance—"

"Yes!" Cody laughed, pulling him into a kiss. "I promise I'll say yes."

CHAPTER

Despite Nate's nonchalance about their relationship, Cody knew they were playing with fire.

He'd already gone more than half the school year without anybody starting a fight with him. That was a record. He figured he'd skated through the first half of the year because of Logan's friendship, but that wouldn't save him now.

Still, Cody was used to the adversity. He'd been pushed around for most of his life. He knew when to put his head down and keep his mouth shut. Just a few more months and he'd be done with Walter Warren High School forever.

But Nate . . .

Nate changed everything. He may have thought he was being subtle, but he gave too much away. He stood too close. He touched Cody too often. His smile said just a bit too much.

For himself, Cody didn't mind. He was used to the rumors, and immune to the word "fag," even though it made Nate grit his teeth. But he had a sneaking suspicion Nate had never been in an actual fight in his life.

It'd be a miracle if that was still true by graduation.

Nate continued buying magazines, even though most of them regurgitated the same bullshit every time. Yes, even straight people could get AIDS. It seemed ridiculous that this simple truth still counted as news, but it did. The *U.S. News & World Report* from January and a *Newsweek* in February both sold the same tired advice: be more careful who you sleep with, and use a condom. The most helpful bit of information arrived a few days after their makeshift dance, when Nate brought him a *New York Times* dated February fifteenth.

"Not quite fresh off the presses, but fresh off the truck that brings the New York newspaper into the back reaches of Wyoming, I guess," Nate said.

There, beginning on the lower half of the front page and continuing for more than a page afterward was what they'd been searching for—"Fact, Theory, and Myth on the Spread of AIDS." For the first time, there were real-world questions with real-world answers. "Can the virus spread through oral sex? Federal epidemiologists suspect it can because the virus is present in semen and vaginal secretions and thus might enter the cells of the body through cuts or mucous membranes in the mouth or throat. However, they have not documented any cases."

Cody read the article start to finish three times.

But while poring through magazines and newspapers, Nate and Cody had been looking for one other thing: a place to go. They kept hoping to find a casual mention of homosexual communities in places other than San Francisco or New York, but they never did. If the articles were to be believed, one might actually think gay men only existed in two cities in all of America, but Cody knew that couldn't be true.

"Forget the magazines!" Nate finally said one day in early March, throwing one across Cody's living room. "We just need to pick a place and hope for the best."

The next day, he brought a giant atlas of the United States to Cody's house, and they sat at the kitchen table and began flipping through its pages.

"What's between Chicago and Wyoming?" Cody asked.

"South Dakota, Nebraska, and Iowa."

"Not Nebraska," Cody said. "Only difference between Nebraska and Wyoming is they got more corn."

"South Dakota doesn't sound much better."

"Okay. So what's Iowa like?"

Nate shrugged, smiling at him. "I have no idea."

The very next day, Cody ditched PE and spent the hour in the school library.

A quick run through the card catalog turned up several books with entries about Iowa. Two in particular seemed promising, and

Cody waded into the aisles, trailing his fingers over the spines of the books as he searched. Once he had a stack in his arms, he settled at one of the desks along the wall and flipped to the pertinent pages.

What he saw took his breath away. Some pictures showed only fields, and some showed rolling hills, and some showed towns and small cities, but in every single case, he saw nothing but green. Miles and miles and miles of green grass and green fields and towering, deciduous trees. He'd never seen so much green in one place in his life. After growing up in the barren, wind-swept plains of Wyoming, where the only green around was dusty sagebrush and a few wind-beaten pine trees with their branches all growing on the leeward side of the trunk, the sight of so much lush vegetation was mind-boggling. Almost miraculous. It looked cozy and rural, and yet Chicago was only a few hours away. Based on the pictures, Iowa winters could be harsh, but that didn't scare him a bit. Not after living in Wyoming. Just the promise of all that green come springtime was enough to make him want to pack up and move the very next day.

One other bit of information caught his attention. The state's law criminalizing same-sex sexual activity and been repealed in June 1976. It wasn't quite the same as "Hey, gay people, we want you here!" but at least they wouldn't have to worry about actually being arrested for what happened in their bedroom.

Iowa. He'd never given the place much thought before, but suddenly, it was the only place he wanted to be.

He dropped the books in the return bin just as the bell rang and headed for Nate's locker, wanting to tell him what he'd found.

But as he rounded the corner, he discovered a circle of people around Nate's locker, and his heart sank. He pushed through the gathering crowd to find Nate backed against the bank of lockers by Brian Anderson. Brad Williams stood only a step or two behind Brian, obviously working as Brian's backup.

"I know it was you!" Brian yelled, shoving Nate backward, even though Nate had nowhere to go. "I know you told your dad."

Nate still had a notebook and his English text in one hand. His cheeks were red, but he was calmer than Cody expected. "I didn't—"

"You must have. You saw us at that party—"

"But I didn't tell my dad. I swear it." He was lying, though. Cody could tell, although he couldn't quite have said how he knew. There was just something about Nate's eyes that told him the denial wasn't entirely honest.

And obviously Brian didn't believe him either, because he poked Nate hard in the chest. "Then why'd he get arrested?"

"I don't know anything about that."

"It was your dad who busted him!"

"My dad doesn't talk to me about his work. I don't know anything—"

"Liar!"

Brian grabbed Nate and slammed him against the lockers. Cody moved fast. He hit Brian from the side, shoving him away from Nate, trying to put himself between them. "Leave him alone!"

His attack knocked Brian back a couple of steps, but he recovered quickly, sneering. "Oh, look," he said over his shoulder to Brad, and to the onlookers. "Nate's trailer-trash butt-buddy is coming to his rescue."

Cody squared his shoulders and stepped forward. It wouldn't be the first time Brian Anderson had punched him, and if it brought the teachers running before they got to Nate, he'd be okay with it.

But the teachers were quicker than he gave them credit for.

"Break it up!" Mrs. Simmons shouted, pushing her way through the gathered students. "That's enough. Mr. Lawrence, you know better than to fight in the hallways. And Mr. Williams, I think your mom has quite enough to deal with right now without having to come down to the school for a conference with the principal."

The rest of the students began to shuffle toward the classrooms. Brian took one step toward Cody, but his eyes were on Nate. "I'll get you, man. You're gonna pay."

"*Mr. Anderson!*"

Brian scowled, but moved away. Nate turned to his locker, and Cody edged closer, noting how Nate's hands shook as he dialed his combination.

"What the fuck, man? You narced on Brian?"

Nate scowled and yanked the locker door open. "Not really. Not like that. Not the way you make it sound."

"What, then?"

He tossed his book inside and pulled another one from the shelf. "It was ages ago. At the end of Christmas break. I'd forgotten all about it."

"So you *did* narc him out?"

Nate slammed the locker door shut and turned on Cody. "Jesus, can you stop taking his side for one minute and listen to me?"

Cody scrubbed his hands through his hair, trying to calm his racing heart. "I'm not taking his side. I'm just asking—"

"I didn't really mean to tell my dad anything, but he was hassling me about spending time with you, telling me you're a bad influence, and I was just trying to tell him it was bullshit. I just wanted him to know those assholes from the Grove aren't the saints he makes them out to be, that's all. And I slipped. I said Brian's name, but I didn't realize he'd know who I meant. I didn't think he was going to go after them!"

"But he did?"

"Apparently. I guess. I don't know."

Now that the moment had passed and his adrenaline was fading, Cody could almost see the humor in it. "You don't know?"

"I have no idea, all right? Like I told Brian, my dad doesn't talk to me about his work. I didn't know anything about it until Brian slammed me against the locker and started screaming at me."

The bell rang, and Nate scowled at the ceiling. "Great. Now I'm late for physics. And you're late for math."

"Whatever." The good thing about being in the degenerate math class was that just about everybody turned up late. "You better find a way to apologize, or to convince him you had nothing to do with it. Either that, or you better be ready to fight him next time he comes after you."

"He won't. He was mad, but I'm sure he'll get over it."

"I don't know, Nate. You can't just assume this'll go away. You heard him—"

"Can we talk about this later?" Nate glanced at his watch, as if he needed it to tell him he was tardy. "I gotta go."

Cody sighed, defeated. "Whatever. Steer clear of Brad, all right?"

"I always do." Nate turned and headed down the hall, but stopped and turned on his heel after a few steps. "Thanks for trying to come to my rescue."

For all the good it did, Cody thought.

Because no matter what Nate said, Cody knew it wasn't over.

It was Monday when Brian caught up with them again. It was a gorgeous March day, and spring was in the air, the breeze warm and the sun high in the cobalt sky. Nate's dad had finally agreed to let him drive the Mustang again, and Cody hadn't needed to wear the thick coat Logan had given him. He had only a zip-front sweatshirt over his T-shirt.

"Maybe we can even put the top down," Nate said as they weaved through the school lot toward his parking spot at the end of the day. He had a notebook and his calculus book with him.

Cody, on the other hand, had nothing but a new pack of cigarettes in his pocket. He'd made it through lunch without one, but he was dying to light up now. "Don't get ahead of yourself," he warned. "It could still snow tomorrow, you know."

And after Logan's accident, he was terrified of Nate being caught off guard, out in a snowstorm with only his Mustang. He figured he'd get over it someday, but not yet. Not when he still looked for Logan's laughing face in the hallways. Every once in a while at the Tomahawk, he still found himself staring down at a sink full of soapy water with tears in his eyes.

"What the hell?" Nate said, stopping short. "I have a flat tire."

Cody eyed the Mustang, slumped like an injured animal on the pavement. "Looks like more than one."

They circled the car, going opposite directions, meeting again on the other side. "All four," Nate sighed. "Guess it's safe to say I didn't just run over a nail."

"It had to be Brian."

"Damn it. I even talked to my dad. He said the bust had nothing to do with what I told him, but not like Brian will ever believe that."

"Now what?" Cody eyed the school. "We could go ask to use the phone in the office."

"My dad's at work. I won't be able to reach him until after five." He glanced up at the sky. "At least it's a nice day. Let's just walk to your house, and I can call from there once he's home."

They started down the street. Cody tipped his head back to let the sun wash over his face. The trees were still bare, but birds chirped and sang, flitting from branch to branch. He and Nate stopped at the curb and waited for a car to pass before crossing toward the empty dirt lot behind the gas station where they'd first met. Cody shook a cigarette out of his pack and lit it. Cutting down as much as he had made him savor each one that much more.

"I forgot to tell you, that day when Brian tried to start a fight with you, I was in the library. I looked up Iowa."

Nate glanced his way, looking hopeful. "And?"

"It looks good."

"Really?"

"Really."

"So, where do you want to go? Des Moines?"

"I was thinking more like Iowa City. It's only three and a half hours from Chicago. They have a university there, and a community college. The book I looked at said the population is about fifty thousand."

"That's not very big at all."

"It sounds enormous to me." But in a good way. Not scary-big. Just refreshing-big. "It looks amazing."

Nate stopped in his tracks, staring at Cody with bright eyes. "'Amazing' meaning you want to go live there?"

"Maybe." But just the thought was making him smile. "If you do."

Nate laughed. "Absolutely." He looked happier than Cody had ever seen him. He reached out and took Cody's hand as they started walking again, squeezing his fingers quickly before letting him go. "I'd kiss you right now, if I could."

"Better not." Cody glanced around to see if anybody might be watching. They were almost to the middle of the dirt lot. It was a big space, a full block wide. It had always reminded Cody of TV shows and movies, where kids gathered to play baseball or football, but the only game he'd ever seen in this particular lot was a group of kids throwing rocks at a stray cat, and once, when he'd only been in grade school, some teenagers fighting.

A shiver worked its way up Cody's spine, the sunshine suddenly not nearly as warm as it had been. His steps slowed.

"What is it?" Nate asked.

Cody glanced around again. The houses on both sides seemed awfully far away, all of them drooping and tattered. Cody guessed at least half of them were vacant. But it wasn't the houses he was worried about. He scanned the edges of the lot.

And there, waiting on the corner near the back of the gas station, Brian Anderson and Brad Williams stood with three other boys from the Grove. Once they realized they'd been spotted, they laughed and started forward.

Cody grabbed Nate's arm to stop him. "Shit." How could he have been so stupid? He should have known to stay on the sidewalk, even though it was a less direct route. It might not have saved them, but it would have at least put them within shouting distance of help.

He turned to check behind them, wondering if they could run, although God knew where they'd go. But no. He didn't know where they'd been hidden, but Tom Watson, Billy Jones, Lance Donaldson, and Larry Lucero were closing in fast from that side.

Brad and Brian had planned it well, from slashing Nate's tires to knowing which way Cody had to walk to get home.

"Is this what I think it is?" Nate asked, his voice shaking.

"If you think it's you and I about to get our asses kicked, then yeah, that's what it is."

"Hey," Brian called gleefully as they closed the distance between them. "Look who it is! The town fags, out for a stroll. Don't let us interrupt your romantic moment, boys."

Cody ignored him, turning in a circle again to see if there was an obvious escape route. The gang was spreading out, moving to surround them, but Brian's group was coming from the right side of the gas station, leaving a bit of a gap to Cody and Nate's left.

"You run," Cody said, trying to pitch his voice low. He pointed quickly. "That way. Get to the gas station—"

"To hell with that. There are nine of them. Even if I could outrun them, I'm not leaving you here."

And in the time it had taken to have that brief exchange, the window had closed anyways.

Cody weighed the odds. There were more of the Grove residents, but they weren't as dangerous. They were spoiled rich brats. Sure, some of them played football, or wrestled, but the three farm kids with Larry Lucero worried him a lot more. They'd be stronger and tougher.

He turned to face them, putting his back to Nate's. Maybe the Grove group would take it easier on one of their own.

Probably not, but it was worth a shot.

Cody's heart was racing, adrenaline making his fingertips tingle. He heard Nate's notebook and calculus text hit the dirt. Cody took one last drag on his cigarette, imagining he could feel the nicotine flowing through his veins. If only it could give him superhuman strength, like Popeye with his damn spinach.

"Just stay out of the way, Cody," Lance said. "It's your boyfriend he wants."

So much for wishing.

Cody sized up the boys he'd apparently have to fight. Larry wasn't much of a threat, although he was certainly the one Cody hated the most. Tom was only a freshman, Billy a junior, but Lance was a senior, and a big one, too. With Logan gone, he was easily the biggest guy in the school.

If he could just take Lance out of the equation, he might have a chance. Then again, if he was only going to get in a few good licks, he's just as soon aim them at Larry.

And as for Nate?

Well, he had to hope Nate could hold his own.

"I've been waiting for this all year," Larry said, grinning. "Finally get to do it, now that Logan isn't here to protect his favorite faggot."

"Fuck it," Cody said. "Let's get this over with." And before the boys in front of him could do anything else, he moved. He threw his cigarette butt in Lance's face, pushed Billy as hard as he could into Tom, and threw a punch at Larry's nose.

It landed too, solid and gratifying as hell.

But it was pretty much all downhill from there.

He fought hard, hitting whoever got in front of him, but after what felt like half an hour but could only have been a couple of minutes, Tom and Billy ended up holding his arms behind his back while Larry punched him several times in the face, then one last time in the stomach. They dropped him on his knees while he sucked air, his brain screaming for oxygen. Behind him, he could hear more punches falling and Brad and Brian laughing. He couldn't hear Nate, but he had to assume Nate wasn't faring much better than he was.

He tried to stand up, tried to turn, thinking he needed to help, but somebody kicked him between the shoulder blades and sent him sprawling in the dirt. One of them landed on top of him, twisting his arm behind his back and pinning him to the ground. Somebody put their foot on the back of his head and pushed his face into the dirt. Somebody else kicked him in the ribs.

"Just stay down, Cody," the person on his back said in his ear. He thought it was Lance, but it was hard to say. "Once Brian finishes teaching your boyfriend a lesson, it'll all be over."

Now he could hear Nate—not talking, of course, but the horrible, painful grunts as somebody punched him, or kicked him. Cody twisted, turning his head, straining to see. Nate was on the ground, surrounded by six boys, all of them taking turns hitting and kicking him.

"Stop it!" Cody screamed, trying to throw the weight off his back. "Goddamn it, you've won, for fuck's sake. Leave him alone!"

Somebody laughed, and then one of the three boys still holding Cody down grabbed his hair and slammed his face into the ground, holding it there this time as Cody squirmed to get free.

"Stop it," the voice in his ear said. Not threatening at all. He was almost pleading. "Just stop, Cody, or it'll only get worse for both of you."

"Hey," somebody said, "you think I can get AIDS from punching him while he bleeds?"

It was said gleefully, obviously meant to be a joke, but a sudden hush fell over them. As stupid as it was, Cody found himself considering the question. Not that either he or Nate was infected, but if they had been, and the boy throwing the punches had split knuckles, would it have been enough to spread the virus?

"Let's go," a voice he recognized as Brian Anderson's said. "I think they get the point."

The weight on Cody's back disappeared, and the only thing he heard was the *thump-thump-thump* of sneakers hitting packed dirt as nine boys ran away.

Cody waited until he heard car doors before dragging himself over to Nate. He was still curled in a ball, holding his stomach, his face covered in blood.

Jesus, he's dying.

But quick on the tail of that thought came a bit of clarity. No, Nate was breathing, moaning in pain, but probably in no immediate danger. He'd taken a lot of blows to his kidneys, though, and Cody knew that could be dangerous.

"Nate, are you all right?" The full surge of adrenaline was hitting Cody now, his vision blurring, his breath coming in gulps. He wasn't sure his words had even come out right. His hands shook as he touched Nate's shoulder. "Nate?"

Nate groaned, turning onto his back, still holding his stomach. He was bleeding from cuts over his eye, from his temple, from his nose, from his mouth . . . So much blood, and Cody tried to think what to do. Nate clearly wouldn't be able to walk, and even with Cody's help, he probably wouldn't make it more than a block. Even now, after all the noise they must have made, nobody had appeared to investigate.

Cody eyed the back of the gas station, weighing his options.

"Wait here," he said, as if Nate had any intention of doing otherwise. "I'll be back."

Vera's eyes went wide when he pushed through the glass door, but she let him use the phone without question. His hands shook so badly he had to recite the number while Vera dialed. He sank to the floor, listening to the rings, hoping against hope that she'd answer.

"Hello?"

Cody almost sobbed with relief. "Mom? I need help."

His mom made it in record time, her tires squealing around the corner. She didn't even stop at the curb, just let her beaten old Duster slam over it before braking to a stop next to them. She jumped out, leaving the ignition running.

"Are you okay?"

"I'm fine, but Nate—"

"Let's get him in the car."

It took both of them to get Nate on his feet. He moaned, his arms wrapped around his ribs, then promptly doubled over and vomited into the dirt.

"Where's he live?"

"The Grove. But his dad's at work. Jesus, Mom. His dad—"

"Talk in the car. We need to get him to the hospital."

They managed to get Nate into the front seat, and Cody grabbed Nate's dropped schoolbooks and wiggled behind the driver's seat into the back. His mom's eyes flashed to his in the rearview mirror as she turned onto the street.

"Who was it?"

"Some assholes from the Grove. Plus Larry Lucero, and a couple of the farm kids. Tom Watson, Billy Jones, Lance Donaldson." It was the wrestling team, he realized. Part of it, at any rate. That was why there was such a strange mix of cliques. They probably all played football together in the fall too. They obviously hadn't included any of the Mormons in their plan, and Jimmy Riordan had either balked or been left out, but wrestling and football were the only things that connected Brian and Brad with the cowboys and Larry Lucero.

"How do you want this to go?" his mom asked.

Now that he was in the car, headed for the hospital, the rush was fading, leaving him limp and exhausted. Her question confused him. He pulled it around in his head, trying to make sense of it. Finally gave up and said, "Wha—"

"His dad will get the cops involved. You want to be part of that?"

"Oh God. Nate's dad *is* the cops. Remember the guy who came to our door when Pete and Kathy reported a break-in?"

He caught his mom's scowl in the rearview mirror. Nate's dad was going to freak. He'd already told Nate several times to stay away from Cody. And the Grove kids all had their daddies' lawyers, and he was pretty sure Billy Jones's uncle was a county sheriff. And on top of everything else, there was the simple knowledge that the blame almost always landed squarely on him. Everybody knew Cody Lawrence was trouble. He lived in the Hole. His mom worked the truck stop. Everybody knew he was a fag. Cody shook his head. "They'll say I started it."

"Did you?"

"Jesus, Mom. How dumb would I have to be to pick a fight with nine guys at once?"

The wrinkles around her eyes seemed more pronounced in the rearview mirror than usual, but he recognized that she was trying to force a smile. "People do crazy things for the ones they love."

Cody's heart burst into motion, but Nate chose that moment to begin coughing—a deep, hacking sound that brought up way too much blood.

"Hang on, kiddo," his mom said.

"I'm bleeding all over your upholstery."

It was the first thing he'd said, and Cody's mom laughed, the same sad laugh she used when a "past due" notice arrived in the mail. "Don't you worry none 'bout the car."

By the time they reached Warren's tiny hospital, Nate was a bit more coherent. He looked worse than ever, though. His entire shirt was blood-soaked, and the left side of his face was already beginning to swell. They helped him out of the front seat with his arm over Cody's mom's shoulders. She waved her hand at Cody, shooing him in the direction of the car.

"There's napkins in the glove compartment. Clean yourself up as well as you can before you come in."

It surprised him. He didn't want to leave Nate, but when he plopped into the passenger seat and flipped down the visor to check the mirror, he understood. His face looked almost as bad as Nate's. His eyebrows and his bangs were caked with mud. His nose had obviously been bleeding at some point, but he hadn't noticed. Now, it had dried all over his mouth and chin. Flakes of it clung to the light stubble on his neck. He looked down at his shirt and realized it was red down to his navel. If he walked into the hospital looking the way he did, they'd make a fuss over him. At the very least, they'd whisper about him. That Lawrence kid from the Hole again, always causing trouble. They'd insist he wait for the cops to arrive.

If he wanted to get out of there with as little hassle as possible, he needed to look less like a victim.

The mud in his hair was red, a mixture of blood and dirt, but things dried fast in Wyoming's high-desert climate. It didn't take much to scrub it out. He dug in the glove compartment and found napkins, plus a few wet wipes from the diner. He also found a warm can of generic soda in the front seat. He drank half and used the rest in lieu of water, scrubbing his face clean. He took off his shirt and put it on backwards, so the blood was hidden in the back. There wasn't much blood on his sweatshirt, so he zipped it up and checked himself again in the mirror. There was a broad, oozing abrasion on his forehead from having it rubbed in the dirt. He combed his hair down over it, wishing he had a baseball cap. Other than that, he didn't look too bad. He'd have a black eye and his upper lip was about twice its normal size, but hopefully nobody in the ER would look at him closely enough to notice.

Finally, he hurried inside.

Nate was nowhere in sight, but his mom was sitting in one of the waiting room chairs. He took the empty one next to her. "What's going on?"

"They've already called his father. He's on his way."

He thought of Nate, somewhere on the other side of the waiting room doors, all alone. "Can I see him?"

"I don't think so. They wouldn't let me go back."

Cody ran his hand through his hair, then remembered he was trying to keep his scraped forehead from showing and shook his hair back into his face. He glanced around the waiting room. A middle-aged couple with worn, haggard faces sat in chairs on the far side of the room, holding hands, their heads together, caught up in their own crisis, and Cody couldn't help but wonder if this was how Logan's parents had looked on that horrible weekend after Thanksgiving. In another corner, two men sat side by side, legs splayed, heads back, their eyes closed, their muddy work boots and company hats marking them as roughnecks from a nearby oil rig. A bunch of nurses and receptionists sat behind the desk, more than were probably needed at such a small hospital, looking busy without doing much of anything. They were trying so hard not to look at Cody and his mother, it must have been giving them headaches.

Now that he had nothing else to think about, the pain was kicking in. His head hurt, and his ribs. But whatever he was feeling, he knew Nate had it worse. And Nate was somewhere in the back, completely out of Cody's reach.

"Should we just go?" He didn't want to, but if he couldn't see Nate, there was no point in hanging around.

His mom's lips thinned, her hands clenched together in her lap. Cody knew she was dying for a cigarette. "Not yet."

He didn't argue. He didn't have the energy. He put his head in his hands and waited without knowing what exactly he was waiting for.

Some indeterminable amount of time later, the door swished open and his mom tensed. Cody glanced up in time to see Nate's dad bearing down on him, still in uniform.

"Cody? What the hell are you doing here? What happened? Where's Nate?"

But before Cody could answer, his mom was on her feet, rushing toward Mr. Bradford. She grabbed his arm and led him away from Cody, talking low and fast. Cody couldn't hear her words, but he recognized the briskness of her motions, the flash in her eyes, the thin set of her lips.

"What?" Mr. Bradford's voice was loud, and everybody in the waiting room turned his direction.

One of the receptionists began circling from behind the counter, whether to intervene, or simply to take Mr. Bradford to see Nate, Cody didn't know.

"That's ridiculous!" Nate's dad said to Cody's mom. "If these boys—"

Cody's mom cut him off, edging forward, her voice still too low to carry, but her anger causing him to take a step backward. He finally glanced again over at Cody. He nodded, rubbing one hand through his thinning hair.

"I can take you back now," the receptionist said to him.

He nodded, his eyes still on Cody. "Okay." And then, to Cody's mother. "Okay. I don't understand it, but if that's the way you want it—"

"It is."

Mr. Bradford threw up his hands and turned away, letting the receptionist lead him through the double doors into the back area. Cody's mother kept her head up as she crossed the room, even though everybody was watching her. She didn't even stop as she passed him.

"We're leaving."

Cody hurried to follow her out the door. The passenger seat was spotted with blood and littered with the napkins he'd used to clean his face. He pushed them all on the floor while his mother punched the lighter, a cigarette already between her lips. He reached for his out of habit, stopped short, glancing her way. It wasn't like she couldn't see the packs in his room, or spot the butts in the ashtray that didn't match hers, but he never smoked in front of her.

"Go ahead," she said. "I think you've earned it."

He didn't, though. It felt too strange. He just watched as she lit hers, sucking deeply before leaning back to blow smoke toward the open window. Only then did she start the car and head for the parking lot exit.

Cody waited for the questions to begin, but they never did. His mom's lips were still thin, her jaw tight, but her grip on the wheel wasn't white-knuckled like it had been on the way to the hospital. He couldn't tell if she was angry or upset or indifferent. He finally cleared his throat and made himself break the silence.

"What did you say to Nate's dad?"

"I told him you weren't there."

Cody blinked at her, trying to wrap his head around that. "You what?"

"I told him you found Nate after it happened. You called me for a ride, but you have no idea who did this or why. I told him Nate may say differently, but if he does, it's only because he's confused about what happened, and I told him that dragging us into it won't do him any good anyway. Not if he wants to protect his son's reputation, and I have a feeling he does."

"Do you think he believed you?"

"No, but I think he got the point."

"Which is what, exactly?"

"First of all, that you weren't the one who beat Nate up."

"And what else?"

She didn't answer right away. She pondered it while she took another drag off her smoke. Finally, she sighed, the smoke blowing out of her nostrils in two fast puffs. "I know Nate spends half his time holed up in your bedroom, but I told his dad that as far as I'm concerned, nobody needs to know about that. And if anybody asks me, I'll deny everything. I'll tell them I've never seen that boy before tonight." She glanced Cody's way and almost smiled. "Wouldn't even be a lie, since I work weekends, and even when I'm home, he always sneaks out after you think I'm asleep."

There was no judgment in her voice. No disgust. "You know about that?"

"His car's at our place more often than not. Your bedroom door's always closed, and you guys are *awfully* quiet in there."

Cody's cheeks began to burn. "That doesn't mean—"

"Of course it does." She chuckled. "When it comes to kids, silence is way more suspicious than noise. Apparently that's true of teenagers too. And the fact that you're suddenly washing your sheets every weekend is hard to miss."

He waited, expecting accusations or a lecture, or maybe to be told how much of a pervert he was, but his mom was silent. "That's it?" he finally asked. "You don't want to yell at me, or tell me I'm a sick pervert, or that I'll get AIDS, or that—"

"Would you prefer that?"

"No, but—"

"I've met plenty of truck drivers like you over the years to know it ain't all bad." She took another drag of her cigarette before tossing the butt out the window. "At least you won't knock up some girl and be stuck here like the rest of us. I wish you were normal sometimes, but only because it'd be easier on you. In my experience, most men are pigs. They'll fuck with you and leave you broken and never look back. Kind of like that boy a few years ago." She shrugged. "But I guess there's plenty of men who'd say that about women, so it don't much matter what I think."

He didn't even care that she'd essentially called him abnormal. "You knew about Dusty?"

She turned toward him, her eyebrows up, as if to say, *Do we really need to go over this again?*

He thought about Nate, and about how hard they'd tried to hide their secret, even though they'd failed. "You told Mr. Bradford about Nate and me?"

"Not quite, but I imagine he'll figure it out soon enough."

Cody's headache was quickly escalating. He leaned back in the seat and tested the abrasion above his eyes. It stung like hell. "But what if he—"

"How Nate's dad handles it isn't my problem. I know that sounds harsh, Cody, but that boy isn't my concern. You are. If his dad tries to get the rest of the police department involved, it'll cause as much trouble for Nate as it does for you. And I've met Billy Jones's uncle before." Her voice was thick with contempt as she said his name. "I won't let some self-righteous hick who got his badge out of a Cracker Jack box try to lay this at your feet just because you're different. As far as I'm concerned, whatever's been happening in your bedroom isn't anybody's concern but your own. God knows the cops in this town ain't never done us any favors."

He closed his eyes, too stunned to speak, both by his mom's easy acceptance and her fierce protectiveness.

They were silent the rest of the drive. Once home, his mom took a bag of frozen peas out of the freezer and tossed them his way. "Knew I bought these for a reason. Put that on your eye."

He sank into one of their kitchen chairs and followed orders. It felt wonderful. He should shower and change out of his bloody clothes, but all he wanted to do was sleep.

"You hungry? I can make you dinner, long as you don't mind generic SpaghettiOs or tuna casserole."

"Tuna casserole sounds great."

"You got it." He had his eyes closed, but he tracked her footsteps across the kitchen to where he sat. "It isn't fair, is it?"

He could think of plenty of unfair things, but it was hard to say which one she meant. "What isn't?"

Her hand settled on his head, stroking his hair. It was something she hadn't done in ages. He'd forgotten how good it felt. "You've been so happy these last few months—happier than I've seen you since you were a boy—but nothing good can live in this town. It all gets stomped to dust in the end."

She kissed him on the head and walked away, and Cody sat there, his face stuck in a bag of frozen peas, thinking how he'd never appreciated his mom as much as he did right then.

CHAPTER
Twenty-One

*N*ate had been to the emergency room before. Granted, that had been in Texas, but he'd needed stitches once as a kid after falling off his bike and splitting his chin open, and he'd broken his arm in seventh grade, and needed stitches again in tenth grade after his cousin's dog bit him. He thought he knew what to expect. But this time, something was different.

"Don't you worry," the first nurse told him after taking his blood pressure and his temperature. "We're calling your dad right now." She handed him a hospital gown. "I'll go out. You undress and put that on, and lie down on the bed there. Then we'll get you cleaned up while we wait for the doctor."

Nate did as instructed, although undressing made his ribs hurt like hell. A few minutes later, the nurse came back, but before she could do much, one of the other nurses called her over. They stayed within sight as they whispered urgently, glancing toward him every few seconds. Another woman joined them—not a nurse, he didn't think, but maybe one of the women from the front desk—and soon they were all whispering, their eyes straying his way more often than seemed normal.

The nurse came back, but this time, her smile didn't seem quite so genuine. She began going through drawers, pulling out cotton balls and gauze pads and a bottle that he hoped wasn't plain old rubbing alcohol—that was bound to sting. Finally, she dug around in another cabinet and came up with a box of rubber gloves.

"Okay," she told him as she opened the box and pulled a couple of them out. "Let's take a look at those cuts on your face."

Nate watched her, puzzled. He knew from TV that doctors wore gloves for surgery, but in all his visits to the ER, he'd never seen them used. "What do you need those for?"

"Just being careful." She was careful, all right—careful not to meet his eyes as she said it.

"I'm not sick."

She gave him a tight-lipped smile. "One of the other nurses went to a symposium in Denver last month. She said they're recommending rubber gloves for everything now. Even sports physicals and dental visits. It's practically routine."

Practically. Except not really. Otherwise, she wouldn't have had to search for them.

She began cleaning the many cuts on his face, fumbling a bit with the bottles and tubes of ointment, obviously unused to having her work impeded by the gloves.

A cold little knot of dread began to form in Nate's gut. He had a sinking feeling he knew what was going on.

"I don't think you'll need stitches," she told him. "That's good news, right?"

"Right."

"The doctor will be in any minute now—"

She was interrupted by the arrival of his father. Nate didn't think he'd ever been so glad to see him.

"Jesus, Nate, what the hell happened?" his dad asked, once the nurse had gone.

"Just some of the guys from school." Trying to talk about it made it all come back to him—the terror and the shame and the pain—and he fought to keep his voice steady. "They slit the tires on the car so we'd have to walk, and then they were waiting for us in the empty lot behind the gas station. Cody tried to—" His dad scowled, and Nate stopped short. "What? Is Cody okay?"

"Better off than you, it seems." But his voice was strained.

"Can I see him?"

"I'm pretty sure he and his mom left already."

"Oh." Nate tried not to sound too disappointed. In some ways, it was just as well knowing Cody wouldn't have to see him dressed in a flowered hospital gown, with one side of his face swollen up like a balloon. Still, he was surprised Cody would leave without even saying good-bye.

"I told you not to hang out with him. I told you it would lead to trouble."

"You busting Brian's dad for cocaine possession didn't exactly help, you know."

"I told you. That had nothing to do with what you said about him."

"Well, try telling Brian that, why don't you? He was too busy kicking me in the kidneys to listen to excuses."

He was glad to see the doctor arrive. At least it would put an end to their argument. But rather than examine Nate, the doctor asked to speak with Nate's father. Again, they stepped away, staying within sight of Nate's bed, but moving far enough away to talk without Nate overhearing.

Nate watched them, waiting. He hurt everywhere. Now that the adrenaline had worn off, he wanted to cry from the pain. His stomach and his back and his face all ached. His face hurt the worst. But it all paled next to the shame he felt, watching them all whisper as they glanced his way. His dad became agitated once, raising his voice to say, "That's ridiculous! My son is not—" before they all shushed him. His dad's jaw clench, the color rising in his cheeks.

"Fine," he said at last. "Just do whatever the hell it is you need to do."

The doctor examined him at last, but not until he and the nurse had stopped to put on the stupid rubber gloves. They took X-rays and ran a slew of tests, all the while giving him that *look*. It was the same look he'd seen thrown Cody's way at school. The same look people had started to give him. He flashed back on his first conversation with Cody about it, and the way Cody had said, *"It's an STD. You even know what that stands for? Sexually. Transmitted. Disease."*

Nobody bothered to ask him if he'd actually had sex with Cody, or if Cody could possibly be infected. No. In a town as small as Warren, there were no secrets. One of the nurses or the receptionists had undoubtedly recognized Cody. Maybe she even had a son or daughter at Walter Warren High School. Somehow, she knew the rumors, and rumors were all it took to make those telltale rubber gloves come out.

Rumors were all it took to make his dad sit on the other side of the room, his jaw clenched tight.

In the end, they told him nothing was broken. They prescribed some mild painkillers, bed rest, and plenty of fluids, and gave his father a list of things to watch for in the coming days, then sent them home.

Nate sat in the passenger seat, an ice pack from the ER over one eye even though it was already swollen most of the way shut. His dad had a white-knuckled grip on the steering wheel. Nate didn't think he'd ever seen him so mad.

"There was never a girl, was there?"

Nate closed his one good eye and leaned his head against the passenger window. "No."

"You told me you were in love."

"I am."

"No, you're not! Whatever this is—"

"I know what I feel, Dad."

"You and Cody—" His words ended in a strangled choking sound.

Nate felt like he should apologize, but for what? For loving Cody? He wouldn't apologize for that. "I know you're disappointed. I know you're probably surprised. I was too, but—"

"Do you realize the risk you're taking? You could catch AIDS!"

"Not from Cody."

"You don't know that."

"Dad." He had to force the words past gritted teeth. "One of us would've had to have had sex with somebody else in order to catch it. Somebody who already had it. Somebody other than each other—"

"Shut up!"

Nate turned to look at his dad, stunned at the venom in his voice. "We don't even do what you're thinking about, and even if we did—"

"I said *shut up*! I don't want to hear about the sick things you do! I can't even look at you right now. I can't—" He shook his head. "We'll talk about it later. Once I've had a chance to talk to your mother. To calm down a bit. I don't know."

Nate was surprised his dad's rejection didn't hurt more. He felt like maybe he should cry, but he was out of tears, his heart a cold, hard lump inside his chest. It was just as well, anyway. Bad enough that his dad knew about Cody. Best not to have him think Nate a pansy too.

He went to his room as soon as they got home and stayed there, curled on his bed, listening to his dad's voice rise and fall as he talked on the phone. He wanted to talk to Cody, but there was no way that could happen. Not yet, at any rate.

He eventually fell asleep. He awoke in the darkness and slowly got to his feet.

He hurt even worse than he had before.

He surveyed the damage to his face in the bathroom mirror. His left eye was swollen shut, the other a livid shade of purple. His upper lip was split and swollen. Bruises stained his face from his forehead to his jaw. His rib cage hurt like crazy. Trying to pee brought tears to his eyes, and seeing the blood in the toilet was scary, even though the doctors had told him it might happen.

He changed into clean sweats and a T-shirt and peeked out his bedroom door. The house was dark and silent. His dad was in bed.

He snuck downstairs. It was two o'clock in the morning, but who knew when he'd have another chance? He took the phone off the cradle and crept into the pantry, closing the door behind himself. His heart pounded as he dialed Cody's number. It was entirely possible Cody's mom would answer. It was possible she'd yell at him for waking her up, or for getting her son in trouble, but he had to talk to Cody.

Cody picked up before the second ring. He didn't even say hello. Just, "Are you all right?"

"I'm fine."

"Don't lie to me."

"I'm peeing blood, I can't see out of one eye, it hurts to breathe, and my dad isn't talking to me." That about covered it. "How about you?"

"I'm fine."

"Now you're the one who's lying."

Cody made a sound that might have been a laugh. "My mom's actually being pretty awesome about the whole thing, but I feel like shit. This was all my fault—"

"Don't be stupid. It wasn't your fault. We just weren't thinking—"

"If I had fought harder—"

"You did the best you could."

"It wasn't enough."

It sounded like Cody was trying hard not cry, and Nate closed his eyes, holding his aching ribs. "It doesn't matter. It's over. I just wanted to make sure you were okay."

"I'm fine. They let me off easy, to be honest."

"I'm glad."

"I'm not," Cody said. Nate wanted to protest again, but Cody didn't give him a chance. "I have your calculus book."

Nate laughed, then regretted it. It made his ribs hurt. "A bit of late homework is the least of my worries."

"Nate, listen to me. We have to cool it. We can't let them see us together. You can't drive me to school anymore. You can't sit next to me in social studies—"

"Stop. Please. I'm not having this conversation right now. I wanted to hear your voice, but I don't want to argue."

Cody sighed. "Okay."

"I love you."

"Oh Jesus," Cody whispered, like some kind of prayer. "Nate . . ." Cody never said the words back. Nate had a feeling he'd never said them to anybody in his life. It didn't matter. He knew well enough how Cody felt. Even if he hadn't known already, he could hear it in Cody's voice.

"I'm supposed to stay home for a day or two, but I'll see you Friday, at the latest."

He felt Cody's reluctance in the silence that stretched between them. Nate understood. As tenuous as it was, the voice on the other end of the phone felt like the only thing they had.

"Cody?"

"Yeah," he said at last. "Okay. See you Friday."

Nate snuck back into the kitchen and put the phone on the cradle. He made a peanut butter sandwich, which he washed down with a glass of milk before going upstairs, brushing his teeth, and crawling into bed.

Despite everything, he felt better.

Cody'd been on the receiving end of ass-kickings before, so when he showed up to school on Tuesday with a black eye and a split lip, he was prepared for the curious stares and the whispers and the occasional snickers as the story of his humiliation spread through the student body.

What he didn't anticipate was the way a small but fierce group of people suddenly seemed to rally in his defense.

It started in PE, when two boys who'd never seemed to notice him before made a point of saying hi in the locker room. One of them even went so far as to ask Cody to be his partner in tennis. Cody was too stunned to do anything more than agree.

In metal shop, Jamie Simpson's younger brother silently picked up his project from the table he'd shared all year with Tom Watson and Billy Jones and carried it over to the open spot next to Cody. He didn't say a word the entire hour other than to ask Cody to pass him the pliers, but his steadfast scowl seemed to speak volumes.

The two Jennifers from Orange Grove stopped by his locker during a passing period, both of them looking embarrassed. "Nine on two's bullshit," one of them said quietly. "I don't care what they think you did."

They went back to ignoring him after that, but they seemed to be ignoring Brad and Brian and the rest of the Grove boys who'd been in the gang just as much.

At lunch, Jimmy Riordan and Amy Prescott, who had apparently become a couple at some point in the last few months, tracked him down and invited him outside for a cigarette with them.

"I would have warned you, if I'd known," Jimmy assured him as they smoked in a recessed doorway behind the gym, where they were sheltered from the wind. "I mean, a couple of weeks ago, Larry started making noise about teaching you a lesson now that Logan wasn't around to protect you, but I thought he was just talking out of his ass like he always does." He shrugged, ducking his head in embarrassment. "He hadn't said anything since then though, so I figured he'd forgotten about it. But I feel like an ass now for not telling you."

Cody wasn't really sure how he was supposed to respond. He settled for, "It's cool. It wasn't your fault."

"How's Nate?" Amy asked.

Cody took a drag off his cigarette to buy him time. He couldn't get the image of Nate's bloody, bruised face out of his head. Then again, it felt like some kind of betrayal to Nate to admit how bad they'd beaten him. "I imagine he's pretty sore today," he said at last. "But he'll live. He should be back at school later this week."

"That was just a chickenshit thing to do," Amy said. "Nine on two? Is that true?"

"Yeah," Cody reluctantly admitted. "It's true."

It made him feel like more of a wimp, having to talk about being beaten up, but as the day wore on, he grudgingly accepted that it was working in his favor. For the moment at least, whether or not he and Nate were gay seemed to have taken a backseat to the fact that it hadn't been a fair fight. This was Wyoming, after all. Two men beating each other up in the name of some backward idea of honor was one thing, but kicking the shit out of somebody who was vastly outnumbered? That apparently stank of cowardice. In a week or two, every student at Walter Warren High School might go back to calling him and Nate fags, but in the meantime, nobody was going out of their way to pat the bullies on the back. Lance Donaldson even stopped him after math, hanging this head a bit.

"I never should have gone along with it," he said. "Brad and Brian— Well, they made it sound more like they were just gonna scare your friend. I didn't really expect them to take it so far."

It wasn't quite an apology, and Cody wasn't sure he would have accepted it anyway, but he had to give the guy points for effort.

The last surprise came from Christine Lucero, who found him at his locker at the end of the day and threw her arms around his neck.

"Oh my God, my brother is such an asshole."

Cody could only stand there, stunned. Christine had always been decent to him, but she'd certainly never hugged him before.

She finally let go of him and stood back to meet his eyes. "Are you okay? Is Nate okay?"

"Uh—"

"Listen, I have the car today because Larry's at wrestling practice. How about if I give you a ride home?"

"You don't need to do that."

"I know I don't need to, but I want to. Besides, you practically live next door."

"Practically next door" was a bit of an exaggeration, since she lived in the more respectable part of the trailer park, but it was also true that it wasn't much out of her way. It occurred to him that she might just be leading him into another ambush, but he decided to give her the benefit of the doubt. Her disgust with her brother seemed genuine enough.

She led him through the parking lot to a gigantic, four-door Buick that had definitely seen better days. The upholstery on the ceiling had been stapled back into place every few inches, and hung in pillow-like squares between the staples, reminding him of the inside of a coffin.

"I'm sorry about my brother," she said as she started the engine.

"It's not your fault."

"I know, but still. I honestly don't know what his problem is. I mean . . ." She sighed and backed out of the parking space, not speaking again until they were headed toward the parking lot exit. "He hates living with our mom, and he's constantly saying how he's gonna go live with our dad. But our dad don't want us now any more than he did when we were kids, and I think it just makes Larry so mad that he doesn't know what to do. It's like the only thing he can think of to make himself feel better is putting other people down."

Cody frowned, considering her words as they turned toward the trailer park. "I guess I hadn't ever thought of that."

"You should hear him at home. He's always going on about the 'niggers' and the 'spics' and the 'ragheads' and the 'fags.' I mean Jesus, like it ain't bad enough we're trailer trash, barely making rent most months, then he has to go talking like that and make us look worse? And then to team up with those assholes from the Grove, as if they're his friends. As if they don't make fun of him when his back is turned. They don't like him any more than they like you. Only difference is, he kisses their asses." She kept one hand on the steering wheel and with the other, reached into her purse and pulled out a cigarette. She put it between her lips and pushed the car lighter. "You know why he hates you so much?"

Cody blinked, wondering if he was really supposed to answer that. "Because, uh, well . . ." He was debating how wise it would be to say, *Because I'm gay*. It felt like everybody knew by now anyway, but it still seemed scary to say it to anybody but Nate.

The lighter popped, and she pulled it out and held it to the end of her cigarette. "Two reasons," she said as she returned the lighter to its plug. "One: I think it pisses him off how you don't care what anybody says, you know? Like, he's trying so hard to make you realize he's better than you, in his mind at least, and you refuse to acknowledge it. And for some reason, he really needs for you to acknowledge it. And then when you and Logan started being friends . . ." They turned into the trailer park, and she slowed down, inching over the speed bumps. The car's shocks were shot to hell, and the back bumper slammed down onto each bump as they passed, no matter how slow she went. "Larry was always trying so hard to impress Logan, and the harder he tried, the more Logan didn't care, you know?"

"Uh, no. I had no idea."

"And that's kind of the second reason he hates you, I think."

"Because Logan and I were friends?"

"Well, yes and no." They drove under the tracks, and she stopped next to his mom's Duster. She threw the car in park, unhooked her seat belt, and turned to face him. "He'd kill me for saying this, but I almost think he had a crush on Logan. I mean, he'd never admit it, but Larry tried *so hard* to impress him, and it was almost too much. Like, there was this desperation there that I never quite understood. I'm starting to wonder if maybe he's more like you than he wants to admit."

Just when he thought she couldn't surprise him more, she went and said something like that. "You're saying you think Larry's gay?"

"I don't know." She shrugged, looking as if she regretted having said so much. "Maybe not. Maybe he's just desperate to fit in."

They fell silent. Outside, the wind blew through the trailer park, rushing across the bare plains. He could hear raised voices from inside Kathy and Pete's trailer.

"It explains about Nate, though," Christine said.

"What do you mean?"

"I mean, I invited him over one night before homecoming, when Larry and I were having a party. Took him into my room—"

Cody's heart clenched at the thought.

"—but he just freaked out. Went running out of there like somebody was chasing him."

"So, nothing happened?" He wondered if she could tell how much he hoped that was the case, not because there was anything wrong with Christine, but simply because he hated the thought of anybody else being intimate with Nate.

"He told me it was some religious thing, and then when he went to homecoming with Stacy, I thought maybe he was Mormon." She laughed and shook her head. "First time that's ever happened to me."

"You mean, first time a guy's told you no?"

"Exactly." She frowned and pushed her cigarette butt out the narrow crack in the window.

Cody pulled out his own pack of cigarettes, just so he'd have something to fidget with. "Can I ask you a question?"

"Sure."

"Doesn't it ever bother you, all the things people say?"

"You mean everybody calling me a slut?"

It seemed odd that he was the one blushing, but he nodded. "Yeah."

"Does it bother you? They talk about you just as much."

Fair point. He wanted to tell her no, but he felt like he owed her the truth. "It does sometimes. I try to pretend I don't care, and sometimes I can ignore it. But yeah, it still pisses me off."

She turned further toward him, curling one knee under her on the bench seat. The car continued to run, the engine a soft hum that couldn't quite drown out the shouting from Pete and Kathy's trailer. "It bothers me too, but not for the reasons you probably think."

She stopped, chewing her lip, and Cody waited.

"It's just unfair, you know? Logan probably had sex with half the girls at our school, and that was okay. Nobody ever had a bad thing to say about him. Brian Anderson's the same way. Brad Williams—hell, the day after I had sex with him, he quit talking to me altogether. Went from calling me twice a day and inviting me over and buying me little presents and telling me he loved me to pretending I didn't exist, just like that." She snapped her fingers. "Ever since then, he and Brian snicker every time they see me, like somehow I should be ashamed of screwing them, but they don't need to be ashamed of screwing me."

"Uh . . ." Cody hadn't ever thought of it in those terms before.

"And my brother. Hell, the only reason he ain't nailed every girl in the school is 'cause most of them have better taste than that. But even if he had, that'd be just fine, as far as everybody else is concerned, right? 'Boys will be boys,' and everybody just laughs about how they're sowin' their oats or whatever. Well who the hell do they think they're sowin' them with? Girls like me, that's who!" She shook her head. Her chin trembled a bit, but she bit her lower lip and took a deep breath. "So guys like Logan and Brad and Brian are just doing what boys are supposed to do, but me? I'm a slut, just because I ain't a total prude. Now, how come they get to do whatever they want, but I'm supposed to be a goddamn nun?"

"I don't know." He was too busy trying to take it all in. He'd always felt a bit bad for Christine, because he knew her dad was no better than his. He'd always thought she should be able to do better. It had never occurred to him how big the double standard was. "It is kind of shitty, now that you mention it."

She sighed, looking out the bug-spattered windshield at the distant highway. "Well, I guess that's how I feel about you and Nate, too. I mean, you guys are eighteen. You're about ready to graduate. Everybody expects that after high school, people will pair up and settle down and get married. Guys like Brad and Brian will have to quit nailing everything that moves, and I have one year left before I have to make some guy put a ring on my finger just so I can start popping out babies, whether I want them or not. And here's you and Nate, just minding your own business, not hurtin' anybody. Just, I don't know, being friends or being boyfriends or whatever you guys are. If one of you was a girl, nobody'd bat an eye. Hell, if you was both girls, people still wouldn't mind. They'd just assume you were best friends. But since you're both *guys*, and you're clearly not out banging all the girls you can land, they decide it's cool to jump you, nine on two. Like somehow that makes them so fucking tough." She shook her head and smiled at him. "The truth is, they're all just a bunch of goddamned douche bags, you know?"

It was said so frankly, in such a matter-of-fact tone, that Cody was reminded of Logan, and he laughed. "They really are." He opened the door, but stopped with one foot out. "Thanks for the ride."

"No problem. And Cody?"

"Yeah?"

"Tell Nate . . . Hell, I don't know what. Just tell him I hope he's back to school soon."

"I will." Cody didn't bother to tell her he was hoping the exact same thing.

CHAPTER
Twenty-Two

N ate's father skipped work the next day. Nate heard him downstairs, pacing the kitchen, talking on the phone for what felt like hours at a time. Nate's stomach grumbled angrily, wanting breakfast, but he stayed sequestered in his room, unable to face the confrontation waiting for him downstairs.

Eventually, his dad called him down for lunch, and later for dinner, but he never sat with Nate to eat. The only time he spoke was to ask Nate for the names of the boys involved. Other than that, he barely even looked at Nate, and Nate returned to his room each time, hanging his head.

His dad kept him home the next day too, and the day after that. Nate began to wonder if it was going to be like this from now on. It was like being in prison, only emerging from his room for meals. At least the physical pain from the beating was receding, the swelling in his face going down, and he hadn't peed blood again since that first night.

His body was healing, even if his heart wasn't.

On Thursday, Nate broke the silence.

"Is anything going to happen?" He was at the table eating the Hamburger Helper his dad had put down in front of him. His dad was at the other end of the kitchen, washing the dishes and pointedly ignoring Nate. "You asked for the names of the boys who jumped us. Did you talk to them or anything?"

His dad sighed, but didn't turn to face him. "There isn't much I can do. I'm not allowed to pursue it myself. I have to give it to one of the other officers, and in cases like this, it comes down to your word against theirs. And one of them has an uncle who works for the sheriff's office." He shook his head. "It's complicated. But the short version is no, it's being chalked up to boys being boys."

Nate considered that, staring at his dad's back. "You think I deserve it anyway, don't you? This is what I get for being gay?"

"I don't think you deserve it," his dad said quietly. "But, like it or not, sometimes things like this happen when you insist on being different."

Nate didn't ask anything else after that. He wasn't sure he could stand to hear the answer.

But on Friday, his father surprised him by coming into his room a bit after three. Nate had been lying on his bed, staring at the ceiling, listening to his copy of the tape he'd made Cody for Christmas. He sat up quickly, turning off the music. His dad sank heavily into the chair by Nate's desk.

"I'm sending you away."

That was it. One simple sentence dropped like a bombshell into the landscape of Nate's life. "I don't want to go."

"It isn't open for debate. I've made up my mind."

"Where are you sending me? Home to Mom?"

"No." There was something about the way he said it. Something about the tightness in his shoulders, and his hands, clenched in his lap. Nate's heart sank. He'd only had one stilted phone call with his mom since the night Greg had answered the phone, but he'd always assumed things would sort themselves once summer arrived and he went home for a visit.

"You talked to Mom, right?"

His dad's head jerked in an awkward nod.

"And?"

His dad sighed, shaking his head. "There's no reason for you to hear the things she said."

Nate swallowed, more hurt by that than he had been by the kicks he'd taken to his kidneys. "Was it that bad?"

"Well..."

Yes, it was that bad, apparently. Bad enough that even his father, who hated the thought of Nate's homosexuality, didn't want to repeat it. At least she wouldn't expect him to call home every week now. He tried to tell himself he didn't care.

"Nate, this is for the best. It really is."

"For who? For you?"

"For you. I've talked to your Aunt Cora." Cora, his dad's sister, who lived in Chicago. His dad had always jokingly called her a "pinko commie," which had nothing whatsoever to do with actual communism. It was simply his dad's way of saying Cora was a bleeding-heart liberal compared to him. "We've planned all along for you to go to Chicago after graduation. After what's happened, we think it's best if you go now. Cora's pretty open-minded about this kind of thing. She's been working all week to get you enrolled in school there. You'll be able to start on Monday, and graduation won't be a problem."

"Wow," Nate said, his voice flat. "Sounds like you've got it all worked out, whether I like it or not."

"I've already booked you on a flight. We'll leave first thing tomorrow—"

"I don't want to go. I don't want to leave—"

"You don't want to leave Cody, I know." His dad stood up and came to sit next to him on the bed. He put his hand between Nate's shoulder blades. It was such a warm, comfortable gesture, a lump rose in Nate's throat. "This isn't punishment, Nate."

"It feels like punishment to me."

His dad nodded. "I can understand that, but that isn't my intent, I promise."

"I'm not leaving."

"Nate, I know you think you love this boy—"

"I *do* love him."

His dad sighed and put his face in his hands. "It doesn't matter."

Nate's heart sank. "What do you mean?"

His dad sat up, squaring his shoulders, rubbing his hands over his head. For the first time, Nate noticed how thin his dad's hair was on top. He noticed the wrinkles on his dad's face, and the gray whiskers in his mustache. It was as if he'd aged ten years overnight.

Had Nate done that to him?

"The thing is," his dad said, his voice low and hoarse, "talking to your mom made me realize that maybe . . . well, maybe I overreacted."

It wasn't what he'd expected to hear. Nate had been prepared for a fight, not for something that sounded like surrender. "What do you mean?"

"I mean, I sat there, listening to the things she was saying—her and Greg both, because he was on the other line—she was talking about some kind of therapy, about camps she's heard about, and Greg said no stinking faggot was going to live under his roof, and then your mom started talking about military school—"

"Dad, no!"

"—and all I could think was, how can she turn on you like that? You're her son. She should take your side over Greg's. She should know how much you'd hate military school. I wanted to tell her she was being a terrible mother, but then I realized I'd done the exact same thing. And so I hung up, and I called Cora."

Nate couldn't believe what he was hearing. It hurt, finding out how his mom had reacted, but now his dad seemed to be having a change of heart? He was afraid to ask about that though, so he stuck to the facts at hand. "What did Cora say?"

"She said she always suspected you were . . . like that. Working real estate in Chicago, she's met all kinds of people. She has friends who are . . . well, who are like you, I guess. And so, I don't know, Nate. Maybe it doesn't matter that you're . . ." He choked, as if he could hardly stand to say the word. "That you're a homosexual."

Nate waited, his heart pounding, trying to figure out what this meant. "You mean, you're not mad anymore?"

"I am. A little. I don't know. Maybe a lot. But . . ." He sighed again, shaking his head.

"You're disappointed."

"A bit. But you have to understand, Nate, it isn't that I love you less. That's what I realized after talking to your mother. It might take me a while to get used to the idea, but you're my son. Nothing can change that."

The words brought a lump to Nate's throat. "Really?"

"I want you to be happy. That's the only thing that matters, but I don't see how this . . ." He stood up, holding out his hands as if to encompass Nate and his room and the entire situation in one gesture. "How can you ever be happy, knowing what people think? Knowing you can't ever get married or have kids? I mean, look at what comes from hanging around with a boy like Cody! Maybe if you met the right girl—"

"I don't think that would matter. And none of this is Cody's fault."

His dad sighed, his shoulders slumping. "That's what Cora said."

Nate waited, unable to think of anything to say that would make the situation any better. "If you're not mad, then why are you sending me away?"

"Because this town is no place for somebody like you. You can't live the life you want to live here. Maybe you really are gay, or maybe it's a phase, or maybe you'll meet a woman and realize what you're feeling right now is just curiosity. But whatever happens, you need to be in a place where there are options. Where you don't get beaten to a pulp just for being different."

In some dark corner of his heart, Nate knew his dad was right. He also knew arguing would get him nowhere. "What about Cody?"

"I know this isn't the way you wanted it to go, son, but I also know this: if what you have with that boy is real, it'll survive. If you leaving town ends it, it wasn't worth saving in the first place."

Okay. That made sense. It hurt, but it made sense. "Can I at least see him before I go?"

"I'll drive you over."

"He'll be at work until eight."

"Then I'll take you over at eight thirty. You can have twenty minutes."

It wasn't nearly enough, but it was better than nothing.

Cody spent the whole week trying to decide whether or not he should call Nate. On Wednesday afternoon, he decided it'd be safe enough. Nate's dad was usually working at that time. But when Mr. Bradford answered, Cody panicked and hung up the phone.

Each night, he stayed up a bit later, thinking Nate might call him after his dad had gone to bed, but he never did.

What if this was it? It was easy enough for Nate to talk about them being together forever when he was naked in Cody's bed, but now that it was out in the open, maybe he couldn't handle it. Maybe he couldn't stand to look in his dad's face and tell him he loved another boy.

When Nate didn't pick him up before school on Friday, Cody's heart sank. At first, he assumed Nate would be back at school, but had simply chosen not to give Cody a ride, but it didn't take him long to figure out Nate was still missing.

Not avoiding him, then, unless he was going so far out of his way to do it that he was ditching school completely.

After school, Cody walked to the Tomahawk, imagining all kinds of scenarios where Nate suddenly went back to ignoring him and hanging with those assholes from the Grove. Knowing he was being an idiot didn't stop the panic that began to fill his heart. He washed dishes that night feeling lonelier than he had in months, knowing Logan would never come to put the bowls on the high shelves, knowing Nate wouldn't be waiting to drive him home at the end of the night.

Business was slow, and Frank sent him home early. At eight thirty, he was sitting next to his mom on the couch, staring blankly at *Falcon Crest*, wondering if he'd at least hear from Nate over the weekend.

Lights flashed across their front window, followed by the unmistakable sound of tires on gravel as a car pulled up outside.

Cody glanced at his mom. She stared back at him, her expression saying, *I'm not expecting anyone. How about you?*

Cody got up and peeked through the curtains.

"It's Nate and his dad." Although so far, neither of them had moved to exit the vehicle. They were just sitting there, talking.

Cody's mom stood up and put her hands on her hips. "Does it look like he's here as a cop?"

"I don't know." But as he said it, Nate's dad gestured toward the trailer, and Nate got out of the Jeep alone. "No. I think it's only Nate coming in."

"Well, it was about time for me to get ready for work anyway." She grabbed her cigarettes off the table and headed for her bedroom. "I'll let you guys have a few minutes alone."

Cody might have been embarrassed if he wasn't so inexplicably nervous. He opened the door before Nate knocked. "Hey."

Nate stopped on the porch, glancing quickly toward his father. "You have a minute?"

"Of course."

Cody stepped back, his heart pounding. Nate followed him, closing the door behind him. Only then, with the door closed, did Nate turn and pull Cody into his arms.

He was shaking, and Cody clung to him, standing on his toes, holding Nate as tight as he could, wondering who was comforting whom.

"Are you okay?" Nate asked in his ear.

"I'm fine. What about you?" Cody pulled back to study Nate's face. The bruises were still visible, although they'd obviously faded. There was no swelling, but the cuts on his eyebrows and lip hadn't healed yet. Worse than the bruises was the look in Nate's eyes.

"I have to tell you something."

Cody's heart sank. His knees suddenly felt weak. He took a step backward, as if that could change whatever it was Nate was about to say. It was bad. He knew that much already. "What is it?"

Nate didn't let him retreat. He followed him, stepping close and gripping Cody's arms. "I know I told you I wouldn't go anywhere without you. I know I said I wouldn't ever leave you again, but..." His voice trembled, and Cody found himself wanting to pull away, not wanting to hear whatever it was Nate had to say. "I'm going to have to break that promise."

"No—"

"My dad's sending me to Chicago."

The words hung there between them while the only good thing in his life fell apart. "No. You can't go! You promised. You said—"

"I know! But it's only for now, Cody. It's only temporary—"

"I knew you'd do this! I knew you'd take the easy way out and leave me! I knew it!" Some part of his brain knew he was being unfair, but he didn't care. All he knew was that Nate was breaking his heart after promising not to, and Cody tried to push him away, fighting to keep from crying. "I knew I'd end up here alone in the end. I never should have believed you! I never should have trusted anything you said!"

Nate refused to let him go. He held on to Cody's arms, and Cody's rage seemed to wash away as quickly as it had come. It wasn't Nate's fault. He knew that, and he could tell by the tears welling up in Nate's eyes that he was grieving too.

"It doesn't change anything," Nate said, his voice hoarse. "All it means is, we arrive in Iowa City separately instead of together."

Cody shook his head. "But . . . I can't stay here without you. I can't . . ." He couldn't manage more than that without bursting into tears, and he didn't want to do that.

"Listen to me. Please? I only have a few minutes."

Cody nodded, letting Nate pull him close again. Letting himself be wrapped up in the familiar warmth of Nate's embrace.

"I don't know what will happen when I get to Chicago. My aunt's already enrolled me in school so I can still get my diploma. And you want to finish high school too. It'd be silly to quit now, with graduation only two months away."

Cody nodded. "May thirtieth." He said it into Nate's shoulder, his voice barely a whisper, but Nate seemed to have heard him, because he chuckled.

"Exactly. That means June first is a little soon, but July first seems doable."

Cody pulled back a bit so he could look up into Nate's face. "For what?"

"For us to meet in Iowa City."

Cody blinked, torn between wanting to believe and not wanting to have his heart broken all over again.

Nate put his hand against Cody's cheek and leaned closer, almost kissing him. "I mean it, Cody. July first, I'll be there. And I'll wait for you, either until you arrive, or until you tell me you don't want me anymore."

"No. That won't happen."

"Then you'll come?"

It didn't matter what Cody said because by then, Nate wouldn't want him anymore. He was positive. Nate would get to Chicago and meet somebody else, and by the time July first rolled around, Cody would be nothing but a memory.

"Cody?"

"I can't—"

"Yes, you can. I'm not giving up on us. I want you to tell me you aren't either."

Cody just shook his head, unable to speak past the lump in his throat. Nate was leaving. That was the only thing he knew. Nate was leaving him behind to die in Warren, just like Logan.

"Tell me you believe me."

"I don't."

"Then tell me how to convince you."

"I wish I knew."

Nate laughed—a strained, sad sound, but a laugh nonetheless. "I swear, you're as impossible now as the day I met you behind the stupid ICE cooler."

Cody almost smiled, remembering that moment. Remembering how he'd envied Nate's car and his house in the Grove and his ridiculous class ring.

And suddenly, he knew.

He took Nate's hand, glancing up to judge his reaction as he slid the ring off Nate's finger.

Nate shook his head. "Now I feel like an idiot. I probably should have thought of that ages ago."

Cody held it tight, not ready to put it on yet, but somehow feeling better, simply holding that piece of Nate in his hand.

Beeeep, beeeep.

The car horn cut into the moment, wiping the smiles from both their faces at once.

"I have to go."

Cody managed to whisper, "Okay."

"Tell me you'll be there. Tell me you'll meet me."

"I will." He'd walk all the way to Iowa if he had to. "I'll be there."

Nate pulled him close and kissed him, somehow putting all his sorrow and all his hope into that one simple gesture. And when he broke the kiss, Cody spoke quickly, wanting to finally be the one to say it first.

"I love you."

Nate's smile actually reached his eyes this time. "When it's dark enough, you really can see the stars." He touched Cody's cheek, kissed him one more time as the horn blared again outside. "I'll see you in July."

Cody waited until he was gone—until the taillights of the Jeep could no longer be seen—before slipping the ring on his finger. The fact that it fit perfectly seemed like a sign, and he was happy to find that his eyes were dry.

"Do you believe him?" his mom asked quietly from behind him.

"I believe he means it right now." He didn't look up from that sparkling blue stone. "But once he gets to Chicago . . ." He shook his head. There were just too many things that could go wrong. He was afraid to hope for too much.

"Better to stay skeptical and be pleasantly surprised than to get your hopes up and have him break your heart."

It seemed wise enough, but staring at Nate's ring, Cody realized one simple thing:

He wanted to believe.

CHAPTER

*T*he nearest airport was in Salt Lake City, approximately 270 miles away. At six o'clock on Saturday morning, Nate climbed into the passenger seat of his dad's Jeep, pulled out his Walkman, put on his headphones, and did his best to pretend his father didn't exist. His clothes and his most valued possessions—namely, his cassette collection—were in suitcases he'd take with him. His father would ship the rest once Nate arrived.

It wasn't until somewhere around Evanston that his dad took a deep breath and said, loud enough to be heard over Nate's music, "I'll keep sending your allowance, as long as you're still in high school."

Nate turned the volume down, in case his dad had more to say, but otherwise didn't answer.

"This isn't punishment, Nate."

"You said that."

"So, why the silent treatment?"

"Because no matter what you say, it still feels like punishment to me."

"Look, you don't want to be stuck with a kid like Cody anyway. He's a bad egg. He's—"

Nate cranked the volume on his Walkman, loud enough that it was a bit uncomfortable, although he'd never admit it. Loud enough that his dad could undoubtedly hear it from the driver's seat.

"All right!" his dad yelled. "Point taken."

Nate hit the Stop button and took off the headphones, letting them hang around his neck. "I wish you'd quit judging him based on who his parents are."

His dad grimaced, gripping the steering wheel and twisting it like he thought strangling it would help. They spent ten minutes like that—his dad glowering and Nate simply waiting—before his father spoke again.

"I have money set aside for you for school. Your mom and I have been saving it for years. Once you figure out which college in Chicago you're going to—"

"I'm not staying in Chicago."

His dad turned his head so fast, the car veered a bit to the right. "What?"

"I'll go there to finish high school, like we agreed. But that's it. I'm eighteen now, and once I have my diploma, I'm moving to Iowa City."

"*What*? Are you kidding me? What's in Iowa City?"

"Cody." At least, he would be. Eventually. Nate looked at the empty space where his class ring used to be. He'd had it on since his sophomore year. He hadn't realized how much he fidgeted with it until it wasn't there. He didn't mind, though. He hoped he never got used to having it gone.

"So you're just going to throw your entire future away over some boy?"

"They have schools in Iowa too."

"And how do you intend to pay for them?"

Nate swallowed, telling himself he shouldn't have been surprised. His dad had always said he'd pay for as much of Nate's schooling as possible. Now, it seemed that help was dependent upon him staying in Chicago. Or, more likely, dependent upon him not dating Cody. "I'll get a job and work my way through, if I have to." It'd take longer, but if other people could do it, so could he.

They checked in at the airport, and his father walked him to the gate. They still had half an hour before the flight boarded, but all the seats were taken, so they stood.

People milled past them, most of them excited about their travel. The smell of burning tobacco reached them from the smoking section. One couple who couldn't have been much older than Nate stood embracing each other, the woman openly crying, obviously counting down the minutes before they had to say good-bye. The overhead system was a constant loop of messages.

"Mr. Preston. Mr. Paul Preston. Please pick up a courtesy telephone…"

Nate wondered if his father was going to speak to him again at all, but he finally did.

"Why Iowa? Why can't he just meet you in Chicago?"

"Cody's lived his entire life in Warren. He's never even been out of the state. I think Iowa feels safer."

His dad pushed his hands into his jean pockets and rocked on his heels, staring down at the floor. "I want you to go to school. You'll do better if you have at least an associate's degree."

"I know, Dad. And I will. I'll just do it in Iowa instead."

"You won't get any help from me. If you insist on throwing away your future for a kid like Cody—"

Nate put his headphones back on and tuned out his father. When they called his boarding group, he picked up his carry-on bag and got in line. His father walked away without saying good-bye.

The flight was a little over three hours long. Three hours, with the man next to him chain-smoking and the lady on the other side telling him about her grandkids. Nate smiled and nodded and tried not to think about whether or not either of his parents would ever speak to him again.

He grew nervous as they landed and taxied to the gate at O'Hare. He hadn't seen his Aunt Cora in almost three years, but he was relieved to find he still recognized her on sight. She smiled and waved, and when he finally reached her, she hugged him warmly. She was far shorter than he remembered, and as if reading his mind, she laughed and said, "Boy, you've gotten tall."

"I guess."

Cora was several years older than his dad, with a petite build and shoulder-length blonde hair that hadn't yet started to gray. She'd been married once, but she'd been divorced for as long as Nate could remember.

"I'm sure you're hungry," she said, as they waited for his bags. "What do you want for dinner? We could order pizza, or I can cook. Anything you've craving?"

"Fried okra and collard greens."

She laughed. "You can take the boy out of the South, but you can't take the South out of the boy."

"If it's too much trouble—"

"I haven't cooked collard greens in years, but Army & Lou's isn't too far out of the way. We'll grab some takeout."

The restaurant smelled like heaven, and Nate's stomach grumbled as they waited for their food. His mouth watered all the way back to Cora's house, his lap warm from the contents of the takeout bag. Cora kept up a constant stream of chatter, pointing out landmarks. But it wasn't until they were sitting across the kitchen table from each other, with the remains of the best Southern feast Nate had eaten in months laid out between them, that she finally said, "Okay, Nate. I know what your dad has planned for you. Now why don't you tell me what *you* have planned for you."

Nate debated, popping another piece of fried okra in his mouth and chewing it slowly. His father had said Cora was open-minded. Still . . .

"Okay," she said. "How about you tell me about Cody."

There was no judgment in her voice, and her expression remained open and friendly. "Really?"

"Really."

"What did my dad say?"

She waved her hand dismissively. "Oh, I don't know. Something about bad eggs and foolish boys and reckless decisions." Nate's cheeks began to burn, but Cora smiled and leaned her elbows on the table. "Did you ever hear the story of Mr. Spangler's station wagon?"

"Who?"

"Mr. Spangler. He was our parents' neighbor when your dad was in high school. He was friends with our parents. They lived in Bossier City at the time, not far from the base. Most of the neighborhood was Air Force families, and they all knew each other. They'd get together for cocktails or whatever. Anyway, when your dad was eighteen, he didn't have his own car, but Mr. Spangler had this old station wagon he didn't use much, and sometimes, he'd let your dad borrow it."

"I think I remember him mentioning it."

"Well, I was off at college, but your dad was a senior at Barksdale High, and the drinking age was eighteen there, of course. So for spring break, your dad asked to borrow Mr. Spangler's car for the night. Said he and his friends were just going out for a few hours. But instead, they loaded up a bag of peanut butter sandwiches and a cooler full of beer and . . ." she leaned forward conspiratorially, grinning, "they drove to Mardi Gras for the entire week."

Nate sat back, stunned. "No way."

"Way."

"But Bossier isn't all that close to New Orleans, is it?"

"It's about a five-hour drive."

Nate laughed. "I take it he missed curfew."

"By a long shot. At first, my parents were freaked. They thought he'd just gone out and not made it home, like maybe he'd wrecked the car or something. But then they found a note he'd left saying he'd be back the next weekend."

"Did they have a place to stay or anything?"

"Nope. Not a thing. They slept in the car and drank like fish and ran out of peanut butter sandwiches before the end of the week, and came home smelling like vomit and stale beer, but they survived."

"I can't believe that! Dad's always so . . . I don't know, so serious and responsible."

She laughed and reached for her glass of Coke. "Maybe now, but not when he was eighteen, no matter what he tries to tell you." She took a sip of her drink and set it back down. "I have a feeling your plan isn't anywhere near as reckless as that. So tell me, Nate."

He did. And when he was done, his aunt smiled. "Okay. First thing's first. You start school on Monday, but once you get home, you can call information. Get the number for the Iowa City newspaper, then call and request a subscription for the next month or two. That way, you can start looking for jobs. I have plenty of real estate connections there. I'll make some calls, see if I can't find you a place where the landlord won't freak about two boys in a one-bedroom place."

"You'd do that for me?"

"Sure. You can take the car on my days off and drive out there. Maybe I'll even go with you. It's only three and a half hours. We can check out the schools and see what you need to enroll. Eventually, you'll need a car. Or a bike, at the very least, depending on how far it ends up being from your apartment to work and school. But for now: graduation, job, apartment, college, in that order." She held her hands up, smiling. "I don't see any reason it can't work."

"Really?" It was funny how hearing those words from an adult seemed to make a world of difference. "What about my dad?"

She leaned across the table and patted his hand. "Don't you worry. All he needs is a bit of time."

Nate wished he could believe her.

Nate found a job working evenings and weekends at a Baskin-Robbins within walking distance of Cora's house. Each weekday, he caught the city bus to school, grateful that it ran on time, and that a student pass was cheap. His new high school was enormous—bigger even than the one he'd attended in Austin—and Nate loved it. With a student body almost as big as the entire town of Warren, nobody cared about one new kid. He kept his head down, did his work, and walked away with a diploma. He didn't bother to attend the ceremony—his dad couldn't get the time off work, his mom wasn't talking to him, and it seemed silly to expect anybody else to travel that far just to hear his name called—but he sent out announcements at Cora's insistence, and to his surprise, money began flooding in. Relatives he barely remembered sent him five-, twenty-, and fifty-dollar bills.

Cora just smiled and said, "Told you the announcements would pay off."

He talked to his dad weekly. The conversations started out awkward, but gradually began to feel normal. Graduation weekend, his dad surprised him by telling him he'd try to bring his truck to him before winter. Nate would have preferred his Mustang, but his dad insisted he'd need four-wheel drive in Iowa as much as he had in Wyoming. He also told Nate he'd still help pay for school.

"That's what the money was always supposed to be for," he said. "I guess it doesn't matter if the school's in Iowa or Chicago, as long as you go."

Nate increased his hours at the ice-cream shop, saving as much of his pay as he could. The Iowa City newspaper arrived daily, and

Nate carefully went through the want ads, circling any job that looked promising.

Eventually, he drove there with Cora. They scoped out the community college and picked up an application package, along with a map of the town, and she introduced him to the man who would eventually be his landlord. He was thin and slightly effeminate, but his smile was warm and friendly.

"I think half the gay men in town live in this apartment complex," he told Nate. "It's not quite Boystown, but nobody'll give you trouble."

Nate filled out job applications, feeling like each one he handed in was a little ray of hope.

The pieces began to fall into place. The only thing missing was Cody.

Nate mailed letters at least twice a week, pouring his excitement into them, hoping to infuse Cody with the same bright optimism. At first, Cody answered, but it wasn't long before the letters stopped completely. Nate's heart grew heavy every time he checked the mail. He called Cody once, with his aunt's permission, since the call was long-distance. Cora had a bright-orange metal stool next to the phone made from an old tractor seat, and he perched on it, his heart in his throat as he waited for Cody to answer, sure that Cody had changed his mind about everything.

Cody said all the right things, but the words sounded false. Nate knew he was lying. He knew something was wrong. The only part of the conversation that rang true was at the end.

"I love you," Cody said, his voice so quiet, Nate assumed he was trying to keep his mom from hearing. "I really do."

Nate closed his eyes, hanging on the words, glad to know that this at least hadn't changed. "I'll see you in July, right?"

"I hope so," was the only answer he got.

Any time he had a day off and Cora didn't need her car, he drove to Iowa City, and finally, early in June, it all paid off. He found a job at a video store, and put down a deposit on a one-bedroom apartment. He worried he was doing it all for nothing—that Cody would never join him after all—but he tried to hang on to hope.

And that very same day, he received a letter from Cody.

It was the first one in two months, and Nate's heart burst into gear. His hands shook as he tore open the envelope. He was thrilled to finally hear from Cody, but he dreaded reading what he said. He had a sinking feeling it contained bad news.

> Nate,
>
> I suck at this long-distance thing, I know. I'm sorry. I think about you all the time, but every time I try to write, I realize I have nothing good to say. You send me happiness, and I hate the idea of sending you anything less than that, but there isn't much of it here to go around.
>
> Our phone doesn't work anymore. I thought you should know that. The number for the pay phone at the gas station is 307-798-6543. I know you can't call very often, but I'll be there every night at seven just in case. Seven my time, I mean. I think that's eight for you.
>
> I know you're probably mad at me for not writing more often, but keep sending the letters, please. I miss you like crazy. It's just hard to hang on to hope in a place like this.
>
> Cody

Nate breathed a sigh of relief. Cody still loved him, then, but something was obviously wrong. It was time Nate found out what it was.

CHAPTER

For two wonderful weeks after Nate's departure, Cody thought maybe the world was finally cutting him some slack.

He had a plan. Shortly after Nate's dad shipped him off to Chicago, Cody fed the gas station pay phone two dollars and called the Greyhound depot in Rawlins to check on prices and schedules.

He almost had enough for the ticket. All he had to do was keep saving money, finish high school, then have his mom drive him to the bus depot.

It seemed so simple.

He quit smoking altogether, even though the cravings at lunch were almost enough to drive him mad. He picked up every shift the Tomahawk could give him, and even started working a few hours in the kitchen, plating up salads and chopping vegetables. The staff dwindled as more people moved away from Warren. Business waned. The entire establishment felt doomed, but Cody only had to make it to June.

People at school had mostly gone back to ignoring him, with the exception of Jimmy, Amy, and Christine, but he didn't mind that one bit. Christine asked about the ring on his finger once, but if anybody else noticed, they kept their opinions to themselves.

Cody was counting the days to May thirtieth, keeping his eye on the prize. Several times a week, he dreamed that he showed up at graduation in his cap and gown, only to be told there'd been a mistake and he had to do his senior year all over again. The anxiety made him more dedicated to his schoolwork than he'd ever been in the past.

He wasn't about to let a bad grade in English come between him and Nate.

But for better or worse, he was still in Warren, Wyoming, where nothing good could last.

Early in April, as a warm wind from the south brought promise of summer, the Tomahawk closed its doors for good. Logan's uncle explained in a quiet monotone what they'd all known: business had been waning for too long. Cody knew it was true, but he was also pretty sure the real issue was that Logan's parents couldn't bear to stay in Warren now that both of their children were gone. Five days later, they'd already packed up and left. A For Sale sign in the front yard of their Orange Grove home was the only thing left to prove Logan and Shelley Robertson had ever lived there.

And just like that, Cody was out of a job.

Four days later, as his mom drove home from the truck stop in the wee hours of the morning, her car sputtered to a stop on the shoulder of I-80. She walked half of the fifteen miles back to Warren before somebody from town recognized her and gave her a ride the rest of the way, at which point she plopped down on the couch, looking tired and wrinkled and far older than she had when she'd left.

"What the hell are we going to do?" she asked. "I can't afford to have it towed, let alone fixed, and I sure as hell can't afford to buy a new one."

She didn't say the rest, but Cody didn't need her to. Without a car, she had no job. The pile of bills on the counter grew a bit each day, her fine for solicitation still needed to be paid, and they now had zero income between them.

They scoured the town in search of work, but there were simply no jobs to be had. The oil and coal booms were long gone, leaving vacant houses and empty businesses. Sometimes it felt like half the town was unemployed, and while Cody knew the numbers couldn't be quite that high, he also knew there were several people sleeping on benches in the park. No work and no money meant plenty of discontent. The bar on the edge of town seemed to be the only place still making money, and the police were the only people who stayed busy.

Warren was dying, and Cody had no desire to go down with the ship, but he needed to leave in order to make money, and he needed money in order to leave.

"If the world didn't suck, we'd fall off," his mom said to him one night.

Cody was beginning to think falling off wouldn't be so bad.

Nate sent letters full of light and sunshine and love, promising that once they made it to Iowa City, everything would be okay, but Cody felt his hope drying up like the grass on the wind-blown plains. He'd promised himself when he said good-bye to Nate that he'd walk to Iowa if he had to, but that was easier said than done. Rawlins was a hundred miles away. It'd take him more than twenty-four hours to walk to the bus station. He'd need food and water, and a place to stay along the way. There were probably rest stops, but did he really want to sleep on a picnic table, with the last of his cash in his pocket and using all his worldly possessions as a pillow?

And what about his mom? That was the other question that haunted him as he lay awake in the night. Without him, she'd have nobody to help her pay the bills. Then again, without him, she'd have one less mouth to feed. Was he helping her by staying, or only making things worse?

He didn't want to tell Nate how bad things had become. Maybe it was foolish. Maybe it was wrong. But Nate's letters were so bright and full of promise, and all Cody had to send back was confirmation that he and his mother were both trash, unable even to pay their bills.

He quit writing to Nate altogether.

Graduation arrived, although Cody didn't participate. Renting the cap and gown cost money, and there was nobody to cheer for him but his mom. He told himself it didn't matter. He'd graduated. He had a diploma. Walking down the aisle didn't actually mean anything.

Except, of course, it did. Somehow, even with his diploma in his hand, he still felt like a failure.

On June first, the phone company discontinued their service due to lack of payment. Although Nate had only called him once since leaving, Cody felt the loss like a hole in his chest. The phone line had been a tenuous connection to his future, and now it was gone. He wrote down the number for the pay phone at the gas station and sent it to Nate in a letter, promising that he'd be there every night at seven o'clock, just in case Nate was able to call.

It felt stupid, but what else could he do?

He and his mom pooled their money to pay the more urgent of the bills. He still had enough for the bus fare, but only barely. On June tenth, he worked up the nerve to knock on Christine Lucero's door and ask her for a ride to Rawlins.

"I would if I could," she said, sounding sincere, "but my car broke down last week." And a few more minutes talking to her was all it took to find out that Jimmy Riordan and Amy Prescott had already left town, headed for new jobs and a new life in Montana.

Cody wasn't the only one desperate to leave Warren. He wished he'd thought to ask them for a ride earlier. Now, there was nobody left for him to ask.

On June twelfth, he stood by the pay phone at the gas station, wanting a cigarette so badly he could hardly stand it. He hated to spend the money, but at this point, what was the point in saving it? He had no hope of getting to Rawlins, let alone Iowa City.

And then, the phone rang.

Nate had waited to call Cody until he had everything in place—the job, the apartment, his new address and phone number. And then he perched on the metal stool with the tractor seat in Cora's kitchen, and watched the clock, waiting for eight o'clock. Finally, he picked up the phone and dialed the number. He held the handset to his ear, his heart pounding.

He felt like everything in the world could be made right, if only Cody would answer.

"Hello?"

It was Cody's voice, although there was a hollowness to that one word that made Nate pause. "It's me."

He heard nothing but the *shhhhh* of the Wyoming wind against the mouthpiece. Nothing else. No answer at all.

"Are you there?" he asked.

"Yes."

Nate laughed, shaking his head, picturing Cody at the gas station where they'd first met, trying so hard to be tough. "I've been counting the minutes until I'd hear your voice, and you're going to make me work for every word, aren't you?"

Cody took a shaky breath. "It's not that. It's just, I have no idea what to say. And I think maybe I need to hear your voice more than you need to hear mine."

And Nate could believe it. Cody sounded so small and so fragile that Nate feared the wind would carry him farther away like some metaphorical tumbleweed.

"I have good news. I found a job, and a place to live. The landlord's nice. He says the whole complex is 'gay friendly,' which sounds stupid as hell, but it's good to know, right? My aunt's going to drive me out there tomorrow. I won't be able to afford long-distance service, which is why I had to call tonight. And I can't talk long, because it'd be rude to run up her bill. But I wanted to tell you in person. Or, you know—" He laughed. "Not in a letter, at least."

"I understand."

"You're still planning on meeting me there, right?"

"If I can."

And then, more silence.

"I know something's wrong. I can tell. And for some reason, you don't want to tell me. You think you have to handle it all yourself, but you don't."

No answer except the wind.

"Cody," Nate said, feeling like he was pleading, like he was trying to urge a scared kitten down from a tree, "talk to me. Please."

For a second, he thought it hadn't worked. He was almost starting to feel angry that he'd gone to such lengths to call Cody only to listen to the wind, but then Cody took a deep breath and started to talk.

"The Tomahawk closed back in April. My mom lost her job a week later. All the bills are past due, and my mom still owes money to the state, but there's nothing here. No jobs at all. We've tried all over town, but there's nothing. I put my name on a list at the unemployment office—they say there are usually house-painting jobs in the summer, but there are at least twenty names ahead of mine, and I might be able to mow a lawn or two, but that won't be more than a few dollars, and the phone's been shut off, and the electricity will be next, and I could pay part of them, but not all, and if I do, I won't have any money left at all. As it is, I have just enough for a bus fare, but it's a thirty-hour walk to Rawlins, and we don't have a car anymore, and, Jesus, of course I want to meet you there. You have no idea how much I miss you, or how bad I want to get away from this godforsaken town, but I can't, Nate. I just— I have no idea what to do. I don't think I can get there, no matter how much I want to. It's just like I've always said. There's no escape from Warren."

He finally stopped, as if he'd run out of gas, or run out of words and hope at the same time, and Nate leaned his head back against the wall, twirling the cord around his finger. He'd used a big chunk of his cash putting down a deposit and first month's rent on the apartment. He couldn't afford to use any more of his savings now, and he wouldn't get money from his dad until fall, and even then he'd have to use it for school, but he refused to give up hope. Graduation money was still trickling in, and he could work full-time over the summer. Somehow, he'd make it work.

"Cody, listen to me: we'll find a way. It may not be by July first like we'd hoped. But as long as you still love me—"

"I do." It wasn't much more than a whisper, but Nate thought he could hear Cody's whole heart beating in those two words. "I do."

"Then we'll figure it out, okay? I promise you we'll find an answer."

"Okay."

"Do you believe me?"

"I want to."

Nate sighed. "I guess that'll have to do."

They talked a few more minutes, long enough for Nate to give Cody the address and phone number for the apartment in Iowa City. They hung up, and Nate sat there, staring at the empty space on his finger, debating.

He wouldn't have to ask for much. Certainly not for money.

All Cody needed was a ride to Rawlins.

Nate took a deep breath, gathering his courage, and picked up the phone one more time.

CHAPTER
Twenty-Five

ody wasn't sure if he felt better or worse after talking to Nate. It'd been good to hear his voice, and his promises, and to hear him say "I love you" a couple more times. At the end of the call, he'd made Cody write down the address and phone number of the apartment in Iowa City. Cody had left the receiver hanging from the cord while he'd run into the gas station to borrow a pen and a bit of paper from Vera. He looked at it as he walked home, trying to imagine how it would feel to know that address and phone number belonged to him.

"Well, he must have called tonight," his mom said when he got home. "You were gone longer than usual."

"He did."

"And?"

She was on the couch, and he sank into their threadbare armchair. "He found a job in Iowa City, and an apartment, and . . ."

"And all you have to do is get there?"

"Yes. But that's easier said than done." But even as he said it, an idea came to him.

The truck stop.

It made his stomach do terrible, twisting things, but it was an option he hadn't considered.

The truck stop was only about thirty miles away. A long walk, for sure, but he could do it in a day. And once he got there, he could find a ride to Rawlins. It might mean hitchhiking, or begging. It might mean . . .

It might mean doing other things.

Even if he made it to Rawlins, he barely had enough for the bus ticket, let alone food along the way. He needed the money, and the truck stop provided a scary yet very real possibility. His mom had done it, from time to time. He could do it too, if he had to.

Maybe.

He thought about it, his heart heavy with dread.

Handjobs wouldn't be so bad, but did men ever pay for those? Blowjobs seemed more likely. He'd only ever done that for two people in his life. Giving one to a stranger would be scary, but probably only the first few times.

And if they wanted more?

He swallowed hard, closing his eyes, trying to imagine it. It probably hurt the first time. Just the thought was enough to turn his stomach. But the potential pain wasn't the worst part. The worst part would be the risk. He and Nate were both safe as long as they only fooled around with each other, but if he did what he was considering, he'd be opening himself up to all kinds of horrible possibilities. He could insist on condoms, but even those weren't foolproof, and anything he ended up with—AIDS or herpes or who knew what else—would be passed on to Nate.

He'd be playing Russian roulette with both their lives in exchange for . . . what? A few dollars? How much did one charge for things like that anyway?

His mom watched TV while Cody went back and forth in his head for nearly an hour about the wisdom of his plan. Part of him believed he might be able to find a truck driver heading east who wouldn't mind driving him the few miles from the truck stop to Rawlins with nothing asked in return. But the more realistic part of him knew it might be a lot more complicated than that.

He couldn't quite decide if he was that desperate yet or not.

He was startled out of his reverie by the sound of tires on the gravel as a car passed under the train tracks and into the Hole.

Not just any car, either. As the car braked to a stop outside their trailer, Cody's heart burst into speed.

That was Nate's Mustang. He was sure of it.

Some stupid part of him lit up, wishing it was Nate, but knowing it wasn't. Still, he rushed to the front door and opened it to find Nate's dad looking back at him, his hand raised and ready to knock.

Not dressed as a cop, though. He was wearing regular clothes.

Cody was uncomfortably aware of the cluttered trailer behind him, reeking of cigarette smoke, and of his ratty jeans and rattier shirt, and his messy hair. He tried to smooth it down.

Nate's dad gave him a nervous smile, and despite his bushy mustache, he looked so much like Nate when he smiled that Cody almost found himself smiling back.

"Can I come in?" Mr. Bradford asked.

Cody looked behind himself at the dirty dishes and laundry and his mom, who was watching them with a scowl, obviously expecting the worst. "How 'bout if I come out instead?"

"Fair enough."

Cody followed him down the rickety steps and over to the Mustang. It was a warm evening, even with the sun beginning to set. Nate's dad leaned back against the driver's door and crossed his arms as he studied Cody. Cody waited, while the wind whistled across the plain and gusted between the crumbling trailers of the Hole.

Finally, Nate's dad sighed and dropped his arms. "I guess we've never quite met. Not on civil terms, at any rate." He held out his hand. "I'm Bruce."

Cody blinked, hoping he didn't look as surprised as he felt. "Cody," he said, shaking Bruce's hand. "But you know that already."

Bruce let him go and returned to leaning against the Mustang. "Are you going to Iowa City to be with Nate?"

"I want to."

"When?"

"As soon as I can, I guess."

"Nate said you might need a ride to Rawlins."

Nate had said that? Nate had talked to his father? Not only that, he'd sent his father to give Cody a ride? "Uh . . . yeah. To the bus station. That's the closest one, other than Rock Springs, but the ticket's a bit less from Rawlins since it's closer to Iowa."

"Do you have money?"

Cody hesitated. "A bit."

"How much?"

Cody tried not to bristle at the question. "Enough for the bus fare." Barely.

"And after that?" Bruce asked. "Enough to eat?"

"I figured I'd take a couple of sandwiches with me." Plus, he was used to being hungry. He just had to get to Nate. After that, he'd figure it out.

Bruce sighed scuffed the toe of his loafer in the dirt. "You're all he talks about. It drove me crazy at first, but now . . ." He shook his head, studying Cody like he couldn't quite figure him out. "It's like he lights up every time he says your name. I don't even have to see him to know it. I can hear it in his voice."

It made Cody smile. He didn't care that it was Nate's dad saying it. He couldn't even find it in himself to be embarrassed. All he could feel was incredible joy at those words. "I know exactly how that feels." And he knew he sounded like a damn fool saying it, but he didn't care.

Bruce sighed again, staring up at the sky as if it held answers, and Cody realized he was fighting tears. Bruce took a deep, shaky breath before he met Cody's gaze again. "This disease. AIDS. It's rampant, and it's a death sentence. You know that, right?"

"Yes."

"You've been paying attention? You know how it's spread?"

"I do."

"You understand that you'll be putting yourself at risk? Both of you?"

"No." Because it wouldn't be like that—the bathhouses and the anonymous sex and the hustlers. It wouldn't be like that at all. It would be him and Nate. "Not as long as it's just us. We'll be fine."

Bruce nodded, looking away from Cody again to wipe his eyes. "Promise me." His voice strained against the tears he refused to let Cody see. "Promise me that you'll both be very, *very* careful. Promise me you won't take risks or get carried away and do something reckless. Because I can get used to the two of you being together. I really can. But I can't face watching my boy die because one of you did something stupid."

Cody couldn't believe it. Bruce didn't hate him. He didn't want to keep them apart. He just wanted them to be safe, and with AIDS tearing like wildfire through the gay communities, who could blame him for worrying?

He wanted Cody to promise they'd be safe. That they wouldn't take risks. For himself, it was easy to commit, but could he make that promise for Nate? Could he tell Nate's dad with a straight face that he and Nate would be together forever, for the rest of their lives, with nobody else ever coming between them?

No. He couldn't promise him a lifetime. But he could promise it for now.

"We'll be safe," he said. "I promise."

Bruce nodded, still refusing to meet Cody's eyes. "There are maps in the glove compartment. I marked out the best route. Don't speed. Pull over when you get tired. Don't sleep overnight at rest stops unless you have to, and if you do, park under a light and lock your doors. Do you understand?"

No, he didn't. He didn't understand what was happening at all, but Bruce didn't wait for Cody to answer. He reached out and took Cody's hand, and he placed the car keys in Cody's palm.

"Nate needs his car. And you need a ride. This seems like the obvious solution." He let go, and Cody stared down at the keys, feeling stunned.

Was Nate's dad really giving him Nate's car?

"Tell my son I love him," Bruce said. "No matter what."

Cody made his way back up the porch steps to his front door, still stunned by Bruce's gift. He'd offered him a ride back to his house in the Grove—it seemed like the least he could do—but Bruce had just smiled and said, "Seems like a good night for a walk. I could use the exercise."

And now here Cody was, with the keys to Nate's Mustang in his hand.

"What was that about?" his mom asked as he stepped back inside.

Cody looked around at the shabby, run-down trailer that had been his home for as long as he could remember. There'd been a house once, when he was just a baby and his parents were still together, but he only knew about it from a few faded photographs. This narrow, cramped space was all he'd ever known. It suddenly felt safe, and the rest of the world seemed incredibly huge and scary.

Cody sank into the armchair. "He gave me Nate's car."

His mom blinked, looking as stunned as he felt. "He what?"

"He said I can drive it Iowa. To be with Nate."

Her fingers flew to her lips, her eyes wide. "I can't believe it."

"Me neither. I mean—" The more he thought about it, the less sense it made. "Why would he do that? He must realize Nate could do better. He must know that, right? Why would he want somebody like me—"

His mom came off the couch, closing the distance between them quickly.

"No." She shook her head, perching on the edge of the coffee table and cupping his face in her hands. It was such a wonderful gesture—so simple, and yet so maternal, that Cody was suddenly fighting tears. "Don't you start believing the things people say. You've been told your whole life that you're a no-good kid, but it isn't true. Bad kids lie and steal and cause trouble, but you've never done any of those things. The only thing you've ever done is had the bad luck to be born to two lousy parents in a place that can't accept you for who you are. You're a good kid who's been dealt a bad hand. You're the only decent thing I've ever managed to create. You're better than you know, Cody. You're better than this whole goddamned town, and if you have a ticket out of here, you take it. You take it, and you run as fast as you can, and don't ever, ever look back."

"Mom . . ." He didn't know what to say. He had no way of telling her how much it meant to hear those words from her. "What about you? All the bills and the rent, and there aren't any jobs in Warren. How will you—"

"Don't you worry about me."

Cody still thought it might be wrong to leave her, but the surety that he'd never have a chance like this again kept him moving forward as he packed his few things. It wasn't until midway through the next day that his mom stopped in the doorway to his room, leaning against the doorframe as he sorted through the last of his clothes.

"Maybe I could go with you," she said. "Just as far as Cheyenne?"

"To your sister's house?"

"I took a chance and wasted two bucks at the pay phone. She thinks she can get me a job cleaning rooms with her at the Best

Western. Says I can stay with her for a couple of weeks, till I find something I can afford."

He found himself smiling, glad that he wouldn't have to leave her in Warren. "It'd be nice to have some company, part of the way, at least."

It cost him a few extra days, but he didn't mind the delay. Not too much, at any rate. It seemed like the least he could do for his mom, who needed time to close all their accounts and pack her own things. He had nightmares nearly every night where some shadowy figure appeared at the front door and told them they weren't allowed to leave.

But they did.

They opted to leave their furniture behind—none of it was worth saving anyway. Half their stuff was packed in garbage bags instead of suitcases, but who cared anyway? Five days after being handed the keys to Nate's Mustang, Cody and his mom climbed into it and left Warren, Wyoming, behind forever.

It was the best feeling in the world.

re you sure you don't want to spend the night?" Cody's mom asked him that afternoon, after they'd finished unpacking her bags from the car. "You could make it the rest of the way to Iowa City tomorrow."

It was true that staying in Cheyenne would have saved him a night in a hotel, but it also would have left an eleven-hour drive for the next day, with the change in time zones working against him.

Besides, he was ready to get the hell out of Wyoming.

"I'm sure."

And there, on the front step of his aunt's duplex, with the wind blowing only a bit less than it did in Warren, his mom hugged him for the first time in ages. He couldn't have said when the last time had been. It felt good. He was glad she was getting a new start on life too.

"Take care of yourself," she said, stepping back to meet his eyes. "And be careful."

"You too."

He climbed back into the Mustang and waved good-bye. And then there was nothing but him, a handful of beaten-up eight-track tapes that reminded him of Nate, and a long, straight ribbon of road. Every mile marker Cody passed seemed to take a bit of weight off his shoulders.

He stopped for the night in North Platte. His motel room was tiny and reeked of smoke, but it was cheap. He topped off the gas tank so he'd be ready to leave first thing in the morning, and then, before going back to his room, he pumped two dollars into the pay phone and dialed Nate's number.

In less than twenty-four hours, it'd be his number too.

The sky was fading to twilight, the stars just beginning to show, and Cody thought as the phone started to ring that it might have been the most beautiful night he'd ever seen.

Nate answered after two rings, sounding surprised, and Cody figured he wasn't used to the phone ringing much at their apartment. "Hello?"

"It's me."

"Cody? Oh my God, where are you? My dad wouldn't tell me what was going on. He said he'd done what he could to help, and I could tell he was all proud of himself when he said it, but he wouldn't tell me what he meant, no matter how many times I asked. Did he give you a ride to the bus station?"

"Uh, no." Cody couldn't stop smiling. "He gave me your car."

"What?" Nate laughed. "I knew he was up to something. He kept telling me I'd just have to wait and see, but—" He laughed again. "Where are you?"

"I'm in Nebraska. I've been looking at the maps your dad gave me. I think it'll be another eight hours or so tomorrow, and then . . ."

"You'll be here?"

It still seemed too good to be true. "I should be."

Nate started to give him directions to the apartment, but Cody had nothing to write on, and the time two dollars paid for ran out way too fast. They were cut off before they even had a chance to say good-bye.

No matter. Nothing could keep them apart now.

Cody went back to his motel room and lay on the bed, staring at the ceiling, so full of joy and wonder that even the spider on the wall and the line of ants under the sink couldn't bring him down.

Of course, his subconscious decided to play dirty.

He dreamed of icy roads where every exit led back to Warren, the Mustang spinning out of control, semis bearing down on him with Logan in the passenger seat, and Nate always just out of reach.

It made for a depressing start the next day, and for the next few hours, he felt sure he was still dreaming. Nebraska stretched on for an eternity, the final bit of road from Lincoln to Omaha seemingly taking him through a time warp straight out of the *Twilight Zone* where he drove and drove but never got any closer to Iowa.

But, finally, he crossed the state line.

After that, his melancholy melted away. How could he be worried in a place filled with so much green? Miles and miles and miles of trees, and real music on the radio, and cute little towns that somehow seemed infinitely cleaner than the one he'd left behind.

He arrived in Iowa City a little before six o'clock. Nate had told him to follow the signs to the university, and so after stopping long enough to put the Mustang's top down, Cody set out in search of his new life. He had visions of finding their apartment, of knocking on the door, having Nate open it with his face full of surprise.

He found the college, but no address that matched the one in his hand. He stopped at several gas stations to check the map in the pay phone phone book, but each time, he found that the pertinent pages had been torn out. He silently cursed the selfish bastards who'd decided their need outweighed the need of everybody else in the world. Finally, he did what he should have done from the beginning and used the pay phone. At least it wasn't a long-distance call.

"You're not far at all," Nate told him. "Wait right there. I'll find you."

Cody went inside and bought a bottle of Coke. He thought he'd wait in the car, but it was hotter than hell in the sun, the air wet and sticky on his desert-born skin. He'd never been one for shorts, always thinking his legs were too skinny and way too white, but he had a feeling Iowa would cure him of that pretty quick. He found a bit of shade behind the ICE cooler.

Less than five minutes later, Nate appeared.

He looked the same, only different. Still blond. Still tall. Still so damn preppy, he might as well have been an extra in *Pretty in Pink*, but there was a looseness about him that was new. His hair was longer, his smile somehow more natural than it had ever been in Warren.

He leaned against the ice machine the way he had the day they'd met. "Hey, man, can I bum a smoke?"

Cody smiled. "Wish I could help, but I quit."

"Me too." Nate edged closer, not quite daring to pull Cody into his arms, but he reached out and took his hand. He looked down at the ring on Cody's finger.

"Do you want it back now?" Cody asked.

Nate smiled and shook his head. "Not ever."

For a moment, they just stood there, Cody thinking how he wanted nothing more than to throw his arms around Nate's neck, but that seemed bold for such a public place.

Nate laughed, as if reading his mind. "You ready to come see our place?"

"Absolutely." He dug the keys out of his pocket and handed them to Nate. "But I think I'll let you drive."

The apartment complex was made up of four giant, boxy buildings, all painted charcoal gray. They looked old, but not too run-down, and they were surrounded by expanses of green grass and towering trees. Cody spotted a playground just past the nearest building.

"It's like we're living in a park." He didn't think he could have loved it more if it'd been a mansion.

"There's a swimming pool too," Nate told him as they climbed out of the Mustang.

"Are the people cool?"

"The ones I've met so far, yeah. The guys right across from us are a couple too. I mean, they're way older than us, like in their fifties maybe, but at least we don't have to worry about them being assholes, right?" He took Cody's hand and led him up three flights of stairs. "This is us. Building B, apartment 413. I don't have much furniture yet . . ."

Cody didn't care. He just wanted Nate to stop talking and open the damn door. He didn't even look around once they were inside. The door was barely even closed before he was in Nate's arms.

He should have been tired after such a long drive, but all he could think about was how good it felt to be here, in their apartment, their space, in a town where nobody knew him or his mother or his past, so far from Wyoming, the wind was nothing but a playful breeze.

"I can't believe I'm actually here."

"And before July first, even." Nate rubbed his back, holding Cody tight. "So, uh . . . this is probably a dumb question, but you didn't go to prom, did you?"

"Ha!" Cody stepped back just enough to meet Nate's eyes. "What do you think?"

"Neither did I, and I know you'll think it's silly, but . . . I thought maybe we could have a prom of our own tonight."

"Like on Valentine's Day?"

"Yes. Only better. I thought we'd go out to dinner first, then come back here. Turn on the music. Maybe light some candles. Dance for a bit. And after that—"

"Yes," Cody laughed, guiding Nate's lips down to meet his. He was pretty sure he already knew what came after the dancing. "I say yes."

References

Articles quoted in this book:

Morganthau, Tom. "Future Shock." In *Newsweek*, November 24, 1986.

Altman, Lawrence K. "Fact, Theory and Myth on the Spread of AIDS." In *The New York Times*. February 15, 1987.
partners.nytimes.com/library/national/science/aids/021587sci-aids.html

Magazines referenced but not quoted:

McCauliffe, Kathleen. "AIDS: At the Dawn of Fear." In *U.S. News & World Report*. January 12, 1987.

Kantrowitz, Barbara. "Kids and Contraceptives." In *Newsweek*. February 16, 1987.

Dear Reader,

Thank you for reading Marie Sexton's *Trailer Trash*!

We know your time is precious and you have many, many entertainment options, so it means a lot that you've chosen to spend your time reading. We really hope you enjoyed it.

We'd be honored if you'd consider posting a review—good or bad—on sites like **Amazon, Barnes & Noble, Kobo, Goodreads, Twitter, Facebook, Tumblr,** and your blog or website. We'd also be honored if you told your friends and family about this book. Word of mouth is a book's lifeblood!

For more information on upcoming releases, author interviews, blog tours, contests, giveaways, and more, please sign up for our weekly, spam-free newsletter and visit us around the web:

Newsletter: tinyurl.com/RiptideSignup
Twitter: twitter.com/RiptideBooks
Facebook: facebook.com/RiptidePublishing
Goodreads: tinyurl.com/RiptideOnGoodreads
Tumblr: riptidepublishing.tumblr.com

Thank you so much for Reading the Rainbow!

RiptidePublishing.com

ALSO BY
Marie Sexton

Winter Oranges
Second Hand, with Heidi
Cullinan
Never a Hero
Promises
A to Z
The Letter Z
Strawberries for Dessert
Paris A to Z
Putting Out Fires
Fear, Hope, and Bread Pudding
Shotgun
Between Sinners and Saints
Song of Oestend
Saviours of Oestend
Blind Space
Cinder
To Feel the Sun
Flowers for Him, with Rowan
Speedwell

One More Soldier
Family Man, with Heidi
Cullinan
Roped In, with L.A. Witt
Normal Enough
Lost Along the Way
Chapter Five and the
Axe-Wielding Maniac
Apartment 14 and the Devil
Next Door

Writing as A.M. Sexton
Release
Return

Coming Soon
Damned If You Do

ABOUT THE

Marie Sexton's first novel, *Promises*, was published in January 2010. Since then, she's published nearly thirty novels, novellas, and short stories, all featuring men who fall in love with other men. Her works include contemporary romance, science fiction, fantasy, historicals, and a few odd genre mash-ups. Marie is the recipient of multiple Rainbow Awards, as well as the CRW Award of Excellence in 2012. Her books have been translated into six languages.

Marie lives in Colorado. She's a fan of just about anything that involves muscular young men piling on top of each other. In particular, she loves the Denver Broncos and enjoys going to the games with her husband. Her imaginary friends often tag along. Marie has one daughter, two cats, and one dog, all of whom seem bent on destroying what remains of her sanity. She loves them anyway.

Marie also writes dark dystopian fantasy under the name A.M. Sexton. You can email her at msexton.author@gmail.com, or find her on:

Facebook: facebook.com/MarieSexton.author
Twitter: twitter.com/MarieSexton
Pinterest: pinterest.com/msextonauthor
Instagram: instagram.com/mariesexton.author